BORN OF MALICE

BORN OF MALICE

XAN VAN ROOYEN

RUADÁN BOOKS

Boston, MA

Born of Malice

ISBN 978-1-968143-14-5 (trade paperback)
ISBN 978-1-968143-15-2 (ebook)
ISBN 978-1-968143-16-9 (audiobook)
Library of Congress Control Number: 2026937325

Edited by R. B. Wood
Illustrations by J Edward Neill
Design/Formatting by Leah Donell

First Edition

RUADÁN
BOOKS

RuadanBooks.com

For those who have been wounded.
Your scars are a testament to strength.

And for Mark, with love, always.

When our eyes close in eternal sleep, bring us safely into the embrace of our ancestors, where we may live in peace or be reborn.

Tsirayan Prayer for the Dead

Table of Contents

Prologue 1
Chapter One, Niki 5
Chapter Two, Zal 21
Chapter Three, Leksi. 53
Chapter Four, Niki 71
Chapter Five, Leksi 87
Chapter Six, Zal 105
Chapter Seven, Niki 123
Chapter Eight, Zal 135
Chapter Nine, Leksi 155
Chapter Ten, Niki. 165
Chapter Eleven, Zal 177
Chapter Twelve, Leksi 189
Chapter Thirteen, Niki 205
Chapter Fourteen, Zal. 227
Chapter Fifteen, Leksi 239
Chapter Sixteen, Niki 261
Chapter Seventeen, Zal 277
Chapter Eighteen, Leksi 287
Chapter Nineteen, Zal 307
Chapter Twenty, Niki 323
Chapter Twenty-One, Zal 351
Chapter Twenty-Two, Leksi. . . 365
Chapter Twenty-Three, Niki . . 377
Chapter Twenty-Four, Zal. . . . 383
Chapter Twenty-Five, Leksi . . . 401
Chapter Twenty-Six, Niki 417
Chapter Twenty-Seven, Zal . . . 425
Chapter Twenty-Eight, Niki . . 433
Chapter Twenty-Nine, Leksi . . 441
Chapter Thirty, Zal. 451
Chapter Thirty-One, Leksi . . . 463
Chapter Thirty-Two, Niki. . . . 479
Chapter Thirty-Three, Leksi . . 493
Chapter Thirty-Four, Zal 499
Epilogue 515
Acknowledgments 517
About Xan van Rooyen 523
Also By Xan van Rooyen 525

Prologue

His skin peeled in thin ribbons, twisting into frayed flowers at his feet. His bones splintered like kindling, and the Nether prince fell. The snow beneath him curdled, blackened by blood and shadow.

"Mother." His voice cracked, the gulf between childhood and adolescence widening as Death's rage sheared scalp from skull. "Please—" he whimpered, but she severed his tongue.

He beseeched with his gaze then, his tears freezing on flayed cheeks, and with fingers like talons, Death plucked out her son's eyes.

The prince wilted, broken and undone. The wind screamed across the frozen veld while the magic of his homeland set his broken bones, stitched torn flesh, and reshaped his organs from gobbets of gore until he was whole again.

But his mother's ire remained a conflagration.

Again and again and *again*, he endured violent disassembly.

He could only gurgle a plea for mercy when Death seized his hand, spread his fingers, and shattered the nacreous gem growing from his knuckle.

Again and again and again, until stone and bone had been obliterated.

Each moment of agony was a seed, the dream of vengeance

blooming within him. Resentment throbbed like a second heart already putrefying, and the prince couldn't help but wonder if perhaps he deserved becoming nothing more than discarded gristle and a fading stain.

The sacred tritone has long been forbidden from use in spellwork due to its unstable nature. It is, in fact, the very antithesis of magic. Dissonance when harmonizing incantations is to be avoided as it can have unexpected effects on the specific spell. While the tritone interval used to be known as the Serpent Tone, this is now considered derogatory and an insult to the Great Inyoti who blessed us with magic.

Excerpt from the foreword by Master Arkani Anjaria Moy to *The Learned Arkani's Principle Guide to Spellwork*

CHAPTER ONE
NIKI

"You do enjoy making things complicated, don't you?" Jaq asked with a jab of her elbow. Harmless teasing, but her question picked at cracked scabs on old wounds.

"You don't have to be here." I frowned at her, trying to focus on the tubes and plates assembled throughout the chamber thanks to Jaq's mathematical precision.

"Of course I do." She touched my shoulder, the contact butterfly soft. "You need me. Without me shimmying you along, you'd still be holed up in your studio." Her tone was jocular but her words stung. The truth always did. Without Jaq, I could've spent another year or more poring over my research with little to show for it.

If anything, I should be grateful she was here, still supporting me and pushing me to test my theories. I should be grateful I had a friend at all.

As much as I'd longed to escape the smothering confines of my parents' cottage and the claustrophobic village steeped in superstition, an annoying part of myself wished that my folks could be here. If only so I could look them in their prayer-misted, devotion-addled eyes and tell them *I told you so.*

If it worked, of course.

Together, Jaq and I surveyed the architectural revelation of rock and metal that used to be the Temple of Inyoti. It was built centuries ago by the faithful who believed those capable of wielding magic must've been born with one of the serpent god's scales lodged in their heart. A scale which conveniently vanished upon death, leaving no trace for physickers to find during autopsies. The temple now stood abandoned on the outskirts of the city, until I'd discovered it while trawling for appropriate concert venues.

The chamber, hewn into the bedrock, had phenomenal acoustics, the reverberation perfect for my experiment. Owned by the city, it had been relatively easy to convince those in charge to lease the derelict building to the university for a nominal fee.

Despite our cleanup efforts, the temple still smelled of bat guano and ancient incense. At least the interior was cool, providing some reprieve from the season's humidity.

"It's going to be fine," Jaq said. "You're annoyingly brilliant, if tediously meticulous." There was an edge to her voice, a hint of annoyance I'd detected before when I was slow to act on new findings, or whenever one of our experiments failed.

"I need it to be perfect." My scalp tingled with apprehension but also excitement. Hope glowed like a fragile ember in my chest, likely about to be smothered by my own ineptitude. My inherent stubbornness prevented me from giving in to despair, though, even if my supervisor was growing weary of my failure, especially given the radical nature of my thesis. She never failed to remind me how funding was hard-won. If I couldn't achieve results tonight, I could wave goodbye to a career in academics.

"It will be perfect." Jaq flashed crooked teeth in a too-big smile and smoothed down the baby hairs on her forehead. She'd combed out the tight curls, leaving her dark hair puffed out thick according to current fashion. She'd also traded her usual billowing shirt and embroidered trousers for formal fitted garb of deepest blue. She looked every bit the Savati scholar.

My tunic was the same shade of indigo, the seams catching at my skin, the fiber gouging 'impostor' into my flesh.

Two years I'd spent studying stochastic models and completing harmonic analyses, poring over historical records in the hopes of finding one of Scryali's scores. I'd lost count of the long days and even longer nights spent dissecting scales and tone series, analyzing tuning systems, all in an attempt to figure out how music alone could be used to control primordial magic. Whatever scant research might've been conducted on the topic in the past had either been burned during the rebellion or was under lock and key at the palace, leaving me precious little upon which to build my own theories. I remained determined, however, my obsession fueled by khat-chewing and the belief that magic shouldn't require some god-given ability to wield, let alone spells or sigils.

In fact, it shouldn't require a human at all. As soon as I proved sound vibration itself was enough to harness the arcane force, I'd start recording my compositions, mastering magic using nothing but a phonograph.

My hypothesis, although not entirely novel—and my khat habit—had vexed my professor, but if it was only a matter of time before someone discovered the technological means to control magic, then why not me? At least Jaq believed in me, had done ever since we bumped into each other at the university library reaching for Adjawaja's treatise on arkano-acoustics—hers a mathematical investigation, mine entirely musical. Jaq and I had bonded over geometry and theories of resonance, debated tuning systems and more philosophical notions about universal resonance. Adjawaja's work toed the line of anathema, but she'd been sufficiently subtle when positing a more direct relationship between musical math and magic; thus, her work had thankfully remained intact and on the library shelf, giving me something to work from.

Considering the magic-wielding arkani traditionally used incantations for extemporaneous spellwork, the answer had to lie in harmonics, in that peculiar oscillation of magic molecules—a theory supported by Adjawaja, if one read between the lines. It was all a matter of acoustics, of resonance. If I could only figure out the exact ratio needed to unleash and control magic, it would change everything and pave the way for a future built on science and technology—a future fair and accessible.

Now, shoving a wad of khat into my lip, I focused my attention back on the musicians warming up on the candle-strewn stage specially erected for this one-off performance. The candles weren't lit yet. None of them were. Once the music started, the oil lamps would be dimmed, and the candles would ignite, one by one in the pattern we'd devised using interweaving melodies.

If my theory proved true, of course.

The hairs on the back of my neck rose in a prickle as the subtle reverberations of the chamber caressed my senses. The aliquot plates and tubes vibrated in sympathy, enriching the sound with complex tone colors. I winced as the algaita player over-blew a note.

"You're sharp." I glowered at the offending musician.

"Apologies." The player licked her lips and tried again, the reedy sound only marginally better.

I chewed on the wad of khat leaves, savoring the astringent sweetness as I rubbed my jaw, hoping the effects of the herb between my teeth would stop the rise of internal dread.

"Niki," Jaq said with gentle admonishment, catching my hand before I could rub fresh lesions into my skin. "We've been over everything a dozen times." She sounded a little exasperated, and I couldn't blame her. "If this doesn't work, it won't be because of a single wrong note—it'll be because the theory is flawed. Which it is not." She glared at me, daring me to argue.

Jaq didn't understand, though. A dry reed, a shift of embouchure, a momentary lapse of concentration, and it would all shatter. As a mathematician, she saw beauty in numbers, but couldn't tell a lute from a lyre, and didn't understand why her off-key singing made me want to plunge needles into my ears.

Tonight's piece, simply titled *Fantasy No. 12 for algaita, marimba, mbira, and Qhembalese kora*, might be a polymelodic disaster, and the death knell of my academic career. Where would I go if the university kicked me out? Skulking back in shame to my childhood village, where all I had waiting for me were ghosts and regret?

Fantasy No. 12, or Dirge for a Foolish Dream.

The musicians squirmed until I nodded, finally satisfied with the tuning. The audience trickled into the temple, bemused by the odd arrangement of chairs and cushions. For months, Jaq and I had studied the structure, calculating the seating to optimize the acoustics.

Tonight, there were no priority seats, no special gallery for the aristocracy, or mats on the floor for the working poor. Silk-clad shoulders brushed those garbed in simple cotton and homemade batik.

While it was impossible to account for exactly how an audience would affect the sound, Jaq had done the math and I trusted her completely.

She took her own designated seat, grinning at the couple of bluebloods pushing past her with brows furrowed, their ears and wrists heavily adorned with gems. The opulent couple hesitated when they found they'd been placed beside a Qhemba family with traditional scars on their faces, flour in their hair, and mud stains on their hems. With no alternative, the bluebloods sat, eyeing the grubby children warily.

This was how it should be and, if I could prove my point tonight, we'd be one step closer to shaping a more equitable society. What a legacy I'd leave, my name known in every household, whispered in awe and gratitude for generations to come. It was all I wanted: to be known, to be remembered, my whole being burning with this singular desire that had become an all-consuming fixation.

The thought dredged up the memory of my parents and the many times they told me I was wasting my time, labeling me a heretic, and disparaging me daily until I made my escape. Just in time too, before an unseasonal plague swept through the village. No lullabies or chicken scratch runes staved off the sickness. No prayers or offerings to their impotent gods, nor faith in the local arkani's spellwork had saved a single soul.

My lips twitched into a smile knowing my parents moldered in silence, their bodies forgotten beneath weeds and deadfall, just two among the many buried that year.

The palace kakakis lowing in the distance pried me from my musings. I waited for the horns to blast all nine notes denoting the hour, and let the audience settle. The anticipation was palpable. The attendees knew they were part of an experiment, and had all given their consent as per university guidelines, but they didn't know the exact nature of what they were in for.

"It's time," I whispered to Jaq.

"Yes, it is," she said, giving my arm a final squeeze before I gestured to the gaggle of first-year students to dim the lamps. It was dark inside the temple, and the light of the gibbous moon splayed through the open slivers of the dome, cutting geometric patterns across the stage.

With the last blast fading, I took up position on the dais

and raised my baton.

The music began with a plaintive melody on the algaita before being traded back and forth between the mbira and kora, notes weaving together to create the requisite harmonies. I kept time, teeth grinding on bitter leaves as I braced for an errant note or skipped beat.

The audience reeled; some gasped, others tittered, but all seemed entranced despite the unexpected dissonance I didn't always immediately resolve. My compositions weren't meant to be pleasing to the ear, they were meant to control magic. Usually, I valued function over form, not minding the resultant dissonance while still doing my best to avoid the dreaded tritone.

This piece was different, though. I'd done my best to thread some beauty into the confounding harmony, which revolved around the traditional scale of the kora. The melodic layers created sequences of perfect fourths and fifths, those stable intervals frequently used to harmonize more powerful incantations. Even so, many audience members clutched their ears, faces twisted in unease and maybe even pain.

I flicked the baton and the musicians responded, adding new sonic stitches to the antiphonal tapestry. Slowly, I surrendered to the music, soaking in the resonance, letting my body and mind become one with the vibrations. A candle flickered, the wick igniting without the use of match or sigil.

Are you sure you want to pursue this line of inquiry? my professor asked when I'd first presented my proposal. *Your music, if successful, could be considered very dangerous indeed. The university can only provide so much protection.*

A risky endeavor, but my name would echo through the annals, eclipsing even the likes of Scryali.

Scryali's claims were initially tolerated by the monarchy, seeing as how they might still serve the greater good, until she denounced the gods and refused the Principles of Inyoti, asserting she could sing the salt from the sea with only a hexatonic refrain.

She also refused to believe magic should be reserved for those born to it, limited to the usually male and affluent students admitted to the university to study spellwork. For disturbing the harmony of society with her heretical beliefs and her dissonant compositions, the king had chopped off her head, burned her research, and banned her music.

Perhaps I was courting a similar fate.

As the algaita returned with the main theme, more candles flared and the audience gasped. My bones thrummed as if in the grip of some large, throttling fist.

"It's working!" Jaq met my gaze, beaming, as the sconce above her burst into flame.

Well, that wasn't supposed to happen. Not yet. We'd made careful calculations, deliberately wanting to ignite one candle at a time to prove we could control the flow of magic, not simply excite the requisite particles.

The lamps caught next—definitely not part of the plan—burning so bright the light hurt my eyes.

Jaq looked surprisingly elated as candles quickly reduced to puddles and wax dripped from the sconce above. Before I could gesture to the musicians to slow the tempo and hopefully reduce the power of the magic, the doors crashed open and a constable's whistle cleaved through the music. Flinching, I dropped my baton as more whistle blows peppered my body like bird shot. The musicians stopped playing and the temple plunged once more into darkness.

"Get those lamps lit," someone bellowed as my eyes grew accustomed to the moonlit gloom.

"By order of the Savati constabulary, you are ordered to cease and desist this unauthorized use of magic!" The sergeant puffed out his chest, straining the buttons of his brown and black uniform, with a badge proudly displaying the constabulary's hyena head insignia.

As more uniformed thugs poured into the temple, the musicians nervously set down their instruments and raised their hands. The audience tittered, some looking amused or irritated while others were terrified. The lamps glowed again, the constabulary and their frowning faces fully revealed.

"Are you Nikima Tjadamo?" the sergeant asked, brusque and frowning.

"I am." I glanced at Jaq hoping to see her looking as perturbed as I felt but her expression was unhelpfully blank.

"Nikima Tjadamo, you are under arrest for the unauthorized use of magic and for disturbing the peace."

"What?" I laughed at the ridiculous accusation. Disturbing the peace maybe, although I didn't see how my concert on the outskirts of the city could upset the harmony of society.

"As I said." With a meaty hand, the sergeant removed a

pair of manacles from his belt, the iron marked with sigils designed to curb the use of magic. The pistol on his hip was far more terrifying.

"This is a fully authorized performance," I said. "We're from the university." I gestured to my indigo tunic. "We have the paperwork." I motioned to Jaq who immediately started digging in her satchel.

"Here it is." She produced the stamped and signed permits, all notarized, in triplicate as bureaucracy demanded. "This clearly states we have permission—"

The sergeant snatched the papers and didn't even scan their contents before tearing them up.

"What are you doing? You can't!" I clenched my teeth, bitter khat squirting across my tongue as cold sweat snailed down my spine.

"Those were legitimate permits granted by the city of Savat's Department of Arkanic Affairs," Jaq said.

"Looked like forgeries to me," the sergeant said. "Scan them." He motioned another constable forward, this one brandishing what looked like a pocket watch or compass. The device was brought close to Jaq, then to me, the needle jumping as it detected magic. The constables exchanged a smug look of satisfaction.

"This one." He pointed at me. "Unlawful arkani."

"No, that can't be—" Jaq began, but her protests tucked tail and slunk into silence when the sergeant gestured for a second pair of manacles from one of the rifle-wielding hyenas.

A buzzing, as if a swarm of bees had taken up sudden residence between my ears, filled my skull while the sergeant continued, reciting a long list of my alleged crimes. Somehow the sergeant's voice kept twisting into the voice of my father as he rattled off all the ways I'd disappointed my family and their gods, his diatribe inflicting more pain than his belt.

My vision narrowed, my focus softening to a blur as darkness licked at the edges.

Dizzy, I grabbed the back of a chair to stop myself falling as my mind raced to form a coherent argument. How could I make this constable understand it was possible to wield magic without being an arkani, that the arkanospy in their hands must be broken or malfunctioning to trace the magic back to me.

Several of the wealthy audience members wailed in outrage, vehemently denying knowing *magic* would be involved in the evening's performance. Those draped in finery and glittering with gems were escorted from the temple; those in muslin and batik were held in place at rifle point.

"I'm not an arkani," I tried to argue, but the sergeant only grunted in amusement.

"Just a fraud with some hidden arkani muttering spells at the candles then." The sergeant smirked.

It had worked. My hypothesis had proven true. I, a laity nobody without a single magical bone in my body and certainly no affinity to the gods, had bent magic to my will. Not entirely as planned, but still!

There was no point resisting as the constable seized my arms and clapped iron onto my wrists. It could be worse. Most arkani had their hands chopped off or tongue removed. Even so, I trembled as metal bit into tender skin. I knew all about the city's efforts to clean up the streets by purging Savat of rogue magic-wielders. I'd even appreciated the constabulary's efforts. The mere existence of arkani was a symbol of inequality. Now though, I wondered how many innocents like me had been unjustly incarcerated. Or worse.

I gasped and struggled to swallow, my mouth arid even as I spat out the wad of khat. Surely the university would come to our defense? I couldn't end up nothing more than a cautionary tale, a broken body mounted on a pike at the palace gates to be pelted with rotten fruit by the public who'd come to blame magic and its wielders for all their suffering—all while still relying on it for mundane daily life. This couldn't be happening. Not now, not when all my efforts were finally coming to fruition.

"Cuff her," the sergeant said, nodding at Jaq who folded her arms in defiance.

Despite my writhing anxiety, I sucked in a ragged breath and spoke in stilted syllables. "This was my doing," I said. "No one else knew the true nature of this event. She had nothing to do with it."

"Are you sure about that?" the sergeant asked. His gaze raked over Jaq. "Seems like an accomplice to me."

"She's my assistant and only did as she was told," I lied, willing Jaq not to argue.

"We'll see." The sergeant gestured to his subordinates.

Jaq hesitated but complied with a sigh, and the sergeant

snapped manacles onto her wrists.

"The others are free to go." The sergeant waved a magnanimous hand over the remaining audience members, who fled before he could change his mind. The musicians followed suit. "But take these two." He gestured to Jaq and me. "Escort them to the palace." The constables hauled us more aggressively than necessary from the temple.

"It'll be all right," Jaq whispered to me, earning sneers from the hyenas.

I couldn't speak; could barely think. My frayed nerves sizzled beneath my skin, my heart racing in syncopated paradiddles. I swallowed, already tasting the rank flavor of the mildewed dungeon where we'd be left to rot—if we were lucky. My mind stuttered, refusing to contemplate the potential torture and gruesome death awaiting us. Surely the university wouldn't see two of their top scholars humiliated like this.

With no family to miss me or friends beyond Jaq, I had no one but my professor to fight for my release. Would she be willing to risk her reputation to save me? And how? The permits lay shredded on the temple floor.

Jaq had connections, though. Perhaps her family would come to our rescue.

Despite the terror turning my insides to water and blood to ice, I couldn't ignore that ember deep in my belly rekindled by my success.

I did it. I used music to wield magic—cast a spell without the need of incantation or sigil. If only the powers that be would listen, I might be able to change everything.

Chapter Two
Zal

Zal watched from the western buttress while his guests reveled, drunk on magic and rebellion. As the host of this lavish affair, he should've been wafting among them, indulging in the revelry. Instead, he gripped the balcony's balustrade as he fought yet another wave of pain.

It flowed like the tides. Sometimes a gentle, if constant, eddy—other times it raged, an all-consuming storm obliterating every thought. He'd lived in pain for over two centuries, and as much as Zal tried to convince himself he'd befriended the ache and throb of his slow-healing body, there were moments of white-hot agony that still took his breath away. Like today, when the sun insisted on overstaying its welcome. He gritted his teeth as seams of scar tissue ruptured, raw and weeping—as long forgotten bruises bloomed anew beneath his pale skin, and old wounds bled again. The pain hurled him back through time to when he'd first gained consciousness in the mortal realm, manifesting as nothing but wisps of shadow peeling off shattered bones, his blood smeared across the mosaics and splashed on the effigies in a temple where Zal slowly stitched himself back together using the prayers of the faithful.

Now, Zal summoned the shadows despite his exhaustion.

They detached from the boughs of the stinkwood and karee trees providing much-needed shade for the humans below, before flitting to their master on thrumming wings. They keened notes only Zal could hear as the solstice sun scorched their edges. Their voices blended with the music burbling from the pavilion, where musicians bowed zithers over the steady accompaniment of djembe drums. The air was ripe with magic, alive with the palpable zing of potential, as if a thunderstorm crackling with lightning were about to break overhead.

However, the sky remained a clear and oppressive blue.

Passing through the gathering, the shadows flared opulent hems and tugged tendrils loose from convoluted 'dos before coming home to roost. They settled on Zal's shoulders, a mantle enveloping him in soothing darkness. He breathed deeper, expanding the gnarled tangle of his rib cage, able to focus again as the pain abated.

From the safety of his vantage, Zal studied those lingering in the too-bright night while his varmints whispered snippets of overheard conversation. Although he cared little for the plight of the lesser beings, humanity had proven a source of endless entertainment with all their petty squabbles and devious machinations. While Zal did his best to stay away from the city's troubles, his acolytes insisted on paddling in the cesspit. If only he could've achieved his own aims without the aid of humans.

It was *good politics*, Ailia reminded him whenever Zal grumbled about celebrating the season antithetical to his being. Good for her, perhaps, as she insinuated herself in the city's governing Synod, concealing her magical abilities so she could play politics. She never would've accomplished this ascension had it not been for Zal plucking her from the mire, had it not been for his mark in her flesh, and his magic granting her the long life required to achieve her ambitions. Not that she would be satisfied until she had a crown on her head.

Foolishly, he'd promised to make her a queen, back when she was just a Qhembalese urchin and he began to build his army in earnest.

He watched her now as she sashayed through the parting throngs: her graying hair dyed black with henna and gleaming with coconut oil, coiled and braided about her face, inexorably succumbing to age. His magic could only delay human senescence for so long.

The shadows spoke in sibilant voices and Zal listened, his gaze raking across his guests. Here, in the safety of his abode, they could embrace their arcane abilities and languish in magic without fear of arrest or worse. There, lounging on a silk-covered divan, was the woman who might've sat upon the Savati throne, had the city not gutted their magic-wielding monarchy. The would've-been princess was currently turning beads of sweat into frozen pearls, tracing the requisite runes across the brow of a young arkani, who had his hand on her thigh.

Motselana hadn't been born when her ancestors were deposed—her grandmother some teenage, magic-weak cousin of the queen who'd grovelled for forgiveness—and yet, Lana hungered for the crown.

Zal had been in the city during the decade-long revolution. He remembered the sound of the axe as it cleaved through the line of royal necks, the cheers of the crowd, who gathered the severed heads, and the young duchess dressed in rags, grateful for her exile as she limped sniveling from the city.

Now here sat that woman's progeny with the fire of sedition flickering in her eyes. There were those among his order who might be swayed to her cause, and he understood why. Half of his acolytes he'd rescued, flotsam plucked from the streets, or saved from the increasing number of conversion camps, since the current government seemed determined to snuff out magic as if it were a weed to be plucked.

Still, his arkani were bound to him and could not be loyal to two masters. He would not allow it.

Anger simmered among the gathered magic-wielders and select sympathizers, rage a sheen of perspiration across magic-slick skin. A stew of resentment spiced with fear—a pot already bubbling over thanks to another clampdown on arkani. In the last few years, the Sodality had seen the university's Department of Arkanic Arts dismantled, all relevant texts either destroyed or confiscated. Now the anti-magic extremists were petitioning the Synod, demanding the city be purged of all arkani—every spell and sigil. It might've already come to pass, were it not for Ailia covertly trying to save herself and her ilk through subtle manipulation of the Synod. At least they acknowledged that magic still had its uses, despite how the Sodality argued society would be better off relying on science and technology instead of a force no one truly understood.

It was all meaningless in the long run. Power waxed and waned as politics spun its inexorable cycles, progress loping forward only to shuffle backward. Not that mortal humans could understand the futility of their abbreviated lives.

The shadows continued to relay all they'd overheard, their report stoking Zal's ire. He released a tendril of magic, and it darted, cobra-like, toward the university professor who claimed exile was better than execution. The sweetmeat in the man's hand turned to glass, chipping his tooth and slicing his lips when he took an unsuspecting bite. The professor cried out, and Zal wiped the gray sludge oozing from his rheumy left eye. Ailia swooped in, elegant and reassuring, tossing a glare up at the balcony before trying to repair the damage done.

Zal withdrew. He'd had enough.

But footsteps sounded on the stairs, each heel tap ricocheting in an unfamiliar rhythm. The shadows swirling against Zal's skin stiffened, shades of darkness imbricating into invisible armor beneath his shirt. Others splayed across the balcony, a subtle and protective rime.

Clenching his jaw, Zal forced his crooked spine straighter, gathering up magic and shadow to appear less like storm-tossed driftwood before leaning on the balustrade.

The stranger approached.

"You shouldn't be here." His voice was the creak of dry branches fractured by a winter gale. "This balcony is private." He feigned disinterest in the interloper.

"Oh, my apologies." A sly smile cut into plump cheeks.

"But I thought it high time I met our mysterious host."

The woman, draped in obnoxious yellow, tip-tapped across the polished tiles, her feet unknowingly snarled in living shadow.

Kazwe Olonza. Vice-chair of the Synod with designs on the high seat, according to Ailia.

"Surveying your kingdom?" she asked.

"No kings, no kingdoms." Zal squinted at the horizon where the midsummer sun spilled livid entrails across the distant ocean. The evening breeze ruffling his shadow-thickened hair offered little respite from the heat.

"Yet here you are in your clifftop palace." She waved a hand, gesturing to all of it. If only she knew how it had taken him the better part of a decade to rearrange the bones of the mountain into this jagged form, how this had once been nothing more than a narrow cave scooped out of the range's lower flank. Memories tore at his mind like wild dogs at a carcass, reminding him of a time when he'd been little more than a walking corpse, sustained only by spite and dreams of vengeance.

"Lord of the Marked," Kazwe continued in a mocking lilt. "Seigneur of Shadow. Baron of the Hinterveld. Va'ili." She gave an insultingly shallow bow.

"So many titles to choose from," he mused, and though none were technically wrong, each scraped jagged nails at tender flesh. He was sovereign of nothing, not until he reclaimed what had been stolen from him. His title and birthright lay a realm away beyond a border he couldn't breach.

And not for lack of trying. He'd spent centuries searching for a means of returning to the land that had so violently disgorged him, burning through his precious stores of magic with nothing to show for it but a trail of dead arkani.

"It's a little ostentatious, isn't it?" Kazwe extended a long-fingered hand, pointing at the ice sculpture below. His acolytes had done it, using water from an underground spring, shaping the ice into a writhing serpent with complex sigils. A similarly spelled faucet protruding like a fang from the snake's mouth allowed guests to fill their cups with chilled water, every draw subtly altering the artwork. It was a spectacular, if frivolous, demonstration of power.

"Ailia likes pretty things," Zal said.

"So I see." Kazwe's gaze abraded him from head to toe before returning to his face. "You know, you're younger than I thought you'd be, and not nearly so ugly."

Zal bristled, his attempt at a smile becoming a snarl.

"Oh, come on. Scars can be beautiful, and what stories they tell." She raised a finger to her own ear, brushing aside a ringlet to reveal the melted remnants of cartilage.

"How similar we are," Zal said, tonguing the empty sockets where teeth torn from their gums had yet to return.

"Rumor paints you a wizened old man locked away to spare the world the horror of your visage, m'lord," she said. "Or perhaps that was your father? Tell me, do you simply inherit the inked followers, passing them down the generations like tarnished silver?"

"They're loyal to me; that's all that matters," he said. Bound by the promise of power. His power, which he'd guaranteed by imbuing each of them with a scrap of godliness when they pledged their fealty. Proof he was who he claimed to be—and a taste of the magic he could bestow upon them once he was fully restored. This splash of primordial power kept them subservient, and desperate for more.

Kazwe raised a plucked brow before turning to look pointedly at the last of the royal spawn. "*Princess* Motselana has followers too—more and more by the day, I hear, and what makes a monarch, if not loyal subjects?" Kazwe glided closer. She smelled of lemon and sandalwood, her breath sweetened by the syrah in her glass. "What makes a god if not worshipers?" Her amber eyes flashed, reflecting the light of the dying sun as it stretched greedy fingers across the balcony.

Perhaps in this new age, the truth mattered less when most had stopped believing. The veil between realms had become annoyingly solidified thanks to humanity's evaporating faith. Perhaps Zal should've been bolder from the start and presented himself as an Ancestor incarnate, but who would believe him a god in this frail form?

He'd learned the hard way when he'd first gathered up the remains of his form made corporeal. Claiming godhood in those early days had only earned him laughter and derision. Had a toothless old woman with one foot in the grave and a heart dedicated to Death not taken pity on a boy she thought the victim of abuse with a damaged mind, he might not have survived, let alone been able to scrounge together enough flesh or wealth to carve out a human existence. Age-addled and devout, she'd believed his claims in the end, directing her prayers to him instead of shrines, and how he'd needed that faith and adoration to restore all he'd lost. He still did.

"Am I a god now?" Zal asked.

"The gods are dead," Kazwe said before inclining her head to Lana sprawled below. "She promises the people freedom and salvation. What can you offer, aside from a new year's party?"

Zal tightened his grip on the balustrade, the stone unyielding beneath his weakened fingers.

"I don't have to explain myself to you," he said.

"Such an enigma," Kazwe continued. "Locked safely away from the Synod. But there are stories about you."

"Tell me about myself, then." Zal had heard a few tales, shared by his acolytes or shed by his whispering pets.

"Let's see." She tapped her glass with a delicate nail. "Your ancestors came from across the desert in a gold chariot pulled by lions, but your blood is cursed, leaving you a sickly recluse like your father before you, and his before that, your lineage… polluted."

Her words chafed too close to the truth.

"Others claim you're the sole survivor of a shipwreck," she continued. "A strange arkani from across the sea. There are even nursery rhymes about a mountain man released from stone by a lightning strike and the relentless pecking of vultures." She laughed, high and piercing. "Personally I prefer the more fantastic tales of a joRanian demon who lost his way." She grinned, flashing her left canine studded with a gem the same gold hue of her eyes.

"A demon? Seems I've been demoted then." Zal sidestepped a determined slant of sunshine. The light would do more than char his pride. Retreating, he shrugged his left shoulder, and the shadows flowed down his arm, coalescing into an obsidian staff.

"Impressive," Kazwe said, raising a thin brow adorned with tiny diamonds, most likely from one of Zal's mines. "Some of the rumors seem true after all."

As the sun gnashed in its death throes, Zal grew increasingly impatient with his unwanted companion. Although Ailia had seemingly managed to repair the damage caused by his flippant magic, the guests below had wisely taken that as their cue to depart.

He watched as Lana extricated herself from the limbs of the arkani turned sycophantic by her attention. Was that how she ensnared her followers? She tossed a long look over her shoulder, pinning Zal in place, a challenge written in the quirk of her lips before she gathered her retinue and sashayed toward the waiting vehicles. Lana had a carriage pulled by a pair of magnificent horses, their traces gleaming against their chestnut hides, the leathers sporting an array of gems too. The would-be queen had done well for herself, carving out a dominion in the winelands northeast of Savat.

The other guests clambered into more modest tumbrels, returning to apartments in the city or seaside villas along the rugged coast.

"It's getting late. You should go," Zal said.

"Oh, I prefer the dark. Don't you?" Kazwe sipped her wine and draped herself across the balustrade, her dress made molten by the dying light.

To some, she was probably beautiful. Tall and proud and slender, her features sculpted from mahogany. She was entirely without magic, though, which rendered her as appealing as stale bread.

"Please. After you." Zal gestured toward the doorway.

"I'm not used to being dismissed." Kazwe's words had bite, and Zal found himself mildly intrigued by this middle-aged woman who'd navigated the convoluted bowels of his home to gain his audience.

"What do you want, then?" he asked. As day finally conceded defeat, the pain gnawing on every joint and threading through every sinew finally relented, allowing Zal to pay more attention to his guest. "I doubt you came up here only to assess my looks."

"No?" She swirled the dregs of her wine before tossing back her head in an inelegant swallow. She dabbed her lips with ring-crusted fingers before speaking. "Given the current attitudes toward arkani, I thought you'd be grateful for a friend."

"A friend?" He'd never had one of those, and wasn't sure he'd know what to do with one if he ever did.

"Look," Kazwe said. "Savat may be ancient and slow to shuck tradition, but no one can stop the march of progress. Our grandparents successfully rid themselves of the monarchy, and the Sodality—through the Synod—is making good on its promise to cleanse the city of arkani."

"Magic will never be purged from the world," Zal said, his shadows stirring as they sensed his irritation.

"Magic is nothing more than science we don't understand yet. And already we're that much closer to answers. Do you know what a corpuscle is?" she asked, but Zal, never one to readily admit his own ignorance, didn't answer. "Soon we'll have the knowledge to either harness magic as easily as steam and coal, just another force to fuel industry, or we'll develop the technology to replace magic entirely."

Zal chuckled, the sound like discarded seashells crunching beneath calloused heels. "As if the gods would allow it."

"The gods are nothing more than footnotes in the history books," Kazwe said. "Faith in the arcane has already been replaced by commitment to progress."

"Then why are you here?" His shadows writhed at their feet, but Kazwe stared only at his face, her gaze boring into his.

"Because Ailia's days are numbered, and yours are too. It's only a matter of time before others on the Synod figure out what she is and that she wears your mark. The city is well aware of how your predecessors, if that's what they were, collected arkani like urchins gather crumbs. Or perhaps like rulers of old cobbled together a militia." Her voice didn't quite lift the words into a question but her brows were raised in twin arcs. "The Synod is aware of Motselana's designs as well. If Lana had her way, we'd return to an era of subjugation by magic. Temples restored, fanes overflowing with offerings to gods best forgotten. It would be terrible regression." Her hand curled into a fist. "And erode all our progress."

"And you tell me this because?" Suspicion needled Zal's gut.

"As much as I want to see our city embrace modernity, I don't believe we should butcher those afflicted with magic."

"How benevolent." Zal's grip tightened on his shadow staff, the scars on his hand pulling taut.

"I came here to ensure you and yours continue to remain peaceful, that you understand why Lana and her desire for the throne is a threat to all of us," Kazwe said.

A threat. She feared him, feared what he was, his power, and those he commanded. She feared he'd side with Lana. If only Zal could assure her he had no desire to attack Savat and couldn't care less about some upstart royal. His battle lay elsewhere. But humans didn't like being afraid.

Fear—admiration. Two sides of the same coin, and while Zal certainly preferred one over the other, he would happily accept both so long as neither came between him and his vengeance.

"A war waged by arkani would be devastating for this city," Kazwe continued.

"Yes, it would." He returned her glare and a muscle twitched in her jaw.

"Our current high-chair is a dogmatic old fool, a devout member of the Sodality, and is no doubt in his chambers right now drawing up legislation to eradicate all arkani for good."

"Your Synod has strange notions of progress," Zal said with

a scoff.

"Well, were I high-chair, I'd find a more diplomatic solution," she said. "Where laity and arkani might work together. Imagine a system where Ailia could serve the city openly as an arkani."

"With a white band on her arm like those registered to the guild and hamstrung by the Synod?" he asked. It would never make sense to Zal that those without magic attempted to govern and restrict those with true power.

"People fear what they don't understand," she said. "I firmly believe that the better we understand magic, the less conflict it will cause. Imagine a future where we could set aside past grievances and work together to use magic for the greater good."

Ailia was right. This woman's ambition dripped from every pore, but Zal had no interest in her proselytizing, not if using magic for the greater good meant making arkani subservient to the laity. The Sodality radicals would never be satisfied until every last arkani was dead.

"If a wealthy man like yourself were to make significant contributions to our efforts," Kazwe began, "fund research perhaps, or similar initiatives, then I believe the other members of the Synod could be convinced to cast a vote of no confidence and see a more capable mind installed as high-chair."

"And in return, no more arkani decorate the palace pikes?" he asked, beyond weary of her presence.

"Exactly. In fact, your estate lies far enough from the city gates not to be a threat at all. Provided we could be assured no army gathered here, we could all live peacefully as we navigated the transition to a more inclusive government. Your mines…" Kazwe continued, but Zal stopped listening as the cramp wrenching his calf juddered up his leg, wringing through thigh, then hip before seizing his spine and unraveling scars across his ribs. Blood seeped into the delicate fibers of his shirt, turning the garment unpleasantly sticky.

The shadows pressed closer too, as if they might absorb his pain. He closed his eyes, reciting the names of his siblings and how he planned to end them, a mantra to cope with the agony.

Slowly, the cramp eased its grip and his awareness of the mortal world returned. The night had grown raucous as insects serenaded the moonrise, jackals barked in the scrub, and rock hyraxes screamed from the outcroppings, their voices echoed by the mountains cupping Zal's citadel in their craggy hands. Magic simmered in the air, roused by the wild chorus.

Zal, too, longed to scream, and might've joined in the nocturnal ululation were it not for Kazwe Olonza.

Only one tumbrel remained, waiting to take its owner far away. A pair of white ostriches ruffled impatient feathers, their harnesses glinting in the glow of lamps spelled to capture sunlight during the day and emit it at night. His acolytes moved among the abandoned tables, clearing away the remnants of the party. As always, his attention was drawn to the sciomancer who wore Zal's mark against his heart.

Emri glanced upward, his long hair flowing like spun starlight across his shoulders. The sciomancer bowed in subtle acknowledgment, his pale eyes gleaming with ghost-sight.

"Are you even listening?" Kazwe grabbed Zal's arm. Pain shot through his elbow and lanced into his shoulder.

His shadows attacked as sharp-beaked shrikes, smothering the woman's screams with a whir of ephemeral wings.

"I don't deal with laity," Zal said as the woman fell, wine glass shattering. "And I don't take kindly to ultimatums."

He didn't stay to watch the butcher birds at work. Come dawn, his fever trees would be spangled with visceral tinsel, a banquet for the carrion eaters.

Zal hobbled down the stairs, his magic too weak on a night this thin to soften the impact of his descent. Breathless, bleeding, and sore, he finally arrived in the cool embrace of his inner sanctum, one of the original caves he'd excavated with his bare hands all those years ago. The windowless walls were adorned with shelving for the bibelots and baubles he'd accumulated during his sojourn in the mortal realm: books and artifacts, art and instruments, polished bone fragments, shimmering geodes, and an assortment of knives.

Lamps flickering with the warm glow of magic immediately soothed his sun-stained eyes. He shuffled toward the nearest pile of cushions, his staff liquefying as he let silk and down cradle his body.

He ignored the invasive wave of emotion extending parasitic tendrils toward his mind. If only he knew how to sever this irksome filament binding blood to blood.

"You look weary, brother," his sister rasped from where she slumped in a jumble of desiccated limbs, her flaking wrists chained to the wall. She shifted, her patchy skull brushing the shelf above. It held illuminated texts telling tales of gods and monsters from the lands north of the infernal desert. His crossing had been torturous, and certainly hadn't been in a golden chariot drawn by lions. He'd been sun-drunk and feverish, stowed away in a merchant's wagon, fleeing for his miserable life from those who'd once worshiped him. In silence and deprivation, he'd endured the caravan's arduous trek toward the promise of Savat and a fresh start.

Ignoring his prisoner, Zal rearranged his malformed limbs, shedding tears of relief from his right eye and another gummy trail of gray from the left.

"There's blood on your shoes," the almost-corpse croaked in the tongue of their homeland, all frost-crackle consonants so unlike the half-swallowed diphthongs of Savati. "Pity it's not all your own. I'll never forget how prettily yours glommed the snow."

A barb of her amusement penetrated his defenses, not that he needed a psychic connection to know how much his sister enjoyed needling him. Despite their previous estrangement, their proximity had revived the tenuous threads stitching Netherling to Netherling.

If his shadows weren't feasting up on the balcony, or if it were any other day of the year, he might've had the energy to relieve his sister of her tongue, again, but summer had torn its claws through his marrow.

When Ailia came, he'd ask her to cast another spell of silence. Or perhaps he'd saw off his sister's toes, if they'd grown back since the last dismemberment. It had been several weeks since their last session and only half her teeth had returned. The shelf above her was lined with all the molars he'd ripped from her jaw in the hopes he'd uproot her secrets. But unlike Zal, Riksa was still attached to their homeland by an umbilical he couldn't sever, a channel constantly replenishing her magic.

He'd tried destroying the connection, cutting off the finger where the Nether-gem grew, a symbol of her heritage. Hers had grown back, a multi-faceted pleochroic taunt. What little Nether-power remained in Zal's veins was all he had, a force bolstered only by prayer and adoration, or abject terror. But no amount of human faith would be enough to repair all the damage. He rubbed the scarred knuckle where a nub of protruding bone remained devastatingly devoid of stone.

Testing his elbow, Zal reached for the carafe of water on the side table and poured a tantalizing trickle into the crystal glass. Existing in the mortal realm rendered their bodies susceptible to thirst, hunger, and sleep. Foregoing these things wouldn't kill Zal, or those like him, but it would certainly hurt, and Zal already suffered enough. Even more now, thanks to their shared sibling connection.

Riksa's anger and increasing desperation felt like gristle caught between his teeth, a constant irritation.

He sipped the water flavored with lemon slices and sprigs

of mint with exaggerated enjoyment. Riksa's bloodshot eyes widened, mouth curving into a rictus before she lunged. The manacles held, spelled with sigils etched into the iron. The floor bore similar runic constructions, painted in arkani blood and refreshed daily to contain her. The spells would otherwise lose their power to keep her captive.

"Do you know what a corpuscle is?" he asked, licking his lips.

"Some new torture device?" Riksa responded, voice like dry leaves crumbling. "How much longer must we play this game until you admit you cannot best me?"

Zal sighed and a rib shifted, slotting into its rightful place with a satisfying snap. "Tell me how to get home, and I'll give you a drink."

No response.

"Tell me why you came to Savat and I'll end your suffering."

Riksa's chuckle turned into a cough as she hacked up a chunk of blistered lung. It seemed Ailia's spells were having some delightful side effects. "You can't kill me."

Not in her current state, but Zal had come to Savat looking for a very specific bit of magic. He'd endured a traverse across the sands and many difficult years accruing wealth in the city before he'd gained the trust and admiration of his first followers. They'd all expired far faster than expected, succumbing to the exhausting experimental spells he demanded they perform in an attempt to claw his way back to the Nether. He'd seen the city endure a revolution and thought he'd lost his chance of finding arkani strong enough for his purposes, but the civil unrest saw many magic-wielders abandoned and in need of rescue.

He'd found Ailia then, and had let his revolving stable of acolytes nurture her bright mind until she was old enough to do what Zal could not, discovering secrets others had left to molder.

While he'd continued to convalesce, Ailia studied forgotten tomes and forbidden texts, translating and interpreting, divining and devising, quickly establishing herself as both a formidable arkani and capable leader. They were so close now—if only Ailia could use her connections in the Synod to gain access to the palace archives.

During the revolution, laity zealots had tried to destroy all royal artifacts. Zal remembered the pyres belching acrid fumes across the city as those entombed, and all their belongings, burned. Magical items that survived the flames were sealed away in the palace, taken over by the Sodality, and deliberately forgotten, their existence denied.

As soon as Ailia gained access, Zal knew they'd find what they needed to complete the spell to strip a being of magic and transfer that power to him. It would render Riksa mortal while restoring Zal to his former might. Then he'd be strong enough to tear open the realms. His lips twitched into a smile at the thought of finally seeing justice served.

"Please tell me you didn't murder Kazwe Olonza." Ailia's outrage preceded her as she strode into the chamber.

"She had no business being on my balcony." Zal took

another sip of water. "If she hadn't tried to threaten me, she might've survived. Though I doubt it, given how dull the conversation was."

"Zal, my love." Ailia knelt beside him and placed a gentle hand on his knee. "Your shadows have made ornaments of her organs. The trees are dripping offal."

"The vultures and crows will take care of that." He took her hand and kissed her knuckles. Her skin was papery and mottled with liver spots, the constellations darker and denser than he remembered.

"And who will take her place on the Synod?" she asked.

"You, of course." He brushed his thumb along her jaw, noticing the wrinkles bracketing her lips. Age had made her elegant where she'd once been pretty.

"That's not how this works." Ailia closed her eyes, breathing in through her nose and out through her mouth before speaking again. "I'm already at considerable risk in my current position. I needed Kazwe. Arkani are dying. An alliance with her was the only way to subdue the Sodality."

"The Sodality is no threat to us." He tucked a lock of hair behind her ear.

"No threat?" She parroted with incredulity. "Haven't you noticed our dwindling guest list, how every year there are fewer arkani? They are killing us. We've already lost two of our own who are no doubt being tortured and will soon be impaled."

"When? Who?" Zal tried to take mental inventory of his order. Would he even recognize them all or know if an acolyte was missing?

"The fact you don't know—" Ailia pursed her lips, her scowl admonishment enough. Zal squirmed as an unfamiliar chagrin curled in his gut. "Kazwe was the only one who might've stood against the high seat," she continued. "The only one who might've been able to secure the release of the arkani, if they still live. And now—you think Kazwe's absence will go unnoticed? That the constabulary won't come bashing down your doors demanding answers? Tell me, Zal." She cupped his jaw, thumb scraping across his cheek a little too hard to be pleasurable. "Will you make worm's meat of everyone in this city?"

Zal leaned away from his lover and her visible disappointment. She looked at him as if he were an irascible child guilty of breaking his mother's favorite vase. If only it had been a vase he'd broken, perhaps…

Perhaps he should've held his shadows in abeyance. He would've, had he been able to. It was Kazwe's own fault she'd been eviscerated.

"Oh dear, little brother," Riksa said. "Seems you're destined to make a mess of things." She jerked but wasn't quick enough to avoid the glass Zal flung at her head. Ignoring the lacerations on her face and crystal shards embedded in her wizened cheek, she turned to lick the splash of moisture from the wall.

Zal watched, sickened by the pang of pity for the sibling he'd rendered so pathetic, which only compounded the guilt aggravating his insides.

"What the Synod does is of no concern," he said. "Once we have what we need to complete the spell, feel free to kill anyone you like."

"And leave the city in turmoil?" Ailia asked. "Bring about another age of—"

"Chaos?" Riksa supplied in Savati, her mouth bloody from sucking on stone. "He can't help what he is."

"A spell of silence." Zal waved his hand in the prisoner's direction and Ailia rocked back on her heels, eyes steely.

"Please," Zal added, his fingers skimming her cheek. He'd learned over the years how much she appreciated tenderness, and it was easy to give this small thing to his oldest surviving acolyte, always so loyal and devoted, to be gentle with this mortal he'd come to love.

"For what it's worth, I'm sorry if Kazwe's death is an inconvenience," he said. "But she was proving most intolerable alive as well."

"An inconvenience?" Ailia clucked her tongue. "This will weaken the Synod, especially so close to First Council. Never mind how that instability will play in Lana's favor."

"What can Lana possibly do?" Zal asked. "Threaten to stop supplying the city with wine?"

Ailia's lips pressed into a thin line as she regarded him with sad eyes, or perhaps she was simply exhausted by the festivities and succumbing to human age.

He took her hand again, kissing the mark on her wrist. His gift of shadow fluttered between the tendons, rising to meet his touch. She softened, her breath warm and cinnamon-scented on his face as she bent her head toward his, their foreheads touching.

"You are a constant vexation," she said and mussed his hair. Zal felt the scabrous pulp beneath his sternum jerk in response, as if it suddenly remembered what it meant to be a heart.

"Give me a moment to prepare." She nodded toward Riksa. "While I do, please have something more than water. Iqno!" she called, and one of the newest members of their order scuttled into the chamber bearing a tray ladened with leftovers from the feast.

Ailia helped Zal to sit up, tutting at the burgundy seeping through his shirt. She stayed until he'd popped the lamb's liver wrapped in caul fat into his mouth. Salty grease exploded across his tongue and Zal moaned in pleasure for Riksa's benefit. She lunged for the tray—or for his throat, it was hard to tell—before being caught by the chains and spell-work.

"Go on, eat another." Her anger was like raw chili in a recent wound. "Have your sport, brother. Enjoy yourself while you can. These won't hold me forever." Riksa stretched a filthy foot toward the sigils, using a heel to rub at the symbol, and stifling a cry as the exposed bone of her returning toes began to smolder. Her desperation shifted into something like excitement. How delusional the captivity had made her.

Zal enjoyed her struggle, despite her peppery emotions infecting his own, and polished off more food, the leaks and cracks in his flesh slowly sealing.

Ailia returned and prepared for the spell. Unlike most

arkani with an affinity for only one element, Ailia was an expert in all. Not quite as naturally gifted as Scryali, but what she lacked in talent she'd acquired through diligent study.

He settled back in the cushions, weariness pouncing like a leopard to clamp its jaws on his throat. He blinked his eyes, resisting sleep, wanting to see his arkani work her magic, but his limbs and lids turned leaden.

"That was effective." Ailia's voice rang distantly.

"I don't understand," Iqno whispered. "You said—"

"Hush. We need to focus."

Hands smoothed his hair, Ailia's he guessed, given the thiouraye scent of her skin, her touch comforting, igniting pleasure in his ravaged body. The same hands then slipped a necklace over his head and the object rested light, but solid, on his chest. A wooden pendant, perhaps, though he couldn't fathom its purpose.

More voices began a chant, melodies like waves lapping at his consciousness. This wasn't a familiar incantation, and certainly not the spell to silence his sister who rasped encouragement. He caught a few of the words, syllables borrowed from the dialects of the gods, elongated and contracted to fit the imposed hexameter.

Magic—his own—coated his tongue with a brimstone piquancy as Ailia opened his shirt, exposing his skin to the cool air of the chamber. His body responded against his will, his magic buzzing in his bones and making his teeth ache.

He tried to call out but his tongue seemed glued in place, mouth furry. He flinched now as Ailia gouged into his skin with a cauterizing finger. It burned, a fire ant trail chewing through his flesh, and the object around his neck warmed and grew heavy.

"Yes, just like that," Riksa said. "How beautifully you bleed, little brother."

Not again. *Never* again.

Zal shook with effort, fighting against Riksa's excitement, which was becoming a smothering glee snarling his thoughts in a psychic net. Instinctively, he summoned his shadows. To his left, an arkani yelped and the incantation faltered and the darkness behind his eyes thickened as the shadows wrapped him in a protective cocoon.

"Thought you said you could handle those," Ailia said, her tone flinty. Zal didn't understand what was happening, but he knew it needed to stop.

"Not quite at full strength yet," Riksa said, and Zal knew then he'd been betrayed.

Again.

The chanting continued, stilted and punctuated by cries and curses as his shadows did their best to protect him against those he'd considered devout.

A new heat burrowed deep, and a flare of purest white soaked his vision, incinerating the hope he was wrong, that the human he'd loved for so long wasn't scorching treacherous sigils across his ribs.

Zal thrashed, his blood made viscous with rage, his resolve shadow-soaked.

The solstice may have reduced his body to a quivering

wreck, but he was still chaos incarnate.

He moved, his hand latching onto Ailia's wrist. Flames licked from her fingers, but he ignored the burn and squeezed. Her bones were spun sugar beneath his fingers. Ailia screamed, the decades riffling across her distraught face like the pages of a book, a story filled with promises of a throne he'd failed to deliver. For so long she'd been the moon to the tides within him, but her too-human greed had eclipsed whatever counted as love in his heartless chest.

"Why?" he asked, the question bubbling unbidden from his depths even as a gout of flame shot from her uninjured hand toward his face. A shadow leapt from his chest and smothered it, all the while the pendant pulsed with a burgundy glow as the magic escaping from his side soaked into the carved wood. Ailia's spell was too strong, Zal's shadows too weak; his flesh unraveled.

"Such a heady bouquet of emotion," Riksa said. "A full-bodied fear with acidic notes of rage and a long, mushroomy finish of shame. We're going to drain you dry, little brother, make you a husk not even fit for the maggots." She spit in their native Nethertaal, the words made ugly by her hideous mouth.

This shouldn't be possible. The spell wasn't ready, unless Ailia had found more than she'd shared.

Of course she had. How stupid he'd been, to leave Riksa with her cunning tongue intact, to trust Ailia would be strong enough to resist his sister's manipulation. She was War, conflict manifested in her presence whether she willed it or not. He and Ailia had simply fallen victim to her aspect. He should've known he wouldn't be immune.

The incantation resumed, the insidious spell excising his power. Using what little strength he had left, Zal flung Ailia away and pressed a hand to the mess of his ribs as if he could staunch the hemorrhage.

"We need your power, not you," Ailia said. How easily she dug her nails into Zal's softest parts, parts he thought buried deep enough to avoid her claws, but this was the woman he'd raised from feral girlhood, who had been by his side for more than seventy years, the woman he had grown to love. She knew exactly how to hurt him.

"You can't wield what's mine." He hissed, tasting snow and copper on his tongue.

Ailia's lips parted in a rueful smile. "No?"

"But I can," Riksa said, her delight nauseating.

The amulet dragged at his neck, his skin sizzling when he tried to tear it off. He flung himself from the cushions, desperate to escape, and toppled, flailing like a fledgling plummeting from its nest. Hard earth slammed into his fragile knees and his shadows puddled around him, trying to soften the impact, weakened as they were by the spell siphoning his power; the spell they should be using on Riksa.

Centuries of planning and careful construction, lifetimes of agony spent preparing—all for nothing. His dream was shredded gossamer, a spider's web left tattered by the fly snared in its midst.

If Zal wanted to survive, he only had one choice. Summoning the dregs of his power, he searched for escape, instinctively reaching out, desperate to find purchase on some muttered prayer, a votive relic, a crumbling altar dedicated to Death and Darkness.

There: a flicker in the gloom, a cold current as tremulous and sickly as his hope. Zal dipped a cautious toe into the stream as Ailia's spell continued pilfering power from his veins. He reached, grasping for the remnant of faith tickling his senses: the damp molder of soil, the must of worms and beetles, the creak of wood protesting the load of earth above it, and there, in the swamp of charnel darkness, he glimpsed the glitter of a Nether-gem.

"It'll hurt less if you don't fight it." Ailia hooked her fingers beneath the leather holding the amulet. He wrenched away, the thong slicing into his nape before it snapped. The pendant skittered across the floor and Riksa lunged for it, but Ailia snatched it up first.

"I don't need either of you," she said.

"No!" Riksa thrashed, shaking the manacles still clamped on her wrists. Her rage burned incandescent, searing Zal's mind, but it also gave him strength.

Ailia's dark eyes turned lambent, reflecting the flames licking up the fingers of her raised hand.

Abandoning pride and dignity, Zal dove into the current, letting the strange undertow drag him toward an unknown destination.

The Principles of Inyoti as recorded by the first arkani blessed by the Ancestors to carry that most sacred fragment of the Serpent God within their hearts. Thus are the tenets upon which we build our society.

First Principle—
Respect for Ancestors and God:
In order to maintain harmony, society must value the wisdom and experience of elders, ancestors, and God. Respect and appreciation must be shown through frequent and proper ritual, prayer, and offerings. All thoughts and actions should be for the preservation of the greater good, society in harmony to honor Inyoti.

CHAPTER THREE
LEKSI

Leksi couldn't remember having ever taken a holiday. Time off simply wasn't a concept she understood.

Despite the fact she was technically immortal, she never seemed to have enough hours in the day. Securing funding for her halfway house was a full-time job the newest Minister of Social Affairs was making increasingly difficult. Never mind how the powers that be would shut her down, lock her up, and throw away the key if they ever discovered what she was really up to.

Leksi startled, spilling ink, as the palace kakakis ululated the hour. The horns bellowed eight bronze blasts across the city. Was it really that late already?

While Leksi appreciated many of the ancient city's traditions, hourly bombast and old-fashioned bureaucracy weren't among them. Why was everything required in triplicate? Her fingers cramped around the pen just thinking about all the initialing she needed to do.

Chewing on her lip, she tried to come up with yet another way to obscure the true nature of The Anchorage. She understood why the government wouldn't want to cough up tax money for an establishment providing sanctuary to those running from arkanophobic conversion camps, but it turned her stomach to see so many of her private donors buying into the Sodality's bigoted rhetoric. She didn't know how much longer she'd be able to hide what she was doing.

Leksi despised magic with every fiber of her being. But sending those afflicted with it off to camps wasn't the solution. Magic couldn't be beaten or starved out of a wielder. The only way for an arkani to overcome their curse was to fully understand their power and master the urge to wield it.

"I know I'm your partner and not your boss," Tamisk said, leaning in the doorway of Leksi's office, albeit little more than a curtained alcove tucked into the back of the old barracks-turned-refuge. "But—"

"But what?" Leksi asked without looking up. She could see Tamisk's unimpressed expression in her peripheral vision. "These are due in two days. I've got nothing but ink splotches for a 'justification.'"

"If I were your boss, I'd threaten to sack you for working too much." Tamisk folded her arms across her chest, bulging biceps exposed by the sleeveless vest she knew Leksi couldn't resist. It was a ruthless tactic aimed to distract. And it was working.

"Then you'd make a lousy boss by Savati standards." Leksi felt her focus drift, her gaze following the ropy trails of Tamisk's forearm veins. Vascularity like that should be illegal.

"I'd be beloved by the unions though," Tamisk said.

"Is there a union for the neurotic self-employed?" Leksi pressed the heels of her hands to her eyes. They prickled, tearing up with fatigue and frustration. Not the kind of fatigue swept away by a good night's sleep either. This weariness settled in her marrow, an unwelcome rodent nibbling away at her stores of energy. And good humor.

"Not yet, but I'm working on it." Tamisk shouldered her bulky form through the narrow doorway to stand beside the cluttered desk.

"If we don't make the deadline, we'll lose this place." Leksi rested her face in her palms and stifled a yawn.

"We'll make it." Tamisk stroked Leksi's hair and Leksi leaned into the touch like a needy house cat. "But you're not going to help anyone by burning your bum black like a pot over the fire."

Leksi smiled. Tamisk was from the archipelago nation of Tsiraya. The idioms in her native tongue, when translated directly, often made for amusing imagery.

"I appreciate your concern for my bottom." Leksi took the taller woman's hand and squeezed. "Don't think it's charred just yet."

"Shall I check?" Tamisk grinned, pulling Leksi from her stool and scooting her hands down the back of Leksi's pants. She gave one set of cheeks a pinch then leaned over and gave the other a series of kisses until Leksi dissolved into giggles.

"Fine, you win." A single night off wouldn't be that cataclysmic, surely.

"Good. Let's go." Tamisk grabbed her hand, hauling her from the study before Leksi could protest. "Actually, maybe you should change."

Leksi glanced down at her rumpled slacks and blouse.

"Stars wept, have I looked like this all day?" She scraped at the splattering of breakfast porridge decorating her shirt.

"Yes. You're adorable."

Leksi gave Tamisk a playful swat on the shoulder.

"But hurry. It's getting late."

"Late for what?" Leksi asked.

"Have you forgotten what day it is?" Tamisk's thick brows drew together.

"Absolutely not, what with the deadline being—" Leksi smacked her forehead. "I'm sorry. I love you. Thank you. One moment." She dashed up the rickety staircase to the room they shared.

No wonder The Anchorage had been so quiet today; all its usually rambunctious tenants were out enjoying the solstice festivities. Given the tradition of costume wearing, it was one of the few days where her charges felt more at ease being themselves, safely anonymous behind masks while out in the city.

Leksi contemplated her clothes rack, wondering if she could get away with long sleeves. Not that cotton would provide much protection in a crowd where dozens of sharp edges could snag her skin. There was a time she'd never have risked being in such a throng in case of injury. Over the years, she'd gotten better at repressing the danger lurking beneath her skin and now she no longer felt the need to hide her hands in gloves either. No one beside Tamisk knew the gaudy ring on her left middle finger was one she couldn't take off. No one, not even Tamisk, knew what it truly meant. She'd tried to remove the gem once, even amputated the finger and buried it six feet under, but the loathsome digit had grown back.

Besides, it was the solstice. Her magic was at its weakest—if she'd be able to use it at all. Magic wielding was like a muscle: it atrophied with disuse, and having not used hers in more than a century, Leksi felt confident her power had withered, becoming as brittle as winter grass and just as easily crushed.

The sun was a bigger concern, the season squelching sweatily and barely half over, but she'd learned to cope with that too. She searched her jewelry box, selecting one of the many necklaces bearing a sigil-etched pendant. She slipped it over her head, letting it hang low and hidden between her breasts. It would protect her skin for a while at least. It was a risk, what with the hyenas roaming the city looking for any excuse to arrest those suspected of magic use, but it was a risk she had to take.

Dressed in a summer frock with pink and purple cosmos flowers embroidered across the bodice, Leksi secured a similarly flowery mask over her eyes and a wide-brimmed straw hat on her head, before slipping her hand into Tamisk's. Tamisk wore an asymmetrical mask stitched from leather that made her look even more roguish.

Leksi hesitated for just a moment before leaving. The forms would be waiting for her in the morning. She could let her hair down for one night.

Savat was a riot of color, a cacophony of laughter and music as citizens from all strata spilled onto the humidity-slick streets to celebrate the season. This discomfort was bearable though, preferable even. Leksi resented how much she longed for darkness and cold, and the reprieve winter always brought.

Tamisk kept a protective arm looped around Leksi's shoulders as they picked their way through the vibrant streets of the Qhemba township, home to the city's poorer denizens of various ethnicity. Among the Tsirayan and joRanian immigrants, there were others who hailed from even further away, come to Savat on merchant vessels, some fleeing dire circumstances or simply preferring the way of life in the ancient city that was oddly permissive of all things except magic. The vast majority of the inhabitants here, however, were Qhembalese, who called the peninsula home long before outsiders came in boats and claimed the land as their own. The outsiders built a city and a palace, established a foreign monarchy, and called it all Savat, an old word that meant something like cradle or womb.

At least there was a Qhembalese representative on the Synod now. Not quite the progress many had hoped to see, but it was better than nothing.

Despite the menacing patrols of the constabulary armed with pangas and cudgels, Leksi detected magic in the air. A fiery tingle across her skin and a subtle aroma, masked by the fragrance of summer flowers cut and fashioned into complicated bouquets. They hung from doorways and dangled from eaves, and many people wore garlands around their necks or single blooms tucked into their hair. All the flowers disguised the stink of the mills, factories, and tanneries clustered to the east as well.

Tamisk drew Leksi close as they passed shebeens serving fruity mampoer and homemade firewater. The pungent tang of the alcohol turned Leksi's stomach and the unwanted parasites inside her stirred. She ignored the gnawing annoyance of her birthright, stamping firmly on the squirming dregs of her magic.

They met up with Tamisk's friends on a less crowded street to listen to the Qhembalese buskers playing single-string bows and percussive rattles. They bought posies for each other's wrists, sipped on ice-slushed lemonade, and sucked on skewers of frozen fruit served from kiosks. Leksi swore she could taste the remnants of a sly spell used to cool the cubes of pineapple and guava. Not everyone in the city hated magic. Leksi ate her fruit and didn't complain about the spell on her tongue. Not tonight when Tamisk was so determined to show her a good time. Tamisk worked hard too and needed this even more than Leksi did.

"You okay here for a bit?" Tamisk asked.

Leksi nodded, her mouth full of icy sweetness. Tamisk beamed before she and her friends joined a crew of dancers gyrating to a frenetic beat. Several among the crew were Tsirayan, their charm bracelets jangling along with the music, same as Tamisk's.

Grateful for the shade provided by the kiosk's awning, Leksi was content to watch, savoring the way her lover's muscles strained against tawny skin sheened with sweat. Tamisk twisted and jived, stomped and pulsed through traditional Tsirayan dance forms all meant to honor the sun and Life. Again, the vermin inside Leksi stirred, an unwelcome reminder she had failed to escape what she was.

The song ended and Tamisk thanked the dancers, touching elbows with each of them before returning to Leksi and showering her with kisses. Leksi breathed her in and licked the salt from her lips.

"How you doing?" Tamisk asked.

"It's a lot," Leksi said. Her senses were becoming over-saturated by sound and color as the various smells wafting from food carts and cafes combined with body odor and the cloying redolence of flowers. Pollinators thrummed among the bouquets, which only added to the noise hacking at Leksi's head.

Not to mention how her hair stuck to her neck, how her dress clung to sweat-pearled skin, or how the sun glared relentlessly from a cloudless sky. She was already turning red and itchy despite the protection charm. It was all too much.

"Ready for some alone time?" Tamisk asked.

"If you are."

With a reassuring smile, Tamisk bid her friends farewell then took Leksi's hand. They headed out of noisy Qhemba, traversing the city. Part of her wanted to see the flower floats that would be lining the cobbled roads leading to the palace, but the crowds would be thickest there. Although the monarchy had been dismantled, the palace endured. The gilded halls perched atop the escarpment overlooking the city now housed the Synod and other government officials instead of royalty. It was also where the main solstice festivities still took place, no longer in honor of the gods but rather in celebration of the people as everyone 'embraced the future' the Sodality sought to shape.

Instead, Tamisk led Leksi toward the sea, south along the peninsula. The clustered dwellings tapered off as the land narrowed, eventually rolling into sandy beaches.

The strands were alight with bonfires and even rowdier revelry. People danced, bodies moving in sinuous shapes along the shore. There was magic in the air, wild and unfettered, seeping from the sea to lap at the shapes carved into the wet sand beneath ignorant feet. There were likely arkani among the revelers, those gifted with the aptitude for wielding yet lacking the know-how.

An untrained arkani could be even more dangerous than a learned one. Not that the Sodality seemed to understand this fact, considering how they'd convinced the Synod to forbid the university from accepting new students. While most spellcraft books had been burned or locked away from the public, Leksi had no doubt textbooks and the odd sigilary had been squirreled away, to be pored over in secret.

The blast of a whistle made Leksi clutch her ears. A youth fled from the fire, pursued by several constables. Tamisk took a step forward, but Leksi held her back.

"Don't," Leksi said, even when the hyenas caught up to the teen and wrestled them to the ground, cudgels swinging.

"It's not right," Tamisk said. "They're just a kid." Others were gathering too, looks of fear and outrage mottling the crowd's faces. No one intervened.

The kid was being accused of using magic. Leksi caught their eye and saw the flames flickering in their depths. She wanted to tell them not to do it, but she recognized the look of defiance on the youth's face as well as the scarring on the teen's cheeks denoting them Qhembalese. The teen started humming, some nonsense vocables born of instinct, and a single spark flared from the tip of their finger. A harmless party trick, but the Synod had a zero-tolerance policy. Leksi had to use her full body weight to stop Tamisk from charging over as one of the hyenas brought a cudgel down across the youth's skull. Another removed the panga from their belt.

The blade fell with a vicious drop, cleaving flesh and bone.

Leksi swallowed her rising gorge, rage and guilt sloshing through her insides as she watched the constables haul the unconscious youth away. The kid's smoldering hand lay twitching on the ground in a bloody puddle.

"This isn't right," Tamisk said again, flinging several curses in Tsirayan at the departing constables. "I wish we could do something."

"We are," Leksi said. "We have The Anchorage. Think about all the kids we're helping. We can't save them all, but we're doing what we can." Leksi held Tamisk's gaze, her heart seizing as her lover deflated.

"It's not nearly enough." Tamisk swatted a tear from her cheek and turned away from the carnage.

In the wake of violence, silence had blanketed the beach. Someone scooped up the kid's severed hand, sobbing quietly.

Leksi couldn't stay, the twisted things inside her far too excited by the bloodshed. In days gone by, lost limbs might've been offered at a fane with Leksi's name on it.

Leksi checked her exposed skin for any sign of damage, for even the slightest nick or scratch, but she was uninjured. The nightmare that had transpired wasn't her doing.

Somberly, Leksi led Tamisk toward the cliffs west of the palace, surprised when Tamisk insisted on picking up a picnic basket from a street vendor along the way. She doubted either of them would have much appetite now.

In the thicker shade provided by umbrella pines and silver proteas along the trail, it was easier to breathe, and Leksi filled her lungs, trying not to think about what would happen to the youth and others dragged into custody tonight. Tomorrow morning the city would be strewn with crushed flowers, the palace dressed in blood and gore. Leksi blinked away tears. Below, the ocean roared and crashed against the rocks, a mirror of her roiling emotions.

They continued along the trail as it wound through the old cemetery. Few people were buried anymore. The dead were either cremated or turned to mulch for agriculture further north where the encroaching desert made life difficult for struggling farmers. The *vrotteland*, some city dwellers called the rural outskirts, as if the increasing heat and lengthening droughts were the fault of the farmers who still clung to old beliefs and danced for impotent gods across the fields.

Leksi touched each headstone, salt-bitten and lichen-gunged, wind-gnawed and time-weathered. Many of the names and dates were illegible. Some were in scripts she couldn't read, others etched with symbols and no words at all. And there, a symbol of her own devising. A grave for a past version of herself. She'd had to bury empty coffins once, reinventing herself in order to remain in the city without raising suspicion.

"Here?" Tamisk gestured to a patch of tufty grass in the shade between graves. The view was impeccable, the air here unclogged by magic or industry and only faintly hazed with humidity.

"It's perfect." Leksi settled cross-legged on the warm earth, and tucked her sandaled feet beneath her skirt. It was later than she realized, the sun already melting into the sea. She glared at the questing fingers of dying sunlight as if she could frown them away.

"This could've been a perfect evening," Tamisk said, as she listlessly unpacked a basket full of Leksi's favorites.

"It mostly still is. Don't let them steal our joy." Leksi popped a banana fritter into her mouth. "You planned this, I see. Did you have an ulterior motive?"

Tamisk blushed and it shocked Leksi's heart, black and shriveled as it was, into a painful throb.

"You never take a break," Tamisk said. "I wanted to make it special."

"It is. Thank you." Leksi planted a kiss on the tip of Tamisk's perfect button nose. There was nothing quite so romantic as a picnic in a cemetery at sunset; Leksi only wished the basket hadn't come with knives. Sharp objects made the monsters inside her restless, and they were already aggrieved by the season, and riled up by the scene at the beach.

"Aren't we being rude though?" Tamisk gestured to the graves. Tsirayans gave their dead to the wild gods of the fathoms.

"The dead don't care." Leksi helped herself to a groundnut pudding. "And I appreciate the quiet."

Cemeteries were never crowded, except for the first day of autumn when families gathered to pay their respects, leaving beeswax candles and other tokens made of chiseled stone, polished wood, shells, sea glass, or bone.

There were no tokens on Leksi's graves. She did her best to ensure no one would mourn her. She'd had friends and lovers over the years, but she always carefully extricated herself from their lives long before she had to fake her demise.

Eventually, she'd have to leave Tamisk too. But that was decades away. She glanced at her lover whose hair was still a rich treacle mop shot through with sun-kissed strands of gold. No gray in sight. Leksi could get away with a few more years before having to magic-up wrinkles with another spelled pendant, even if the use of any magic pained her.

The breeze was a sticky kiss of brine, tousling Tamisk's bangs hanging like daggers over eyes the color of nutmeg. It slipped its fingers up the frothy hem of Leksi's dress, and she resented how much she loved its cool caress—an unwanted reminder of the home she wished she hated. Leksi sighed, trying to relax and forget the images of brutality seared into her mind.

"Doesn't seem fair to be happy when so many suffer," Tamisk said.

"It's not," Leksi said. "But wallowing in grief doesn't help anyone. We're doing what we can to help. We deserve this moment for ourselves."

A tentative smile tugged at Tamisk's lips as Leksi popped another fritter into her mouth. "Despite everything, right now, in this moment, I'm happy."

Leksi sucked in a deep breath. There, the faintest tickle at the back of her throat, an almost sneeze teasing her nostrils.

The graveyard vibrated with a soft resonance she felt as a rumble beneath her palms, as if she was caressing her purring cat. Not surprising, when the bones of long-dead arkani infused the soil with magic as they decayed. Eventually, their essence would trickle back into the veins of energy webbed beneath the skin of the world. The sun slipped below the horizon, unspooling gold thread across the waves as twilight skulked closer. The earth juddered.

"Did you feel that?" Leksi asked.

"Just a tremor," Tamisk said, spooning rice into her mouth.

Another ripple, this one stronger. It undulated through Leksi as if a jagged stone had been skipped across her brain. Magic, powerful and undeniable.

"Are you sure?" Leski asked.

"It's nothing," Tamisk said. "Just the rumblings of old gods who don't want to be forgotten." She kissed Leksi and all concern dissolved in the taste of sweet coconut. Then Tamisk pulled away, breathless, and reached into one of the many pockets of her trousers. "Guess I should seize the moment despite the night's unpleasantness." She revealed a small wooden box, delicately carved in the Tsirayan style.

Leksi stilled, every muscle taut as a harp string. She should've seen this coming.

"I love you, Leksi. I love you with all the salt in the sea," Tamisk started, voice deepening with sincerity. The words turned Leksi's insides into the mush of fermenting fruit.

It wasn't true though. Tamisk loved a version of Leksi sculpted by dishonesty. Their life together was a fiction, beautiful lies stitched into a fragile tapestry. She'd never expected anyone to love her as Tamisk did. But it wasn't the *real* her; no one could love that. Tamisk would jump in the nearest skip and hightail it back to Tsiraya if she knew the truth of what tainted Leksi's blood.

Leksi eyed the knives. How easily she could nick her skin and release the nightmares festering inside her. Some dark part of herself wanted to see Tamisk recoil in fear, but Leksi throttled the instinct. She was better than that. She had to be.

The box cracked open and Leksi's chest did the same.

A silver set of earrings with garnets swirled black and red lay beside a needle to do the piercing if Leksi said yes. Nestled beside the earrings was another trinket bearing a similar gem, the bauble waiting to be added to Tamisk's bracelet.

Now the question, hanging in the space between them like a butcher's blade. No matter how Leksi answered, it would destroy them both.

Another rumble, the cliffs heaving hard enough to scatter

their picnic and shake squawking birds from the trees. In the wake of the tremor, there was silence. No chirrup of insects, no cry of gulls or croak of disgruntled crows, no rustling in the undergrowth from crepuscular critters. Then a roar as the waves rushed back to shatter against the cliffs, spray exploding high above their heads and dousing the edge in foam.

This was a power Leksi thought she'd left behind almost five hundred years and half a world ago. It was so irritatingly familiar, its unwanted presence making her teeth itch.

"We have to go," she said, scrambling to her feet.

The nearest headstone split in two and Tamisk screamed, a sound Leksi had never heard before from her usually stoic lover.

"What's happening?" She clung to Leksi, who desperately checked her hands for any sign of blood on the off chance she'd caused this.

Again the ground seethed, a fault-line ripping through the sod. The earth heaved and a ghoulish limb scrabbled through roots and soil.

Tamisk screamed again and Leksi shifted, placing herself between her lover and whatever creature was being vomited up from the bowels of the earth. A head emerged, hair knotted with decomposing leaves and disgruntled earthworms. A face streaked with dirt, eyes blinking away grit before its gaze fixed on Leksi with soul-searing intensity; one eye an icy swirl of color, the other a clouded gray. In his hand, the ghoul clutched Leksi's discarded gem-nobbed phalange.

She froze, every sinew cinched to snapping. The monsters

tamped down in her marrow scraped her insides raw, roused by the magic spilling from the desecrated grave.

Lips, bloodied against teeth too white, curved into a rictus as Leksi's name—her real one, comprising eight foul syllables in the whip-snap tongue of their homeland—fell from her brother's mouth.

Current arkanic theory states that arkanisticated substances contain arkana, which can be understood as a force within 'magical' corpuscles. When excited, that is vibrated with the correct frequency, these particles de-arkanisticate and release magic, which is absorbed by the air as well as living matter. Once released, this arkanic force can be controlled and even transmuted by those competent in spellwork.*

Excerpt from *Doubts and Paradoxes: An Argument for Magical Corpuscles* by Robera Bololo

*Whether these corpuscles were created by a deity or simply exist within the natural world is not within my purview, nor relevant to the scientific understanding of this phenomenon.

CHAPTER FOUR
NIKI

The darkness lay thick as molasses, impenetrable and suffocating, and yet I wanted to take a long swallow. Perhaps it was simply fear and dehydration making pencil shavings of my mind, but I swore I saw the darkness twitch as if it were some living creature.

"Jaq?" I called out once the constables departed. "Jaq, are you here?"

"Don't." A stranger's gruff response came swift and categorical. "Speak and they'll take your tongue."

Cautiously, I traced the cracks along the stone, the unnecessary manacles on my wrists clinking. I whispered into mold-slimed gaps in the masonry. Nothing. If Jaq was in a similar cell somewhere, she couldn't hear me, was too terrified to answer, or perhaps they'd done something terrible to her—I squeezed my eyes shut, trying to block out the nightmarish thoughts. This would not be where I sounded the final cadence of my brief existence, some imperfect echo fracturing into silence as I turned to rot and dust. Forgotten.

How naïve I'd been to believe in the city's justice system, as if every arkani pinned like a dead bug outside the palace gates had received a fair trial. Jaq and I had both believed having the right permits and a scholar's indigo robes would protect us. My hubris had been shredded while being dragged blindfolded and gagged through the palace by constables who'd only offered snide remarks about ridding the city of yet another arkani.

I fell into silence, counting breaths and waiting. I kept away from the walls, not wanting to feel that mildewed touch. The thin layers of my clothes did nothing to protect me from the filth and damp. Alone in the darkness, I had no defense against the wisps of childhood memory slithering into my mind.

The tentative caress of the shadows was a familiar one, transporting me back to the cellar where I'd been imprisoned for whatever minor irritation I'd caused my parents. The cellar was preferable to the woods though, where they'd hauled me beneath the thatch of trees festooned with trinket offerings to the elemental gods. There they'd bound me to the stump of a lightning-felled jackalberry, hoping they'd return at dawn to find me god-touched and suddenly capable of magic.

Dawn only ever brought bitter disappointment.

Excelling at school had seen me beaten or banished to the cellar less frequently, but my parents never stopped praying for a different sort of child. I'd done everything I could to earn their love, to make them proud. It was never enough. And now, all those hours poured into academics might still amount to nothing. No one was coming to save me.

My thoughts spiraled as I began to hum the tune borrowed from Scryali's *Ditty for Zither*, now known as a children's rhyme. It was the same melody I'd hummed to pass the hours spent between sacks of moldering potatoes, or wondering if a leopard would find me tied to a tree.

At least the dungeon had good acoustics. Every cough, sigh, whimper, and fart from other prisoners reverberated while the clink and scrape of iron chain provided a percussive accompaniment. As I waited for an unknown end, I composed. An ode to the stinking bucket in the corner, a threnody for my delusions of grandeur, a dirge of degradation. Perhaps if I were an arkani, I'd be able to assemble the scattered fragments of sound into a spell to ward off the chill or combat my despair.

Perhaps my parents had been right after all, and the gods had finally risen from their indolence to punish me for the heresy of my pursuits.

Grabbing fistfuls of hair, I rocked back and forth, manacles jangling. I tucked my head into my knees, trying to breathe through the panic rising like a spring tide, engulfing me in cold sweat. I lapped at my own tears as if the brine would slake my thirst.

A swift death, however painful, would be preferable to slow decay.

I gave into sleep then; there was no point being awake. Sleep at least brought dreams of sharpened pikes and an end to misery. It should've been a nightmare, but dreams of dying had always proved a comfort. As a child, my greatest fear was that I'd somehow become what my parents wanted, acquire the ability to wield magic and yet remain a disappointment.

Death was preferable.

An indeterminate amount of time later, I slid from sleep

to waking. My mouth was fuzzed with the moss of dehydration, breath sour and stomach gurgling on nothing but bile. I dragged a hand through my hair, fingers streaked with filth and scabbed with an array of tiny wounds I didn't remember acquiring. The chains dangling from the too-tight manacles chimed, and I winced as the hard edge of the cuffs bit into my skin, already rubbed raw.

I paused, studying my fingers limned in gray. As I took inventory of my broken nails, the murk grew brighter, the shadows thinning. The dull thud of heavy heels drew closer until each footfall echoed like a gunshot.

The lantern light was searing, and I squinted, momentarily wishing for darkness.

"This one," a constable said, and the bars of my cell screeched open.

Rough hands jerked at the chains, the manacles biting deeper. I cried out and received a slap across the face.

"Another sound and we'll take your tongue." The constable flicked open a folding knife, the blade glinting.

Gritting my teeth, I stumbled behind my captors. I tried to take in my surroundings, making mental notes of the layout, and surreptitiously peering into gloom-choked cells in search of Jaq. Most held nothing but the withered remains of a corpse, the smell barely registering given the general miasma of rot and excrement.

A face loomed behind the bars of one cell, eyes peering from gaunt sockets, cheeks hollow and the nose a crooked ruin from multiple breaks. As I stared, the prisoner wrapped their remaining skeletal fingers around the bars. They licked their cracked and bleeding lips, gaze beseeching, but said nothing. The prisoner's gaze followed me in silent protest as the hyenas lugged me toward the narrow staircase.

My heart soared despite the difficulty of the climb. I was a child again, my mother standing silhouetted in the light from the kitchen, door open and welcoming me back up into warmth, if not love.

I felt it now, the automatic loosening within my chest as I ascended. The university must've interceded on our behalf. No doubt an official apology and significant compensation for the erroneous arrest would be waiting at the top of the stairs.

"Surely you can remove these now," I said when I staggered up the last step.

The answer was a fist smashed against my jaw. I toppled, stunned. I'd never been struck, not like this. The beatings of my childhood were a lifetime ago, and neither of my parents, despite their many other failings, had ever hit me with their fists.

Weak and reeling, I didn't resist as the constables dragged me down a long, dim corridor. My ears were still ringing when they deposited me in a room that smelled impossibly of fresh cut flowers. A heavy door slammed shut, the sound falling like a hammer on my already throbbing head as I struggled to regain composure.

"Oh, Niki." A familiar voice cracked with emotion. Jaq's gentle hands soothed filth-crusted hair from my face, and I wept at her touch. Her wrists had been bandaged, her hands whole and fingers unscathed.

"I'm so sorry," she said, and I exhaled in relief. She still had her tongue. "I tried to tell them, but they wouldn't listen." She held me as I continued to sob in relief. "Come on, you're safe now. Or you will be, if you do what they say."

A wooden door at the opposite end of the room whispered open, admitting a tall and stately person I recognized but couldn't immediately place. There was an insignia embroidered in mauve on the lapel of the person's otherwise gray kaftan: the sigil of annulment used by magic-wielders to negate a spell. The same sigil was etched into the manacles still clamped on my wrists.

The symbol of the Sodality.

It wasn't easy drinking tea with shackles hanging heavy from bloody wrists, but I was parched and didn't care if I sloshed the honeybush brew all over the plush carpets. Nor did I care as I scalded my tongue, downing one cup only to have Jaq refill it. The three of us sat on cushions around a low table as if we were at a high society tea party, and not a few rungs up from the dungeons.

"Please, help yourself." The Sodality member slid over a tray of pastries. I wanted to flip the silver, to scatter the tartlets, and hurl the teapot across the room.

Instead, my stomach urged my hand toward one of the

sweet treats commonly eaten at solstice. I crammed it into my mouth, swallowing a mouthful of apricot jam and cream, and even licked my filthy fingers. I ate three more before I managed to scrounge up enough courage to face my captor.

"Who are you?" I asked, seeing Jaq wince out the corner of my eye. She sat tight-lipped, the food untouched on her own plate. "And what do you want?"

"I'm here to make you an offer, to give you the opportunity to save yourself," she said.

"I'm not an arkani. Tell them, Jaq."

"Just listen to what she—Our Esteemed," Jaq added with a sideways glance at the woman, "has to say. Please," she said softly in the same tone she used when trying to explain why the math wouldn't support my musical theories.

Our Esteemed? She certainly wasn't my esteemed.

"I'm not an arkani," I said again.

"Perhaps not," the Esteemed said. "Tell me, Nikima, do you follow the Principles of Inyoti?"

I'd learned them like every child at school and had them beaten into me at home. The ideology had allegedly been a gift from the Serpent God to the first arkani, our Ancestors, blessed to carry a scale within their hearts. A society could be built on worse, but I'd always questioned the need for the gods in those principles. Surely people could just be decent to each other.

The Sodality, however, didn't acknowledge Inyoti at all.

"I live according to the laws of Savat," I said.

"If you did, we wouldn't be having this conversation." The

woman stirred honey into her tea.

"Why does it matter if I believe in the principles?" I was exhausted, my exasperation starting to show.

"For far too long, Savat has lived in the grip of an archaic belief system. While we, the Sodality, acknowledge the positives contained within the principles, we also believe it's time for change," the Esteemed said.

"The One True Path," I said, trying not to sneer.

"Yes," she said. "The One True Path provided by our understanding of science and technology, not superstitious nonsense. Discovery, innovation—I imagine you might agree with the idea that every one of us has a duty to contribute to the betterment of society, to leave a legacy that ensures the continued path of progress for future generations."

It was hard to argue with that, but I had to wonder who got to decide what counted as bettering society.

"What about magic?" I asked. "That's not superstition. It exists. We can see it at work." I glanced at the lamps, searching for sigils, but found none.

"Magic is simply a force we don't fully understand yet, but your performance tonight certainly proves it has nothing to do with gods, doesn't it?" She sipped her tea. "You said so yourself; you're not an arkani, and yet you used fire magic," the Esteemed continued.

Unlike the Sodality members I'd seen on the city streets, this woman hadn't shaved her head leaving only a single stripe of hair down the middle—the hairstyle meant to denote the One True Path. Instead, her dark tresses were woven into a tight braid from crown to nape, revealing her right ear, which bore a burn scar.

"Actually, I'm not even sure the elemental affinities are relevant," I said, unable to stop myself.

The Esteemed grinned. "See? It's exactly that keen intellect of yours we think would be better used in the service of the people."

"In the service of the Sodality, you mean." I hadn't meant to sound so petulant, but this whole exchange irked me. All I'd ever wanted was to serve the people. Magic without the need for higher learning or birthright nonsense, providing greater equity for all. Whether it came from the gods or not seemed immaterial. It was a force we could use if we learned to wield it more fairly.

"I'd like to make you an offer." The Esteemed topped up my cup.

I was about to interrupt when Jaq gripped my knee, squeezing hard.

"Just listen," she said.

Fighting the urge to argue, I nodded and sipped the tea, swallowing my protests.

"If you forget the university, we'll forget these charges against you," the Esteemed continued. "Pledge yourself to the Sodality and you'll be granted a research position right here in the palace where you'll be free to conduct experiments as you wish. No permits required, no bureaucracy, no restrictions. You'll also have unlimited access to all the archives, including the forbidden texts of the former royals."

My mind immediately filled with images of the legendary palace library, that gilded trove of knowledge both magnificent and functional that would put even the university's shelves to shame. I could already smell the antique tomes, fingers twitching at the thought of getting my hands on all that abandoned wisdom.

"That's a very generous offer," I said. Too generous. There had to be a catch, and yet the hunger in my belly snarled with want for so much more than fruit pastries.

"We've had our eyes on you for a while now," the Esteemed said. "We've been impressed with your work and feel you'd make a considerable contribution to our own research."

"Most of my experiments have failed," I said, the admission lacerating. Even the most recent experiment hadn't exactly gone to plan.

"Your methodologies show promise, methodologies we have, in truth, not been able to replicate ourselves, let alone master, but we believe you're on the right path to unlocking the secrets of magic."

"And what methodologies have you employed, aside from executions?"

"Niki," Jaq said, my name a warning.

"I agree with you," the Esteemed said. "The executions are unnecessarily cruel. Perhaps it'll be your research here that allows us to find less violent methods of subduing wayward arkani without resorting to impalement."

I considered the Esteemed's words. While our methods diverged, our ultimate goals seemed more or less aligned. *More or less.* I'd never had any political aspirations beyond wanting to understand the mechanics of magic to improve life in Savat.

"So you get my research and expertise, but what will I get in return?" I asked, momentarily forgetting the manacles on my wrists.

"You are unbelievable," Jaq said with a sharp inhalation.

"You mean besides getting to live and work without restrictions?" The Esteemed raised an incredulous brow and I swallowed hard. I had no right to ask for more and yet I couldn't stop myself.

"Will I be able to publish my findings?" I asked.

"Those will be shared exclusively with the Sodality," the Esteemed said.

Of course. I would be trading one prison for another. One that came with tea and tarts, and hopefully a bath, though.

As if reading my thoughts, the woman added, "You'll want for nothing."

Except freedom. The thought whipped a welt across my mind.

"And if I don't agree to these terms?" I asked.

Jaq muttered something incomprehensible under her breath and shook her head.

"Then there is little I can do considering the charges against you." A frown creased the older woman's brow. "And you'll likely be found guilty of using unauthorized magic in public, branded an arkani, and—"

"No," Jaq said before turning to me. "Think about what this opportunity means for your research, Niki, for your legacy?"

"What legacy, when the Sodality will own my research?" I scoffed.

"At least you'll live," she snapped. "Or has this all been about your ego?"

I balked as Jaq's words sank barbs into me.

"Isn't figuring out how magic works and how everyone can use it more important than personal accolades?" Her words carried a vehemence I'd never heard before. She'd always seemed ambivalent, but perhaps I'd misjudged her. She was right. The plight of the people mattered more than seeing my efforts lauded, even if it meant I'd never be known, or remembered. Why did that chafe at me like a dry pumice stone on tender skin? Why couldn't I shed this desire for acknowledgment even when my life depended on it? I gulped down another mouthful of tea.

"What if—" I started, but doubt gathered like storm clouds. *What if I fail? What if I'm wrong?*

"Our concert already proves at least some of your theories are right. You're so close now. All our hard work would've been for nothing if you refuse." Jaq bit her lip, a flash of familiar irritation on her face. "I've spent the better part of a year neglecting my own studies to help you with yours," she said. "You owe me this."

Guilt needled my heart as she took my hands, seemingly unfazed by the muck and blood on my fingers. "Think about what you could accomplish with all the Sodality has to offer."

Far more than what I'd achieve at the university.

"Besides, they'll kill you if you don't agree," she deadpanned. "Please, Nik. If not for yourself, then do this for me. Don't let everything I sacrificed for you this past year go to waste." Her gaze bore into me and I had to look away as I tried to untangle individual emotions from the flurry of feelings pummeling my insides. I did owe Jaq. Although I'd never asked her to, she had set aside her own pursuits to help with mine and now I had a way to repay her.

Closing my eyes, I hummed the comforting Scryali tune, my mind churning. Death or acquiescence. It was no choice at all. I couldn't deny the excitement stirring inside me at the thought of getting my hands on all those ancient, forbidden texts, never mind the possibilities of what I might accomplish without needing to appease my professor.

"Unlimited access to any resources I want," I said, glancing at Jaq who nodded encouragement. "No restrictions on experiments or performances?"

"None whatsoever," the Esteemed agreed.

"Access to the latest recording technology and to whatever research the Sodality has already gathered on magic?"

The woman's expression soured a little. "You aren't in any position to make demands. That said..." The air between us crackled with tension as she seemed to deliberate. When she opened her mouth, I braced for condemnation. Instead she chuckled. "You drive a hard bargain for someone in chains, but I think we can arrange that. Especially if it means we'll be able to announce a breakthrough at First Council."

"First Council?" I gaped. "But that's only a few weeks

away."

"Seventeen days to be exact," the Esteemed said.

Three days I'd been in the dungeon then. It felt so much longer.

"Seventeen days?" I laughed at the preposterous suggestion. "Perhaps in seventeen months…"

"This is non-negotiable," she said. "And given the relative success of your latest performance, I'm sure you'll provide us with something we can use to reassure the people."

"You're serious. You want me to come up with something in seventeen days?" I gawped. It had taken me years to achieve this much, and it was barely anything at all.

"Yes."

"It's impossible," I said, dread unfurling like a suffocating blanket from my toes to my neck.

"For your sake, I hope it isn't." The Esteemed bit into a tartlet.

"What if Niki can't do it?" Jaq asked and I really wished she hadn't.

"Then the Sodality may have no need for arrogant young scholars who think too highly of themselves. Perhaps another night in confinement would provide the necessary motivation—"

"No. It's fine," I said. "I can do it. By First Council." It was absurd to think I could deliver anything of value in such a short time, but if I at least tried, perhaps I'd be allowed to live.

"Excellent," the Esteemed said. "Then we have a deal."

"Could I have the terms of this agreement in writing,

though? Signed and notarized. In triplicate," I asked. I needed some assurance the Sodality wouldn't renege on their promises.

Jaq snorted, in derision or disbelief, I couldn't tell.

The Esteemed's eyes narrowed. "Careful, Nikima. Audacity is only admirable in small doses." She stood and gestured for a nearby constable who grudgingly unlocked the manacles on my wrists.

"I'll be happy to get started as soon as I can get a bath and some clean clothes," I said, hoping she wouldn't notice my trembling hands.

"Of course." She smiled, but her next words cut me to the quick. "I sincerely hope you don't disappoint us."

Chapter Five
Leksi

For a moment that stretched into eons, Leksi stood transfixed, staring at the malformation of limbs that was somehow her little brother. She thought she'd escaped her family, the Nether, and the literal death-grip of her mother. Yet, despite the centuries and realms between them, one of her siblings had managed to track her down.

"You," Zal snarled the word, glowering as if this was somehow her fault. Then his eyes rolled up into his head. He pitched forward and Leksi reacted involuntarily, catching him before his head hit the ground.

"Who—what—how?" Tamisk stuttered through all the question words, none of which Leksi knew how to answer.

"Go home," she said.

Tamisk folded her arms across her chest. "That thing crawled out of a grave like some corpse-puppet and—what are you doing?"

"Ruining a perfectly good blanket," Leksi said as she bundled Zal into the fabric, leaving the remains of their picnic for the crows. No amount of bleach would rid the fibers of Zal's stench, the stink like stars spilling their hideous entrails across the void. It was the reek of pure chaos, of entropy, and enmity.

"Leksi." Tamisk squeezed her eyes shut and bashed her fist

against her forehead, the thing she always did in moments of frustration.

"Either go home and forget about all this, about *me*, or—" Leksi stumbled over her words. A voice in her head told her not to give Tamisk a choice, to let this be the end of the relationship, a violent but effective severing of what could never be.

They'd been together almost ten years now, far longer than Leksi had ever played house with a lover before, their roots and boughs pleached in some parasitic embrace. Tamisk had become the unwitting host, oblivious to how she was slowly being strangled to death.

"Or what?" Tamisk darted a furtive look at the yawning grave Zal had clambered out of with all the grace of a necromancer's first conjuring.

Leksi's brain hadn't gotten that far yet. She only knew she didn't want Tamisk anywhere near the corrupting force of her little brother, and she definitely didn't want him anywhere near The Anchorage. But there was nowhere else she could go.

She eyed the cliff. It would be so easy to roll Zal over the edge and be done with him, but something tugged inside her chest. They were still connected, still their mother's children, linked by blood and magic. She wouldn't be able to do him harm. She could walk away though. Leaving him here wasn't the same as tossing him into the sea.

"We should help them. They're hurt and obviously the victim of sinister magic," Tamisk said.

Leksi choked back a bitter laugh as her gaze met Tamisk's. Her lover was so earnest in her desire to help, in her naïve judgment of the Nether entity Leksi cradled in her lap. But she was cradling him and he was injured. Her breath hitched with unexpected panic. The sensation was familiar, bringing back a warped nostalgia of childhood. It felt like her life was unraveling, but it wasn't. It was merely the proximity of her brother and his particular brand of magic.

Tamisk no doubt felt it too, that slow discombobulation and loss of self.

"Fine, help me up," she said and Tamisk reached for Zal, taking some of his weight off Leksi so she could get her feet underneath her.

"Who is this and how the Depths did they climb out of a grave?" Tamisk cast a worried look into the thickening shadows.

"No idea," Leksi said and once more fought the urge to send Zal tumbling from the cliffs. Something warm and unpleasantly wet was soaking through the blanket and into her skirt where her hip pressed against Zal.

"Stars wept, he's bleeding." That explained the stink and dizzying sense of vertigo. His blood shimmered where it fell, red turning an oily black glossed with magic. She had no idea what his undiluted power would do to the mortal world, the havoc it might cause. She gathered the blanket closer, hoping to prevent more seepage.

"He? You know him? Should I go for a doctor?" Tamisk took a shuddering breath. "Should we get him to the hospital? If I run back to town, I might be able to wave down a tumbrel."

"No, just help me get him home." The one place Leksi didn't want to take him. There was no way this wouldn't end badly for her and yet, that nagging, gnawing familial connection pulsed between them. She resented how much she'd missed it, how much she wanted to hold him close and ask how their family was, if Mother had sent him to look for her. It was far more likely he'd come to the mortal realm for his own nefarious reasons than to run errands for Death.

"But Leksi, he's seriously hurt. We can't—"

"He's my brother," Leksi said.

Tamisk stilled, shocked into momentary paralysis by Leksi's admission.

"You lied to me," she said.

Oh so very many times, but this wasn't the place for a domestic spat.

"Please, Tam, believe me when I say he wouldn't want doctors. And they wouldn't do much good anyway. Please, trust me."

"Trust you?" Tamisk's expression warped from shock to hurt to anger before finally settling into resignation. She started gathering up the detritus of the aborted proposal and Leksi said nothing when Tamisk pocketed the discarded box of earrings.

Leksi couldn't imagine anyone else not being reduced to a quiver of piss and snot at the sight of a monster crawling out of a grave, especially one related to the person you shared a bed with, and yet, Tamisk remained rattled but resilient.

Together, they managed to lift Zal's bulk onto their shoulders. As a youth, he'd been lithe and well-muscled from his misadventures across the Nether, but he was so much smaller now, as if something had chipped away at him, reducing him to cinders.

He grunted in pain, barely conscious. Tamisk probably could've carried his weight alone but he was oddly shaped, as if whatever path he'd taken between the worlds had broken then poorly reassembled his limbs. They trudged through the cemetery, Tamisk hesitating before they emerged in the surrounding neighborhood.

"The constabulary will have questions," she said.

"Just another reveler who over-indulged on the solstice," Leksi said.

"But he's bleeding."

The burgundy stain had spread across the blue-gray blanket and utterly ruined Leksi's dress as well. Magic peeled away from the fibers in sparking slivers.

"A drunk reveler who fell down on his own bottle and gashed his belly?" Leksi said, but Tamisk only raised her eyebrows. "Fine, go get a tumbrel."

Leksi grunted with the strain as Tamisk relinquished Zal's body, then took off down the street, stout legs pumping. There'd be tumbrels waiting near the beaches to transfer the hordes home. Even so, it would be safer to disguise the extent of Zal's injuries. Something subtle, the tiniest of glamours to turn heads away. Surely she could manage that much.

Reluctantly, Leksi flexed a muscle she hadn't used in far too long. Nothing happened. "Come on," Leksi bit out through gritted teeth. "I know you're there, you bastards. Don't make me beg." She closed her eyes, focusing on the power she regularly smothered. The vermin twitched as she slowly released that internally clenched fist, then surged. Leksi cried out as she fought to regain control. She was too weak. Her monsters were ravenous and it took all her remaining strength to wrangle them back to dormancy.

Lesson learned.

By the time Tamisk returned with a tumbrel drawn by a pair of tired-looking mules, Leksi was sweating and swaying from exertion, a migraine pounding at her temples.

Tamisk pried Zal away and got him slumped across the seats in the carriage that was little more than a cart. It was only meant to carry two, but Tamisk slid the driver another handful of coins when they complained, then bundled Leksi in beside her.

It took almost an hour before they stumbled into The Anchorage, the place she'd called home for two and a half lives now. She'd remodeled the original barracks, gradually transforming it first into a coffee house, popular with poets and minstrels, then to an inn, before refurbishment had been complete and she'd started taking in strays.

Two years ago, Leksi had finally cleared space in the wardrobe and allowed Tamisk to move in. She'd never allowed anyone into her private sanctum, not since she'd been forced to share a home with her terminally dysfunctional family. Living with another, and a human, had been an adjustment. A decision she was starting to regret.

Together, Tamisk and Leksi managed to wrestle Zal across the threshold. Ansa greeted them at the door with throaty mewling, her sea-foam gaze flicking to Zal, her tail twitching. If anyone was home, they'd probably be comatose until well past noon. The sudden and unwanted image of the youth's severed hand popped into Leksi's mind, and she hoped none of her charges had succumbed to the constabulary tonight.

"What now?" Tamisk lit the nearest lamp, the light chasing away scampering shadows.

Leksi frowned at the filth sloughing from the body propped against the wall. Filth and magic. "Water," she said. "He stinks."

"It'll take an age to heat," Tamisk said.

"Cold is fine." His veins, like hers, were lined with frost.

Without arguing, Tamisk lit another lamp and handed it to Leksi before disappearing into the kitchen. Leksi shoved her barely conscious brother into the communal washroom at the back of the building and Ansa followed, hissing at the shadows that once again pressed closer.

Leksi muttered something in the language she hadn't spoken for the better part of a century, words falling from her tongue like flakes of rust. The shadows were her brother's, but they retreated at Leksi's command.

"Are you awake?" she asked, still using Nethertaal, her gums stinging. Considering the swath of silence between them, perhaps she should've come up with something better to break the ice, but Zal was bleeding on her pristine floor and there were beetles in his hair.

He only groaned in response.

"Can you stand by yourself? Here, use the wall." She raised his hand and braced it against the wooden logs. The finger she'd hacked from her hand a lifetime ago tumbled from his grasp.

"That's what drew you to me?" She inhaled sharply, mentally berating herself for being so careless.

He didn't deign to answer, or perhaps simply lacked the power. She half expected him to fall, limp and useless, but his grip held, gnarled fingers finding purchase in the gap between beams. His hands were scarred, as if his flesh had been used as a scratching post by a grumpy lion.

He seemed to gather himself then, reeling in his magic and, gingerly, Leksi released his weight, waiting for him to straighten.

He didn't.

He did, however, open his eyes: one clear and brilliant, flecked with hues of color that had no name. The other was gray, clouded, and oozed similarly gray tears. His angular face caught the jaundiced glow of the lamp and Leksi sucked in a breath. She remembered him young and beautiful, sculpted from darkness and ice. The circumstances of his birth had never shown on his face, their mother's rage and devastation manifesting only in the nature of Zal's magic. Now, though…

"What happened?" she asked, hands hovering above the scars laid in a lattice across his cheeks as if his skin had been peeled and patched and peeled again.

Zal held her gaze as he brought his bare heel down on the finger bone between them. The gem had long since lost its radiance, nothing but a pale pebble on even paler bone.

"I didn't want it to be you." His voice was the growl of a brewing tempest as he twisted his foot, crushing the remains of gem and digit.

"Be grateful. Riksa would've shoved you off the cliff," Leksi said, meaning to tease, but the words had too much bite, and Zal flinched as if she'd struck him. "Did you get mauled by a pack of ghouls?" she asked.

He said nothing, his silence unnerving. It wasn't like him. As a kid he'd never shut up. The chaos inside him kept him constantly chattering, switching from one topic to another fast enough to make even a demigod's head spin. Even the dead, forever trapped in the Nether, grew weary of his incessant babbling and rambunctious presence.

"Zalix?" Leksi asked, and waved a hand in front of his face.

He blinked and grimaced, about to respond when Tamisk entered with two buckets filled from the kitchen taps. She dumped them both in the tub standing on curled cat paws.

"Anything else?" she asked, casting a cautious but curious glance at Zal.

"Coffee, please," Leksi said. "It's going to be a long night."

"Technically, it's the shortest," Zal said, his feeble attempt at snark proving he was in fact alive—as alive as any of Death's children could be.

"Just wash." Leksi spit in the language of their homeland, jaw aching from the sharp consonants, and sinuses ringing from the overtones not meant to reverberate in a near-human body. "There's soap on the stand." She pointed in the direction of the tub.

Slowly, Zal dropped the blanket, and Leksi sucked in a breath. His body was littered with scars, the flesh knotted and skin pulled taut in places where the bones beneath weren't sitting right. He limped forward, clearly in pain, with a hand pressed to a fresh wound clotted with dirt. His hip and thigh were scabbed burgundy, smears of blood standing in garish contrast against his pale skin.

The damage was far more extensive than she'd previously thought, and old, too. He'd been hurt, brutally—tortured, perhaps. He should be healing, but the wound extending from chest to ribs was still bleeding, as were other, more minor injuries, all leaking magic. They'd have to do something to contain it, and soon.

Zal's pained inhalation as he slid into the water felt like rusted wire catching at her palms. Someone had hurt him deliberately and catastrophically.

"Is that a sigil?" she asked.

"Surprised you recognize it," he spoke through gritted teeth, and Leksi bit back a retort.

"Was it one of us?" she asked instead.

A moment of stillness, tension thrumming in the air as he considered. The water sloshed over damaged flesh, and Leksi fought the urge to aid him.

"Not this time," he said.

Her anger flowed like vinegar. She may have chosen to leave her family, she may have been grateful to escape her mother's clutches and the suffocating obligation of her birth, but she had never wished any harm upon her siblings, even when they embraced their nature while she could not. That someone else had dared to hurt Zal made her blood bubble and monsters writhe.

"No need to unleash any nightmares on my account." His words sent a rash of gooseflesh up her arms. She'd forgotten how sensitive they were to each other, to the Nether essence they shared even if it manifested differently within each of them.

Gently, Leksi tested that withered connective tissue, prodding at the edges of his power.

"Careful," he said. "I'm not fully myself."

She pulled back, her senses returning to the real world where the scent of her lemon and pine soap had finally begun to mask the stench of blood and graveyard muck.

"What then?" she asked. "Did you piss off some powerful arkani with a penchant for sadism?"

He rested his elbows on his drawn up knees, face hidden by tangled hair. "Do you know how to work an annulment sigil?" he asked, and she bristled at his evasiveness.

"You disturbed a rather lovely picnic and ruined my evening, you know, never mind the stains you've left on my floor. The least you could do is give me a straight answer."

"Perhaps we could stop the chaos seeping out of my veins first?" he said, panting as if merely speaking was too much.

"Stars wept, Zal. What happened?"

"Annulment sigil." He glowered with his good eye.

Leksi wanted to argue, but his pain was a wing with broken

feathers batting at her senses, so she sighed and crouched beside the bath.

"I haven't done proper magic in centuries."

"Even then, you were never any good at it," he said.

"Do you want my help or not?" she snapped.

"Like this." He traced the sigil in the grime caking the edge of the tub. "*Exactly* like this." He traced it again then tapped his chest.

"Why can't you do it yourself?" she asked.

He said her name then, each ugly syllable a lash slicing to the bone.

"Don't call me that. I'm Leksi now. Just Leksi."

"I'm not strong enough to do this by myself. Please. Leksi." His lips quivered and an icy frisson throttled her body.

"Not sure it'll work. I don't know what I'm doing," she admitted.

"Just try."

"Where, just on top of this other one?" she asked, reluctant to touch him or the wound, or to wield magic when she'd devoted her life to its banishment.

"Yes." He closed his eyes as he lay back, exposing his scar-riddled chest. "There's an incantation too. Try to sing along."

"I can't sing."

"Everyone can sing," he bit out.

Taking a deep breath, and once more trying to relax her grip on the magic inside her, Leksi glanced at the scum-written sigil before drawing it gently across the damaged flesh of her brother's chest.

He sang, his voice surprisingly pleasant as it dipped and weaved through a repetitive melody. She tried her best to follow, earning a one-eyed scowl from her brother when she fell out of tune.

Nothing happened.

"Again," he said. "Try harder." He sang and this time the melody felt less like pebbles on her tongue.

When nothing happened after three genuine attempts, Leksi coughed and Zal sighed, defeated.

"You'll need to find me an arkani," he said. "One that can hold a tune."

"How about, thank you dear sister for hauling my naked body out of a literal grave and bringing me home, providing me with soap and water, and—"

"Clothes?" he interjected.

Leksi released a string of vitriolic curses she hadn't used since leaving the Nether. It would've blistered human ears had there been any within hearing range. Ansa meowed from where she stood watch at the door, gaze riveted on Zal as if the cat knew who to blame for Leksi's outburst.

"Take what you must." Leksi indicated the drying rack and the load of laundry Tamisk had hung that morning. "You'll find bandages in the cabinet. I'd appreciate it if you didn't leak all over my floors again."

"Find me an arkani then," he hissed, the sibilant words of Death's language.

Leksi stomped out of the washroom, irked by how easily he

slid beneath her skin. It was his nature to sunder and dysregulate, an aspect no doubt worsened by the wound on his chest.

She had no idea where to find an arkani willing to work healing magic without asking questions, without risking their neck if the constabulary discovered their illicit casting.

Leksi followed her feet to the kitchen, where Tamisk sat tapping her fingers against the table while the samovar boiled—the aroma of coffee, comforting. Tamisk turned and Leksi wanted to clasp her hands, but her own were bloodstained, dirt outlining the creases.

"It's fine." She held up her palm. "None of it's mine."

"It is decidedly *not* fine," Tamisk said as Leksi scrubbed in the sink—careful not to break the skin and stopping only when her hands were their usual milky pallor.

"Your brother?" Tamisk asked, and Leksi concentrated particularly hard on drying her hands. "Is this something..." She chewed over her next words like a mouthful of spoiled cream, then spat it out as if it tasted just as bad. "Are we in danger? Is this something to do with the past you refuse to talk about?"

"Not now, Tam, please." Leksi sighed.

"We have kids living here. If he puts them at risk, I have a right to know. We have a responsibility—"

"I know." Leksi slumped in a chair and propped her elbows on the table before burying her head in her hands. "My family is complicated. We're estranged. I've never lied about that."

"Your brother crawled out of a grave during an earthquake," Tamisk said, big eyes wide and arms folded as she regarded Leksi. "Is he a magic-wielder? Is that why you're so anti-magic?"

Leksi wanted to laugh, or cry. Instead, she tried to take calming breaths, imagining the petals of a protea opening and closing. It was a trick Tamisk used with their charges to soothe panic attacks.

"Leks, please," Tamisk said. "If you let me in, maybe I can help." She deserved answers Leksi didn't know how to give. The truth would fracture the life they'd built together, but she could hardly deny who and what she was with her brother bleeding in their bathtub.

Leksi, she'd called herself ever since she'd escaped the frosted prison of her mother's realm, the abbreviation of her full name translating to something like *dream*, as if she could turn her fantasies into reality and escape what she was. But she was the very antithesis of dream, and it was time Tamisk knew the truth.

Later, though; right now there was the small matter of casting an annulment over her leaky faucet of a brother.

"I promise I'll tell you everything," Leksi said, hoping it was a promise she would keep. "But my brother, Zal. He's hurt."

"I'll fetch a doctor, one from Qhemba who knows to be discreet."

"No," Leksi said, trying to be gentle. "He needs an arkani to annul the spell cast on him." If his magic continued to flow unchecked, then it wouldn't only be the inhabitants of The Anchorage at risk.

"We can't." Tamisk shook her head. "After everything…

considering all we stand for."

"I wouldn't suggest this if it weren't serious. If it wasn't dire, in fact." Leksi paused, giving Tamisk time to absorb the blow.

"We can't risk bringing an arkani here, and we certainly can't risk going to one. If we raise any suspicions, we could lose everything." Tamisk clenched her fists, muscles cording in her forearms.

"We could ask one of ours," Leksi said softly. "Salja has a gift for healing."

"Absolutely not," Tamisk said. "We swore to protect her and all the others under our roof. Unconditionally." She enunciated every syllable, and Leksi knew there was no point in arguing.

But they had to do something, otherwise the life they'd built—and what little protection they could offer to those in need—would end up in ruins in the wake of Zal's destructive power.

Chapter Six
Zal

The songs had pulled him into consciousness, hymns to Death whisper-hummed by the penitent placing peeled scabs, boiled bones, red beads from freshly pricked fingers, or teeth still gooey from raw gums on the crude altars. While the devotion of the faithful bolstered his strength, he couldn't use the offerings to heal his wounds. He tried and failed, his flesh rejecting the foreign objects.

He'd waited, feeding ravenously on prayer, before he could muster his shadows. Like crows, he sent them scavenging for the remnants of his shattered form. He'd tried and failed to fit each shard into place, but the damage was severe and his body, cut off from replenishing magic, resisted his efforts.

It wasn't until the crone, Gafina, with her cataract-veiled vision and heart full of Death's longing, took pity on the misshapen boy she assumed had been abandoned by a family unable to love his twisted limbs and scarred visage. She'd scraped so very close to the truth.

Buoyed by his shadows, Zal had let her trundle him in a barrow to her shack in the slums on the outskirts of the city, where her careful ministrations and daily invocations to the god that had spurned him soothed his injuries and let him convalesce. Gradually, he forced the false assembly of parts into a composition resembling something more like a person and less like a butcher's leavings.

And here he was, once more a battered, broken thing, at the mercy of another. Only this time there'd be no vigils or vespers to help knit his wounds.

Had he guessed the stream would lead to his sister, Zal never would've taken the plunge. She'd rejected her family when all they'd ever done was love her.

"Leksi." He rolled the abbreviation across his tongue, feeling the softened edges of her true name. It still left a terrible aftertaste. She'd always been the favorite, had always had Mother's love, and yet she'd thrown it away. And for what? To play human?

Zal closed his eyes and let the cold water slosh over his head as if he were back in Death's womb. He waited, until the heaviness of the sorrow spawned by Ailia's betrayal morphed into righteous fury. He had no use for sadness, but rage would let him gather his aching limbs, grit his teeth against the pain tearing through his chest, and rise from the muddy waters, renewed with bitter purpose.

Ailia was a powerful arkani, her natural talent enhanced by years of dedicated study, but she was still human. She wouldn't be able to wield his power. It would corrupt her mind, overwhelm her, destroy her, if Zal didn't destroy her first.

Clean enough, he rifled through the contents of his sister's cabinets, finding lavender oil, feverfew, and some other salves, as well as the promised bandages.

"What are you looking at?" Zal glared at the fluffy feline

regarding him from the door, tail twitching as its slanted gaze turned toward the shadows roosting like bats in the rafters. Of course Leksi would have a cat. They were Death's creatures, after all.

A small mirror allowed Zal to study the sigil on his chest, his gray pallor made worse by the hazy glass. The sigil comprised four separate runes, one for each element, and a messy fifth. He traced the inflamed skin as if some residue of the spell might cling to the frayed edges.

Ailia had found a way to complete the spell. Almost. He'd escaped just in time. While she'd stolen a considerable amount of his power, she hadn't taken it all. There was a chance he could fix this, find Riksa, and inflict this spell on her instead.

He should've known Ailia's ambitions rivaled his own, should've seen through the ruse instead of being blinded by adoration. Blood seeped, smoking faintly where it landed on the floor. Wisps of raw magic dissipated into the ether, lacing the air with chaos. Zal didn't care about the havoc such spillage might cause when soaked into soil or inhaled by human lungs; he only cared that he was weakened.

The cat padded closer and paused, sniffing, then lapping at a puddle of his blood. Its tail flicked and curled in sigil-like formations. Zal waited for the cat to sprout wings or explode into roaches, but it only regarded him with burning eyes and red whiskers, tail still twitching.

Ignoring the cat, Zal dressed the wound as best he could with a witch hazel tincture and a calendula ointment. Nothing more than hedgerow flower-craft, but it would have to do.

He couldn't afford to lose more magic. The slightest effort left him light-headed, and several fractures had reopened in his healing bones. Even lifting a shirt over his head proved utterly exhausting. After a third unsuccessful attempt, he gave up and settled for a pair of loose-fitting trousers before limping barefoot from washroom to kitchen, the feline following in his wake.

His shadows flitted against him, stitching darkness across cuts and scrapes, sinking into bones to temporarily bind and mend. He listened to their whispers as they recounted their journey from cemetery to Anchorage. He was in the city now, far from the comfort of his citadel; in the city where they banned magic and impaled arkani.

He wondered where Ailia would go, trying to view her plan through her eyes. Armed with his power, she might think herself strong enough to take on the Synod and Sodality single-handedly. Or perhaps this was all part of some greater plan with Motselana.

Zal sighed, battling against another wave of weariness. The sun must be rising and, although the season had officially tipped toward winter, the summer remained a relentless foe.

Beneath his palm memories caught like cobwebs, ghosts trapped in aging timber murmuring pleas and sorrow. He understood their lament, their desire for freedom, for the solace of Death's realm. He picked at a splinter, debating whether or not to set the spirits free. Were the ghosts a comfort or an annoyance to his sister? The splinter caught beneath his nail and a single bead of blood stained the loosened fibers, opening a doorway for the trapped dead.

He rested his head on the wall, letting the tremulous spirits momentarily bolster his strength. They flowed through him, a rejuvenating trickle filling depleted capillaries and oozing along desiccated arteries.

He'd had a heart once, but his mother had ripped it from his chest, the black gristle left shredded in the snow. It was a part of him he'd never been able to heal. Perhaps it was easier to survive with only the memory of it beating behind his ribs, though the absence of the organ had done little to spare him feeling.

Grief congealed in that cavity, thick gobbets of unwanted sentiment. Ailia was nothing to him now. Her betrayal, a death sentence he couldn't wait to carry out.

Zal pushed away from the wall, cradled by his shadows as he headed toward the kitchen. There, Leksi and her paramour sat in silence at a lamplit table.

Without looking up, Leksi poured coffee into a mug and pushed it toward an empty chair. She didn't bother trying to hide her resentment of his intrusion, and he didn't bother masking his disgust at everything she'd become.

Gingerly, he eased his body down, ignoring Leksi's scrutiny. The cat twined around his legs, vibrating with a noisy purr that only seemed to further irk his sister.

"Anything to eat?" he asked, gritting his teeth against the weight on his aching joints when the cat leapt onto his lap. When Leksi didn't respond, he added, "It would help me heal." The bandages on his chest were already stained.

It was the human who got up and ladled spoonfuls of forever soup into a bowl from the pot simmering on the stove. Zal inhaled the aroma of bone marrow and rosemary, his twisted innards twitching in need.

Gratefully, he took the bowl. The human had tattoos on their hands, the shaky lines faded and blown out, but still recognizable as the sigils of the salt gods, the progeny of Water, and Zal's cousins. If his sister insisted on making a pet of a laity, at least she'd picked a more interesting one. "You're Tsirayan," he said in the Salt tongue. "Coral Clan?"

"You speak Tsirayan?" The human seemed impressed. "And yes, Coral Clan, or I used to be." The human rubbed the blurred ink on their fingers. "I'm Tamisk, and use *she*, *her* in Savati."

Like the language of the Nether, the Salt tongue had no gendered pronouns.

"Call me Zal. *He*, *him* when needs must."

"Someone sure did a number on you, Zal." Tamisk switched to Savati, her gaze on the gnarled topography of his torso.

"An arrogant arkani thought she could rob me of my magic," Zal said between bites. There was little point in lying.

"So you are a magic-wielder," Tamisk blurted, the disgust clearly written across her face. He glanced at Leksi, who responded with a scowl and folded her hands to hide the white agate growing from her knuckle. How had she explained that to her lovers, he wondered, while fighting the urge to rub his own denuded joint. His gem had never returned.

"The arkani failed, right?" Leksi asked. "Please tell me she failed."

"The sigil is incomplete, but still problematic." Zal didn't want to admit just how deep the wound ran.

"Is it even possible?" Leksi's forehead creased in contemplation. "Can an arkani strip you of your power?"

"Theoretically," he said, choosing his words carefully in case he gave this estranged sister inconvenient ideas. "She imbued an amulet which is still drawing on my power, hence my need for the annulment."

Leksi shot a questioning look at Tamisk, who shook her head. Interesting.

"That only explains the most recent marks," Leksi said.

"It looks like you were tortured." Tamisk's soft voice was at odds with her size and impressive musculature. "Did the constabulary do this? Were you held at a conversion camp?"

"Tortured, yes. Repeatedly," he said. "But they are very old wounds." He caught the fleeting impressions of the emotions flitting across Leksi's face before her features settled into a mask of resignation. She reached a hand across the table, but he only stared at it. He didn't want her pity or her care; he needed nothing from the sister who had rejected her family and abandoned her home. Instead, Zal pointedly stroked the purring cat curled in his lap and took a tentative sip of the coffee. He'd expected some cheap, barrel-scrape variety, but this tasted of dense jungle with notes of volcanic histrionics. It had clearly been imported from well north of the desert, from verdurous nations beyond the empire of joRania.

"Did you deserve it?" Leksi asked, and Tamisk muttered

something in the Salt tongue Zal didn't catch.

"Mother thought I did," he said.

"Mother?" Leksi recoiled. "No. She was never cruel."

"When you left, you broke her heart. She was different after that. Violent and spiteful in her grief—none of us were left unscathed." Resentment burned through his veins, as toxic as snake venom leaving a trail of necrosis in its wake.

He studied his sister's face: the strong jaw they all shared, her cheekbones wide and so like their mother's, where Zal's were more like razors. She had narrower eyes which made her look permanently unimpressed, and thin lips sculpted by the frigid breath of their father. Zal's lips were fuller, his mouth wider. He was taller too, had always been the tallest of his siblings, willowy where the others were stout and built for strength. Still, they were all variations on a theme.

Leksi looked older now, her skin a veneer blemished by her pretense at humanness. Such false imperfection felt like vile mockery, given the state of his own visage.

His ashy hair had been black once, thick and dark as midnight where hers and the rest of Death's children sported shades of russet gold. Leksi had either dyed or spelled hers an insipid shade of brown though, dulling the natural color. He wondered how long she'd been in the city, camouflaged among unsuspecting humans, and if she ever longed for the cool embrace of home. He wondered if she ever regretted her choice to leave the way he regretted that day at the river.

Zal closed his eyes and drew unsteady breaths into lungs as spongy as mushroom rot. "I just need an arkani who can do the annulment," he said. If he had any hope of going after Ailia and recovering what she'd stolen, he needed to stop losing magic. "You owe me that much," he added.

"I owe you nothing," Leksi said, but she wouldn't look at him.

"In Tsiraya we have a plant that's supposed to help temper spellwork," Tamisk said. "A shore weed we call tapak-zony."

"Curse-breaker?" Zal raised a skeptical brow.

"The Savati call it scale leaf, for the myth about serpent scales giving the arkani their power." Tamisk shrugged and a muscle twitched in Zal's jaw. How easily truth and history curdled into superstition.

"And does this hexless algae work?" he asked.

"Reed family actually, and yes, I've seen it curb lesser spells at least," Tamisk said, her gaze falling on Leksi's gem growing like a wart from her knuckle. "Not all curses can be cured though."

Ah. A simple excuse for the growth, easily believed, but lacking in imagination. He'd expected more of his sister.

"Where do we get scale leaf?" Leksi asked.

"I still have some," Tamisk said. "It's not the freshest, but it should work. I know a dealer in Qhemba where we could get more, if you find it useful. Give me a moment." Tamisk strode from the kitchen, her heavy feet thudding up the back stairs.

Zal glared across the table at Leksi, the tension like an over-tuned zither string stretched to snapping.

"A curse, really?" he asked.

"We are the literal embodiment of curses," Leksi said. "You

had an entire world to disgrace with your presence; why here? Why my city?"

"*Your* city?" He had, up until a few hours ago, considered it his. "I've been here almost a century."

"Try five, little brother."

Five hundred years in the mortal realm—Zal couldn't comprehend how she'd endured the stink and swelter of it. A testament to her hatred of the Nether.

"The mortal realm is vast, and yet we both wound up here," she said, gaze narrowed.

"Savat is ancient and soaked in magic," he said, slipping back into their mother tongue. "Perhaps something drew us to the city."

"You believe the rumors? That the Serpent sleeps deep below Savat?" A grin teased the corner of her mouth.

Zal shrugged, regretting the movement when it cracked the scabs on his chest and fresh blood oozed through the bandages. The cat tried to lick him clean, but he gently set it on the floor despite how much it hurt his crooked spine. The cat's eyes danced with impossible color as it mewled in protest.

"Zal—"

"You rejected us." He spat.

"It's been centuries, have you been holding a grudge against me this entire time?" Leksi asked.

"You made it so easy."

"You were never this bitter, Zal. Whatever happened—whatever you did—I'm sorry I wasn't there."

"So you could've joined Riksa in her gloating as Mother

broke my bones and tore out my eyes?" Zal asked.

"Where was Mezra?" Leksi asked. "They would never have allowed it. Not even from Mother."

The pet name of their eldest sibling sent a lancing pain through the hollow of Zal's chest. He couldn't speak. He could barely breathe, consumed by welling memory.

Dead, Zal wanted to say, but the children of Death couldn't die, they could only be condemned to eternal torment, which had become Mezra's fate, thanks to Zal.

"Your gem—" Leksi said and Zal raised his middle finger for inspection. An agateless spur of bone curled from the flesh.

"Here." Tamisk returned and Zal lowered his hand, sending the memories scuttling back into corners like cockroaches. "Easiest option is to smoke it." She placed a tin of rolling paraphernalia before him. "I know the tincture is considered stronger, but that has to be injected. If this doesn't work, we could try that."

Zal deftly rolled the dried leaves into brittle paper then leaned forward, lighting the spliff from the lamp's flame. He took a deep drag, and his shadows pressed closer, becoming a protective mantle moments before footsteps sounded outside. There was a single thump at the door, followed by subdued laughter.

Tamisk huffed and rose from the table. "I'll see them sorted. You deal with this." She gestured in Zal's direction before trudging from the kitchen.

"Trouble?" Zal asked, inclining his head toward the door.

"Teenagers," Leksi said. "They're under my protection.

You will not interfere with them." She raised a pointed finger.

Zal took a slow drag. The smoke was tangy, the spliff leaving a sweet residue on his lips. He felt the tell-tale tingle at the edge of his awareness, the magic of another becoming palpable to his demigod senses. He thought it was the power of the Salt gods laced into the weed, but no, this was more immediate.

"You gather arkani strays? How noble." He ashed into his soup bowl. "Any capable of an annulment spell?" He cocked an ear toward the door where Tamisk's voice rumbled with admonishment amid giggles and slurred apologies.

"No," Leksi said too quickly. "Especially not in their current state. Is the algae working?" she quipped.

He patted his fingers against the bandages, drying now. "Less oozing," he said. "How long will it last?" He studied the contents of the tin. There were leaves for another spliff or two at most. And while the weed might curb the effects of the spell, it couldn't reverse the damage or restore his stolen power.

"Not long enough," Leksi said. "And you can't stay here."

"Wouldn't dream of it," he said, pleased to see her expression sour when his barb hit its target. "Besides, I need to find an arkani."

"What about the one who did this to you? If she attempts to wield your power, she could destroy this city. You need to fix this," Leksi said as if it were some kind of revelation.

"I'm glad you understand the scope of the problem, dear sister." Zal stubbed out the cherry, slipped the tin of remaining scale leaf into his trouser pocket, and rose on unsteady legs. "But without that annulment spell, I'm nothing but a tapped beer barrel waiting for her to draw a draught." He teetered, hand braced on the back of the chair, his fractured bones humming instead of screaming thanks to the scale leaf providing a soothing balm on his senses. "If you care so much about this faithless city, you might consider helping me."

Leksi groaned and thumped her fists on the table. "I almost had the life I've always wanted."

"You always had everything I wanted," he said. "They all loved you, even Riksa." The words tore from his lips. "And you threw it all away, you discarded us—" The thought screamed through his head, the torus rippling across their connection and making Leksi wince.

She touched her fingers to her temple. "I don't think you'll ever understand."

And he didn't care to. "If you won't help me, then I need to go back to my citadel to find someone who will."

"You have a *citadel*?" she said. "Seems you've done all right for yourself despite appearances."

If only she knew what it had taken for Zal to scrape himself from the floor of that temple, to cobble together the shattered parts of himself, how he'd devoured Gafina's prayers and devotion, and it still hadn't been enough. Not even when he'd revealed the truth of his divinity, when she'd offered herself body and soul to him, not even when he had sucked every last drop of adoration from her bones.

He had needed so much more than one old lady's love, and

he'd found it, slowly, and by degrees. Even so, every use of magic had opened old fractures and shredded freshly seamed skin. The pain was indescribable, unimaginable, and nothing compared to what Mother had inflicted upon him. Until Ailia's betrayal.

Leksi whimpered, swatting at the tears tumbling down her cheeks as Zal's anguish flooded their connection. Abruptly, he shut it off, stoppering his feelings and memories the way he couldn't seal the rift in his chest.

Leksi strode across the kitchen and rummaged in a cupboard before pulling out a stoppered bottle. "Fireweed brandy. For me, not you." She took a swig and Zal tried to straighten, but a rib dislocated again, the cartilage shearing away with every breath as the magic he'd been using to hold himself together dissipated from his chest wound.

He staggered and Leksi swore, but caught him.

"You abandoned me once," he said. "Will you do it again?"

"That's not fair, Zal."

"Neither was my exile, but here we are." He gripped her arm, broken nails digging into her skin as he fought a wave of nausea and forced his bones into place through sheer will alone. "Help me or Ailia will destroy this city and this life you seem to hold so dear. Help me find an arkani to stop this spell, and you'll never see me again."

Her lips parted, but she paused, brow furrowed in contemplation.

"This spell, if completed, would've stripped you of magic?"

"So Ailia believed," he said, not quite ready to admit his

vulnerability. "When Mother exiled me, she severed my connection with home. I can't replenish my power."

"Could this spell be used on others, and remove a person's magic?" Leksi asked, almost wistful.

"Rendering them entirely powerless," Zal said. "If not killing them."

"I see," she said, sending a wave of hope along their tether. Did Leksi think she could somehow use the spell against him? Zal wouldn't allow that. He'd destroy her precious city, even himself, before he allowed a sibling to usurp his power.

"The more time we waste, the greater chance of Ailia trying something foolish with my magic," he said, drawing the shadows into a staff with a jerk of his wrist. Armed with both his and Riksa's magic, Ailia would be too powerful for any mortal arkani to combat, and far too much for Zal to take on alone. "If you want to save this city, you'll need to help me."

She pursed her lips and shook her head.

"Suit yourself, but don't blame me when this city gets reduced to rubble by mishandled entropy." Zal took a few faltering steps toward the door.

"Wait," she said. Zal kept walking.

"Storks and spirits! Zal—" His full name fell from her lips, sizzling through the air and stung his skin like a lover's kiss. "Just… wait. You can't go traipsing about Savat half-naked."

If only she knew how he'd haunted the alleys and gutters of joRania. After he'd taken all he could from Gafina and the few friends in her community who'd believed him a demigod, he'd been driven from the slums by those who saw him as a soul-sucking parasite. They weren't wrong, and he'd fled, limping and ragged with nothing but Gafina's meager treasures to his name. He'd survived as a half-blind, hollow-cheeked mendicant, loitering beside temples by day to feed on prayers, and sleeping in cemeteries where proximity to the dead brought a modicum of comfort at night. But Leksi didn't need to know this sordid history, nor the trail of destruction left in his wake.

He let her dress him then, her hands surprisingly gentle as she slipped a long-sleeved shirt over his thin arms, then pulled socks and boots onto his feet, even if they were a little small.

"So you'll help me?" he asked.

"As if I have a choice," she said, and Zal couldn't help the relief—or gratitude—trickling across their connection. "You'll need this too." She tied a thong around his neck with a pendant spelled to protect him from the sun. "Not a word," she said when he raised an incredulous brow.

"Hypocrite," he whispered, watching her prickle at the insult she couldn't defend, even as he tucked the pendant out of sight.

"I'm already regretting this," she said as, together, they stepped into the searing light of dawn. For a moment, Zal could pretend it was like old times. For a moment, the two of them were off to explore the ghost-riddled realm of the dead, and not on a dire quest to save the city from imminent demise thanks to his own poor judgment.

Since magic has multiple applications across numerous different fields, the term 'industrial magic' (and consequently 'industrial sigils') is used to denote that magic bound by both rune and spoken incantation for less extemporaneous purposes within various industries. Note: industrial magic always requires both incantation and sigil for processing, manufacturing, energy management, and safety, and should only be administered by a trained arkani with the requisite industrial specialization.

Excerpt from *A Treatise on the Utilitarian Application of Magic: Demystifying Spellwork for Industrial Purposes*
by Synara Makhezi

CHAPTER SEVEN

NIKI

The gray fabric chafed, both the rough seams and the dull color grating at my skin.

My scholar's indigo had been reduced to ash, tunic replaced with the uniform of the Sodality. I remained a prisoner, albeit a clean one now, and well fed too.

A fresh-faced young man clad in Sodality gray led Jaq and me through the disorientating corridors of the palace. Jaq's relief when I finally accepted the deal had bordered on excitement. It had since subsided into a stoic hopefulness I struggled to emulate.

"Did you know they began building this a thousand years ago?" the jolly apparatchik asked.

"Was it really that long ago?" Jaq trailed her fingers along the smooth stone wall.

The Sodality favored a more ascetic lifestyle, and had stripped the palace of its previous opulence. There was beauty in the austerity, though, the denuded sandstone striated with natural shades of beige and ocher. Our escort seemed chiseled from the rock too, his skin the same shade of sandy brown, his shaved hair the dull red of clay.

"It was a fortress long before it was home to royals," he continued as if he were a tour guide and not a jailer. "A bastion against marauders and slavers and all those wanting to claim Savat for their own. It's been renovated several times throughout the ages. This wing is the oldest."

"Fascinating," Jaq said, but I couldn't tell if she was being sarcastic or earnest.

I wasn't in the mood for a history lesson. If anything, the lecture only made me feel even more trapped, a child locked in the cellar at the mercy of others. Only this time I'd agreed to the captivity.

"You know a lot about history, ah—" Jaq hesitated.

"Yatto Makhezi." Our escort gave a little bow.

"Makhezi?" I nearly tripped over my own feet. "Any relation to Synara Makhezi?" A brilliant scholar at the university, whose work on sigils I had admired before the stress of her position had necessitated she take a leave of absence. She'd never returned, though, and I'd subsequently forgotten all about her. Until now.

"My mother." Our guide smiled. "She works here too."

"Here?" I asked. Had she been recruited by the Sodality? Forced to join as we had, or had she willingly given up tenure for the promise of unfettered research?

"I'm sure you'll meet her at some point." Yatto winked. "Ah, see this mosaic—" Our chatty escort continued as we meandered, our path eventually taking us up a narrow staircase no doubt intended for servants during the age of thrones.

"Look." Jaq paused at a narrow window made for archers. "Isn't it breathtaking?"

I would've been more impressed were we on a tour of the

library, but I still peered through the slit in the stone, across the vast expanse of the ocean. We were higher up than I realized, and in the western wing, where the palace perched at the edge of sheer cliffs dropping down to a turbid churn. The warm breeze whistled through the window holes and storm clouds gathered on the horizon. I might've been able to appreciate the view a little more, were there not an invisible sword at the nape of my neck. Another day almost done, and the impossible deadline loomed closer, accentuated now by the blasts of the palace kakakis, announcing the hour. Panic welled within me, and the storm rumbled its first warnings as if in response to the ululating horns.

"Here we are." Yatto exited the stairwell, and we emerged in a well-lit corridor that smelled quite strongly of citronella and lavender. "Back in the day, this wing was used by scholars and archivists, scribes and suchlike. The young royals would've had lessons in the very rooms you'll be working in." He gestured to a series of studies much like the chambers in an anthill, some of which seemed more like laboratories. None of them had doors. There was no privacy here, and no way to conceal research from watchful eyes.

If these had been used by scribes and the like, though, we couldn't be far from the library, from knowledge, from answers, from producing results that would see my life spared.

Several people were already at work. Each of them gray-clad and scowling, distinguishable only by skin color and hairstyle. Unlike the true adherents with their hair shaved in a single stripe down the center of their skull, many of these wore braids or 'locks or had stuffed their tresses under caps. I scanned the researchers for Synara Makhezi, but either she wasn't here, or my poor memory for faces meant I didn't recognize her.

"This is yours." Yatto gestured us toward one of the larger laboratories. The floral bouquet was even stronger here, undercut by an unpleasant ripeness as if we were in proximity to a latrine.

Several workbenches bearing scientific and musical paraphernalia had been arranged around a central table, which bore a lumpy mass concealed beneath a shroud. My attention snagged on the phonograph in the corner though. Unlike the one I used back at the university, this was a more recent model based on arkani Tomaya Edilele's original invention.

"No spells or sigils," Yatto said, noticing where my attention lay. "Testament to amagical technology." He beamed as I lamented, stewing in my own hypocrisy.

Eventually, technological inventions might catch up to their arkanic counterparts, a process my own research might help expedite, but a spell-free phonograph would have to have the cylinders manually changed every few minutes, and said cylinders would wear out that much faster without the benefit of preservation sigils.

Tearing my gaze away from the machine, I studied the rest of the room, grimacing at the pervasive odor.

"What is that?" I pointed at the shrouded lump, anxious sweat already peppering my skin. "And why does it reek?"

"Your first test subject." Yatto smiled, his teeth a jumble

behind his thin lips. "Our Esteemed thought you might like to start with an autopsy. No better way to know how something works than to take it apart, neh?"

I swallowed my rising gorge. I dissected harmonics, not flesh. I wouldn't even know where to begin with a body, and it was unlikely I'd discover something no physicker ever had.

"Can't I just read the report from the palace mortician? Surely this isn't the first body studied here?" I asked, trying not to gag.

"Hardly, and yes of course, but our Esteemed thought you'd appreciate the opportunity to see these things for yourself. Sorry about the smell." Yatto waved his hand at the corpse. "We had a few complaints, hence the botanicals. You get used to it, though."

I'm not sure I wanted to.

"Ah, right on time." Yatto's gaze slipped past me, and I turned at the sound of wheels creaking across stone. Another gray-clad Sodalite approached with a trundling cart piled high with codices and even scrolls. I grimaced. Scrolls were unwieldy at best, if not wholly indecipherable, and I was already on an impossible deadline. I wouldn't have time to transcribe all those hand-written findings. Never mind translate any texts not in modern Savati.

"What's all this?" Jaq asked.

"Research, as requested."

"You're bringing it to me here?" I asked. I'd imagined trawling through the palace library, spending hours at an antique writing desk in the sanctified silence of that hallowed ground. "Can't I peruse the archives in my own time?"

Yatto grunted with amusement. "Only the most learned members of our order may enter the library. But you can trust our archivists to provide you with whatever resources you need."

I very much doubted that. Despite the Esteemed's promises, the Sodality was not giving me unfettered access.

"This should be more than enough to get you started. Wouldn't want to overwhelm you." Yatto grinned again, and I swayed in place, grinding my teeth together. "Of course, I'll be here to assist, as well."

"You?" I blurted.

"Just completed my third year of physicker studies," he said, raising his chin with sudden pride. "Considering my experience with living specimens, I think I can handle the dead ones, should you not have the stomach for it."

"I'm a musicologist, not a butcher." And certainly not a torturer. "I don't see why I need to delve into a corpse at all."

Yatto cocked his broad head at me, eyes narrowing. "If you're trying to replicate spells by circumventing the need for incantation, sigil, and arkani, wouldn't it be prudent to understand both the spells and the wielder in order to eradicate them?"

"I can read a report." I bristled at his tone, clenching my fists until my nails—recently clipped as they were—dug crescents into my palms.

"I assumed a researcher of your caliber would want to see firsthand. My mistake."

"It's not a question of—"

"We all want the same thing," Jaq interjected, digging her elbow into my side. "Less arguing, more investigating." She gave me a pointed look, and I bit my tongue.

"Shall we get to work then?" Yatto beamed once more.

"Right now?" I thought I'd have time to get my bearings, to peruse the texts, to familiarize myself with the lab, to settle into my quarters and adjust to my new life before having to apply my recently trauma-gnawed mind to the Sodality's demand for answers. But that seemed a luxury I would not be afforded. Of course not. I was a prisoner here, and my deadline was a death sentence.

"Days are long, but time is short," Yatto said with an infuriating glimmer of mirth in his eyes. "And best we cut them up while fresh."

"Them?" I asked in a hoarse whisper. "There's more than one?"

"Arrests are so frequent now, we have plenty of fresh meat," Yatto said as if he were replenishing a pantry.

"Could we have some coffee brought up?" Jaq asked, and I could've hugged her. Now if only she could procure more khat for me, and maybe a nose peg.

"Your wish, my privilege." Yatto turned to his compatriot with the cart. "Coffee, and snacks," he demanded. "It's going to be a long night." The Sodalite ducked their shorn head in a shallow bow before pattering back the way they'd come.

I uncurled my fingers, grazing my fingertips across the leather-bound books.

"Nothing about Scryali?" I asked, disappointed.

"Oh, there's a lot more where this came from," Yatto said. "Didn't want to overwhelm you with too much too soon."

As if I had the luxury of easing into this new academic track.

"I'd like to see everything pertinent to my inquiry," I said. "Especially everything you have on Scryali. Her work has always been a special interest of mine."

"And relevant to our cause, I hope," Yatto said.

"She believed she could work magic without using incantations or sigils, so yes, I would say highly relevant." I plucked one of the books from the cart.

"I'll personally ensure you get all materials related to Scryali, then." Yatto gave a teasing bow as I opened the cover of the codex in my hands, pleasantly surprised by the neat Savati script inking the page. Something released inside me, too, the tension unraveling as I sank into the familiar comfort of research. I might be a captive, but I had access to secrets and proprietary research no other musicologist in the world would likely ever see.

Decoding Incantations and the Magical Idioglossia by Samiela Ngakula.

I'd never heard of Ngakula, my curiosity piqued as I flipped through the pages discussing the nature of the arkanic idioglossia. Everyone knew the words used for spells were said to have come from the gods, the more powerful phrases sacred and not for the laity, but here Ngakula posited a relationship between phonetics and resonance that questioned whether the words themselves carried meaning or were simply vocables to help shape sound. A plausible notion, if what Scryali believed about the incantations being unnecessary altogether proved true.

I skimmed the words as panic tore again at my insides. It was all too much. This was just one book, one cart! I'd never be able to read everything before First Council, let alone conduct my own research. Dark spots speckled my vision. It was getting harder to breathe.

"Easy, Nik," Jaq said. "You're all right."

"It's too much," I said, my voice an embarrassing squeak.

"We'll figure it out. We'll come up with a plan." She took my hands and pried the book from my tightening fingers. "Yatto and I will help you sort everything into piles. Let's start with the most pertinent topics, yes?"

I swallowed, still struggling to fill my lungs.

"Focus on what's important. No distractions. No going off on your usual tangents," she said brusquely.

It's what we'd done six months ago when I'd started pursuing the temple composition. Incendiary spells only, she'd said, helping me to focus on something simple and easily measured.

I let Jaq guide me now toward a work bench cleared for reading.

"I can't do this," I said.

"You can." She squeezed my fingers. "Because you have to. It'll be just like at the university, only with sea views." Her lips twitched into a smile.

"And better resources," Yatto added.

"Let's start with our most *burning* question," Jaq said, and I exhaled a chortle.

"Why did my composition work, but not as planned?" I said.

"Precisely." She snapped her fingers. "You can do this, Nik. You're so close to figuring it out. I believe in you." She squeezed my hand hard, then harder. "I know you won't disappoint me." She released her grip, and I shook out my sore fingers.

"Okay," I said, taking a calming breath, and immediately choked on a mouthful of pungent citronella. "I need everything about ignition spells and fire magic." I dabbed at my watering eyes.

"You got it." Jaq started rummaging in the cart, piling up relevant tomes for Yatto, who grumbled something incoherent at the growing tower. I wasn't listening, though; I was still trying to convince myself I could do this. I had to. My life—and Jaq's—depended on it. Perhaps with all the resources at my disposal, this task wouldn't be so impossible after all. Perhaps I'd be able to save us both and salvage my legacy, too.

Chapter Eight
ZAL

A few hours later, Zal stood amid the ruins of his home. Ailia's betrayal had broken more than his heart. It had cleaved a wound through the very bedrock, the mountain cracked and lopsided.

He pressed a hand to his chest and breathed through the loss, inhaling the reality of the damage wrought by greed and self-importance. He should've seen the avarice in her eyes, tasted it in her kisses, and felt the true hunger in her touch. Naïvely, he'd believed it was him she'd wanted, when all she'd really desired was what lay beneath his skin and festered in his bones.

"It must've been magnificent, before," Leksi said, eyes wide beneath the broad brim of her sunhat.

Despite himself, Zal felt a jolt of pride at his sister's words, even if magic shimmered in a mirage-like suspension above the rubble, the stench of spilled entropy souring in the sun. Loose scree danced, ferried along invisible currents curdling the air. Zal reached for a hovering stone, which exploded in a shower of razor-edged petals at his touch. The splinters embedded in his fingers, minnow-darting through his flesh.

"It's worse than in the city." Leksi nudged a cautious toe at a lump of congealing sediment. His blood splatter had left a trail of oddities, all minor transmogrifications where raw chaos tainted the earth.

"Nothing I can do about it now," Zal said.

"You didn't think ripping through space and time would have consequences?" she asked.

"I was fighting for my life," he said. Zal hadn't cared one jot about humans in that moment.

"It's mildly impressive you managed it at all given your… injuries," she said.

Zal cut his sister a sidelong glance. "You've never done it?"

"What? Sundered reality to take a shortcut? No, I haven't." She fingered the chain around her neck, rubbing at the pendant. "I only use magic when absolutely necessary."

"You've never tried to return home?" Zal asked, his nascent hope already fizzling.

"Never," she said. "Have you?"

"I can't," he said. "I was exiled. All doors are closed to me." The puddle at his feet squirmed and sprouted legs, transforming into a legevaan. The lizard flicked its forked tongue and blinked quartz-dazzled eyes before lumbering away on granite claws to terrorize the hyraxes gathered on the cliffs.

"Why do you even want to go back?" she asked. "Live your life here. Savat is brimming with life and potential and—"

"A government bent on snuffing out magic, skewering arkani, and eradicating faith in the old gods," Zal said. "Yes, it's quite the paradise."

Leksi's sigh turned into a yawn. She'd complained several times about the lack of sleep on their mule-trek from the city, but sleep would have to wait until they'd found a way to stop him leaking magic.

"I doubt I could open a door to the Nether even if I wanted to," Leksi said. "When it comes to any sort of magic, I'm out of practice."

"We all make choices," Zal said as he stalked through the wreckage, his joints protesting every movement. He kept to the shadows provided by the mountain, searching for survivors or the mangled body of Ailia. If she'd fallen victim to her own spell, it would save him from having to kill her. "When you channel all your energy into self-denial, of course you'll have nothing left for anything useful," he continued, irritated by the sun and this sister who had everything he craved and was so keen to toss it all aside.

"Self-preservation," Leksi said. "And I don't need magic when I have technology."

"I'm surprised you haven't shaved your head and donned the gray." He stumbled over a corpse, the limbs sprawled like the tangled leaves of the desert kharos plants. The eyes, turned toadstools, rose on ocular nerves and swiveled to look up at him.

"One of yours?" Leksi asked, and Zal nodded, hating how he recognized, but couldn't name, the acolyte turning to foliage.

He reached into the folds of the fleshy leaves and coaxed free the sliver of magic he'd given this follower. It burrowed into his palm and Zal sighed with relief, the pain easing ever so slightly with the return of his magic.

"What about that one?" Leksi pointed and Zal squinted

against the glare to follow her line of sight. A head bobbed above the rockfall, then another, survivors popping up like meerkats on the lookout for predators.

Zal disentangled his foot from the corpse-kharos and limped forward, leaning heavily on his shadow staff as he searched the dirty faces, trying to name them.

There were only five, and none were Ailia or Emri.

His sinews tightened at the thought of the sciomancer dead and twisted into some aberration among the ruins.

The others watched his approach, silent in their careful regard as he hobbled closer with Leksi hovering at his side, as eager for the cool embrace of the mountain shadow as he was. They passed the grove of trees where the remains of Kazwe Olonza were woven among the thorns. Only two trees still stood, their boughs strangled in offal turned to leafy vines by the magic impregnating the air. A crow cawed, flapping wings ending grotesquely in human fingers.

"Who needs Nightmare when you've got Chaos," Leksi said, eyeing the misshapen corvid with obvious disgust.

"Va'ili!" One of his acolytes called out, cradling a bloody arm. "Va'ili, you live."

"No thanks to you," Zal snarled, every word exhausting. "You have all betrayed me."

"We would never." The acolyte dropped to their knees sending up a puff of sparking dirt. Zal caught the crackling energy with a swipe of his fingers, drawing the loose charge back into his flesh.

"Where is Ailia?" he bit out.

"I d-d-don't know," the acolyte stammered. "Va'ili, please—"

Zal lurched forward and grabbed a fistful of the acolyte's hair, wrenching their head. The skin gave way, releasing with the creak of splintering wood. The acolyte blinked up at Zal before toppling, their skull split open like a geode, revealing a sparkling hollow.

"That is vile." Leksi gestured to the scalp dangling from Zal's hand. Instead of blood, it dripped rubies, which hit the dirt and coalesced into the segmented body of a scorpion before scuttling away. Zal dropped the mass of hair. It splashed where it fell, and from the fast-evaporating pool, a wisp of darkness rose: the scrap of his power released in death. It stained his fingers, squirming beneath his nails to settle once more within, and again he grew stronger.

"You gave away pieces of yourself?" Leksi asked, incredulous. "You can do that?"

He felt her jolt of excitement along their tether and found it nauseating. He'd done it out of necessity, when he'd had nothing to offer but a sliver of power as a promise of more. Perhaps he'd only been able to give away pieces of himself because he was so loosely stitched together.

"A gift to the faithful," he said. "A promise of future reward to those in my order."

"Or a shackle," she said.

"Isn't that what all promises are?" He raised his gaze, regarding each of the remaining survivors. Perhaps not all of them had turned against him. Perhaps some still remained loyal, and might've even been ignorant of Ailia's plot. Perhaps he could resurrect his original plan just as he'd resurrected himself.

"So you what, bound a bunch of fanatics to your will with shards of shadow in the hopes you'd raise an army to take on Mother?" Leksi asked, gleaning insight from their connection.

Put like that, it sounded like nothing more than the spiteful dream of a recalcitrant child.

"What's it called?" Leksi asked. "The Cult of Chaos? Zalix-ism?" She taunted. "Actually, that last one has a nice ring to it."

"You're one to judge," he said. "When you've gathered your own merry band of sycophants."

"Hardly the same. I help the lost and discarded, the abused and disenfranchised."

"Who all hold you in high regard, who *worship* you," Zal said.

"It's not the same. I don't brand them with shadow and demand veneration." Her guilt prickled along the edge of his awareness as she turned away. They were demigods after all, living in an age that had abandoned faith in favor of science and industry. They both thrived on adoration in whatever form it was given, adoration or fear.

Zal turned back to the quivering acolytes. "Where is Ailia?" he asked again, his voice as sharp as the edges of the broken skull at his feet.

"She's gone," a familiar voice drifted from what remained of the archway leading into the mountain. Emri emerged, silver hair held back in a braid that snaked over his shoulder.

Zal started forward and Emri waited where the shadows were thickest, where the cool exhalation of the caves would soothe Zal's sun-ravaged skin, and where Zal would be strongest. Emboldened and empowered, he seized Emri by the throat and shoved the sciomancer against the flaking cliffside.

He felt his power move within the other, a flutter of darkness staining the pale brown skin of Emri's chest. How easy it would be to plunge his fingers into flesh, nails whittling bone to release the nugget of Nether implanted there. His fingers tightened, two knuckles dislocating and several ligaments shearing with the effort. The pain only made Zal more determined to throttle the truth from the too-pretty arkani.

"Where is she?" Zal stared into the black depths of Emri's eyes, swirled with the opalescence unique to the ghost-touched. There were so few of them in the world—most drowned as infants or abandoned in the wilds. If Emri's family had loved him, they would've killed him, but Zal refused to pity the man who might've been complicit in his undoing.

"Gone," Emri croaked, struggling against Zal's grip. "She vanished. As did you. We didn't know what happened. The aftermath—we surmised Ailia tried the spell, and failed." He swallowed, throat bones grinding against Zal's palm. "We searched everywhere. Found no trace of either of you. So many dead or… different." He gasped.

"Did you know Ailia planned to betray me?" Her name sliced across Zal's tongue. "To use the spell against me?"

"No." Emri met his gaze with neither fear nor guile. His lashes were long and thick, and for a disorientating moment Zal wondered what they'd feel like against his lips. "Forgive me, Va'ili, I didn't know," he whispered. "If I had… Forgive me."

Forgiveness? The spawn of Death were not in the habit of such a thing. Zal and his siblings were made for war and terror, spite and vengeance, destruction and damnation. Zal tightened his grip, tendons screaming in protest. Emri remained stoic in his grasp. The man, though slender, possessed a wiry strength. He could've easily overpowered Zal, especially in the daylight with the fangs of summer buried in the Netherling's bones. Emri barely moved, not a single twitch or tremble except for the ragged rise and fall of his chest as his lungs fought for breath.

Perhaps it was a side effect of Leksi's unbridled curiosity and compassion infecting his will that made Zal peel open his grip, when every fiber in his being wanted to snap the sciomancer's spine and make the man pay in Ailia's stead.

Zal slid his hand down the ink-stained flourishes on Emri's throat to the exposed V of his tattooed chest. He pressed his hand to the smooth skin, fingertips prickling as the power he'd gifted the sciomancer rose in greeting. With ragged nails, he grazed Emri's skin, dug in deeper but stopped before he drew blood.

"I am yours," Emri said, his voice a deep rasp. "I will always be yours."

Zal couldn't feel the sciomancer the way he could his siblings, but there was an earnestness in the man's expression and a heaviness to his words that made Zal want to believe they were true.

"While this is rather touching," Leksi said. "Think we could continue this little reunion indoors? Also, you're bleeding again."

"Some of the inner chambers are still intact." Emri took Zal's injured hand and gently maneuvered himself so Zal could rest his weight on the sciomancer's shoulder. Zal swallowed a whimper, wanting to sag into Emri's arms, but he would not show any more weakness.

"And what about our prisoner?" Zal asked. Without Riksa he'd be left with even less and no way to replenish his magic.

"Mostly gone too," Emri said.

"Mostly?" Zal asked at the same time as Leksi asked, "What prisoner?" Her curiosity was a weevil burrowing into his awareness. Dread too, though Zal wasn't sure if it was hers or his knowing there was no way to escape the fact he needed the sister he hated the most.

The mountain enveloped him, alleviating some of his agony. In the depths of the earth, further from the sun and closer to the borders of his birth realm, Zal's wreck of a body began to knit itself back together. The freshly returned magic helped too, as did another spliff of the scale leaf.

He smoked as they meandered through the system of excavated caverns, the structure inspired by termite architecture. So many of the tunnels had collapsed, his world a dilapidated ruin.

When Zal had first arrived in Savat, following rumors of

a powerful and defiant arkani making a mockery of both the Savati monarchy and all musical conventions of the time, he'd had nothing but the stolen wealth he could carry in his pockets and a single drawstring bag. It took years of ingratiating himself with the Savati aristocracy—proving himself worthy of notice despite his physical disabilities—before he'd been able to secure his position in the city. He'd needed a home, an estate. Something impressive, mythical even—a citadel carved from the mountain, first with Zal's bare hands, and then later with arkani magic. Over the better part of a century, the citadel had grown into a magnificent underground sprawl. And yet, those decades of work had so easily been undone with one errant spell.

"How bad is the damage?" Zal asked.

"We recovered what we could from the rooms that remained accessible." Emri gestured to the neat piles of food and scrolls, books and blankets lining the violet-lit corridors. "The chambers adjacent to your own seem the worst off, but we're making progress. We weren't sure if you or Ailia would return, weren't sure what had happened at all." Emri's shoulders slumped at that, as if he could've predicted Ailia's treachery.

"Don't be so hard on yourself," Leksi quipped. "Zal doesn't actually blame you. He's angry with Ailia. The betrayal cuts deep and—"

"Enough," Zal growled. "Stay out of my head." He tamped down their connection but couldn't fully extinguish it. It was a flame that guttered but refused to go out no matter how many times he tried to smother it.

Emri glanced from Zal to Leksi and back. "You're psychically connected?"

"An irksome side effect of being siblings," Leksi said, and Emri's eyes widened as he digested the revelation.

"Leksi, this is Emri," Zal said. "Emri, meet my sister, Leksi."

Emri raised a delicate brow in question, no doubt waiting for the command to seize and shackle, the way he'd done with Riksa. Zal was sorely tempted by the idea, but employing less brutal tactics with Leksi seemed wise, given her ability and his weakened state.

Receiving no command, Emri turned back to Leksi and bowed from the waist. "It's an honor to meet a daughter of Death."

"Is it?" Leksi asked.

"Ghost-touched as I am, yes," Emri said. "The Ancestors honor me, and they are, after all, spirits of your domain. You are the gods of my affinity."

Zal's next breath came a little easier, buoyed by the devotion exuded from the sciomancer. It was nothing but a drop in a dry bucket long emptied by the faithless, but Zal swallowed it hungrily all the same.

Leksi did too, the zing of pleasure gleaned from Emri's belief in them sizzling between them.

"About the spell, Va'ili, I take it Ailia didn't complete it," Emri said.

"No, not quite," Zal said as they arrived in his personal chamber. He shuddered at the memory of Ailia's hands as he surveyed the damage to his inner sanctum. Shelves had collapsed, the treasures he'd gathered over the years reduced to smithereens. The remnants of Riksa's teeth and dismembered digits lay sprinkled like salt across the bloodstain on the fractured floor where he'd torn through the fabric of the world.

His shadows detached as ribbons from his hair, swooping down to pry his spilled magic from the stone. Zal breathed deeply, his expanding lungs forcing ribs and spine back into place, allowing him to stand a little straighter.

The wall below the shelving was laced with fissures, the manacles loose in their moorings with only the desiccated hand, snapped at the wrist, dangling from the chains. The containment circle had been destroyed, and Riksa had escaped. Perhaps she'd gone after Ailia, seeking vengeance for the arkani's betrayal. Which meant she had a head start. Zal couldn't let Riksa get her hands on Ailia or the amulet; couldn't risk her claiming his power for her own.

Leksi ran her fingers over a particularly valuable illuminated text Zal had acquired in joRania.

"Va'ili indeed," she said, her jealousy a feather touch against his perception before she stomped on her own feelings. "All this time, you've been living like a lord in your subterranean realm."

Zal ignored her petulance as he finished the spliff and turned to Emri. "The spell, though incomplete, remains problematic," Zal said. "As you can see."

"He's leaking like a bloody faucet," Leksi chimed in.

"Ah, hence the scale leaf," Emri said. "If it's helpful, we

can always procure more." The man's care was genuine. He'd always been loyal and deserved more than angry rebukes.

"How about an annulment spell?" Leksi asked. "Can a sciomancer do that?"

"It is not my expertise," Emri admitted. "But of those that remain, I'm the most likely to succeed."

Zal eased himself into the chair opposite the one he'd been assaulted in, his gaze drifting to the disembodied hand. He rubbed his burning eyes, scraping gray gunk from the one that refused to heal, his body determined to reject the orb no matter how many times he'd plucked it out and channeled magic to begin its regrowth.

"You are the only one I trust to try," Zal said. "The only one I trust at all." He looked up at Emri, surprised by the pride on the sciomancer's face—even more surprised by the warm rush of appreciation for the man permeating his usually frigid insides.

"You honor me." Emri dropped to his knees at Zal's side, his all-black attire already streaked with dirt and dust. "I cannot promise it will work, but I will do my best. I will need a moment to prepare and—"

"Storks and spirits, tell me this isn't what I think it is." Leksi crouched beside the hand. The middle finger still bore its gem. Mezra's had been laced with blue where Leksi's was white. Zal's had been a swirl of myriad shades to rival his eyes, and Riksa's was striped with fiery bands of orange. Zal rubbed his bare finger, massaging the swollen knuckle. The gem had never grown back, and probably never would.

Leksi grasped at her own hand as if hiding the stone would change what she was. "Why do you have our sister's hand?"

"I had use for her," Zal said as Emri wisely took his leave.

Leksi touched the skeletal phalanges and shuddered. "The spell Ailia performed on you, tell me you weren't planning to strip Riksa of her power?"

"I'm happy to lie if that's what you want."

"Stars wept, Zal. Why?"

Zal regarded her with as much disdain as he could muster. "Can you not see the damage done to me? I was exiled, cut off from our home, disconnected from everything. I cannot heal. For centuries, I have existed in anguish, all because..." He choked, not quite able to say out loud what he'd done. It had been a mistake, a miscalculation of a youthful demigod still learning the limits of his power. "If I could heal, if I had more power, perhaps I could find a way to return home," he said, not sure when he switched to Nethertaal.

"I can't help you." Leksi rocked back on her haunches. "Not unless you tell me what egregious thing you did to deserve this." She waved a hand in his general direction.

Of course she believed he deserved his mother's ire, and perhaps he did, but not that—not exile.

"You wouldn't want to help me if you knew," he said.

"I'll do anything to save the innocents of this city and those I love," she said with scalding sincerity.

"If you're ready, Va'ili," Emri interjected. "Then perhaps we could begin?"

"Please do." Zal gingerly rearranged his limbs so Emri

could remove his shirt and gain access to the stained bandages.

Emri sucked in a breath but said nothing, his touch tender as he pried away the bandages and bathed the wound with cloths spelled for healing with carefully embroidered sigils. He used imbued water as well, the spelled liquid soothing where it made contact with Zal's butchered chest.

"Can you feel this?" Emri pressed a finger on the wound and Zal shook his head, his flesh numb.

"How did you even find her?" Leksi asked.

Zal didn't answer immediately, too focused on Emri, who sliced open his own arm, letting blood trail down his finger before he drew a new sigil over the one still suppurating on Zal's chest.

"I'd been searching for a strong arkani for the better part of a century, finally drawn to Savat when I learned of an impetuous magic-wielder terrorizing the monarchy. Her name was Fetrina Scryali," Zal said over Emri's baritone hum. "When she proved a disappointment, I sought others and eventually found Ailia." That was oversimplifying the numerous years he'd spent establishing himself in Savat, but his sister didn't need to know the details. "Ailia was a gifted arkani, but more than that. She burned with a hunger I understood."

She'd bitten him the first time their paths crossed, fighting him with all the ferocity of a honey-starved ratel tangling with a puff adder, her body sparking with magic she couldn't control. She'd been an urchin, fending for herself in the poorest part of Qhemba. Zal had saved her, raised her, educated her, loved her. He'd believed she was invested in his cause and loyal beyond all measure.

The lump of gristle in his chest spasmed as memories welled like pus from a wound.

"I was actually asking about Riksa," Leksi said. "But do go on."

"Yes, well, Riksa and I shared the same quarry," he said. "She was careless, stumbling into my territory." Zal squirmed as Emri's magic plunged into him, a hornet sting penetrating to the bone. Sweat dripped from the sciomancer's face, translucent hairs caught against sticky temples. His lips trembled as veins and tendons strained against the skin of his forearms inked with asymmetrical geometry.

With a final groan, Emri withdrew. "I'm sorry, Va'ili," he said, panting. "The annulment won't take. I'm not in my element here."

"Would a different arkani be able to do it?" Leksi asked.

"Perhaps." Emri mopped sweat from his brow with his sleeve before pressing a gooey poultice to Zal's chest. Zal leaned forward, letting Emri wrap clean bandages around his body, savoring the gentle brush of the man's hands. "But I don't think so. Ailia's spell wasn't finished and you can't annul what isn't complete. That's just how magic works." He held Zal's gaze, eyes turned mesmeric in the bruised glow of the lamps. "The spell can only be completed or undone by the one who wrought it. Without Ailia, there is nothing we can do. I'm sorry." He looked down and Zal fought the urge to catch his chin and raise his head, wanting to gaze once more into the man's ghost-glazed eyes.

"What's in the poultice then?" Leksi asked.

"Bitter aloe and devil's claw to relieve pain and prevent infection," Emri said. "Charms to promote healing and stop swelling. I wish I could so more."

"Thank you." Zal gripped the sciomancer's hand and gave a squeeze of genuine gratitude. "If we're going to hunt down Ailia, I'll need more scale leaf."

"I'll send Dzika and Pfumi to acquire more," Emri said, naming acolytes Zal couldn't conjure faces for. How deeply he must've wallowed in the mire of his own misery to become so detached from his followers.

"We?" Leksi raised an incredulous brow.

Zal was saved from having to respond when an acolyte, Dzika or Pfumi perhaps, charged into his chambers.

"Apologies, Va'ili, but Emri said you wished to be informed immediately if we found more survivors."

"Who?" Emri asked, binding the cut on his arm with a strip of black cloth as he rose to his full height, looking every bit the commanding officer.

"Iqno," the acolyte said, and cold fire ignited in Zal's veins at the same time he detected a twitch in the tether to his sister. Her expression remained inscrutable.

"Bring her to me." Zal rose from the chair, anger strengthening his depleted energy. "In chains, in pieces if you must, so long as she can talk and explain her treachery."

If Iqno knew where Ailia had fled, or what her next move would be, Zal would pry it from her even if he had to divine the answers from her entrails.

The Principles of Inyoti as recorded by the first arkani blessed by the Ancestors to carry that most sacred fragment of the Serpent God within their hearts. Thus are the tenets upon which we build our society and foster community.

Second Principle—Interconnectedness & Communal Responsibility:
I am because we are. Individuals are inseparable from the community. Individual well-being is inextricable from the well-being of the society within which they live. Everyone has a responsibility to contribute to the greater good and overall well-being of society, creating a harmonious existence for all.

CHAPTER NINE
LEKSI

Leksi had never considered herself the jealous type. She'd lived far too long to indulge the occasional flares of insecurity that came with loving things and wanting things and pretending to be human.

But now, jealousy fermented in her gut. She'd slogged for decades to build The Anchorage, to put food on the table, and save those tossed aside by society, struggling to make ends meet and begging for government scraps. And all the while her miscreant brother had lived like a lord, waited on by devout arkani, wanting for nothing.

Except his own petty vengeance.

While they strode—well, Zal still limped despite the scale leaf, poultice, and Netherly ambiance of the dwelling—Leksi took inventory of the recovered items. She never imagined the feral godling she'd known in the Nether might one day turn scholar, but there were enough books in the piles to rival the university stacks. Between those lay luxurious tapestries, many hailing from countries and cultures half a world away. There were jars of imported delicacies propping up paintings and sculptures, an abundance of jewels, and myriad other tokens of wealth Leksi could only marvel at. Her hands itched with the desire to pocket a bauble or two. With so much, surely he wouldn't miss a few trinkets.

Pride stayed her twitching fingers even while she ran mental calculations. There was so much she could do for The Anchorage and her wider community with a quarter of the wealth on display.

Stifling another yawn, Leksi followed where Emri led. While her body required less sleep than the average mortal, she'd grown used to nightly naps, and breakfast. Hopefully, one of Zal's pets would think to feed them soon.

They had to take a circuitous route thanks to rockfall, but eventually stepped into a courtyard of sorts where an opening in the rock high above let in a beam of natural light. The narrow spear of day was a shock to Leksi's system after the comfort of being underground and sheltered from the season. It illuminated a single marble statue.

"We couldn't move her," the acolyte Emri had called Pfumi said.

A shadow shifted on Pfumi's throat, a gray smudge against the deep brown of her skin visible above the neckline of her shweshwe. At least Zal didn't impose a uniform on his followers like the Sodality did, forcing everyone to dress the same, heads shaved to denote the one true path to enlightenment. Science, apparently, although it looked a lot like meek obeisance.

Emri approached the statue. Zal hung back, his unbridled rage pounding against her skull. Leksi stayed close to her brother, annoyed by her inability to watch him teeter without reaching out to steady him. If only he'd tell her what he'd done, perhaps then she could hate him and leave him to deal with the consequences of his actions alone. But she didn't hate him, never had, and she couldn't imagine what atrocity he must've committed to warrant this level of suffering.

Zal shifted beside her, no doubt sensing her jumbled emotions. His own rage and a new foul flame sizzled across their connection.

"So much hatred," Leksi said.

"Iqno conspired with Ailia," he said, his gaze trained on Emri as the sciomancer continued to study the sculpture. Leksi studied it too. Iqno wasn't the most unique of names, but dread calcified in Leksi's gut at the familiar features of the artwork.

Then it moved and Leksi swallowed a rush of bile. It wasn't a statue; at least, it hadn't always been. Like the distorted bodies outside caught in the torus of her brother's magic, Iqno had been altered. The girl had changed, and long before she'd been caught in the blast radius of misguided spell-work. Leksi couldn't help feeling a little responsible for that, but she reined in her guilt before Zal could detect it.

"Can she talk?" Zal asked.

"She's alive, at least," Emri said in his warm baritone, having placed tender hands on the acolyte turned sculpture, but his gentleness belied a strength Leksi had seen written in the corded sinews of his straining arms when he worked magic.

She'd never met another sciomancer. Few survived infancy, let alone into adulthood. And certainly not in Savat or in Tsiraya. There were places north of the desert where the ghost-touched were tolerated, and others where they were kept like pets, appreciated only as oddities for entertainment. Emri could not have been born in Savat with those eyes. Given his countenance and the faint lilt to his accent, she guessed he came from across the desert.

The sciomancer continued his examination before saying, "Her lower body is fused to the rock, but her torso is flesh. She should be able to talk." He cupped Iqno's face, pressing long fingers into the hinge of her jaw to force her mouth open. Her tongue and teeth were intact.

"You were always Ailia's little shadow," Emri said. "Did you know she schemed against Va'ili?"

Leksi paused outside the ring of light, watching as tears spilled from the girl's eyes. Despite her best efforts, Leksi hadn't been able to save all those afflicted by magic who whirled into her orbit.

"Please," Iqno stammered. "I only did what she told me."

"Pfumi, fetch a hammer and chisel," Zal said, and the acolyte dutifully scurried away. Iqno's stony gaze skated past Emri to land on Zal who stood cloaked in living shadows that roiled with rage and hate. "Let's see how easily one draws blood from stone."

"Look at me! You cannot hurt me," Iqno said, her voice cracking like thin sheets of shale. "I'm already dead."

"Not quite," Emri said softly.

Pfumi returned and Zal nodded at the sciomancer who accepted the proffered tools.

Leksi didn't want to watch what she knew would happen

next, but her monsters stirred at the promise of pain, filling her with a giddy anticipation she found repulsive even as it locked her in a chokehold.

Emri dragged the chisel down the statue's flank. Iqno screamed and Leksi shuddered, her parasites writhing in glee. Blood welled in the gouges, crystallizing into bulbous grapes Emri smashed with a swift blow of the hammer. Iqno screamed again and Leksi's monsters roared, gnashing at her innards, their claws snagging at the confines of her skin.

Zal snapped his fingers and Pfumi brought a stool for him. He sat with a grunt, leaning heavily on his staff, his eyes bright with malice—even the one leaking gray crud.

This was not the brother she remembered. He'd been mischievous, but never cruel. If anything, it was his constant ebullience that had been most annoying, his relentless energy so out of a place in the land of languor. At worst, he'd been prone to bouts of sullenness, trailing after their mother, always hungry for the affection she'd never been able to give.

Not that Leksi could blame her for her disinterest in Zal, but it wasn't her place to divulge the secret of his existence. Try as she might, Leksi had never been able to broach the topic with her mother. Instead, she'd been forced to watch dysfunction erode familial bonds, the discord between her parents poisoning them all until she couldn't take it any more. She blamed her father, too. Leksi hadn't been the only one who'd witnessed her mother's indignity at the hands of Time. The breeze had become a storm that night, a blistering gale raging across the frozen veld, her father's rage and indignation nothing but bluster that eventually petered into apathy.

Emri gouged another groove with the chisel, and Iqno's cries reverberated in the cavern, and again, Leksi's monsters writhed in ecstasy. Leksi hadn't wanted to be what her mother had made her, what the realm demanded of her. She'd left to escape this very aspect of her nature. She couldn't stand by now and watch Zal torture the girl already suffering for her duplicity.

"Stop!" Leksi stepped into the sunlight, her monsters instantly cowering. "Before you reduce her to bloody rubble, let me try."

"You?" Zal asked, genuinely surprised by her sudden interest.

"Some of us don't need blunt instruments." Leksi held up her hand, letting it curl into a claw as if she had any intention of loosing the forces within her. Suspicion dripped from her brother as thick as syrup.

"Oh please. As if I'd usurp whatever power you're after." She rolled her eyes.

Zal studied his sister, straining toward her and, this time, she opened the connection, letting him see there was no deception, only desperation.

"I want to find Ailia as much as you do," Leksi said. "Before she destroys this city and the life I've built. And before your leaking magic unravels reality any further." She hoped he'd understand how deeply she loved Savat, and Tamisk, and the odd little life she'd cobbled together. She hadn't realized just how much she treasured what she'd made until it was on the brink of destruction.

"I'm not leaving," Zal said.

"Fine. Stay. Hope you're ready to face your fears." Leksi held her breath as she goaded her monsters to the fore.

Predictably, Zal flinched, and pulled his shadows closer as if they'd be enough to protect him from the nightmares lurking in her blood.

"You have an hour," he said. "If I don't have answers, I'm coming back with a hammer. Pfumi, watch from the door. Hear everything. Emri, with me."

Zal rose, his joints audibly popping.

Emri regarded Leksi with a cautious curiosity as he set the tools down at her feet.

"You should know, sciomancers do more than converse with the dead. I put Riksa in chains," he said as if he were whispering across silken sheets and not issuing a threat. "I'd rather not see another Princess of the Nether succumb to such a fate." His words sent a deluge of dread rushing down Leksi's spine. The magic within her instantly stilled as if a strange hand had somehow reached inside and petted her nightmares into submission.

"I understand," she said, and Emri withdrew.

She waited for them all to leave; the echoes of their footsteps faded before she turned back to the statue.

"It is you," Iqno said, head lolling on a flaccid neck. "I don't understand… why are you here?"

"I just want to talk." Leksi pulled up her brother's discarded stool. "To understand what happened. Can you tell me?" She needed to know how the girl she'd rescued from a conversion camp almost a decade ago had ended up in the clutches of her brother's cult. Leksi needed to understand exactly how she'd failed Iqno so she'd never do it again.

Iqno's chest heaved with a strangled breath as another sliver of flesh petrified.

"I want to help you," Leksi said.

"Like you wanted to help me then?" Iqno asked. "By making me hate my magic, by forcing me to hide who I was?"

"No, that's not…" Leksi sighed. "I'm sorry," she said. "I'm sorry I didn't help you well enough then, but I can now, if you let me."

"Can you undo this?" the girl asked, a slow tear trailing crystals down her cheek. "Do you serve Va'ili?"

If lying was what it took, so be it. Leksi had already lied her way through a dozen lifetimes. But perhaps a nugget of truth in this moment might serve her best. "I'm your Va'ili's sister."

Iqno made a strangled noise as if there were gravel caught in her throat. "You?"

"Believe it or not, not that it matters. All that matters now is stopping Ailia before she does something foolish that'll destroy Savat."

"I—" Iqno's response turned to a coughing fit as she hacked up chunks of zircon. "But don't you see?" she managed with a rueful smile. "The destruction of this god-forgotten city, that's exactly what they want."

Spells are simple in that function dictates form just as the purpose dictates the affinity. There is no 'fire' magic or 'water' magic—the difference lies in how the energy released from the arkana particles is employed. If you wish to cool and quell, use water sigils. For warming and igniting, fire sigils are best, and so on.

Excerpt from *Doubts and Paradoxes: An Argument for Magical Corpuscles* by Robera Bololo

Chapter Ten
Niki

"Is that absolutely necessary?" Yatto asked, gesturing to the phonograph.

The music player was currently grumbling through the third repetition of the echo-song I preferred for concentrated study as we continued to wrestle with the corpse.

"Yes," I said. "Your Esteemed wants answers. This is how she gets them." The call and response of the music provided a predictable rhythm that steadied my hands. My assistant, some sullen Sodalite with a pimple-pocked face who refused to speak to me, had the arduous task of resetting the reproducer whenever the music stopped.

"How about a little variety then?" Yatto asked. "At this point, I'd rather listen to screaming." He twirled the scalpel between his fingers, never missing an opportunity to remind me that he preferred carving up living flesh.

"No. Shall we continue?" If I had to suffer Yatto's presence, he could endure my choice of music.

Having grown up slaughtering chickens and the occasional goat, I hadn't considered myself squeamish, but prying open human ribs was nothing like skinning a rabbit or gutting a fish.

My pits were soaked, my shirt clinging to my back in the humidity of the laboratory despite the open windows letting in the summer breeze. It did alleviate some of the stink of decay and herbs at least.

We'd been at it for days now, our mornings spent hacking our way from head to toes on one cadaver and then another. I hated to admit the work was easier with Yatto's assistance, and with only fourteen days until First Council, I couldn't afford to refuse his help even if his patronizing instruction left me bristling. Having gleaned all I could from existing autopsy reports, I did my best to follow diagrams in physicker textbooks as, together, Yatto and I navigated the viscera, looking for anomalies others may have missed.

While I spoke Savati and could haggle a decent price on fresh fish in Tsirayan, I'd never learned the language of anatomy. It was an extinct tongue physickers had preserved for the nomenclature of their profession. At least it used the same alphabet as Savati, so I could read it. Not that it helped all that much when I couldn't tell one arm bone from another, which Yatto found endlessly amusing.

Worst of all, for all my gruesome excavations within the arkani carcasses, I'd so far only achieved staining my shoes with stomach acid and ruining two perfectly good shirts. Yatto had come prepared with an apron.

Like those before us, we'd found no sign of a scale fragment, of course, nor was there anything to suggest why some arkani proved more adept at one elemental form of spellwork over another. As far as we could tell, there was no special organ in an arkani's throat altering the sound waves during an incantation, no additional gland to explain an arkani's magical abilities, nor was there any immediate evidence of structural difference in bone or muscle.

"This is a colossal waste of time," I said. Either the answers lay concealed deeper within the tissue, in some hidden lobe of the liver or worm-fold of the brain, or there were simply none to be found. "No wonder the physickers of old believed the arkani were God-touched."

"An archaic and ignorant belief," Yatto said, wiping gore on his stained apron.

"And you're sure this one could actually wield magic?" I gestured to the corpse. Perhaps none of the poor sods we'd had the displeasure of dismantling were true arkani, and merely the victims of bigotry and paranoia. "If hands are typically removed upon suspicion of magic wielding, I'm just wondering what evidence you might have of their arkani ability."

"The word and witness of the Savati constabulary," Yatto said tersely. "No further evidence is required."

"Indeed. What a fair and robust judicial system we have," I said, despite Yatto's scowl as I turned my mind to less depressing thoughts, like resonance.

It was the only thing that explained why I, a non-arkani, had managed to channel any magic at all. Were arkani like aliquot strings, vibrating along with the unseen force of magic by some quirk of physical composition? Perhaps I'd been looking at this all wrong, searching for a peculiar structure within the body when it was the physique in its entirety that mattered.

An individual's unique physiology as a whole could explain why certain spells were easier for some arkani than others. I scrutinized the carcass before me with renewed interest. With so many possibilities, there was no way I'd solve this mystery in just fourteen days.

"That's quite the butchering," Jaq said, startling me so hard I dropped what I thought was either the gallbladder or the spleen. Whatever it was hit the floor with a squelch that made me grateful I'd skipped breakfast.

"I am always thorough," Yatto said, smug even when spattered with offal.

"I don't know why we did this." I kicked the pulp toward the buckets huddling in a mushroom clump beneath the table. I pitied the cleaners who came in each evening to mop up my mess, most of them former prisoners who'd chosen to commute their sentences by working unpaid instead. Here, though, there were no spelled brooms or rags to ease their labor.

My expressionless assistant eyed the slop but dutifully changed the phonograph's cylinder as she'd been ordered to, once again filling the lab with the crunchy sounds of an inexpertly recorded percussion ensemble.

"You've still got time," Jaq said. "First Council—"

"I'm aware, thank you very much." As if I could forget how quickly time crept toward its zenith. I felt no closer to answers. If anything, I was at an even greater loss. My world had been upended, my routines disrupted, my methods in disarray. My previous approach had been slow, but productive, without the anxiety-inducing pressure of delivering answers by an arbitrary deadline. And without the infuriating presence of Yatto Makhezi.

"Niki can now name a few more body parts at least," Yatto said with a smirk. "Best to stick with music though," he added.

"I intend to," I bit out.

"What about the papers we sorted?" Jaq asked. "Nothing in any of those?" She pressed the back of her hand to her mouth as if she could avoid the stink I barely noticed now.

"Too much," I said, regarding her over the mushy remains of the corpse. She looked comfortable in Sodality gray and didn't seemed to mind our wardens nearly half as much as I resented them. "That's the problem," I continued. "There are too many variables, too many unknowns. I have no idea which path to pursue. How are you doing?"

She'd been similarly tasked with solving mathematical quandaries, not entirely related to magic, though.

"All right, I suppose," she said. "Although it'll certainly cost a whole lot more to expand existing infrastructure without the use of arkani and their magic." Her face scrunched the way it always did when she had to admit an uncomfortable truth. "I see why some people remain proponents of industrial magic. It does have its uses."

"Nothing human labor can't achieve," Yatto said, rubbing a hand along the strip of hair bisecting his scalp.

"Magic certainly has useful applications," I added, applications far more interesting than building factories and *railroads*. "Jaq, what do you make of this bruise?" I pointed to a discoloration on the cadaver's thigh where we hadn't cut it open to pry out the bones.

"It's lividity," Yatto said. "We've been over this."

"But it doesn't look like the other bruises," I said. This one was gray instead of the violet-yellow marks where manacles had damaged wrists and ankles, or where a heavy fist had fractured the orbital bone.

"Perhaps you missed a spot when you washed the body," Yatto said, and for a moment I wished he was the corpse on the table.

"*This* is lividity." I gestured to the bruising caused by pooling blood on the underside of the body. "This is different. Observe." I pressed on the mark and it darkened at my touch, almost as if something under the skin gathered at the pressure. "That's not how bruising works."

"Didn't realize you were such an expert," Yatto said, folding his arms.

"Cut it open?" Jaq suggested, ignoring him. "Excision or whatever."

I gave Yatto a pointed look. I'd suggested we do exactly that, and he'd refused even though it was the only anomaly I'd managed to find. *I'd* found it, though. Not him.

"Go on then." Yatto handed me the scalpel and I hesitated.

"Come on, Nik. We need answers," Jaq added. "Otherwise we both end up back in chains."

We were more likely to end up skewered at the palace gates.

"It's not fair they've tied your fate to mine," I said as I took the blade before snapping at my assistant, "Get paper and ink. Note down everything I tell you to and make your own observations if you can. You are literate, right?"

The assistant's lips pressed into a very thin line at that before nodding. For the first time I realized her lack of verbal communication may not have been out of surliness but rather the result of disability or difference of the mind, and here I was treating her the way Yatto treated me.

"Sorry, of course you are. Please, take notes," I amended and she nodded. Yatto only rolled his eyes.

"I was your accomplice, remember," Jaq said, watching as I approached the bloated limb. "Of course our fates will be the same." She continued, but I stopped listening to focus on the grim dissection.

The flesh parted, each side peeling away from the scalpel as I sliced deeper. I didn't expect blood to well—I knew enough about exsanguination now and the characteristics of putrefying tissue—but the viscous substance pooling around the scalpel was a disturbing surprise.

The music ended. The only sound was the scratch of my assistant's pen on paper and Yatto's sharp intake of breath.

"Lividity?" I asked, and he answered with a scowl.

"What the vrot is that?" Jaq asked, startling me with the curse as she leaned closer.

"Ink?" Is this what happened to tattoos when skin began to rot? I had no idea.

"That's not a tattoo," Yatto said.

"I think that's—look out." Jaq slapped my hand away when

the stain *moved* as if it were alive and had jolted awake.

I dropped the scalpel and kicked it away from me, but there was no point. The black substance rose, an edgeless globular puddle hovering in the air in utter defiance of every physical law I thought I knew. My assistant stared aghast, the pen sliding from her fingers to splatter ink across the floor.

There was a bizarre pull in my blood, something akin to hunger but less defined. I didn't feel it in my stomach, nor did I feel it in my throat like thirst. This was in my bones, a need thrumming in my marrow. I raised my hand, reaching for the suspended gobbet of living shadow as it impossibly seemed to reach for me.

"No!" Jaq smacked my hand down with a book she must've seized off my reading table before she swung again and sent the gobbet flying into the phonograph. The contraption erupted in a shower of springs and screws.

Cautiously, I approached the remains of the music player. Dark wisps rose from the carnage like smoke, but I smelled no fire, only the crisp sharpness of cold as if a sudden and invisible frost rimed every surface.

"Don't get too close," Yatto said, sounding genuinely afraid.

"Is it gone?" Jaq asked as I toed through the damage.

"Seems to have evaporated."

A sudden and spontaneous de-arkanistication? If only Bololo were here to lend me her perspective.

"I need to report this," Jaq said and I gave her a puzzled look. "I mean, you need to write this up. As soon as possible." She shot a glance at my assistant who bowed, deferential to

Jaq in a way she'd never been to me.

"We need to tell my—the Esteemed what we found."

What *I* found, but I didn't correct her. My attention snagged on the wax cylinder where the grooves and bumps were stained black.

"I'll start my report," I said. "Could you ask for some cleaners to be sent up? I think I've discovered all I can from our dead friend."

"Arkani aren't our friends," Jaq snapped, eyes hard as stone. Then she blinked again, seeming to recover from whatever had temporarily possessed her. "Sorry, I'm—that rattled me."

Oddly, Yatto placed a hand on her back as if he meant to reassure her. "I'm fine," she said, shaking him off. "I should get back to my own lab."

"I'll find someone to help with the cleanup. You start the report," Yatto glowered at me as if this were somehow my fault.

As Jaq strode from the laboratory with Yatto in tow, she cast a long look at the body, her expression inscrutable. As soon as the two of them were gone, I plucked the damaged cylinder from the mess of phonograph parts, careful not to touch any dark splotches.

My assistant crouched beside me, and tucked the pen she'd been using behind her ear before speaking with her hands.

This is dangerous.

"What do you mean?" I asked, grateful for the classes I'd had on Savati sign language at university. Some believed the hand-spoken language was innately dangerous, using gestures which could be misconstrued as sigils. More than one unlucky Deaf person had been accused of magic and found themselves silenced when ignorant constables chopped off their hands before realizing they were signing, not casting.

I've seen these marks before, she signed, *the arkani who have them are powerful.*

"Not powerful enough to evade capture or death."

Be careful, she signed.

"I will. But how do you know about this?"

She chewed on her lower lip, fingers trembling a little before she gestured, *I had a friend who became marked. He was different after that.*

"Different how?"

Strong, she signed. *Strange.*

I wanted to know more but a pair of cleaners arrived, cutting short our conversation.

"I'll need a new phonograph," I said. "Can you find me one?"

My assistant considered a moment. *Is that smart?* she signed, then shook her head and gestured again, this time crossing her hands as she pulled them away from her forehead. *Is that wise?*

"No great scientific breakthrough ever came from being cautious," I said, and she cocked her head at me with a far too disparaging look on her face for an assistant. Then again, I didn't know much about her. It was easy to dismiss her given her small stature and lack of speech, but perhaps I'd done her a disservice.

"What would you do?" I asked.

Be careful, she signed back immediately, repeating the gesture a third time for good measure. She dithered for another moment before adding, *I'll get the phonograph.* With that, she hurried out of the laboratory, leaving me alone with the cleaners and my thoughts.

Again, a shift in my marrow, this time accompanied by a perturbing sense of loss as I studied the smeared wax. Carefully, I cradled the cylinder. Perhaps it would tell me what the corpse could not.

Chapter Eleven
Zal

"Do you trust your sister?" Emri asked when they were alone and out of earshot. He kept his voice low, as was his way, necessary when echoes traveled like ripples through the caves.

"Not at all," Zal said, considering. "But I know she wants to protect this city for her own baffling reasons."

"And what do you want, Va'ili?" Emri asked, his elbow brushing against Zal's when the tunnel narrowed.

"What I've always wanted. This changes nothing," he said. "Ailia must've completed her research. The sigils and incantations have to be in her notes. If we find the spell, we can still use it." Stripping Leksi of her power would undoubtedly prove more challenging given the nature of her magic, but it could be done.

Zal tightened his grip on the shadow staff, imagining all he might achieve with not only shadows at his command but a cadre of nightmare-inducing monsters too. Of course the beasts might not be eager to bend to his will, but they were creatures of the Dead, and Emri had already proven himself more than capable of hobbling Death's minions in the mortal realm.

Distantly, he heard the scrape of stones being moved, the grunt of human effort, and the thrum of spells as his surviving acolytes continued restoration efforts.

"Ailia's chambers are currently inaccessible, but we're working on it," Emri said, then chewed pensively on his bottom lip. "Va'ili, there's a chance we may find Ailia, crushed—"

"She lives," Zal said sharply. "I'd know if she perished." He'd feel it, he was sure. She'd been imbued far longer and with far more of his magic than any other human, even before she'd attempted the power-stealing spell.

Emri bowed his head. "Then suppose she escaped, do you know where she'd go?"

Zal had underestimated Ailia's ambition once before. He wouldn't do it again. With Kazwe's innards decorating his thorn trees, the Synod was ripe for the taking. Ailia would have the gall to do it too. He couldn't help how his heart swelled as he imagined her marching up to the palace, blood spattered and dust-smeared, to single-handedly overthrow the government, believing herself invincible with the amulet dripping chaos around her neck.

Ailia had always been equal parts cunning and courageous. It had made her dangerous and irresistible. But she was also clever, and striding into the palace to annihilate the Synod wasn't her style. Kazwe's death may have given her an opening to seize power, but the Sodality would no doubt have similar ideas.

Ailia would need time and a safe place to hone her new magic. Even if they could access her chambers and find some personal item for a tracing spell, Ailia would've no doubt taken precautions against that. She always shrouded herself in all manner of cloaking spells in case she crossed paths with a sensitive arkani or arkanospy-wielding constable at the palace.

"Va'ili?" Emri touched his shoulder, and Zal leaned into the touch when Emri didn't remove the gentle weight of his hand.

"I'm less concerned about Ailia than I am about Riksa," Zal said as their meanderings lead them back to his desecrated chambers. Riksa's hand taunted from where it dangled. She'd need time to recover from her recent mutilations; however, if she managed to take the amulet, it would not only expedite her healing process but also strengthen her own magic.

Zal had no doubt Riksa would seek revenge on Ailia, and he refused to let that happen. He touched the skeletal finger, tracing a tattered strip of flesh to the gnarled protuberance where Riksa's gem remained fixed to the bone.

"Emri," he said, the name like honey on his tongue. "Can you use this for a tracing spell?"

"Divination is my specialty, Va'ili," Emri said with a flicker of mirth in his opalescent eyes. Such insolence from another acolyte might've triggered rage, but Zal found himself smirking.

"It's even easier when tracking one of the living dead," Emri added.

"I'm surprised you didn't think to do it already then." Zal eased himself onto the nearest chair, resenting every aching joint as they crackled like hearth logs with his shifting weight.

"I did," Emri said, "But the spell might damage or even destroy the hand. I wasn't sure how sentimentally *attached* you felt to the appendage."

Zal winced as his chest spasmed with an unfamiliar fit of laughter. Ailia had rarely made him laugh, their love a flame. She always burned so bright with life despite the struggles of her childhood leaving pockmarks in her soul. Emri, however, was kindred. Zal gathered shadows; Emri hoarded ghosts. The man understood darkness and death. He carried the weight of grief, understood absence as a looming presence, and knew loss as a constant, if unwanted, companion.

"Do what you must." Zal waved dismissively at the hand. "Where we find one, perhaps we'll find the other. If not, then at least we can interrogate Riksa." Her name, abbreviated as it was to spare Emri's ears, caught in Zal's teeth like fishbone.

"Do you wish to watch, Va'ili?" Emri asked. "Or perhaps you wish to do the honors?" He removed a ceremonial blade from his trouser pocket and handed the knife hilt-first to Zal. The blade was made of uniquely patterned steel with a tooled leather handle. Zal had seen the sciomancer's knife before, but never paid attention to the details.

Now, Zal took the blade, appreciating the expert craftsmanship of whichever desert smith had clearly forged it. Emri rolled up his sleeve, revealing a forearm littered with geometric wounds cut delicately between the snaking bands of black ink and old scars. The tattoos covered even older marks, ones inflicted on the sciomancer against his will.

"Here." Emri tapped a patch of skin near his elbow where

the lines were silver and not the raw pink of recent bloodletting.

Zal set the blade to Emri's flesh and carefully dragged the edge along the designated line, absurdly finding himself unwilling to hurt the man.

"Thank you," Emri said, and Zal lifted his gaze from the welling burgundy, mesmerized as the luminescence in Emri's eyes clotted in the pale pleats of his irises. Zal licked his lips, his shadows restless as the sciomancer rose with blood trickling onto his fingers.

Emri plucked the hand from the chains, letting his blood soak into Riksa's abandoned bones. Then he dropped to his knees and began to sing. The sound was formidable, a deep thrum permeating Zal's bones, his body responding as if it were the head of a drum struck by an invisible hand.

As usual, his pain abated in the tonal caress of Emri's magic—his joints slipping into swollen sockets, and sinews loosening their tourniquet on taut muscles. Even the burning in his chest where the sigil sat dulled to an almost pleasant warmth. Magic enveloped Emri in an opaque mist, all ghost-breath and spirit-tangle, a buzz of frequencies like a swarm of bees, only more mellifluous. It reminded Zal of the Nether, of the ghost-songs sung by the dead across the tundra, accompanied by the burble of the river and occasional percussive beak-clacking of his mother's storks.

Euphoric, Zal sank into Emri's vocalizations as the harmonies swelled, layers upon layers reverberating in the chamber. Emri's voice split—or perhaps he'd cajoled the dead into song as a whistle tone incantation sliced through the tapestry of sound. The words sounded like Nethertaal, but the idioglossia of Emri's unique magic remained gibberish. It wasn't unlike the argot of the incantations used by trained arkani. The 'language of the gods' the arkani claimed to use was merely a conglomeration of all the god-spoken dialects.

Emri's power was something else though. Like all ghost-touched, he could commune with the spirit-world, sharing visions, impressions, and knowledge with the departed like whey dripping through cheesecloth. He could summon and dispel the ghosts clustered around him with ease, his command over spirits stuck this side of the veil extending to all the living dead—demigods included. But Emri couldn't open a passage between the realms.

Zal had made him try once, years ago when he'd first recruited the lost and broken sciomancer to his cause. The spell had left Emri unconscious, coughing up blood from shredded vocal cords and bleeding from cataract-thickened eyes for days while Zal had been left sulking in guilt and defeat.

Emri's song continued, and Zal's shadows stretched toward the cloak of wraiths. The ghosts reached back in moribund greeting and Zal shivered at the contact, a frisson of ecstasy unfurling down his spine.

With thin fingers, Emri traced sigils in blood across Riksa's hand, working a spell he hadn't learned from textbooks or some guild-arkani at the university. This was another reason the ghost-touched were feared. Unlike others who required years of dedicated study to master their magic, sciomancers were living conduits, inheriting power directly from the Ancestors, an ability unregulated and ungovernable.

They'd been venerated once, the custodians of faith and culture, but times changed, and people had embraced modernity. Now, babies born with moon-glow eyes and star-bright hair were drowned or left out for scavengers.

Too soon, the incantation faded into silence, the vibrations in Zal's own body shuddering into unwanted stillness as the spill of ghosts at Emri's feet receded, a retreating glow sealing the wound in his arm as they settled once more beneath his skin.

Zal's shadows lamented the loss of their play friends, probing gently at Emri's limbs as if to coax the spirits free again.

"That tickles," Emri said, gently brushing the shadows from his shoulders.

"Did it work?" Zal asked, more bereft than his pets as pain skulked back into his body.

"I followed her path as far as I could." His eyes dimmed as his magic guttered, the visions he'd gleaned evaporating. "She fled to the city, doubling back multiple times before heading north. Her trail fades after that." He frowned, and rolled his sleeve back down.

"As if she left the mortal realm?" Zal asked. Just his luck she had the ability he craved all this time. Despite numerous attempts with increasingly inventive encouragement, neither Ailia, Emri, or Zal had ever been able to get Riksa to open a door to the Nether. He'd started to believe she was incapable of returning, but he'd underestimated her stubbornness and pain tolerance.

"No," Emri said. "More like the trail becomes obscured, diffuse. I've never seen anything like it."

Zal swore under his breath.

"Could she have found Ailia and the amulet?" Emri asked. "Could it be some effect of your magic interfering with my spell?"

"Possibly." Zal's magic was unpredictable, even for him. "At least we know she went north."

Emri knelt beside Zal, needing a moment to recuperate after using his magic. "But why?" he asked.

Zal had no idea what Riksa wanted.

"There's nothing north of Savat except farmland and the desert."

And eventually the joRanian empire. Not that Zal thought she'd venture that far, not in summer without a means of protecting herself from the season.

"Might she have other allies?" Emri asked, his eyes closed as he leaned back against Zal's chair. Zal resisted the sudden urge to run his fingers through the sciomancer's hair.

"Perhaps," he conceded. No matter the torment, Riksa had refused to divulge her secrets. The fact she'd conspired with Ailia at all meant she was clearly after something: power, dominion? Zal struggled to puzzle out her motives. She had the Nether and the favor of Death; what more could she want in the mortal realm? Unless his sister believed the legends that arteries thick with untapped magic lay below Savat—the remnants of the Great Serpent, some claimed.

Zal's mines ran deep, the deepest this side of the desert, and yet none of those excavations had ever hit a vein of raw magic. Perhaps they'd simply not plunged far enough, or perhaps the mines were too far north and the true power pooled beneath the peninsula.

"Va'ili?" Emri's fingers brushed Zal's elbow.

"I don't know," he forced through clenched teeth, resenting his own ignorance.

"We'll figure it out." Tentatively, Emri placed a hand on Zal's shoulder and pushed him back a little. Zal wanted to resist. He'd only ever surrendered to Ailia's touch, for all it had gotten him. He wasn't sure he could ever trust another mortal.

"Your wound is weeping," Emri said. "The spell still siphons your power. I can't imagine any spell working across realms. The amulet must still be here."

"Then there's still a chance…" Zal trailed off, breath netted in his lungs, when Emri set about redressing the oozing sigil.

"I'm sorry I failed you, Va'ili. I should've seen Ailia's duplicity; I should've intervened. I wish I could heal you now, but that is not within my power. Truly, I am sorry, and do not deserve your forgiveness." His voice feathered into a whisper. "I'm no longer worthy of your gift." He pulled away and Zal whimpered, wanting the sciomancer's touch to linger. Emri tugged open the laces of his shirt to reveal the flutter of shadow above his heart. Zal's gaze traced the symmetrical lines of his full-body tattoo where they lay like the bars of a cage trapping a sparrow. "I saw you reclaim the fragments of your power. I saw how it helped you. Please, Va'ili, take back what is yours." Once more Emri offered Zal the hilt of the ceremonial blade. "I don't deserve it."

Before Zal could respond, the heel-slam footsteps of Nightmare thudded through the cave, heralding Leksi's arrival.

"Oh, am I disturbing?" she asked as she stomped into the chamber with Pfumi a step behind, looking distraught.

Emri regarded Zal, eyes wide in question.

"Keep it," Zal said. "Redeem yourself, if you can." *Please, never give me cause to want to hurt you*—he kept the thought to himself, although a grunt from his sister suggested something had leaked along their tether. How he wished he could sever it for good and keep her out of his head.

A spark of white fire glinted in the sciomancer's eyes before he rose. "As you wish, Va'ili." He bowed low and Zal gathered his strength, such as it was, before turning to face his sister.

"Learn anything interesting?" he asked.

"First, I need you to promise me something," Leksi said.

"Of course you do." Zal squeezed his eyes shut, the left one throbbing. Braced for her inevitable request for power, for some portion of his magic or perhaps the right to absorb Riksa's, he asked, "What is it?"

"The spell Ailia used on you," she said. "When this is all done, I want you to use the spell on me."

It took several moments for Zal to process her words. "What do you mean?" He probed the air between them, grasping for explanation, and sensed only the faint stirrings of her hope.

"I mean, I want you to strip me of my magic," she said, and Zal shook his head, trying to dislodge the shadows that must've congealed in his ears to muddle her words.

"I don't understand."

"Stars wept, Zal, are you really this dense?" Frustration flooded their shared connection. She sighed and tried again, "I want you to make me human."

Chapter Twelve
Leksi

When Leksi first fled to the mortal realm, she vowed to stay out of human affairs. She had determinedly avoided politics, drifting from one country to another doing her best to avoid wars and revolutions, never able to linger a few decades anywhere in case people noticed her lack of wrinkles. All she wanted was a quiet life of small pleasures.

Then she'd bartered passage on a merchant ship and come to Savat.

She'd fallen in love with the city, unable to resist the inexplicable feeling of home she felt the moment her feet hit hard earth. Perhaps the old legends were true: the veil between realms did feel thinner here. And so Leksi had settled in Savat, avoiding the fanes and temples—especially the ones dedicated to her mother—ripe with their gruesome offerings. Proximity to the Death shrines only energized the inner vermin she was trying so hard to subdue.

Leksi hadn't cared when a shift in sentiment saw the fanes abandoned and gods forgotten. She'd been grateful as her monsters withered into dormancy. When a radical group of fanatics began preaching against magic and religion, she hadn't been too concerned. She'd weathered the storms of changing political and philosophical rhetoric for centuries. It was only when the streets of Savat turned slick with blood that she'd felt a prickling concern for the city she adored.

When the remains of the aristocracy resolved into the Synod, which—much to the Sodality's dismay—still welcomed non-royal arkani in positions of power, the war against magic began in earnest.

As much as she abhorred magic, Leksi couldn't do nothing while fanatics abused, maimed, and murdered those cursed through no fault of their own. The Anchorage had always been a haven for the city's flotsam. Long before she'd started taking in magical strays, she'd helped the mendicant and maligned, serving free supper to those in need. When the city pivoted toward rebellion, Leksi's tavern became home to anarchists and dissidents, always a refuge for those considered 'other.'

It was how she'd met Tamisk, who came to perform at a poetry evening, an immigrant like herself trying to forge a new path free from gods and magic and familial expectation. Leksi had been immediately drawn by the woman who wove achingly beautiful metaphors into unforgiving political tirades. Despite lacking knowledge of the intricacies of Tsirayan poetry, she'd been no less entranced by Tamisk's delivery. It was a dance of fingers, the repetitive motions visual rhymes which rose and fell like the waves in dexterous punctuation of spoken words.

Together, they'd transformed The Anchorage from a tavern and soup kitchen into a home for youth like Iqno, sent by her family to a Sodality-run conversion camp. Together, Leksi and Tamisk slipped into camps to rescue those left beaten bloody in pits, exposed to the elements without food or water for days. The cruelty was intended to prove neither gods nor Ancestors cared for the magic-cursed, that magic was a scourge and not a gift.

Iqno was badly sunburned and delirious when they'd smuggled her to safety. They'd tended her wounds—the physical ones healing quickly, the invisible ones, well… Leksi had always feared they'd scabbed over with resentment. When Iqno vanished one night, Leksi had feared she'd see her body skewered outside the palace. For months, she'd checked the faces of every fresh corpse, relieved when none were Iqno.

Instead, the girl had succumbed to a far worse fate, and Leksi had watched her die.

Leksi glared at Zal, her own resentment bubbling through her veins. If she'd escaped the life Death had preordained for her, she could escape the calamity of her brother, too. If the city didn't succumb to an arkani drunk on chaos first, an arkani who never would've threatened the life Leksi had built were it not for Zal's failings.

"You want to be human, but why?" Zal asked, as if he couldn't begin to fathom her reasons for wanting to shuck her godhood.

"Because I'm sick of magic," she said. "I'm sick of being what Mother made me. And I'm tired of living forever."

Zal visibly balked at her words as surely as if she'd slapped him. "I—" he started, but she cut him off before he could deny her request.

"You planned to strip Riksa of her power. It's the same spell Ailia used on you. Clearly it can work, so don't pretend it won't."

"The spell theoretically strips away magic," Emri said when Zal remained staring at her as if she'd sprouted two heads and a pair of wings. "We just have no idea if it can be survived," Emri added with a cautious glance at Zal.

"I guess we'll find out," Leksi said far more flippantly than she felt.

"You'd willingly give up your magic?" Zal asked, and she could almost taste his greedy desire soaking their connection.

"Yes, eventually, but not before we deal with this mess you've made." She pointed her finger at his chest.

"Even if it ends you?" he asked.

"Yes," she said, even if it meant abandoning Tamisk, and all those who depended on her at The Anchorage. Without magic, she could live a mortal life unencumbered by the daily battle against her inner beasts.

And if she perished—she had no idea what happened to a demigod dismantled by an ancient spell ridding them of magic. Perhaps she'd be like sand on the beach, a trillion tiny pieces scattered across the realms. Perhaps then she'd finally be free.

"If my existence causes others pain, then I don't deserve to live," she continued. "All this time, I've tried to mitigate the harm I've caused by being what I am, but it isn't enough. It can never be, not unless I change the very fabric of my being."

"How altruistic," Zal said, his scarred lip curled in a sardonic snarl.

"Tell me Zal, how many lovers have you watched grow old and die?" she asked, changing tack.

She felt his grief flare in cold anguish, but her brother quickly smothered his emotions. It seemed he understood well enough though, that time, for both of them, was a battlefield littered with broken hearts.

"No." He curled his swollen fingers into a fist that must've pained him. "I can simply chisel answers out of Iqno myself."

"You're welcome to try, but it might be hard for her to say much of anything now."

"S-she turned to stone. All of her," Pfumi interjected. "And then she… she crumbled." The arkani held out a handful of sparkly dust. Silica, quartz, and a pair of diamonds, all that was left of Zal's sycophant.

"For what it's worth, I think she genuinely believed Ailia acted on your orders. She never intended treachery," Leksi said.

Rage twisted Zal's features. "Then you'll have your wish." He raised his gaze from the pile of grit at their feet to meet Leksi's own. "When this is over, I promise to suck out every last drop of the magic you possess."

"Thank you," she said. "Now, any chance of refreshments? I'm famished." She glanced between Emri and Pfumi as she knotted her trembling fingers in the voluminous sleeves of her blouse so Zal wouldn't see how affected she was.

"Pfumi," Zal gave the order and the acolyte disappeared.

Emri remained, shadow-like at Zal's side.

"What did Iqno tell you?" the sciomancer asked.

"That there's a plot to blow up the palace during the First Council meeting, to eradicate the Synod—if not the Sodality—all in one big boom." Somehow she'd managed to keep her voice steady while breaking the news, despite how her mind churned over all the horrible ways such a plot could go wrong. So many innocent lives were at risk. Tamisk, and all those she'd promised to keep safe at The Anchorage.

"First Council is in less than a week," Emri said.

"It is," Leksi said, her heart stalling as she calculated how little time they had to avert disaster.

Zal frowned, while Emri remained stoic, his expression betraying nothing. Androgynous and gracile, the man could've been pretty were it not for his cemetery gaze and ghoul-gray hair falling like scrim about his shoulders.

"To what end?" Zal asked.

"Seems the former monarchy would like to take back control of the city," Leksi said.

"Motselana?" Zal seemed genuinely surprised. "She's behind this?"

"According to Iqno at least."

"And what does that have to do with Ailia?" he asked. "She was actively trying to keep the peace. She was upset with me for killing Kazwe Olonza."

"You—what?" Leksi shouldn't have been shocked by this, but she'd hoped her brother might have a little more self control, or at least choose his victims with a bit more care for the consequences. “Zalix!” She caught herself before uttering his full name blistered mortal ears.

“She overstepped the limits of my hospitality,” he said.

“So you murdered the woman?” Leksi raised an eyebrow, and Zal shrugged.

“The point is, Ailia wouldn’t want to destroy the Synod,” he said.

“I’m not sure you have any idea what Ailia’s true intentions are,” Leksi said. “What does she want? Do you even know?” She staggered when raw emotion flooded the connection between them. It was a dark riptide of guilt and anger, of bitter regret and something teetering perilously close to admiration even while its edges smoldered with ire.

Zal sucked in a breath with a grimace, pressing a hand to his side where ribs audibly popped. It was the sciomancer who eventually answered.

“Ailia has always wanted a crown,” Emri said. “To be queen.” He glanced at Zal as if for confirmation, and her brother nodded.

“So Ailia isn’t in league with Lana then,” Leksi said, the gears in her mind grinding smooth. “She could be using the former monarch for her own agenda, to get rid of the competition so she can swoop in to save the city, a savior to be adored by the people even as she assumes control.”

“Perhaps,” Zal admitted, about to say more when Pfumi returned carrying a tray.

“We can still access the spring.” The acolyte offered Leksi a cup. “But it’ll be a while before we can prepare a meal again.

Apologies, Your Deathness," she said.

"Oh, absolutely not. Call me Leksi."

Pfumi bobbed an awkward curtsy and Leksi tried not to roll her eyes.

"Thank you, Pfumi." Emri took a cup. "Can you ensure the others prioritize clearing Ailia's chambers as well?"

"Of course," Pfumi bobbed again. "Va'ili." She handed Zal a cup before making a swift exit.

"Ailia has always been ambitious," Zal said, wheezing. "But this?" He shook his head as the wheezing turned to a mirthless chuckle. "I might've been impressed if she hadn't thought to steal my power too. She's gone too far. This is… it's—" he stumbled over the words and slurped from his cup.

"Madness? Risks plunging the city into chaos?" Leksi supplied. "Did it never occur to you when slipping your shadows under human skin that prolonged exposure to your magic might unravel a few threads in mortal minds incapable of enduring your proximity?"

"It's not as if I'm plotting to ruin the city so I can claim the ashes for my kingdom," Emri said, in a voice as thick and velvety as Tsirayan coffee.

Leksi scowled at the ghost-touched, his eyes an unsettling shimmer as if they reflected a constant stream of moonlight from the realm of the Dead. "You haven't been alive long enough to feel the effects," she said. "Have you even seen twenty summers yet?"

"Almost forty," Emri answered, then pressed a hand to the layered black fabric swathing his chest. "Being imbued by

Va'ili slows our aging and bolsters our abilities."

"My brother truly is the epitome of generosity," Leksi said.

"You could've done the same," Zal quipped.

"Bought loyalty and addled the minds of those playing at worship?" Could she have granted longevity to the lovers she'd watched succumb to age, thwarting Death by simply slipping a little magic under their skin? A splinter that would've no doubt festered. "Let me guess," she continued. "You promised Ailia the crown in exchange for her adoration. Tell me, Zal, was it her bloodthirsty ambition that drew you to her in the first place?"

Zal said nothing, which only confirmed Leksi's suspicions. "It seems we cannot escape our nature. Not while Mother's magic flows in our veins."

"And you'd purge that, would you?" He glared at her with his mismatched eyes, one holding the birth and death of stars, the other red-rimmed and crusted with a gangrenous gunge. "You'd change your fundamental nature, your very being?"

"Yes," she said, setting down her empty cup. "You have no idea how long I've dreamed of dying."

"A dream of death?" Zal smiled, and Leksi wanted to gouge her nails through his smug expression, to add a few more scars to his already puckered cheeks. The monsters inside her thrilled at the promise of violence, thirsty for blood and devastation.

Violence wouldn't help, though. It rarely did. Instead, she pressed each finger tip to her thumb in slow succession on one hand, then the other—another of Tamisk's tricks—counting breaths until she felt calmer, though the vermin within her still thrashed against the cage of her flesh.

"Back to the main problem," she said. "It makes sense Ailia would show support for Motselana's plan if she intended to use your magic to increase the damage of the gunpowder. The bigger the boom, the greater the need for a savior, and the deeper the people's gratitude."

"Ailia loves this city," Zal said.

"Has it loved her back?" Leksi asked.

"It will when she heals their wounds and tends their hurts, as long as no one knows she was the one who caused the injury," Zal said.

"I should've known she was planning something," Emri said, his usually blank expression peeling away like sunburn to reveal a red-hot shame burning across his cheeks. "I never thought her capable of such duplicity."

"She fooled us all," Zal said.

"So how do we stop her?" Leksi asked.

"I'm surprised you think we should. Without the Synod and Sodality, there'd be no wounded strays for you to rescue. Or do you enjoy collecting broken things?"

She ignored the barb. "Without the Synod and Sodality, we'll either be at the mercy of the arkanic aristocracy yet again, or an egomaniac. Either way, Savati society regresses."

"Lana may be more of a traditionalist," Zal said. "But Ailia…"

"…is the egomaniac who'll blast Savat into oblivion if she tries to wield your power," Leksi interjected and Zal promptly lost the argument.

"Even if the city could survive a chaos-fueled detonation," she continued, "Ailia cannot become sovereign and bring back the old magical ways, placing arkani over others." While Leksi found much of the Sodality's radical notions repugnant, she'd been holding out hope someone able to stand up to their extremism would come to power in the Synod and bring the much needed equanimity to Savat's government. Crown-coveting Ailia would definitely not do that.

"You truly abhor magic that much?" Zal asked, as if the mere idea were a personal affront to his delicate sensibilities.

"In all its guises. And while I might not agree with the Sodality's methods, I understand their desire for an egalitarian society."

"Such self-loathing," he tsked as if he didn't hate himself in equal measure, albeit for different reasons she had yet to extrapolate from their sibling entanglement.

"There is nothing to love about what we are," she said.

"Death is always so unfairly maligned as if it, and we, were not essential to keep balance in the universe."

"Balance?" Leksi scoffed. "We were made to cause harm." She slipped into Nethertaal as her emotions got the better of her. "There is nothing balanced about that, and certainly nothing to cherish."

"I wasn't made like that," Zal said. "Chaos isn't inherently—"

"You are the product of pain, brother. Your existence is the result of ultimate suffering, thanks to the man who inflicted you upon our mother."

Zal's confusion was palpable as his brow knitted once more into a frown, his many scars bunching in stark relief. "What do you mean?"

Leksi hadn't meant to divulge the secret of his conception. Especially not now, when she needed him amiable, despite all the simmering animosity within him. She'd always worried what he'd do if he found out. He'd always been unpredictable with a fickle penchant for destruction, his moods capricious. And now with the mountainside already soaked in raw chaos magic and Zal's mind a cyclone swirl, she had no idea how he'd respond to the truth of his creation.

"All that matters is finding Ailia as soon as possible," she said.

"No." Zal gathered himself out of the chair on driftwood legs. "I want to know what you meant."

"While you are many things, darling brother, stupid isn't one of them," Leksi said. "And wallowing in self-pity isn't going to help us recover your stolen magic."

"Tell me." Zal's gaze narrowed, his shadows bristling in an oily lick of darkness like some threatened animal flexing its ruff. Emri placed a cautious hand on Zal's arm and Leksi braced, prepared to see the arkani shredded into viscera by fang-mouthed Nether beings, but Zal seemed placated by the touch. "You wouldn't have mentioned it if you didn't want me to know. So go on then, twist the blade."

Even if they didn't share a father, they'd both been born of Death, with Grief—the midwife—plucking them from the amniotic Waters of Consequence, only to toss them screaming onto a cold, dark shore. Anger was fuel; sorrow, a grave. Leksi chose her next words carefully.

"What is entropy," she said, "but chaos over time until death." Her heart twitched, her monsters shivering in eager anticipation of his reaction.

"Time?" Zal asked, his bright eye flashing.

"Surely you remember when he came to the Nether." When he'd strolled back across the frozen veld as if his original violation meant nothing. "He came looking for you. His progeny."

Zal remained unblinking, his eyes like stars in their death throes. Even as she watched, a seam of scar tissue opened at his temple, leaking red like a tear. She'd expected to feel some echo of her brother's shock, but the tether between them lay dormant. Whatever Zal was feeling, he'd managed to tamp it down, denying her his pain. Or perhaps he felt nothing at this revelation, and that scared her even more.

Then he cleared his throat as he slumped back into the chair.

"Perhaps Ailia has gone to Lana," Zal said in Savati, steering the conversation into calmer waters. "She still needs Lana's gunpowder and followers to execute her plan."

"Va'ili, Motselana's estate is north of the city," Emri said as if that meant something more significant.

"Indeed," Zal said. "Perhaps we should pay the would-be queen a visit."

"We do have time," Emri added.

"And then?" Leksi didn't want to think about what would happen when they found Lana and Ailia. Ailia would die, of that she was sure, and Leksi wouldn't waste her breath trying to convince her brother to spare the traitor, but Lana—perhaps Zal might scrounge up a kernel of mercy for the ambitious woman.

"I need more scale leaf," Zal said. "I don't think—" He grimaced, his knuckles whitening where they gripped the shadow staff. "Did you manage to get more?" he asked.

"Not yet, Va'ili," Emri said. "I've sent those we could spare to look for some. It's not so easy to find."

"I can get more," Leksi said, which would give her time to explain all this to Tamisk, to perhaps make amends, or at the very least end things in the way Tamisk deserved. It would take an hour or so to get back to the city, more than double that to get scale leaf and return. "If you're serious about paying Lana a visit, then we can meet in the northern foothills at sundown. It'll be easier for us to travel at night anyway. Do you have horses?"

Emri nodded.

"Then I'll be off. Until then, try not to wreak any more havoc," she spat at her brother before turning on her heel. She expected to feel his anger, hatred even, but it was sorrow that soaked through her defenses. Shedding unwanted tears, she fled the cave, running to the waiting tumbrel and rousing the mules dozing in their harnesses. She was desperate to escape her brother's agony scraping her insides raw. His pain placated the vermin inside her, but Leksi found no pleasure in it.

"Come on, now." She smacked an obdurate rump and only hurt her hand. The mules weren't dozing—they were dead, having fallen prey to the feral magic infecting the mountainside. Their hides had turned to sandstone, their long lashes now delicate slivers of some black mineral Leksi couldn't name, thatching their eyes shut forever.

With fresh tears blinding her vision, the sun a constant castigation, and doom gathering on the horizon darker than a summer storm, Leksi had no choice but to run back to the city she wasn't sure she could save.

Maintaining the correct hexameter matters more than the words. Vocables sharing a similar phonetic structure can achieve the same results as traditional incantations using the so-called 'language of the gods.' The resonance the sounds produce matters more than the intrinsic meaning of the words when it comes to activating magic.

Excerpt from *Decoding Incantations and the Magical Idioglossia* by Samiela Ngakula

Chapter Thirteen
Niki

While wax cylinders were far more durable than their tin predecessors, especially when spelled for durability, whatever foul substance had escaped the confines of the cadaver's flesh had proven erosive.

The embossing on the cylinder, which should've been a recording of my favorite echo-song, had been corrupted. The wax had blistered in some places, bumps like hives rising in jagged patterns, while new furrows had been gouged into the wax in others.

I traced a finger along the surface of the disintegrating wax, careful not to touch the fading stain. At least the Sodality had been in possession of several phonographs and had granted me the use of another, although not without admonishment for damaging expensive equipment.

Stifling a yawn, I cast my gaze out of the narrow window. The nighttime horizon still glowed despite the late hour, taunting me with a reminder of my looming deadline and how little I had to show for all my days steeped in viscera and scouring useless tomes for any mention of aberrant corpse-shadows.

Perhaps I held the answer in my hand, or at very least, a clue.

A soft rapping sounded at the door. I opened it to find Moli on the threshold. She held out a drawstring bag in one hand and a small basket in the other. Taking the bag of khat, I invited her in, feeling only mildly awkward about having my assistant in my private chambers. It wouldn't have been appropriate at the university, but I doubted anyone cared about propriety here.

You use too much, she admonished with her hands as I prepared a pouch of the leaves. *You should eat. I brought dinner.* She set the basket on the one corner of the narrow bed not strewn with papers and books.

"Thank you," I said, my stomach grumbling. Had I eaten anything at all today? I delved into the basket, delighted to find crispy samosas filled with fragrant curry, dried apricots dusted with sugar, aniseed sweet-buns baked a delectable golden brown, and a bottle of fermented goat's milk to wash it all down. "You are too kind."

Eat. You need to take better care of yourself, she signed as I bit into the first samosa, savoring the explosion of turmeric and cloves, masala and cinnamon.

"I'm sorry," I said between mouthfuls of pastry. "I've treated you rather poorly."

She raised an eyebrow and helped herself to an apricot, waiting for me to continue.

"You've been kind when I didn't deserve it, and incredibly helpful with my research." In fact, I'd wholly underestimated her. Had I taken the time to get to know Moli, I would've discovered far sooner how she'd been a student of the Arkanic

Arts, an arkani-hopeful even though her inability to speak meant she could never independently wield magic. Her sigil work was exceptional, however, so as long as she could be paired with a verbal partner, she would be able to cast spells. It was her substantial knowledge of sigils and her rare ability to combine functions across affinities when crafting her own sigils that had piqued the Sodality's interest. When the Synod—at the Sodality's urging—shut down the university's department of Arkanic Arts, Moli had been brought to the palace to continue her work: work on hold now since she'd been assigned as my assistant, forced to watch me blunder and fumble.

"If anything comes of all this." I gestured at the sprawl of paper with a half-eaten samosa. "Rest assured you will be credited."

She eyed me incredulously. *I don't want credit,* she spoke with her hands. *I want to find answers so we can be free.*

"Likewise," I said, although I had no idea if the Sodality would relinquish their hold on me—on any of us—if we proved useful to their grand designs on the city.

Pilfering another apricot, Moli jerked her chin toward the waiting phonograph. *Did you listen yet?*

"I was just about to," I said, taking a swig of the milk, deliciously cold despite the soupy heat. I didn't need to see the bottom of the bottle to know it would be etched with a cooling sigil. Magic certainly had its uses, some even the Sodality seemed reluctant to give up.

Be careful, she signed, her gestures made sharp with vehemence. *You're walking a dangerous path.*

"I have to."

Take precautions. Protect yourself from exposure to—I don't know, she signed before heading toward the door.

"You won't stay and listen with me?"

She seemed to consider before shaking her head. *I'm not too proud to admit when I'm afraid. Good luck.*

"Thank you again, Moli. I'll see you tomorrow."

She nodded before signing *be wise*, which had become the parting gesture she always bestowed on me, as if repetition alone would be enough to make it so.

After hurriedly finishing dinner, I slipped a pouch of khat between my lip and gum, then turned my attention back to the phonograph. Gently, I eased the stained cylinder into place, turned the crank, and lowered the reproducer. A moment before the stylus touched wax, I paused.

My room here in the palace was smaller than my suite in the university housing complex, but the walls were stone, offering better insulation from my neighbors and the outside world. If this were some sort of malfeasant spellwork, others would likely be safe, but Moli had a point about needing to take precautions.

Abandoning the machine, I scrabbled through the other items Yatto had agreed to bring from my rooms at the university, including a sound-muffling headset I'd devised for noisy environments and the effects of certain incantations. It pinched my ears, but if it protected me from vile magic, then I'd happily endure the minor discomfort. Armed with a pen and a notebook, I turned the crank with a clammy hand. My heart raced in anticipation and, carefully, I set the reproducer to the cylinder.

At first, nothing but the grumble of gear and spring, which I made a note of anyway, then a crackle and chirp, followed by a low soughing as if a sad wind whistled a lament through broken bricks. I jotted it all down in a mix of words and doodles, a notation of my own devising, as I hurried to keep pace with the changing sonics.

The whistle faded, replaced by a growl like the rutting grunt of a lion sliced into uneven divisions by a locust-screech. The warping of a bowed string bent out of true by a careless finger, perhaps? Or maybe an artifact of the previous recording lingered despite the ruined embossing.

A tapping followed then, the pattern disrupted by the metallic bellow of a bell, the echoes scattering across the rumbling susurrus of waves against the shore. Then the wind again, accompanied by a buzzing so low I didn't hear it as much as I felt it in the roots of my teeth. The pitch dropped lower still, and the accompanying sensation became a hornet sting, permeating gum to penetrate bone as if a dozen spiteful insects were injecting venom directly into my marrow.

Just when I knew I couldn't take it any more, when the scream trapped between my gritted teeth was sure to tear loose and summon my gray-clad keepers, the recording stopped and all sensation ceased.

I felt oddly bereft without the zinging inside my veins, and dazed, my thoughts muddled. My notebook wasn't much help either. My doodles were a mess, my usual spider-scrawl reduced to chaotic scribbles, words and symbols piling atop each other. The notation was all but meaningless, and yet seemed oddly familiar, like something I should know but had somehow forgotten.

I turned to a new page, reset the cylinder, cranked the machine, and listened once more, again doing my best to jot down notes. This time I attempted to dictate pitch and rhythm, struggling to keep time or divine the key.

Twice more I repeated the exercise before I deemed it safe enough to ditch my ear-pinning headpiece and listen without hindrance. By then, the cylinder was crumbling, the wax friable and the shadow stain fading as gritty chunks fell away with every repeated play. Still I persevered.

This time, I closed my eyes, listening without the distraction of trying to capture the sound on paper, letting myself just *feel.*

The sounds were less distinct now, made fuzzy by the failing wax, and yet I felt them, the sensation visceral, my body resonating in sympathy like an unstruck tuning fork brought into proximity of one already thrumming a note. As scientifically improbable as I knew it to be, I couldn't help but feel as if this stain had something to say, as if it were trying to communicate with me. All things vibrated. If magic was made of vibrating corpuscles, then could primordial magic actually have a voice?

The frequencies slithered around me in a serpentine embrace and I surrendered, letting myself move with the music as I hadn't since I was a child, before inhibition and formal schooling required stillness of body and mind in order to learn.

Now, tight muscles loosened as I swayed to the music, my hand moving the pencil involuntarily across the page. When the music stopped, I considered what I'd drawn. It vaguely resembled a sigil, but not like any of the many I'd studied. I'd need to ask Moli to decipher it for me, if she could.

The kakakis sounded Final Hour, a single drawn out blast announcing the quiet hours between now and dawn. Sleep was hardly an option for me, though—not tonight, and not with less than two weeks until my inevitable doom.

Tentatively, I touched the cylinder, hoping it would survive another play. The wax turned to crumbs beneath my touch, the scoria smoking with faint gray wisps. I needed more. There were answers here, the magic trying to tell me something.

I gave myself a mental shake. What an unscientific notion, but some shadow substance had been released from the corpse, and it had altered the recording embossed on the cylinder. I hadn't imagined that, even though I had no way of explaining it. Thus was the nature of magic, for now. If this strange scrap was willing to share its secrets with me, then I was prepared to listen.

The stain had faded, taking those secrets with it into the ether. I needed another shadow, and knew exactly where to find one.

Armed with a satchel full of fresh cylinders courtesy of the palace stores and with a fresh pouch of khat tucked into my lip, I hesitated. For over a year, Jaq had helped me navigate every quandary. Perhaps she'd know better now, as well, and help me puzzle out the meaning in the strange sounds I'd heard. If anyone could find errors in my thinking, it was her.

The sky was as dark as it could get this time of year, the waning moon turning the ocean slick with silver and illuminating the palace with a cool light. I padded softly down the sleeping halls toward Jaq's room, mentally rehearsing what I'd say and how best to present my findings, such as they were.

I rounded the corner and froze. Yatto stood outside Jaq's door, leaning casually against the jamb with one arm raised. He wasn't in his usual Sodality kaftan, but instead wore loose trousers and a shirt with a plunging V-neck, showing off the coils of hair across his chest.

It was a menacing stance and I wasn't sure how to approach. Then Jaq stepped out to greet him. I expected harsh words, expected her to shove him away the way I'd seen her handle unwanted attention on those rare occasions we'd been out at a student pub, and once even in the university library when a boy had leaned in too close over a textbook.

Instead, Jaq sidled into him, peering up into Yatto's leering face with an equally hungry grin on her lips. She curled her fingers into his shirt and pulled him into her room, the door snicking shut behind them.

So much for her being the voice of reason.

I'd hoped not to have to go alone to the dungeons, had hoped I'd never have to wander into the stinking darkness again at all, but at this late hour, I didn't want to rouse any higher ranking members of the Sodality, especially not if that got Jaq into trouble for fraternizing with Yatto.

Retracing the steps I'd taken the day I'd been hauled from the mirk, I managed to find my way back to the entrance. My fingers trembled as I tried to light the lamp. Moonlight had so far provided enough illumination for navigating the sleeping palace, but I'd need flame to guide my path in the subterranean depths. If only I could get the vrotting wick lit. Instinctively, I began to hum the conjunct melody I'd composed for the algaita in *Fantasy No. 12* and could've sworn I felt my fingertip warming where I held it to the unlit wick. Sleep deprivation and the overuse of khat were clearly taking their toll. Before I could hallucinate myself singing fire from my finger, the lamps in the room brightened and a figure swanned into the room. I couldn't make out the features of the silhouette in the doorway until my eyes adjusted to the glare.

"Esteemed," I said, further words deserting me as my brain struggled to conjure excuses or explanations.

"So eager to return to the dungeons?" she asked, a wry smile playing on her lips. She wasn't wearing the Sodality gray, either. Instead, she wore a brightly colored dress with a dazzling geometric print in reds and blues. Her hair was pinned in loose ringlets, her damaged ear hidden, and her face studded with decorative gems. She looked regal and imposing, and—Finally, I recognized her.

"You're Kazwe Olonza," I said, blinking as if I were seeing an apparition.

She'd been at more than one university event, most recently at last year's annual award ceremony where I'd been somewhat surprisingly—if not miraculously—granted funding for another year. She'd given a speech about the need to support endeavors that benefited the city and would have a positive impact on the technologic future. While she politically leaned toward the rhetoric of the Sodality, I never would've imagined her the leader of the group.

"Indeed." She touched her hair, then smoothed an imagined wrinkle from her dress. "Upon occasion, I have to don a different hat."

A different hat? This was far more than that. This was an entirely duplicitous existence. The Synod specifically and deliberately did not allow members of the Sodality to sit on the council. It was meant to be an impartial governing body. No arkani. No Sodalites. Just laity who might sympathize with one side or another but had no personal affiliations either way. Of course, the only way they'd truly know if someone was a Sodalite was if that person proclaimed it by donning the gray and shaving their head. Perhaps there were arkani keeping their identities similarly hidden. Now that was a truly unsettling thought.

While I was hardly in favor of the previous arkanocracy, a Savat given over to the extremism and paranoia of the Sodality could prove just as damaging.

"How can you serve the Synod and lead the Sodality?" I asked, my mind struggling to reconcile this revelation. This woman had been watching me; she'd known who I was and all about my research long before the constabulary had dragged me to the dungeons.

Had it all been a fabrication? A way to get me working exclusively for the Sodality, to control me and my research? Anger pooled in my belly while a cold trickle of sweat ran down the back of my neck.

"I don't serve the Synod," she said, removing a woven fan from her belt. The colors of the blade matched her dress while the leather handle was dyed white. "The Synod serves the Sodality." She waved the fan languidly. "And the Sodality serves the best interests of the Savati people."

The arkani impaled at the gates might argue the latter, but I wasn't about to contradict the woman who was arguably the most powerful person in the city.

"I see," I said, needing to fill the tense silence. My situation suddenly seemed far more precarious. Did Jaq know? I would've given anything in that moment to speak with her. I should've shoved Yatto aside and demanded Jaq's attention. I certainly shouldn't have come here alone, not without understanding the full picture. I was good at details, easily consumed by minutiae, a trait even my professor had remarked on. It was a trait that had been useful in my research, but now the failure to see what had been right in front of me this whole time could end up costing me my freedom, if not my life.

"Might I ask why you were heading to the dungeons?" the Esteemed asked.

Kazwe Olonza, vice-seat of the Synod.

The Esteemed, leader of the Sodality.

My head hurt, fatigue gnawing at my brain despite copious quantities of coffee and khat.

Olonza repeated her question and this time I managed to fashion a response, honest but careful. "I've learned all I can from the dead arkani. I was hoping to find a fresher specimen," I said.

"In the middle of the night?" She narrowed her gaze at me.

"I'm on quite a tight deadline," I said, and she smirked.

"And what have you learned?" she asked, her gaze sliding to my satchel where a cylinder protruded from the flap.

"Nothing I suspect the Sodality doesn't already know." I was speaking too quickly.

"Indulge me." Olonza's eyes were as cold as metal.

I nodded, swallowed, tightened my grip on the strap of my bag, wondering how best to put into words my discovery. Would this woman think me insane for attempting to commune with magic as if it were some sentient entity? It was what had sealed Scryali's fate after all, the arkani convinced she could converse with sunbeams, and coax new stars from the ether.

Had Scryali heard the voice of magic? Had she lost her reason, not because of some malady of the mind, but as a result of listening to the impossible music of arkana particles? If so, perhaps it was only a matter of time before I, too, lost control of my faculties.

Scryali, though. So much of her work had been lost when she was executed. So many of her compositions had been considered too dangerous, any and all notation destroyed. If something of hers had survived, it would've been kept under lock and key within the palace, archived along with all the other forbidden texts on the subject of magic, the archive I now had unlimited access to. If I could unearth some of her scores, perhaps—

"Nikima, need I remind you of your situation here?" Olonza snapped.

"No, not at all." I didn't have much to show her except my scribbled attempts at notation and the sigil-like squiggles. Grudgingly, I removed my notebook and turned the page.

"An interesting shorthand." She raised a judgmental eyebrow at my scrawl. "But what's this? It looks like a sigil." She touched her chest where the embroidered symbol of the Sodality would've been had she been wearing her uniform.

"I'm not sure what it is yet, but I think it might be connected to the mark on one of the arkani I studied."

"A mark like an odd bruise?" she asked.

"You've seen it?"

"Not all arkani we arrest are marked like that. Some in our order think it might indicate a contamination of sorts, the result of poor spellwork or malfeasance."

An interesting notion, and not one I'd considered. If magic were a force made up of arkana particles, then perhaps not all particles were alike. Some might even cause harm, infecting the unsuspecting arkani wielding from a blighted source. But what source? And how might those harmful particles be distinguished from the rest? Once again my mind whirred, thoughts ricocheting from one possibility to another. Had Scryali been marked like that? Moli said her marked friend seemed stronger, and stranger. What sort of infection could make a person *better* at magic?

So many questions and far too little time to find answers.

"Precisely why I wanted to study it more closely. I hoped to find another marked arkani already in custody," I said.

"You were going to just stroll into the dungeon and demand an audience with one of our prisoners?" She waved the fan in a slow back and forth that was oddly calming.

"I had hoped to make a request of Yatto Makhezi but he was—indisposed."

Olonza's expression soured. I should've said he was sleeping and I didn't want to disturb him. I didn't want Jaq to get in trouble for indulging the man's dalliances.

"Lucky I found you, else you might've ended up bludgeoned and back in chains. Come on then." She snapped the fan shut and strode past me, retrieving my lamp where I'd left it on the floor before leading me into dank darkness. This time I managed to quash my fear and follow without cowering or whimpering or smelling the rotting potatoes of my parents' cellar.

Less than a bewildering hour later, I found myself back in my laboratory with the sea breeze streaming through the open window and a very much alive arkani strapped to my table. No Yatto this time, thankfully, although that meant I had to wield the scalpel by myself on a living specimen. A pair of guards were stationed outside, in case the prisoner proved dangerous.

I doubted that, considering they'd had both their legs broken, their tongue removed, and their head bashed so hard they were unconscious.

All necessary precautions, Olonza had said while accompanying me to the laboratory. Couldn't have an arkani escaping, she'd said, not even one with broken fingers and a missing tongue.

Now I stood alone with the ravaged body of a magic wielder, mind still ringing with the peculiar strains of the stained cylinder. As gently as I could, I sliced away at the rags covering the skeletal body. It barely seemed human any more, reduced to a jumble of twig-like limbs and a collection of wounds in various states of suppuration. The smell was no better than a corpse, the work all the more grim since the person's heart was still beating. I made a mental note to ask Moli to replenish our citronella stores in the morning.

I began my inspection with the hands, bathing the filthy skin with a warm cloth soaked in mint-laced water in case dirt hid strange bruises. It also seemed the least intrusive place to begin my ministrations.

My hands trembled as I worked, and I longed for the calming strains of the echo-songs. The phonograph, retrieved from my room by a grumbling guard, sat ready and waiting for a cylinder should I manage to find another stain and pry it free from living tissue.

As I fell into the rhythm of soaking and washing, scrubbing and wiping, I began to relax. The knot of my thoughts unraveled as I hummed. The tune was Scryali's, of course, the familiar shape of her melodies a soothing caress as I subvocalized the refrain, hoping to channel a little of her prowess too. It didn't work, though. Having cleaned and examined every inch of visible flesh from toes to forehead, it seems the arkani was only blemished by a stint in chains, all bruises and abrasions, scars and freckles entirely ordinary and bereft of magic.

I needed to turn the body and examine the back, but the restraints made that impossible. For all my sponging and prodding, the arkani remained unconscious. Even if they woke, I doubted they'd have the strength to pose a threat with their damaged appendages.

Glancing at the guards, I loosened the leather straps and set about rearranging the kindling limbs so I could roll the body. I'd only need to do one side at a time. It was awkward work, but eventually I managed to prop the arkani on their side, exposing ladder-rung ribs and a sharply divoted spine. Shoulder blades arced like wings beneath their papery skin. There were wounds where bone cut through too-thin flesh, old scabs splitting as the arkani drew shallow breaths.

There were bruises on their back, too, some the angry violet of recent contusion, while others had already yellowed.

Working my way from nape to buttocks, I pressed on each discolored splotch and found nothing out of the ordinary until I came to one congealed in the hollow of the arkani's lower back.

I pressed on the bruise, startling when its frayed edges raveled at my touch. A thrill of fear and excitement sent a rash of tingles across my scalp. It was the same sensation I experienced when a particularly exquisite piece of music pierced my brain.

Perhaps if I'd been less myopic in my focus, if I'd remembered the body on my table was a living specimen and not a corpse, perhaps I would've been more cautious before picking up the scalpel and making the first incision.

The body jerked when I sunk my blade into flesh, arms flailing as a moan broke from the arkani's bloody mouth. The blade caught, slicing skin pulled too taut over bone, gouging deeper than intended given the arkani's struggle. They speared me with their gaze, dark eyes murderous as they flung a feeble fist toward me. Despite their malnourished state, they were surprisingly strong and their punch clipped me hard on the jaw. I staggered back, still clutching the dripping scalpel. Gathering my wits, I darted back to the table, reaching for the restraints and hoping to regain control of the prisoner before the guards punished us both.

I grabbed one arm, but the arkani lunged at me, mouth open to reveal blackened stumps of teeth, some still sharp and snapping toward my face as a hand with jagged nails scrabbled at my face. I stepped back and the arkani toppled the table, landing in an ungainly sprawl and screaming when their shattered legs met cold stone. The guards shoved past me, reaching for the howling arkani, naked and bleeding and clearly in agony, yet still fighting.

They squirmed and rolled, scraping fingertips raw against the stone in bloody trails. I stood back, cowering against the wall, clutching the scalpel as I watched as if from a tremendous distance while the guards kicked and punched. My vision swam, as if I were watching a mirage, the violence I'd caused nothing but a trick of the light.

A crunch, then silence.

Silence, except for the blood pounding in my ears.

Silence, except for the heavy breathing of the guards.

Silence, except for a whispery scratching in my ear like the feeble scraping of a cricket's leg.

"Still want this?" One of the guards asked, toeing the crumple of flesh that had been a person. A person with family and friends, purpose and potential, dead now because of my careless ineptitude.

I shook my head, not trusting myself to speak for the gorge rising up my throat.

"We'll send for cleaners then," the second guard said. "Perhaps we can escort you to your room?"

I nodded, letting the guard pry the scalpel from my hand. Beneath a crust of blood, my fingers looked discolored. Perhaps another trick of the light or a figment of my shocked brain. I wiped my hand on my trousers, desperate to remove the arkani's blood from my skin and glanced at my fingers again.

Definitely bruised. Perhaps I'd been hurt in the scuffle without realizing it.

"All good?" the second guard asked.

If the guards saw, I might end up a puddle of mashed remains like the poor sod I'd been so keen to dismantle. Shoving my hands into my pockets, I nodded and let the guards lead me from my laboratory without glancing back at the arkani I'd all but murdered. I balled my stained hand into a fist, hoping I was wrong, but I felt it move, a millipede crawling up my fingers, as whatever I'd absorbed from the arkani burrowed its way through my arm.

The Principles of Inyoti as recorded by the first arkani blessed by the Ancestors to carry that most sacred fragment of the Serpent God within their hearts. Thus are the tenets upon which we build our society.

Third Principle—Empathy, Compassion, Dignity:

It is important for everyone to cultivate understanding and concern for the lives of others in order to achieve harmony despite differences. People are inherently equal in their worth and their dignity must always be respected. Individual identities are to be celebrated so long as those identities do not cause discord within the community.

Chapter Fourteen

Zal

A boiling river flows through the Nether, cutting a serpentine trail across a veld of snow and ice. The brutal currents are called many names by the humans whose mouths cannot shape the syllables of Nethertaal without cracking their teeth or blistering their tongues. Despite the many variations, the meaning remains the same.

The Waters of Consequence.

Upon death, a soul is plunged into the depths, submerged until judged.

If a soul is deemed worthy, a marabou stork plucks the soul from the burning flow and tosses it back to shore to be reborn in the realm of the living, or to remain a free spirit in the Nether.

The damned are drowned. Over and over again. Heads pecked by merciless beaks driving them beneath the torrents, talons crushing the dead into silt and sediment where sharp-toothed scavengers take their full. Excreted in fragments and filaments, the souls eventually reconstitute only to be judged again.

Over and over the cycle repeats until the soul has been purged, punishment complete, and is flicked ashore, or condemned once more to tumult. Each time, a little less of the soul survives, tattered shreds consumed or boiled away, lost and forgotten, until nothing remains.

Zal regarded the chunk of rock in his hands. Since Leksi left, he'd helped his acolytes clear the rockfall. This mostly consisted of him watching over his able-bodied followers as they dug and lugged heavy stone away from the entrance to Ailia's chamber.

He rolled the rock across his palm, this one jagged where the pebbles of the Nether river were worn smooth by time and ghosts. He closed his fist around the stone, letting the edge bite into the flesh of his thumb.

It had been a childhood pastime to hunt the marabous. The massive storks were hideous creatures, with their bald heads and long, savage beaks. They carried a fleshy pouch around their necks where they kept trophies and trinkets. Sometimes a snatch of soul stuff, or more often a token left at a fane, transported by prayer to wash up as litter on the shore. Finger bones and shiny beads, blood clots and polished teeth, all dangled around the storks' featherless necks.

Every bird was massive, taller by double than Zal or any of his siblings, who all seemed so small and fragile next to the imperious flock of Death's undertakers. When the storks flapped their wings, they billowed their father's power into the mortal realm: sky-devouring, roiling storms that assaulted the living.

Their father, not mine, Zal thought, and squeezed his fist.

The siblings had made sport of taunting the baleful birds—Zal always the most reckless, who risked eternal suffering to snag a feather. When plucking pinions no longer proved challenging enough, Zal had dared Mezra to pinch a trinket from the neck pouch of Grief, the largest and ugliest of their mother's pets. Mezra had agreed on the condition that the loser give themself to the river. The fact they'd been born in those fiery waters meant nothing; all beings were susceptible to Consequence.

"Va'ili, here." Emri pressed a cool cup into Zal's empty hand and Zal drank, his corporeal form crying out in a thirst he'd been ignoring. "We've cleared passage into Ailia's chambers. We found her notebooks." Emri tapped a stack of leather-bound journals beside him. "Sadly, there's nothing here that might help us reverse the spell she used against you," he said, as softly as always. "I have Pfumi looking for more. We will find a way."

"Thank you," Zal said, making no move to rise.

Instead, Emri joined Zal in the wreckage of his hubris. Dust painted the sciomancer's black attire in illegible calligraphy as Emri folded his long legs to sit criss-cross like a child, his knee touching Zal's. Like drawn to like, Zal's shadows scampered toward the sciomancer. His ghost-glow aura shimmered a little brighter at Zal's proximity. The contact was soothing, not that Zal deserved it.

Inflicted.

The word gnawed at him like a hyena with a fresh carcass.

He knew what his sister insinuated, and, despite how much he wanted to reject the notion, it settled within him leaden and true.

Zal had never felt wanted by his mother. He saw the way she doted on Mezra, indulged Riksa, and fawned over Leksi. When it came to him, however, she barely tolerated his presence and rebuffed all his attempts at affection. He might've believed he was simply not meant to be loved, but Mezra had held him when Mother pushed him away, had distracted him with adventures when Mother twisted her lips in disgust at his antics. He didn't blame her. How could anyone love the product of such violence?

"Va'ili." Emri pried open Zal's hand where he clutched the stone, hard enough to slice the skin.

"Have I ever told you about my childhood?" Emri asked, easing the rock from Zal's grasp. His blood smoldered where it melted into the earth.

"I only know you hail from the southern reaches of the joRanian empire," Zal said. joRania was Savat's closest continental neighbor, and where Zal had been summarily ejected from the Nether.

"I'm from a nomad clan," Emri said. "For generations, my people moved between the cities and southern oases, trading wares or performing for coin."

"You were close to your family?" Zal asked.

"I never knew them," the sciomancer said. "If my parents could've known I'd been born as I am, they would've had me deep in the sands, then held me face-down in a dune."

"They would've murdered you?" Perhaps Zal should be grateful his mother had chosen to birth him at all.

"It would've been a mercy," Emri said, and took a sip from

his own cup. "My family was unlucky. They had me in one of the cities where the ghost-touched are seen as easy access to the Ancestors, to healing and protection."

"Living muti," Zal said.

"Precisely. While customs differ across the empire, many keep the old faith, and consider a physicker's godless medicine anathema. Many joRanians believe the touch of a sciomancer a direct blessing from the Ancestors and a guaranteed cure. If mere touch isn't enough, then using the flesh or blood, consuming it…" he shivered and trailed off.

Zal had traveled in several of the Empire's southern cities, each more resplendent than the last, dripping wealth thanks to the black gold welling from the desert sands.

In his experience, most joRanians embraced pleasure and luxury, revering the gods and ancestors through hedonistic revelry as much as prayer and offerings. Theirs was a society built on the belief that hard work would be rewarded with wealth, and if you weren't reaping rewards, then you weren't working hard enough. There was nothing you couldn't buy in the larger cities—everything and everyone was for sale.

"The Yekkä have little power in joRania," Emri continued. "The nomads always struggled for their independence, refusing to bow to the rule of the empire. Shunned for the shape of our eyes and our ways, we're tolerated only because of the goods we trade."

"The secrets of your metal-work?" Zal asked, gaze drifting to the ceremonial blade on Emri's belt.

"And weaving, jewelry, oryx milk, cheese, and meat.

Herding and trading is how they survive on the periphery as conditions grow more severe every year. If I'd been born in an oasis, I might've been kept a secret, but when the city midwives saw my eyes—" He paused, and Zal didn't need a psychic tether to feel the man's pain. "My parents refused the offer of coin. They wouldn't part with me, and for that, they died."

"How do you know all this?" Zal asked gently, before the answer presented itself in the sheen of Emri's gaze.

The sciomancer smiled, a rueful, broken twist of his beautiful lips. Zal fought the urge to wipe away the hurt caught in the corners of the sciomancer's mouth with his thumb.

"At first, I felt like a treasured pet," Emri said. "Purchased by one of the wealthiest families in one of the largest cities."

Zal respected Emri's choice not to name either, and he wouldn't ask.

"I wanted for nothing," he continued. "A happy child living alongside others I considered my siblings, even if none of us looked alike and none looked like me. As a child, I was educated with the others—learning to dance and sing, to read and write. At night, though, I was paraded at parties. Sometimes I was made to stand on a pedestal where people would come to touch me, to stroke my hair, my face, more—" Emri shuddered, and Zal wished he could reach back in time to break every single one of those hands.

"It was only when I was older that I began to understand the whispers in my head and the magic in my blood. I realized then that children shouldn't be treated as I was. I hated it, being fondled in strange houses, the attention, the demands—" He swallowed. "If I was lucky, they took snippets of my hair. Others wanted more: keepsakes and tokens, muti to continue the healing they thought I provided after I was whisked away." He pressed his hand to his forearm, to the scars hidden by black fabric and ink, where the greedy had felt entitled to pieces of his body.

"I ran away, following the directions of my ancestors." He touched his temple. "It took several attempts before I found my clan. They were afraid of me, and for me. They saw the scars, knew what I'd endured, but they feared what would happen to them if they sheltered me." He paused for a moment, and unexpected rage gripped Zal's insides. How he'd delight in making those who hurt the young sciomancer suffer. How he longed to break them only to heal them, and do it all over again, the same way… the same way… that day in the snow… Zal sucked in a steadying breath, focusing once more on the man beside him.

"My family rejected me," Emri said. "Told me I was dead to them and gave me this knife." He held up his ceremonial blade with the leather handle. "They told me to do what my parents should have done the day I was born: to end my pitiful existence and pray the gods were merciful. If I died I'd be reunited with my parents—perhaps even plucked from the river and given a second chance." His voice, already so low and soft, dropped lower still. "The next time I ran away, I didn't stop until I reached Savat, paying my way however I could." His gaze flicked to Zal's, and Zal read the challenge in them, as if Emri was daring Zal to judge him for doing whatever it took to survive.

Never. Not when Zal had done far worse.

"I understand," Zal said, and the sciomancer exhaled in seeming relief. "We all do what we must." He had consumed the old lady Gafina and her pious friends, sucking the life from them to heal his fractured body. He'd cheated and stolen, maimed and hurt and traded in flesh—his own and others'—to cobble together a life in the mortal realm. If their paths had crossed centuries ago before Zal had wealth and standing, he might've used Emri to his own advantage, the way he'd used so many others, sparing little thought for the suffering he inflicted. Perhaps Leksi was right, and Death's spawn had been made only to cause harm.

"You thought you'd be treated better in Savat?" Zal asked.

"No one was going to carve away pieces of me to soothe a headache, at least," Emri said. "If I was discovered, they might kill me outright. That seemed better." He rested his hand beside Zal's, skin grazing skin equally speckled with the burgundy of Zal's blood. The color had leached into the ink coloring Emri's long fingers, the black turned to rust.

"Suffice it to say, I know what it is to be a victim of circumstance," Emri said, the Savati syllables a susurrus. "To be a child born different."

"It's not the same," Zal said.

"Perhaps not, but whether we're born out of love or violence, we're not to blame for any of what follows. You didn't ask to be made as you are, and neither did I."

"Your father didn't rape your mother," Zal said, the admission a dull spoon in a cruel hand scooping out his insides. His words hung in the air above them, a scythe about to swing. "Now at least, I understand why my mother couldn't stand the sight of me. I must've been a constant reminder of her pain, an incessant source of anguish. I must've made her miserable just by existing, and all those times I sought her attention, her affection—" Zal struggled to retain his composure; he would not survive the strain of tears. "Imagine looking into the face of your child every day and being reminded of *that?* I truly have been the embodiment of suffering since the moment I was conceived." His laughter was brutal and humorless, a hammer to his brittle ribs.

Chaos, entropy, tumult over time unto Death—he was his father's child.

"I understand what it feels like." Emri took Zal's hand and gently squeezed. Zal held his breath. "Like someone has torn open your chest and ripped out your heart," Emri continued. "An evisceration." If only the sciomancer knew how literally Zal had experienced exactly that. "I felt so helpless," Emri said. "So worthless, paralyzed by a mix of anger and self-loathing."

"You were a victim," Zal said.

"And you weren't?"

Zal pulled away, calling his shadows to him as he forced his body to rise despite freshly broken bones.

"Please, Va'ili, haven't we both been punished enough for what we never asked to be?"

Emri hadn't deserved to be used, to be sliced up like some prized fruit, but Zal? He'd goaded his sibling into damnation, a Netherling game taken too far with his uncontrolled chaos inadvertently causing the demise of his sibling, robbing Death of the child she'd actually wanted. Now Zal understood why his mother had unmade him. Perhaps she'd been waiting for an excuse to release all her pent up hurt and hatred, to inflict on him what had been inflicted on her.

Zal exhaled, his knee buckling with an audible crunch. He cried out, toppling into Emri's arms, tears like acid cutting down his cheeks.

"You can't go on like this," Emri said, easing Zal down to the ground again and propping him against the nearest wall. Zal tilted his head back, eyes closed as if he could block out the reality of his circumstances.

"Perhaps we could try something different," Emri said, and Zal cracked open a lid sticky with salt and grit. "I've been thinking about the nature of Ailia's spell, the one you intended to use on your siblings. While I can't reverse it, I think there might be a way to modify it, with your permission, Va'ili." He ducked his head, the gesture respectful where from another it might've seemed obsequious. "You already share a psychic link with your sister, correct?"

Zal nodded.

"Then I don't think it would be too hard to expand that to a physical connection as well. It was the first part of Ailia's spell."

"Explain," Zal said, his mind frayed by pain and waning

purpose.

"I think I could bind you to your sister in a way that allows you to draw on her magic, to heal yourself and give you the necessary strength to find Ailia. If Leksi is willing, of course."

"Would the bond go both ways like the psychic one?" Zal asked.

"I think so," Emri said. "The spell is not without risks."

"What's to stop Leksi from draining me dry then?"

"Her abhorrence of magic," Emri said. "She wants to be human. This would at least provide her a temporary reprieve from her own power."

One she might realize was a mistake and then steal every last drop of magic from Zal's failing body, but Emri was right. He couldn't go on like this. Scale leaf wasn't going to be enough to get him to Lana or fuel the vengeance slowly changing course but burning just as hot within him.

"You sure you can do it?" Zal asked.

"I will try." The sciomancer lifted Zal's injured hand to his lips and placed a reverent kiss on the aching knuckles. "No one gets to choose how they are made, but we do get to choose who we become," he said with scalding sincerity. "And what we do in life." Zal met the sciomancer's ghost-glazed gaze. "That's why I came to Savat: to start afresh and forge my own path. And you can, too."

Chapter Fifteen
Leksi

The city was crawling with hyenas.

Sweat-drenched and sore-footed, Leksi kept her head down as she approached the western gates. Given the holiday, there were few people queuing on either side of the colossal arch strangled by jasmine.

There was a new tension in the air, though—the pressure of a storm about to break. The constables seemed more concerned about who was leaving than entering, searching a waiting tumbrel by disemboweling every suitcase and satchel. Several people sat manacled in the sun, heads bowed, some faces bruised by law enforcement fists.

"State your business," one of the city guards draped in a gray-green cape demanded when she attempted to pass through the gate.

"Returning home. I live in the city." She gave her address, hoping it wouldn't raise any suspicion.

"By order of the Synod, residents must return to their homes and stay indoors."

"Why?" Leksi asked. "What happened?"

The guard ignored her, and Leksi knew better than to push her luck. The thunk of a cudgel meeting flesh and a cry cut short by another blow drew their attention to where a hyena, in the company of a Sodalite, was beating one of the manacled prisoners. The Sodalite wore the uniform gray robes of the order, but their hair was cut in an unflattering bowl instead of shorn in a single stripe. On their arm, they wore the white band denoting them a member of the Arkanic Guild in service of both the city and Synod, their spells and sigils weaponized against the unruly masses in an act of astounding hypocrisy.

With the guard distracted, Leksi hurried through the arch. Her heart lurched as she forced tired feet toward the sanctuary of the home she'd chosen—the one she'd made despite the odds.

With Olonza dead, the city's leadership would soon be in disarray if her absence hadn't already been noted. Perhaps that's why the gates were closed. To lose a representative this close to First Council could only prove… chaotic.

Now that one of the more reasonable voices in Savat had been silenced, it was only a matter of time before the last moderates on the Synod were replaced with gray-clad, magic-hating extremists. For the first time, Leksi questioned her determination not to get involved in human politics.

"Damn you, Zalix," she wheezed as she took a more convoluted route to The Anchorage, darting down narrow alleys to avoid patrols.

This was why you didn't turn city officials into tree baubles.

She sifted saliva turned bitter as brimstone through her gritted teeth, her mood blacker than Death's darkest night as she contemplated the violent vagaries of human existence, never mind the role she and her family had played in all that across the centuries. Leksi wondered what would happen if she revealed her true nature, proving the gods hadn't faded into impotence despite the Sodality's claim and the people's waning faith. Would anyone even care?

The detritus of last night's festivities littered the streets. Flowers lay crushed, petals drifting in the breeze wafting off the sea. Remnants of food and drink gathered in the ruts and gutters too, and strange flowers sprouted from the paving—the petals white and furred, some tumbling like silky hair over charcoal stems.

Frostweed. It grew in abundance in the Nether, but Leksi had never seen it in the mortal realm, had all but forgotten it existed even though she used to weave flower crowns with it as a child.

A rat darted across her path, aiming for the patch of frostweed, and promptly imploded. Leksi froze, not sure she could believe what she'd seen. She stepped closer to where the rat had met an unexpected demise. The air took on a slippery sheen, like a smear of cooking grease—only it hung vertically, suspended on invisible strings a finger's width above the cobbles. The tip of the rat's twitching tail remained on the stone; the rest of it had been reduced to a scatter of red.

Fighting a wave of nausea, Leksi pressed the back of her hand to her mouth. This was chaos magic: her brother's leavings corrupting the natural order of the mortal realm. She glanced up and down the street, relieved to see it deserted. While the day after the Solstice was always spent nursing headaches and lazily picking at leftovers, she was grateful for the

Sodality's ordnance to stay home. She didn't want to see what happened when a person stepped into a puddle of entropy.

Tentatively, she grazed her fingers through the air, searching for the edges of the magical remnant. She didn't want to absorb it herself, and definitely didn't want the burden of her brother's magic in her bones, but she couldn't leave the splotch here for some poor child to stumble across.

She felt it, plucked at it, but it stung her fingers as if she'd stuck her hand into a wasp's nest. Cursing, Leksi recoiled. She didn't have time to worry about a single dollop of destruction, not with the entire city at risk.

Regretfully, she stumbled on, hoping they'd be able to rectify this situation before people got hurt. If they could undo the spell and restore Zal's power, then he'd be able to recall all his feral fragments.

She hurried as fast as her aching feet would carry her, past more patches of invasive frostweed and gruesome remains. There were other anomalies too, where bricks had turned liquid and melted like wax from buildings. Rats sporting feathers, antlers, or even a single human ear scuttled past her along cobbles turned to fulgurite. Leksi paused at a window shimmering with a vista from a foreign city, space and time bending against the crooked pane. Wherever Zal had bled, so oddities had bloomed.

He'd bled at The Anchorage—in the bathtub, in her kitchen!

Hiking up her skirt, Leksi ran the last few blocks, skidding to a halt at the door already warped and festooned with the trailing weeds of her homeland.

"Tamisk?" She stepped carefully across the threshold. The brittle scent of cold and death greeted her as she stalked into the disconcertingly quiet interior.

The bathroom was a veritable grove, overgrown with the icy plants. Her skin prickled as she made her way to the kitchen. Chittering, as if a troop of vervet monkeys gathered in the beams above, broke the silence. She had to squint to see the smoky tendrils of the ghosts.

No doubt her brother's doing. To banish them, she'd have to use her magic. Zal thought he was so clever, but he was only as irritating as he'd always been. Memories of him roosted like the dislocated spirits in the rafters of her mind, fluttering restless wings, demanding her attention. She refused to give in, though—refused to let herself feel any guilt for escaping her fate, even if it had wounded her mother so deeply Death had become cruel instead of inevitable.

There had been so many ways she could've revealed what Time did to their mother. As a Netherling herself, Leksi hadn't fully understood what she'd seen that day beneath the shimmering trees. She and Riksa had been chasing spirits, children grappling with their growing power. She hadn't recognized the figure sitting beside their mother, a slender man with the waves of thick dark hair Zal had inherited. She hadn't understood when he'd pinned Death to the snow, or why she'd frozen in place—in time. After, the wind had turned to a gale and torn up whole trees, sending them cartwheeling across the tundra as the stranger strolled through their realm.

He'd scared her, this god who could hold her motionless and stall her existence. She'd wanted to run after him, beat her Netherling fists against him, and unleash the monsters still cutting their milk teeth inside her. Her monsters grew fangs that night—and sharper claws, too.

Later, when Leksi had found her mother—Death's belly already tender and swollen—she'd been too afraid to ask. When Zal was born and her mother wanted nothing to do with him, Leksi had known for sure the circumstances of her brother's making. None of that was Zal's fault, but this mess he'd made with Ailia was entirely his own doing.

Leksi stomped on a clump of frostweed, letting anger incinerate all her pity and regret.

"Tamisk?" she called out again as she stepped into the kitchen. The stove had gone out, the stew cold in the pot. The samovar remained where they'd left it last night—the brass turning to sludge like melting butter. Was it truly only last night that Zal had upended her entire world?

Ansa sat in the middle of the kitchen table, her head tilted toward the ghosts. Her tail twitched back and forth like a scythe through the air. The cat, at least, seemed unmolested by her brother's magic, except—the cat's gaze settled on Leksi. Her once sea-foam green eyes were the same swirl of unnameable color as Zal's now.

Leksi backed away as the cat lifted a paw and began to groom fresh blood from the unsheathed claws.

"Salja, Zadi, Bofile?" Leksi called the names of their tenants, terrified of what the continued silence might mean with a chaos-addled cat in the house. She didn't want to contemplate what else Zal's bodily debris might have done to her charges.

"Here," a muffled voice responded.

"Tamisk, thank the stars." Leksi strode through the kitchen to her office, kicking aside more clumps of invasive flowers.

Tamisk sat hunched over Leksi's desk, the floor littered with paper going back decades, torn from the immaculate records Leksi kept filed away in the wooden cabinet. It had been a gift from Tamisk, the cupboard doors featuring an exquisitely carved sea-serpent motif with polished cowrie shells for the handles.

"What are you doing?" Leksi asked, dismayed at the mess.

"Trying to understand." Tamisk brandished a sheaf of papers.

"Understand what?"

"How I could've fallen for a liar." Her skin glistened where the light caught her wrist. Scales protruded wetly from her skin and trailed up her veiny forearm before disappearing beneath the rolled cuff of her sleeve.

The consequence of Zal's dribblings no doubt, a consequence that Tamisk of all people did not deserve.

"Where are the others?" Leksi asked.

"Somewhere safe. I sent them away when things started to change." Tamisk pointed at the frostweed. "My friends in Qhemba took them in despite the risks. Kazwe Olonza is missing. The hyenas are on the hunt. They think some rebellious arkani abducted her." Tamisk's usually strong voice sounded brittle and breathy.

"Abducted?"

"One theory." Tamisk shrugged stiffly. "The Synod's morning bulletin said the city is under magical attack." Her gaze dropped to the creeping patch of frostweed again. "No one is supposed to leave their homes until the constabulary finds those responsible. They're breaking down every door." Tamisk still hadn't looked at Leksi. "They have Sodalite arkani with them. Magic-wielders tracking down their own kind. Lies on lies like barnacles on a whale." Her words were spears piercing right through Leksi's shriveled heart. "The kids couldn't stay here. If they're found, they'll be dragged back to the camps, or to the dungeons."

If not immediately skewered and displayed as a warning to others, but Leksi kept the thought to herself.

"You did the right thing," Leksi said. "I'm grateful to your friends."

Tamisk grunted. "A lot of people are going to get hurt in this search until they find Olonza."

"They won't find her." Leksi sighed, wishing she could tell the hyenas how futile their hunt was. "Kazwe Olonza is dead."

"Dead?" Finally Tamisk turned to face her, all color drained from the usually stoic woman's cheeks.

"Dead as driftwood." Leksi used one of her lover's Tsirayan sayings.

"How do you know?" she asked and Leksi briefly reconsidered her commitment to the truth.

"My brother killed her. Unintentionally, but she's no less

dead."

For several excruciating moments Tamisk said nothing while staring at Leksi, as if she could whittle away lies from truth with her gaze alone.

"I did say he was trouble," Leksi said.

"You didn't say he was a *murderer*." Tamisk's voice cracked.

"I didn't know." Leksi cleared her throat. "Anyway, were you looking for something specific?" she asked, hoping Tamisk would let her change the subject.

"Answers," Tamisk said slowly. "I tried to respect your privacy. I understand how it is to carry family pain buried in your bones—but magic?" She sucked her teeth. "I've seen things since we've been together—had little suspicions, but I ignored them all. I loved you."

The past tense hit Leksi like a punch, her head reeling. She felt it then, that strange ebb of adoration, a depletion as if her organs were being sucked dry of some vital fluid.

"I saw you doing good," Tamisk continued. "Everyone is entitled to their secrets, as long as they don't hurt others. And you were helping people, so I didn't ask about your pendants, but now—" She muttered a curse in the Salt tongue. "What are you?" she asked. "I want the truth, not this nonsense." She flung the records at Leksi. The papers floated, caught in currents of wraith breath, the irksome dead chuckling as they toyed with the fabricated history. "Not a single son or nephew? No relatives arguing over the inheritance? All your aunts just expire at fifty-five? I recognize the names; I've seen their headstones."

"I can explain," Leksi said.

"Explain this!" Tamisk lifted her shirt.

Instead of the muscular belly Leksi loved to nibble, coral now bulged from flesh, ribs turning into reef. "I've seen what's happening in the city. I went for more tapak-zony, and I saw things I can't explain." She fingered the delicate seafan protruding from her hip bone.

"This is because of Zal," Leksi said. "His magic is causing the anomalies. The city isn't under attack. It's just my brother. He can't help what he is."

"And what is that, exactly?" Tamisk asked, nostrils flaring.

"I'm not sure you'd believe me if I told you," Leksi said, hating herself for twisting this back on Tamisk. She'd abandoned the Salt ways only after she believed the god of water had abandoned her.

Leksi had never met the uncle who ruled all water, who'd conjured his children from foam and current, freshwater silt and brackish bog, the same way her own mother had produced children with the capricious god of the air.

"Try me," Tamisk said, letting her shirt fall back down to cover the sprouting corals.

Leksi clenched her fists, opening and closing them several times as she tried to find the words she'd never spoken to a human before. Leksi wasn't sure how Tamisk would feel knowing she'd been sharing a bed with the progeny of Death all these years.

"Are you some sort of arkani?" Tamisk asked in a hoarse whisper.

"Worse, I think," Leksi said. "We're not even human."

Tamisk stilled, her body rigid and gaze unblinking as she regarded Leksi with agonizing intensity. "What?"

"Please, I only came for more scale leaf," Leksi said. She should've been begging for Tamisk's forgiveness, not asking for more favors. "It's all that's keeping even worse things from happening to this city." She ground her heel into the frostweed at her feet. The crushed petals chimed morosely as they met their end. "I'm sorry. I shouldn't have lied to you. I never meant to draw you into all this. Like you said, I've been trying to do good. It's why I left the Nether in the first place."

"The Nether?" As if rousing from a deep and troubled sleep, Tamisk finally blinked. "The Nether, you mean like Davakany?" She used the Tsirayan word for the Realm of Death. "You are—you are god-spawn?" She choked on the words, gulping at air like a shore-stranded fish.

"Not our preferred term, but accurate," Leksi admitted. "Demigod is better."

"It can't be." Tamisk dragged trembling hands through her hair. "All this time. How could you keep this from me?"

"I wanted to protect you."

"Protect me? You've been the biggest danger!" Tamisk yelled, but her words snagged in her throat and she wretched, hacking up bits of sea sponge Leksi feared had once been lung.

"I never harmed you," she said, trying to stay calm. "And I never meant to hurt you. I left the Nether. I rejected everything," Leksi said. "The same way you left Tsiraya and rejected the Salt gods."

"We are not the same, adri-raka," she spat, and Leksi flinched at the Tsirayan word for demon. Not that demons existed—not the way humans imagined them, at least. Leksi gripped her biceps, squeezing, and felt the monsters—the *demons*—shift inside her, ever ready for bloodshed.

"I love you, Tam."

"No. If you ever did, you wouldn't have hidden this from me and let me live a lie. You're god-spawn. A demigod," she corrected, despite the circumstances. Tamisk shook her head as she rifled in the bag slumped beside the desk and withdrew a large sachet of leaves. She flung it at Leksi who snatched it from the air, momentarily having to wrestle it from the mischievous ghosts. "You have what you came for. Now get out," Tamisk said, voice uncharacteristically venomous.

"Please, Tam. I'm still me—" But she wasn't. She wasn't even in her true form. Everything about her life in the mortal realm was a lie, and Tamisk deserved so much better.

"I have no idea who you are." A glossy tear welled in the corner of Tamisk's eye, then fell. The pearl tinkled as it hit the desk before rolling onto the floor.

Cursing her brother for the umpteenth time, Leksi sucked in a deep breath, preparing to launch into even more apologies when the heavy stomp of horses sounded in the courtyard.

Bloody hyenas. And they might have an arkani with them. Tamisk couldn't be discovered in the presence of someone they'd peg as magical, and definitely not with pearls falling from her eyes.

"We have to go," Leksi said.

"I'm not going anywhere with you." Tamisk snapped.

"This isn't a fight you can win." Leksi grabbed the woman's tattooed hands and ran her thumb across the knuckles. "They'll see your changes. They won't understand."

"This is punishment," Tamisk said. "My mothers were right. The ocean lives in my veins. There is no escape from the Salt gods." Her gaze seared into Leksi as she pressed a hand to her side where the bright edges of the seafan had torn holes in her shirt.

"If you get arrested, who will be there for Salja or Zadi or all the others like them?" Leksi said. "You can't help them if you're locked up, or dead."

"And who's fault would that be?"

"I don't want you to get hurt," Leksi said. "I couldn't live with myself if anything happened to you because of my brother."

"*You* happened to me." Fresh pearls congealed on Tamisk's lashes like dew on a spiderweb. She wrenched away and grabbed her satchel. "I'll go. For the kids, not for you." She swung the bag over her shoulder.

"Quick. Out back." Leksi gestured, but Tamisk was already striding toward the rear of the building as the front door creaked open.

"Constabulary! Come forth!" a deep voice shouted, destroying the sanctity of The Anchorage which Leksi had managed to preserve for several generations.

Tamisk paused, anger and maybe something a little like regret smoldering in her eyes. "I did love you," she said. "I hope you can fix this."

Such a pathetic petition—and yet it settled on Leksi like a prayer. With Tamisk on her way to safety, Leksi strode toward the cudgel-wielding fiends daring to cross her threshold. The monsters in her blood writhed in eager frenzy. It would be easy to unleash them with no one but her enemies in the house.

Ansa wouldn't be affected, fearless as she was.

With any luck, Leksi wouldn't need to use her own magic when she had Zal's sloppy scraps and a gaggle of ghosts at her disposal.

"Constables," she said, stepping into view. "Please do come in."

Escaping the locked down city proved complicated and time-consuming.

When the kakakis blasted for a third time since Leksi had stalked away from The Anchorage, she'd seriously considered swimming out of the city. The ocean around the point was treacherous, the massive waves smashing against rocks and reefs, or hiding brutal riptides. Thankfully, she'd managed to skulk north and pass unmolested through the gate when a caravan of farmers returning with the remains of Solstice wares took umbrage at being searched.

Taking advantage of the commotion, she'd tugged her

obdurate mule beneath the scalloped arches tangled with yellow creeper before any of the guards could stop her. Now the beast was proving the greater problem, refusing to do more than a gambol despite how much she cajoled or threatened.

She hoped Tamisk was somewhere safe. Leksi only had herself to blame for how badly things had gone between them. This was the price she paid for playing human, for believing she could've had the life she didn't deserve. Adri-raka—demon, evil-doer. Leksi couldn't argue, even as the word left welts on her heart. For all her not wanting to hurt people by merely existing, she'd done just that, and hurt the one person she would've chewed off her own arm to protect.

She closed her eyes as she sucked in a mouthful of sultry air, momentarily allowing herself to wallow in the memories of the constables screaming and the arkani failing to defend them from a ghost attack. In the end, she didn't need to unleash her monsters; the spirits had been enough.

She doubted she'd ever be able to return to The Anchorage, not when her home had been so thoroughly desecrated. She opened her eyes, blinking away the image of Ansa, whiskers clotted with the gore of the arkani's throat she'd torn open.

This was all Zal's fault, all because of a silly little boy's need for vengeance. Had it been her, Leksi would've said good riddance and embraced her life in the mortal realm. She wouldn't be desperately trying to claw her way back to the family that didn't want her. But Zal had always been desperate for affection from the one person who'd never been able to give it to him. No wonder he'd bought the devotion of humans instead—such as it was.

The sun was a smear of melted butter across the horizon by the time she arrived in the foothills, sweat-glazed and reeking of pack-animal. Groves of proteas and feathery fever-trees hugged the hillsides, providing little shade. The sky was streaked with cloud, though, wisps gathering like thread on a spindle into woolly bundles that blocked some of the menacing light. Soon it would be dark—not the deep night of winter or the Nether, but gloom enough to soothe her burning skin and aching body for a few hours.

She could've been wandering the hills all evening, were it not for the connection she shared with Zal. Even though she resented relying on it, she let her thoughts unspool along the invisible filaments like a questing insect feeler.

Guided by the tether, she kicked her mule over a rise and followed the wind of a dried-up stream until she found them hunkered in a patch of sparse shade.

A trio of horses grazed nearby, their coats the speckled gray typical of the local breed developed by the Savati monarchy. The horses must've cost a small fortune, not that Zal was skint. She'd seen what likely amounted to only a portion of his wealth in the caves and adorning his acolytes.

Another pang of jealousy jabbed her in the gut. All this time she'd struggled to keep a roof over her head while her brother lived in the lap of luxury. Not that all the gold and gems in the world could save Zal from himself.

Stopping the mule near the horses, Leksi dismounted in an ungainly sprawl of limbs. She'd never quite mastered the art of riding, especially not on bow-backed nags.

"I'm afraid he's getting worse," Emri said by way of greeting—not looking too well either, his freckled nose sunburned and lips wind-chapped. "Did you manage to find more scale leaf?"

Was it too much to expect even a minor inquiry into her well-being?

"Here." She tossed the sachet at the sciomancer, nodding acknowledgment at Pfumi, who sucked pensively on the gold ring piercing her lower lip. Leksi stomped on the urge to rip it out.

"Thank you." Emri bowed, fingers touching lips and heart in a show of respect.

That was better. Leksi did like being appreciated, as any human would. It wasn't more than that. Enjoying the sciomancer's deference had nothing to do with her being a demigod in want of worship. The void left in Tamisk's wake wouldn't be filled by her brother's gnathonic pets anyway.

"How are things in the city?" Emri asked.

"Terrible," Leksi said. "It's in lockdown while the hyenas tear through every household searching for Kazwe Olonza or her abductors."

Zal grunted in amusement from where he lay in the dirt, head propped on a saddle bag. His face was hidden by a hat similar to her own; only the band on his was bedazzled with gems where hers held wilting flowers.

"We had to abandon The Anchorage," she said. "It wasn't safe, especially not with frostweed blooming from your bloody trail. There are oddities springing up all over the city." She nudged Zal with the toe of her boot and fought the urge to kick him in the ribs. Breaking his bones would only provide a fleeting release for her growing fury. Hurting him wouldn't solve any of their problems, and the joy she took in it was the precise aspect of her nature she'd been fighting for centuries.

"Oddities?" Pfumi asked.

"You saw what happened at the citadel," Leksi said. "More like that, and worse."

The arkani wrapped her arms around her chest as if a self-hug would do a damn thing to change the colossal mess Zal had made.

"Thirsty?" Emri offered Leksi a water skin and she snatched it, greedily downing the contents. It must've been spelled to keep the water cool. So be it. She'd broken so many of her own anti-magic rules of late; this no longer seemed such a travesty.

"I could've used some of that," Zal said, his words coming out in wheezes.

Grudgingly, Leksi knelt beside her brother while Emri rolled a spliff. "You sound like a dying gnu."

"Keep your pity." Zal's eyes opened to narrow slits as he squinted up at her. Sweat peppered his brow; his hair hung lank and greasy, and his shirt glommed to his wizened body wet with perspiration and blood. "Your anger tastes better," he said.

"You do give me plenty to be furious about."

Gritting his teeth, Zal sat up a little straighter, leaning

against the trunk of the protea. He shuddered in the aftermath of even that minimal movement, and Leksi wasn't sure if she wanted to punch him and see him crumble, or offer him comfort.

After Pfumi lit the spliff with a spark of magic from her fingers, Emri crouched down to press it between Zal's lips. Fatigue shadowed the man's ghost-sheened eyes, and his hands trembled.

"When last did you eat or sleep?" Leksi asked. She could survive without either far longer than humans, but her corporeal form fared better when she gave it rest and sustenance. And both were currently lacking.

"I'm fine," Emri said. "Thank you for your concern," he added with a respectful bow.

"Now then, dear sister." Zal inhaled deeply, the frown on his forehead smoothing as the drug took effect. He rubbed away a crust from his putrefying eye before speaking again. "We recovered some items from Ailia's rooms." He blew a smoke ring toward her face.

"Research scrolls, journals, and spell books," Emri continued. "We may have found a better temporary solution than scale leaf."

"Go on." Leksi rocked back on her haunches, bracing herself for the inevitability of having to participate in more magic.

"Before magic can be transferred, a bond must be forged, similar to the one you already share with Va'ili." Emri spoke with his hands, his fingers tracing connections through the air. "The second layer to that is the physical connection, allowing the siphoning and permanent relocation of the power. That's the part of Ailia's spell we don't have. But we believe that with a minor modification we might be able to adjust the psychic connection the two of you already share. If you'll allow it."

Leksi raised a skeptical brow. "So Zal and I could share magic with each other?"

"Exactly," Zal said. "Temporarily, of course."

"Wouldn't my magic just leak right out of you as well? Or have you got some magical cork in your saddlebags?" she asked.

Emri's lips twitched, grin or grimace, Leksi wasn't sure. Pfumi remained silent, watching.

"Ailia's spell was specific to Va'ili and chaos magic," the sciomancer said. "I don't think yours will behave the same way, mostly because Va'ili won't actually be absorbing your power, simply borrowing it."

"Consider it practice for when you give up your power for real." Zal glared up at her, his pupils blown wide from the scale leaf. She liked him better incapacitated and half conscious.

"Our psychic connection goes both ways though," Leksi said. "That means I could finish what Ailia started."

"Is that what you want?" Zal asked, baleful as always.

"Hardly," Leksi admitted.

"That said," Emri began, "it may be wise to have a way to deny Ailia from what remains of Va'ili's power."

"Stars wept, just call him Zal," Leksi said.

"Only if Va'ili wishes it," Emri said, glancing at the Netherling in question.

"Does the title annoy you?" Zal asked.

"Immensely." Too late, Leksi realized her mistake.

"Then Va'ili I shall remain." Zal grinned around the spliff, and Leksi seethed.

"Fine. If all else fails, I slurp up what's left of Zal's magic—even if it ends him," she said. "Hard not to hope it does." Leksi already regretted agreeing to this ridiculous plan. Not that she had a choice. Not with the constables on the rampage and with every passing minute shuffling them closer to potential doom as Ailia and Motselana planned to destroy the city.

"It won't come to that," Zal said. "I won't let it."

Resisting the urge to roll her eyes, Leksi turned to the bruised-eyed sciomancer instead. "Are you sure you're up for this?"

He nodded, convincing no one.

"What do you need from me?" Leksi asked.

"Only your blood and patience." Emri patted the ground beside him.

Leksi crouched beside the sciomancer, who had propped open a weathered notebook bound in strips of leather, the cover marked with a convoluted sigil she didn't bother trying to decipher. Emri removed a small knife from his belt, the blade flecked with rust or dried blood.

"Please give me your hand," he said, and Leksi acquiesced despite the voice in her head begging her not to.

It whispers, itches, burns… insect voices, sun kisses… I hear it, feel it… it wants, it hungers… his power or mine? …open my veins, bleed it out… listen, listen, listen… hear the god-chord… I am life, unceasing desire, I am aquiver, I touch the sky and caress the fathoms… I am god, I am nothing, the voice of the universe, reducing all to chaos… reviving, engulfing, quenching… the primordial power released, a liberation divine profane arcane… I am nothing, I am god, I am god, I am…

A surviving fragment, allegedly from the notebook of Fetrina Scryali, date unknown; text incomplete due to fire damage

Chapter Sixteen

Niki

It itched with the fury of a hundred chigger bites.

A fire raged inside my skin, and scratching only made it worse. I'd used my nails, my teeth, every abrasive substance I could find in the laboratories until I scraped my skin bloody.

The itch persisted, the shadow flitting out of reach and evading capture, sifting through my flesh, sinking deeper when I gouged at the stain with sharp objects. There was no alleviation.

I woke up scratching at night, reduced to screaming into my pillow in frustration and exhaustion. My usual trick to combat midnight restlessness proved ineffectual as well. It was hard to hum Scryali's comforting ditty and soothe myself to sleep with the cricket screech of the shadow's voice looping endlessly in my mind—as if the sound had somehow embossed itself on my brain, my gray matter nothing more than a wax cylinder.

I couldn't concentrate when awake either, the touch of sunlight only exacerbating the flames in my flesh, the noise in my skull unceasing.

After the second sleepless night, I'd plunged my elbow—the gray smudge having taken up residence in the crook of my arm—into a jug of cold water. Finally, relief! Now I kept a filled bucket beside my bed, doing my best to sleep with the stained body part submerged. This proved more challenging when the shadow fluttered across my stomach or spread itchy wings across my shoulders.

I'd lost so many days to the mental fug of sleeplessness. I'd tried to keep myself focused by chewing on khat and downing coffee as I pored over codex and treatise, even delving into ancient texts yet to be copied from their original scrolls—ones I doubted even the oldest professors at the university knew existed. Several weren't in Savati, though, and I made a separate pile of those, already wincing at the thought of asking Yatto to arrange translation.

With so much knowledge at hand, surely I'd find the answers.

Days became nights became dawns again, kakaki blasts no longer registering as the passage of time was rendered all but meaningless.

In my laboratory, I'd taken to sitting in the breeze, the cooling kiss of air mildly soothing but not nearly enough. Moli had graciously procured a fan which took up far too much space and emitted an annoying buzz as it whirred, sending papers flying if I wasn't careful, but it at least provided some relief from the relentless itch.

I might've not survived were it not for Moli who kept me fed and watered, chiding me even as she refilled my coffee cup or brought me more khat. She'd also done her best to analyze the sigil I'd doodled while listening to the shadow music. It wasn't one she knew—in fact, she thought it could be wholly unique, a prospect both exciting and terrifying. She assured me she'd conduct her own experiments to try and figure out its purpose, although without an accompanying incantation, she wasn't sure she could.

My own shadow stain remained a mystery. It certainly seemed to have substance, as if multiple particles had glommed together to form something resembling a primitive organism. The old myths posited the notion of a scale implanted in the hearts of the first arkani. They might've been onto something, explaining the concept of a magical infection with their primitive knowledge of the world in the only way they could. It didn't have to be a literal scale shed by a literal serpent, though. What if primordial magic was nothing more than a parasite, infecting and changing human flesh until, many centuries and scions later, some of us had evolved to cope more easily with the invasive particles?

Primordial magic as a living entity, then. Not sentient—that was one step too far—but even mindless plants could track the sun and retreat from unwanted sensation. That was all the stain did, avoiding my scratching and stabbing. That it could move so freely in my body was another uncomfortable mystery. It wasn't limited to the subcutaneous region of my flesh, nor did it seem confined to my network of veins and capillaries, given the speed with which it flitted about. I was no physicker, but I had scoured all the same textbooks the likes of Yatto used in their studies, and yet I remained no closer to an explanation.

With only seven days until First Council, I couldn't afford to be distracted by this new tangent.

I removed my foot from the bucket of tepid water and studied the ink-splash currently adhered to my ankle. I'd so far managed to hide the blemish by lying to anyone who cared to ask, telling them I had a condition which left my joints red and swollen.

The itch was starting again, and I ground my teeth, rubbing that familiar spot on my jaw as I pondered amputation. A physicker would have to work quickly to sever the limb before the shadow could dart away to coil in some vital organ I wouldn't survive without.

No doubt Yatto would oblige if I asked him to swing an axe at my leg, but I worried the Sodality might think it wiser to aim the axe at my neck if they knew I bore an affliction usually reserved for arkani.

If only I could excise the mark, perhaps I'd be able to listen to it again—piece together more fragments of the sounds, learn the strange language so I could better understand the nature of this shadow song. I thought Ngakula had been onto something. I hadn't heard anything like words from the shadows—not even vocables. It sounded more like birdsong and the vocalizations of animals—all clicks and whistles and grunts.

Moli had gone trawling for research on Scryali as requested and had left a neat, if slim, pile on my laboratory desk. The material was disappointingly scant. A few scores had been kept, works commissioned by the crown with gimmicky flourishes befitting a royal party. Nothing too revolutionary in any way. There were also a couple of treatises written by her detractors, determined to refute her claims and repudiate her abilities. We had copies of those in the university library, and I had already all but memorized their contents. There were, however, fragments from what claimed to be Scyrali's personal journal. The pages were fire-eaten, torn, and faded; the writing that had survived the burning was mostly illegible except for a few nonsensical passages.

This damn itch! "Moli!"

She raised her head from where she'd been scouring the dense writings of Synara Makhezi, still trying to puzzle out the nature of the shadow sigil.

"I need more cold water. Please," I added.

She whisked away the bucket without a word, leaving me rubbing at my leg, nails tearing skin from my ankle bone.

Carefully, I set down the preserved papers to give my ankle the benefit of all ten fingernails. The shadow shifted, vanishing as I broke skin. I sighed, not about to strip naked in the laboratory to trace the shadow's flight.

Given a brief reprieve, I leafed through Scryali's journal again, carefully parting every page. The ones at the center had fared far better than the others, only the very edges charred, their contents otherwise intact if smeared.

"It whispers, itches, burns..." I read, a frisson rippling across my skin.

I swallowed hard and shut the book, opening and closing my fists as I counted my breaths, trying to calm my racing heart.

The itch returned, this time at the base of my skull. I

changed the angle of the fan, ensuring a delivery of cool air directly to the back of my neck. Then I opened the book again, thumbing gently to the page in question.

Beside a raving screed about being god or nothing, a sample of notation had survived. I stared at the symbols Scryali had invented to indicate the precise articulation she demanded of her players. Many of those symbols had been incorporated into the modern notation system currently employed by composers across the continent, but those weren't the ones that interested me.

With trembling fingers, I retrieved my own notebook, pinning open the pages with my elbows so I could compare the scrawl I'd written while listening to the shadow music.

The doodles were alarmingly similar, but I had never seen this composition before and had no way of being influenced by Scryali's work. Her scribbles, like mine, became dense knots of intersecting lines—nonsense filigree that meant nothing in music but—I turned the page and my blood instantly laced with hoarfrost as I stared at the pages. The itch spread across my scalp as if a hand with long fingers had slipped into my hair and started pulling.

Her final, unfinished work. The work she'd claimed would end the world. *Ode to the Apocalypse*, she'd called it, or *Shadow Song*.

There it was, in black on beige.

Shadow Song.

The work was begun, the notation a slanting cascade of notes and symbols spilling over several pages, until the score gave way to fire damage. I studied the intricacies of the notation, my gaze darting between my own notebook and Scryali's as the sensation on my scalp increased in intensity.

"Hear the God-chord," I said out loud. "Hear the God-chord." I repeated the phrase over and over, my own incantation—a spell to reveal Scryali's secrets and unlock my understanding.

The symbol—the sigil—I thought I must've invented or somehow intuited from the bizarre music glared up at me from Scryali's papers. Over and over again, it appeared at regular intervals, a feature of the composition, though I doubted any musician would know how to interpret the symbols if handed these sheets.

The shadow sigil.

Scryali's. Mine. Both of us devising the same twist of lines generations apart with nothing in common beside our love for music and fascination with primordial magic. And perhaps a shadow stain.

It whispers, it itches, it burns, she'd written, and I knew exactly what she meant.

I startled when Moli materialized beside me.

"Ever heard of the God-chord?" I asked. She shook her head as she offered me the refreshed bucket.

Someone else must've read Scryali's scribbles before. Surely some other scholar had been intrigued enough to investigate the sigil and Scryali's claim of divine harmony. I couldn't be the first or only one—but would such research into a known heretic have been allowed to endure? Perhaps I truly was on my own.

With the itch and accompanying aural assault intensifying once more, I gratefully took the bucket from Moli's hands, stepped away from the table and the precious notebooks, then tipped the bucket over my head.

"Happy Solstice," Jaq said when she swept into the laboratory with Yatto in tow.

Solstice? Already? I glanced out the window, trying to remember how long it had been since I'd heard the palace horns announce the hour. It was late. The sea rippled like oil on glass, the waves scintillating with the dregs of sunlight. There was so little time left for me to understand all I thought I knew, never mind come up with something sensible to share with the Sodality—something that wouldn't see me back in chains or impaled.

"What's all this, then? Did you find something?" Yatto peered over my shoulder.

"Maybe." I leaned protectively over my work, not sure why I felt the need to hide it from this man. My hair was still damp from its earlier dousing. The sensation of wet clothing sticking to my skin was unbearable, but a welcome distraction from the itch now loitering in my lower back. "Did you bring me those translations?" I asked him.

"These things take time," he said.

"The one thing I don't have."

"Not the only thing." His lips curled into a snide grin. "Seems you're lacking in linguistics too."

"Meq bisaq misa'aqa," I responded with one of the few joRanian phrases I knew.

"What does that mean?" Yatto glowered.

"That you should learn more languages," Jaq said as she cut her gaze at me. "Anyway, if you figured something out, please do share." She cleared a spot on the corner of my desk before hopping up to sit, far too at ease in my personal space.

"What about you?" I asked. "Made any breakthroughs?"

"Maybe," she echoed, and Yatto grinned, exuding a smugness I couldn't stand. I really wished he would go kiss a scorpion—preferably a deadly one.

"Nothing conclusive just yet," Jaq continued. "But I'm confident I'll have something by First Council." She smoothed back a baby hair. Her tight curls were braided in a single queue dotted with fresh flowers down the middle of her scalp and tied off with gray threads at the nape of her neck.

I frowned, wondering how much of the Sodality's rhetoric Jaq had swallowed, and just how much her willingness to accept their claims stemmed from whatever was happening between her and Yatto.

"Come on, Nik. Give us a hint." She nudged me, and I could smell the peach alcohol on her breath. She must've been out celebrating. "You were never this stingy with your research before," she added.

"My life never depended on it before," I snapped. No one

had offered me the chance to escape the palace. I'm not sure I would've noticed even if they had, though. The last few days had been a blur.

Usually on the Solstice, I actively avoided the crowds and fracas as the city succumbed to revelry. I much preferred remaining holed up at the university, windows open to let the festivities trickle in in manageable doses.

"All the more reason to share your theories, neh?" Yatto said. "Consider it a precursory peer review."

"I'm not sure I'm ready for that," I said.

"Come on, Nik." Jaq sounded exasperated. "Let me see." She moved as if to pluck the top page from my pile. While I tried to intercept her thieving fingers, Yatto swiped the pages from my unprotected side, laughing in victory.

"Scryali?" He quirked a critical brow. "Thought she was a nutter; delusions of godhood and all that."

"Give it back." I fumed, and the itch extended fiery fingers up my spine as the noise in my head grew louder too, exacerbating my fury.

"Scryali was a powerful arkani before her mind broke," Jaq said, looking genuinely interested as she shuffled the remaining papers on my desk, turning them to get a better look at the score I'd been working on. "But are you any closer to figuring out what went right—and wrong—during your concert?" she asked.

"Yes, thanks to your mother actually."

"What?" Jaq startled.

"His mother." I nodded at Yatto. "Bololo's theories on

magical particles coupled with the sigil work of Makhezi—I think it's starting to come together. Actually—" I turned back to Jaq. "I could use your insights. While Moli has been a tremendous help—" I gestured to my assistant who shrunk away from Yatto—"I've always appreciated your mathematician's opinion on these things." I pointed at the symbol I had yet to find in any other tome or treatise. Moli and I had scoured every codex and even dug through the remaining scrolls in search of any mention of the God-chord, and yet we'd found nothing. If the translated texts didn't reveal anything helpful, then I'd truly be at a loss.

"This is the key to Scryali's work," I began. "It makes a frequent appearance in her final score, but there's no description of what it does or how it should be interpreted. She obviously knew what she meant and could direct players accordingly," I said and took a breath. "I think if I could figure out what it means, I might unlock—" I stumbled over my words, having come perilously close to admitting my own infection. "Unlock the secret to her success," I said, hoping Jaq wouldn't notice my hesitation.

"Looks like a sigil. Isn't that just regular arkani craft?" Yatto said derisively.

A distant rumble punctuated the tension between us, the air echoing my annoyance. The western horizon remained clear, which meant a storm must be brewing in the east or perhaps drawing up from the south. Unusual for this time of year.

"No," I said. "Because there's no accompanying incantation, and it's not like the score itself is magic. The symbol is some sort of musical mark; it denotes something in the sound." My mind churned over what was supposition at best. There had to be more research on Scryali and her use of harmony.

"Like a certain pitch?" Jaq asked, her eyes shiny with interest now and not alcohol. She did enjoy a good puzzle.

"Or an instrument, a key—I'm not sure," I admitted. "Perhaps if I had greater access to the palace library and didn't have to rely on archivists, I could find exactly what I was looking for myself."

Yatto's lips tightened into a thin line as he folded his arms.

"Because if I knew what this meant then maybe I could—" *maybe I could complete her composition.* What an arrogant, foolish notion, and yet the thought slithered into my mind. This was a composition she claimed could end the world—why would I even want to do that? And yet, I couldn't help but imagine the legacy that would leave, the power I would have if I managed to harness the ultimate magic. I shook my head, trying and failing to dislodge the odd desire settling in my bones like a bullfrog in a muddy puddle. *I am god,* Scryali wrote. *The voice of the universe.* And I could be that too, if I figured out how to wield magic without the need for spells. "There has to be more on Scryali," I said. "Someone must've done this sort of research before."

"Perhaps," Jaq said. "But I imagine that after Scryali's execution few would've been brave enough to delve into her methods, and any existing material on her was most likely destroyed back then. I'm sorry, Nik." She sounded genuinely remorseful. "Perhaps we can figure this out together. We already know sigils are usually composed of runes," Jaq continued and Moli took a tentative step closer, nodding her head. "Each component of a sigil adds to the function of the spell, right?"

A symbolic representation of the accompanying incantation, Moli signed and I translated for the others. *The spell required to keep a lamp burning requires the runes for ignition, light and warmth, and one for the duration as well.*

"So four or five runes would create a single sigil," Yatto said, proving he could count.

"But in the context of music, could this sigil have different parts too?" Jaq said as she traced the shapes within the sigil.

There are no runes I recognize, Moli signed, *but it's possible there are runes I don't know, or that Scryali had the ability to create her own.* She cut a cautious glance at Yatto.

"Now that's a terrifying thought," he said. "Good thing they chopped off her head."

"Thank you for your valuable contribution to this discussion," I said as the crickets in my skull grated discordant noise onto my thoughts, as if the frequencies were turmeric and my mind a bubbling pot of curry.

My overwrought mind was boiling, about to overflow, until something clicked inside my brain with a mandible snap. Different parts making up the whole. Of course!

"Perhaps it's like the way chords are made of discrete pitches but also intervals," I said, thinking out loud. "Runes could be like individual pitches, combined into a sigil the way notes make a chord."

"Are you saying this represents a chord?" Jaq tapped the

sigil.

"Perhaps." I rubbed my jaw. "Scryali wrote about something she called the God-chord."

"Raved about, you mean," Yatto made yet another meaningful contribution, but a rumble interrupted my response. This time the ground shifted beneath our feet as if some massive creature had flexed its muscles beneath the skin of the earth. Yatto stumbled, my papers scattering as he opened his hands to catch himself on the desk.

"What the vrot," Jaq said as the ground heaved again, the motion accompanied by a sizzle in the air as if lightning had flashed through the chamber.

Or not lightning at all. I looked at my left hand, my fingers black as if I'd stuck them into cinders. Gray wisps rose from each fingertip, the itch becoming searing pain. My veins bulged, flickering with an orange glow as if fireflies were trapped within my skin.

The ground shook once more and Moli grabbed my wrist, plunging my hand into the sloshing bucket, giving me a worried look as she did so. The water bubbled around my appendage as if it were forge-heated metal and not human flesh. Thankfully, the icy water brought instant relief.

Moli regarded me with concern but said nothing, both her hands currently occupied. I looked down at the papers Yatto had scattered and choked back a sob. Not only had hours of work bled away in rivulets of ink thanks to the spilled water, but Scryali's notebook lay face down in a puddle.

"You blithering, damnable idiot," I said and sank to my

knees. At least my hand no longer smoldered, the fingers flesh-toned once more. Either the shadow had dissolved in the dousing or had retreated into my tissues to harass me later.

Blinking away tears of frustration, I scraped soggy mush from the floor, trying to salvage something, anything—but the work was lost and Scryali's notebook was beyond saving. I cradled the ruined tome, a tide of grief rising inside me the way it never had for my dead parents. This was the true loss, and I had no time to mourn it. I glowered at Yatto, preparing to fire off more insults and curses, but the swell of emotion was so overwhelming, the noise inside my head disorientating and painful. I couldn't force a single word through my gritted teeth.

Jaq knelt beside me and placed a tentative hand on my back, rubbing soothing circles between my shoulders. "I'm sorry," she said as if this was her fault and not her hulking brute of a boyfriend's. "It's a minor setback, that's all. You did it once, you can do it again. All that knowledge is already in your head." She gently tapped my forehead. "You've still got time to figure it out."

Not nearly enough. A year wouldn't be enough for the rigorous and thorough pursuit of this inquiry, and all I had was a week.

Seven days from now I'd have either solved the impossible and proven magic could be subjugated with music alone, or I'd be back in chains. Either way it would be over, my life and life's work inextricably linked to doom in a bizarre hemiola.

'I am god; I am nothing.' I was starting to understand.

Chapter Seventeen
Zal

Zal missed the stars.

Lying in the dirt, staring at the sky, he dredged the constellations of the Nether from his memory, mapping them onto the clouds which had thankfully drawn darkening curtains across the lingering twilight.

He tried to relax as the arkani worked, tried not to let the memories of all the times he'd laid out in the snow-crusted veld with his siblings as a Netherling crowd his beleaguered mind. Remembering hurt worse than the sigil oozing in his chest, worse than Ailia's betrayal—perhaps even worse than the truth of his conception.

He'd known something like happiness once: the camaraderie of his siblings and the solace of the Nether.

Emri sang, his voice rich and mellow, while Pfumi provided a reedy descant, and the intricately woven melodies sent a pleasant tingle down Zal's spine. Emri had already scratched the requisite sigil into Leksi's right palm and now completed its mirror image on Zal's left. The blade only scraped the surface, barely drawing blood. The wound didn't need to be deep to secure the bond.

Emri gestured for the two of them to hold hands, sigil to sigil. Leksi hesitated but wrapped her fingers around Zal's, the cut to cut contact stinging when Emri pressed their hands together even harder. Pfumi joined the awkward clasping, their voices blending until the harmonies dwindled to a single monophonic tune. They chanted it on repeat—a looping sequence of six tones.

Zal was exquisitely aware of Leksi's emotions, their psychic connection unavoidable as the spell opened a new channel between them. He caught glimpses of her memories too, no longer mere impressions but vivid flashes of her lived experience. The years flashed before him: her travels and travails, her desperation and resilience, her hope and fear and determination as she forged a path for herself in the human world, reinventing herself over and over again, every new iteration trying to undo the mistakes of the past. How hard she'd tried to avoid what she was, and how often she'd failed.

He witnessed it all: the wax and wane of her human lives. Her love for Tamisk glowed hot and bright, a reflection of what he thought he'd felt for Ailia.

As his sister's regret became his own, so his pain became hers, and he felt her magic stir. He called to it as he called upon his shadows. Although her creatures were sculpted from the same primordial effluvium, they were distinct in their aspect. Zal's shadows weren't malevolent, satisfied with hijinks and mischief, confusion and commotion. Her monsters required a far darker diet and they were starving.

"You have to release them," Zal said.

"Never," Leksi said through gritted teeth.

"They're yours. I can't command them." And he hoped she

saw the truth of it, how Emri's spell hadn't given him power over her nasty pets.

"You need to let go," Emri said. He and Pfumi were both shaking, sweat pouring down their faces like tears. "You have to allow the connection."

"Promise me you won't use them," Leksi said, but before Zal could respond, her hold slipped.

Zal cried out as her magic flooded his veins, a surge of power he hadn't felt since he'd been jettisoned from the Nether. A frisson of near-orgasmic bliss seized his body, spine arching, joints creaking as they were forced straight, sudden breath expanding rotting lungs now awash with tissue-healing magic.

Delirious, he let the sensation soak him, marinating in the afterglow.

A drop of warmth hit his cheek and Zal opened his eyes, his vision clearer than it had been in centuries, to see blood dripping from Emri's nose.

"I'm sorry, Va'ili." Emri released Zal's and Leksi's clasped hands to wipe away the mess. Zal licked at the sciomancer's blood where it had dribbled onto his lips, savoring the tang of death laced in copper and salt, then reached up to tuck a loose strand of silver hair behind the man's tattooed ear.

"Thank you," he said, and Emri held his gaze for what might've been several heart beats, had Zal's chest not been hollow. The sciomancer slumped then, head hanging between his knees as he sucked in ragged breaths.

"Are we done?" Leksi asked.

"Yes. The sigils will keep your powers bound," Pfumi said.

Leksi released Zal's fingers and inspected her palm. Zal did the same, tracing the neatly cut edges of the sigil. Emri's work was as meticulous as always.

"Did it work?" Leksi asked.

Zal inhaled, braced for pain. When no sinews snapped, no joints protested, or muscles sheared with the effort, he pushed himself upright and rolled his neck, the resulting pops alleviating stiffness. He continued to stretch, testing every limb, braced for agony that never came. He almost wept in relief.

"Better," he said and studied his hands. Some knuckles were still swollen, but he could ball his fists. "I feel—" He touched his face, finding the old scars smoother and softer now. He prodded at his eye. While his vision had cleared and the orb no longer streamed tears of gritty mucus, the socket remained tender. "I feel whole."

Only the suppurating sigil Ailia had carved into his chest remained an open wound. He rose to his feet, not needing the assistance of his shadow staff. His legs were stronger, bones sitting true in sockets, muscles knitting back together as Leksi's power fueled his rejuvenation.

He marveled at being able to stand upright without hot blades stabbing into his ribs or hips. His shadows frolicked at his feet, similarly replenished by the infusion of magic.

Zal released a chortle and when even that didn't hurt, he began to laugh. Body-bending, belly-roiling laughter poured out of him as he raised his hands to the sky, remembering what it felt like to be a god.

Emri's face was a mask of blood as he trained his ghost-sheened gaze on Zal, as if the sciomancer were seeing him for the first time. His awe rippled toward Zal, stroking his skin and sinking into flesh. *Yes,* Zal wanted to say, *this is who I truly am, and more besides. Behold my greatness!* But Emri's eyes were red-rimmed. Scarlet tears stained his lashes and dark bruises pressed into his sockets below.

"Va'ili." Emri touched his lips then heart, where Zal knew a piece of his own shadow-magic dwelled. Benevolently, Zal rested his hand on the sciomancer's head. For the first time, Zal could appreciate every exquisite facet of the man without a greasy film obscuring half his vision. Emri was even more beautiful than Zal had realized, despite the blood on his face. The whole world was: the colors brighter, every detail crisp and magnificent. If he'd experienced the mortal realm like this, perhaps he too could've learned to love it as much as his sister did.

Then he turned to Leksi, who seemed a little paler than usual. "It's not that bad, surely," Zal said. "I've barely taken a sip of your power."

"I saw what happened," she said in Nethertaal, her voice devoid of emotion. "You and Mezra. The river. How could you, Zal?" Her voice broke and the hollow where his heart had been twinged with a phantom ache.

"It was a game," he said. "We played it all the time." A game Zal always thought he'd won on his own merits, until that day when Mezra teased Zal about his failure, taunting him, his sibling revealing Zal had only ever won because Mezra let him. "It wasn't my fault," Zal said, with a childish petulance he despised.

"You pushed Mezra," Leksi said.

"They fell." A result of their pride, and innate maliciousness.

"Stop lying to yourself. I saw your hands," Leksi said. "You pushed Mezra back into the water. You let Grief take them. You let the storks peck them bloody and hold them under. You watched them come undone." Her accusation scorched hotter than the midday sun.

"No. It wasn't like that," Zal said, but she was right. It wasn't an accident, not the way he'd claimed when his mother questioned him. There was no denying he'd shoved his smug, grinning sibling back into the river, his hurt and fury obliterating all thought of consequence.

"And now Mezra will suffer eternal torment all because you couldn't bear the thought of losing a stupid game."

"I know," Zal said.

"You did deserve what Mother did to you." Her words were elephant thorns impaling him with white-hot fire.

"I know," he said again, finally admitting what he'd denied for far too long. He'd watched Mezra unravel, the Waters of Consequence churning with the shadows he'd summoned as a tempest roared through the surrounding willows, the fronds whipping the storks to a violent frenzy.

"Nothing you can ever do will make up for that," Leksi said, and he felt her tug on the power they shared as surely as if she'd knotted her fingers in his hair, wrenching out chunks by the root.

A ligament snapped in his ankle and pain flared up his leg. "I deserved to suffer," he said, holding her gaze. "But destroy me now and good luck saving your beloved city. If you help me stop Ailia, though, then I'll give you what you want. I'll make you human."

Leksi pulled again and his rib popped, the bone shoved brutally out of place. He dropped to his knees with a groan, Emri beside him immediately offering to help.

"All that talk of not wanting to harm others," Zal said, glaring up at the sister who was Death's double. "But you're just like Mother."

Pressure grew in Zal's leg, the jaws of a beast closing on his femur, but Leksi relented and the maw released.

"You live on borrowed power," she said, looming over him. "Don't make me regret trusting you. Remember, I know what you truly fear, little brother, and I will conjure your worst nightmare if you betray me." Her words were caustic, the syllables blistering the air and making Pfumi cry out. Emri only wiped away a fresh dribble of blood from his ear.

As Leksi dusted herself off, Zal felt a thin stream of power return, healing the most recent damage. He dragged a hand through his hair, surprised when his fingers met the resistance of waves growing back thick and tangled. He had no doubt that if he failed, Leksi would rip him apart from the inside out. For all that she rejected her heritage, she was Nightmare, and had always been the best at inflicting pain on others.

Chaos, however, didn't need to be suffering. It was disruption, but also untapped potential. He glanced from his sister to Emri, who sagged against Zal in exhaustion. Perhaps there were different ways for Zal to use his newly replenished power.

No longer needing the staff, he let his shadows dissipate and sent several flitting back toward the city—bat-shaped and swift—to be his ears and eyes, and to watch over the woman Leksi loved.

It was the least he could do.

Chapter Eighteen
Leksi

They rode through the too-brief night in silence, seemingly content to keep their own company.

Leksi was decidedly not content, and was in no mood for conversation. She hated her magic and couldn't wait to be rid of it. She hated the idea of her brother being able to use it even more. It was *her* magic. They were *her* monsters. She'd never felt so protective of her power before, but then, no one had ever threatened it.

She glared at Zal's back, resentment brewing inside her. She couldn't stop seeing her hands—Zal's hands—shoving Mezra into the river. She winced remembering the surprise on Mezra's face, their shock morphing into terror as the currents pulled them under and the storks skewered their body beneath the flesh-sloughing ripples.

Again Zal drew on her magic, the sensation like a noodle pulled through sticky sauce by a hungry mouth—only the mouth wasn't hers, the sauce was her flesh, and the disappearing noodle left her feeling inexplicably bereft.

Best you get used to it, she berated herself. This was what she'd wanted, what she'd yearned for. Only she hadn't wanted to lose her magic in drips and drabs, a slow siphoning like an amputation meted out in sawn-off increments. She wanted the axe to fall and cleave away the unwanted limb in one fell swoop. She wanted to be fully purged: of magic, of her incorrigible brother, of her repugnant heritage, of everything she loathed about herself.

At least she no longer had to wage a battle of wills with the mule. Pfumi had given up her horse, the arkani returning to Zal's citadel with the nag while the rest of them rode into wine country.

The night was loud: insects screaming and birds jabbering. Distantly, a jackal howled, greeted by the yips of desert hyenas come south in search of easy prey. The horses didn't like that, tossing their heads and prancing as if ready to run, but no animals would venture too close. Their instincts kept them at bay, rightfully afraid of Death's children.

Leksi wondered what Tamisk was doing, if she still lived given the reef sprouting from her bones. Leksi hoped she'd managed to find her friends and The Anchorage kids; she hoped they were all safe and not fending off the constabulary. Or perhaps they were, right this minute, fighting for their lives, their bodies succumbing to the effects of chaos magic. Horror after horror invaded her thoughts.

"Stop it," Zal grumbled. "You're giving me a headache."

"I can give you worse." She reeled in her power until she saw him slump forward with a grunt, his pain a shimmer along their connection. She almost smiled, but caught herself. Despite how much she detested her little brother, she would not be cruel. She would not become like her mother. Not if she had a choice.

Zal had suffered enough and, if she were being honest, the blame wasn't his alone. Mezra was the embodiment of ambition and greed, of reckless desire and jealousy. She had no doubt they'd goaded Zal into lashing out. None of them were immune to their own natures and the dark purposes for which they'd been born.

Relinquishing her sanctimony, Leksi released her magic, her breath easing as her brother's pain lessened. If only she could do something to alleviate the sciomancer's obvious discomfort as well. Zal had insisted they all eat before they continued, but trail food had done little to revive the man who now swayed in the saddle, his head drooping when he nodded off. Zal rode alongside him, propping him up when required.

It galled Leksi to see Zal treat someone so gently after all the damage he'd done.

Guided by the ghosts in his head, Emri had navigated them along large gravel roads devoid of travelers this time of night. Now he turned them onto a rutted track cutting through scrub. Zal swore when Emri toppled again.

"With my power in your veins, can't you feed more magic into the scrap inside him?" Leksi asked.

"Not really." Zal almost sounded apologetic.

"I'll be fine," Emri said, his voice thin as rice paper. "Nothing coffee or sleep won't cure."

"But what I can do..." Zal's shadows thickened into supports to better hold the sciomancer in place, wrapping the man in an oily embrace.

"Thank you, Va'ili," Emri said, and tender emotion flitted

along their shared connection, almost making Leksi smile before she remembered how much she hated her brother. Of course he'd be drawn to Emri. Zal had always enjoyed collecting pretty things: stones, flowers, souls—his trinkets spilling from the columbarium in their mother's palace in the Nether, destined to be forgotten and left for Leksi to clear out the clutter. She'd seen the shelves in his cave chamber, too. Old habits died hard—or not at all it seemed—and the sciomancer was hardly ugly.

They rode through the night, sharing the waterskins, and even ate breakfast in the saddle. When dawn vomited fire across the veld, Zal handed out ostrich biltong and ripe peaches, making sure Emri ate before taking a bite himself. He scowled when he caught Leksi smirking at his display of kindness.

Leksi was grateful for her long sleeves and wide-brimmed hat as another sweltering day splashed mirages across the landscape. There was nothing she could do to stop the sweat from soaking her skin and making her itch. She wished she'd exchanged her dress for trousers before leaving The Anchorage. Her hiked-up skirts left her legs exposed to the grilling force of the sun and the protective amulet around her neck could only do so much to combat the burn.

"We're almost there," Zal said, who was being vicariously subjected to her growing discomfort.

"Thank the stars," she said, not sure how much longer she could take any of it.

"Thought you wanted to live your life in this wretched

realm," he said softly, with more surprise than judgment.

"Some things are worth suffering for," she said, although she doubted Tamisk would ever want her now that she knew the truth. Regardless, Leksi had to at least try to make amends.

By the time Motselana's estate came into view, Leksi had grown more accustomed to Zal feeding on her magic, as if a lamprey were attached to her sternum. Her palm ached a little though the sigil was barely a graze, easily dismissed by laity, who wouldn't know what they were looking at.

"Have you been here before?" Leksi asked as they passed by a pair of stone sentinels—twin baboons with bared fangs—marking the entrance to a long drive cut through cultivated rows of grapes. Somewhere in the distance, a thatched roof rose above the vines.

"Never," Zal said. "My only dealings with the monarchy happened at the palace."

"You had dealings with the monarchy?" Leksi asked.

"Briefly. I tried to convince them to spare Scryali's life."

"Scryali?" Leksi balked. "That was over a century ago. How did we not sense each other? How did we never cross paths?" Had they discovered each other sooner, she might've ended up in chains in his citadel instead of Riksa.

"With so much magic in Savat, and you deliberately smothering your own, is it any wonder we couldn't sense each other?" Zal asked. "Besides, I've stayed out of the city and away from humans as much as possible. I learned early: it was better to hide my face and true identity. It was easier to let my followers handle any city business."

"Where were you before Savat?" Leksi asked, genuinely curious now.

"joRania," he said. The name of the northern empire seemed to jolt Emri, who visibly stiffened. Breakfast and a few brief naps had somewhat revived the sciomancer, but his eyes remained shadowed, his face wan and hairless, except for the slender brows the same color as his moonspill hair.

"I've been to some of the coastal cities," Leksi said. "They're more god-fearing there; I thought you would've liked that. Why come to Savat?"

"I needed a powerful arkani. I heard rumors of Scryali, but it wasn't until I heard a performance of her music that I became intrigued. The emperor instantly banned it, the dissonance heresy. But there was something familiar about the harmonies, something in her music that made me want to know her."

"You wanted to recruit her," Leksi said.

"I came to Savat and became her patron," Zal said. "To encourage her experimentation."

"Stars wept, are you the reason she went mad?" Leksi had been aware of the irascible arkani who thought herself a god, but she'd been too wrapped up in her own affairs at the time to spare it much thought.

"I have since learned that humans don't fare well soaked in my magic," Zal admitted. "I've learned to share smaller pieces of myself with those I value." His gaze flicked to Emri.

"Well, your petitions for mercy clearly went swimmingly," Leksi said. "It was a public beheading, was it not?"

Zal didn't respond. A muscle twitched in his clenched jaw, but Leksi felt the pulse of anger and a flare of regret along their tether. She bit her tongue, catching the apology between her teeth before it could spill from her lips.

"That's odd," Emri said, and Leksi followed the sciomancer's gaze to a tangled swath of plants.

"Is something wrong?" Leksi studied the grapevines. They were overgrown, some withering, many browned by the sun. Several were clustered with grapes while others were still shedding flowers. She had no idea if that was normal or not. Her knowledge of wine was limited to her preference for a bitter red.

"Hard to say," Emri said. "But this is not how well-tended vines should look."

"Perhaps Lana's preoccupation with insurgency has caused the neglect," Zal said. "And we suspected Riksa headed this way."

"Riksa?" Leksi startled. "Is she part of this explosive plot as well then?"

Zal shrugged and mopped sweat from his forehead with the stained hem of his shirt. His cheeks were prickled with dark stubble that only highlighted the shiny slashes of scar tissue like a patina across his cheeks.

"Let's find out." He nudged his mount into a trot and the others followed, Leksi bouncing painfully in the saddle.

Thankfully, the jolting of spine and bruising of buttocks only lasted a few more minutes before they arrived at the main house. Its walls were whitewashed beneath heavy thatching. Unlike the grapes, the house was well maintained, with wooden shutters painted a minty green. They reined in the horses beside an elaborate marble fountain. The statue in its center had the body of a snake and six separate faces, denoting the gods.

"Wonder which one is Mother," Leksi mused.

"The ugly one," Zal said before swinging down from the horse as if he weren't a ragged assembly of broken parts held together by borrowed magic.

He seemed totally unaffected by the arduous hours spent on horseback while Leksi was exhausted. She slid, jelly-limbed, to the ground, using a stirrup and a handful of mane for support. For all his seeming exhaustion, Emri dismounted as lithe and graceful as a cat. How he wasn't doused in sweat and close to heatstroke clad neck to toes in black remained a mystery. The traces of dried blood at his ears were the only evidence of his troubles. Perhaps the ghosts kept him cool, breathing down his neck with morbid halitosis. If only being Death's spawn afforded Leksi a similar ventilation system.

"Do you hear that?" Zal asked.

A hack and grind echoed on the wind with an accompanying judder radiating up from the earth. She thought the quiver was thanks to saddle-weary muscles, but the rumble beneath her feet reminded her of the night Zal clambered out of her grave. There was an irksome tingle in her back teeth and fingertips too.

"Construction?" Emri asked. "They did want to build the railroad through her land."

"They what?" Leksi asked.

"It's one of many reasons Lana has been against the government. The Synod plans to build a railway connecting Savat to joRania and beyond." The way he pronounced the empire's name tickled Leksi's ears, reminding her of the Yekkä nomads she'd encountered during her travels once.

"Lana objected, of course," Zal said. "Didn't want to give up her ancestral home on land the Synod claimed now belongs to the government since the monarchy was deposed."

"I had no idea." It seemed Leksi's determination to stay out of human politics had made her oblivious to far more than she knew.

"Or perhaps she means to build herself a palace right here," Zal said.

"That would certainly be an affront to the Synod," Emri added, sharing an almost-smile with Zal.

A moment later, they were greeted by a horde of baying dogs with monstrously large heads, ruffs up and tails wagging. A human ran after them—a worker judging by their dirty and disheveled clothes—although Leksi doubted she looked much better.

"I don't think Ailia's here," Zal said. "I would feel her. The pull would get stronger." He pressed a hand to his chest. "If anything, it seems to have weakened."

"Are you sure that's not because of my magic?" Leksi said, eyeing the dogs who instinctively kept their distance.

"Not impossible," Zal conceded.

"Good day to you," Emri greeted the farmhand. "We

request an audience with the crown-in-exile, the Lady Motselana."

"Her Highness isn't receiving guests," the farmhand said, polite but firm. Their skin was polished obsidian, their head shaved and cheeks marked with the ritual scars denoting their Qhembalese heritage.

"She'll receive us," Emri said. "Tell her Va'ili of the Citadel is here."

The farmhand cocked their head, either unaware or wholly unimpressed by this introduction. Their gaze flicked briefly to Leksi and Zal before resting again on Emri.

"You're the ghost-touched?"

Emri nodded, and Zal took a protective step toward the sciomancer.

"Leave the horses." The farmhand whistled a piercing note and a lanky youth appeared. "You can wait inside." The farmhand snapped their fingers, cowing the dogs before showing Leksi and the others into the house while the youth took the horses.

The interior was blessedly cool and dark, the structure a sprawl of chambers spilling from one to the other through archways without doors. She'd expected opulence: lavish displays of wealth and ostentatious fittings. She'd anticipated art acquired from across the ocean, artifacts purloined from far-off cultures, bowls of cut flowers or trophies of exotic beasts mounted on the walls—but there was none of that.

In fact, the home was sparsely furnished without even a rug on the earthen floor.

"Interesting aesthetics," Leksi said as the farmhand led them into a day room. Here at least there were lounge chairs and a table holding a pitcher of water.

"Those with true power have no need to flaunt it," Zal said, and Leksi almost choked, wondering what he thought his citadel sculpted from a mountain and all his gem-embellished worshipers said about him then.

"Please help yourself while you wait." The farmhand gestured to the water jug before disappearing up the staircase.

Leksi didn't need to be told twice, pouring three glasses and downing hers in two swallows before the others had yet to take a sip. She flopped onto the nearest chair, grateful for the cradle of plump cushions. It took a moment for her to notice the juddering had stopped; the tingle in her teeth and fingertips had not.

"What was that?" Emri asked as he eased himself onto a settee.

"I've felt it before," Zal said. "At my mines."

"You have mines?" Leksi asked, not sure why anything about her brother surprised her anymore.

"It feels like earthworks. Like digging," Zal went on.

"Machines or magic?" Emri asked.

"Both. Originally, only arkani with the affinity for earth could move rock and soil. I hired a few to open the ground, then workers went in with shovels and pickaxes," Zal said. "Nowadays, there are machines spelled by arkani that make the process faster and more efficient. There are still workers, of course, but fewer are required and the worst of it can be done by machines."

"Careful, brother. Next you'll be advocating for the replacement of magic with technology," Leksi said.

"I admit I can see the benefits of it. There are times it certainly seems to be more efficient, and—kinder." Zal took a sip of water as if to wash the word from his mouth. "I just don't think technological progress should be at the expense of magic, and I certainly don't believe humans need to forget the gods or execute magic-wielders in order to 'embrace the future.'" He parroted the Sodality's slogan.

"You genuinely surprise me," Leksi admitted.

Zal seemed about to offer a riposte when Motselana strutted into the room, dogs padding behind her, looking every bit the queen she was not.

Not yet.

Emri immediately rose; Zal sprawled.

"You grace me with your presence," Lana said with a strained smile, its edges splintering when she regarded Zal unraveled across the settee. The infusion of Leksi's magic had done wonders for both his visage and his countenance. Anyone who'd known him from before Leksi's intervention would be amazed by the transformation, but he still remained a shade of his former self.

"You honor us with your hospitality," Emri said with a shallow bow. "Arriving as we did unannounced."

"The least I can do for friends." Lana made the word sound more like a threat than an epithet of welcome. The woman was stately in periwinkle blue trousers impeccably tailored to hug her hips and accentuate the curves of her legs. Her white blouse was spotless and similarly shaped to fit her with complex beading across the bodice. The capped sleeves left her plump arms bare. The tattoo from shoulder to wrist on her right arm was subtle, the coffee-brown ink only a shade darker than her skin.

Subtle as the color was, the image was not. The serpent coiled around her biceps and wound down her forearm, its forked tongue splitting along her middle and index fingers, rippling across her dimpled knuckles. Like her royal predecessors, Lana declared her devotion to Inyoti, the Great Serpent god from which even Leksi herself had supposedly come.

"Is Ailia here?" Zal asked, not bothering with small talk or politeness.

"Ailia?" Lana's smile wavered. "Why would she be here?"

"We heard you were planning to blow up First Council together," Leksi said. There was no point wasting time with niceties when the city was already succumbing to chaos.

"I'm sorry, who are you?" Lana gave Leksi an imperious once-over and Leksi returned the favor. The would-be queen was younger than she'd imagined. Leksi did the mental arithmetic, trying to remember Savati history and the family tree of the royals, to figure out exactly where Motselana fit on the baobab spread of relatives. The granddaughter of a lesser princess, Leksi thought, which would make her thirty—thirty-five, perhaps. She looked at least ten years older than Emri, but then she was neither ghost-touched nor shadow-stained.

"Lana, this is my sister, Leksi," Zal said as he finally stood.

Lana's gaze snapped from Leksi to Zal, her eyes widening as he straightened to his full height, hair falling in a shaggy black halo to his shoulders. He'd grown since Leksi had last seen him in the Nether, a long-limbed youth on the cusp of adulthood and gangly in any form. No longer wizened like an old man, he looked every bit the demigod, albeit one in need of a thorough scrubbing.

"You're looking well." Lana blinked. "I… forgive me, I thought—" She stumbled over her words.

"You thought what?" Zal took a step toward her, shadows thickening the air around him. The dogs growled, hackles raised and lips curling.

"Ailia mentioned you've been battling a long illness." Lana rested her hand on the largest mutt's head. "At the party, I saw you on the balcony. I assumed—forgive me. I'm glad to see you recovered, although…"

"Yes?" he prompted and Lana's smooth forehead creased with a frown.

"Forgive me, Va'ili, but you look like you've been dragged backwards through the bundu by an angry rhinoceros."

Zal grinned at that. "Worse, actually, but I survived."

"You too. And you smell." She glanced at Leksi, wrinkling her button nose.

"Perhaps her Ladyship could arrange baths for her guests," Emri suggested, sickeningly obsequious.

"Gladly." She whistled: two short blasts that startled Leksi so hard she almost dropped her cup. A maid appeared a moment later, bobbing a curtsy at each of them in turn while Lana rattled off orders for baths and fresh clothes to be arranged. Food, too. Leksi's stomach rumbled in eager anticipation.

"Now about your plans to rid Savat of the Synod," Zal said, once the maid had disappeared.

Snapping her fingers, Lana commanded the dogs to lie down. Only once the pack had belly-flopped did she sigh and sashay over to the table. She poured herself a cup of water before responding. "Ailia wasn't supposed to tell you."

"Why not?" Zal asked. "I've always supported her political endeavors."

Leksi caught the sly roll of Lana's eyes. "Ailia said your attention lay elsewhere." The would-be queen seemed to choose her words carefully, and a flare of irritation sizzled along the tether as Zal grew increasingly impatient. "She said you didn't care about what happened in Savat unless it served your own aims. Va'ili," Lana added.

"I can be single-minded in my goals," Zal admitted.

"Selfish and incorrigible, were her exact words, I believe." Lana downed the water and Leksi couldn't help but appreciate the audacity of the woman. "But if you say you're here to help, then I appreciate it. I'm a practical person, unlike my forebears who got lost in pomp and ceremony."

"Did we say we were here to help?" Leksi cast a questioning glance at her brother, wondering if she'd missed something.

"If Ailia's not here, where is she?" Zal asked without so much as a glance in Leksi's direction.

"At the palace attending to Synod business, I imagine," Lana said. "We don't need her until the night before First

Council."

"How exactly do you plan to pull off this seditious plot of yours?" Leksi asked.

"We each have our role to play. I procure the explosives and organize transport, while Ailia will ensure our targets will be in attendance, and she'll see to the necessary spells, ensuring the damage is contained."

"Contained?" Emri asked as he perched on the settee again. Leksi refilled his cup and then her own.

"I want to remove those who stand in my way," Lana said. "Not flatten the city."

Just as they'd thought, Queen Lana to the rescue, only Ailia must have wanted the glory for herself.

"Thanks for that," Leksi quipped. "But what exactly do you hope to achieve by eradicating the Synod? You'll still have the Sodality to contend with and a crown-hating public against you. You think they'll welcome back a monarch so easily?" Magic they might be more open to, considering the majority of Qhembalese had never fully swallowed the Sodality's rhetoric.

"Of course," Lana said. "If Ailia plays her part, then both the Synod and the Sodality will be eliminated." She smiled, lines crinkling around her dark eyes. "Two birds, several kegs of gunpowder, one fiery eradication."

"So simple," Zal said.

"It doesn't need to be more complicated," Lana said. "The people just need to understand how corrupt the Synod has become, poisoned by the Sodality. Many never gave up the old ways, just hid their allegiance. And the rest only need to be reintroduced to the Principles of Inyoti."

"The Sodality believe they follow the One True Path," Emri added.

"Heresy!" Lana spat, and stroked the serpent on her arm. "My arkani ability may be weak—a consequence of my diluted blood and the general lack of faith diminishing the omnipotence of our gods—but we can change that. We can return to the old ways and restore the gods to true power."

The ground jostled beneath their feet as the whine and grind began anew. Leksi noticed the scuff marks on the toes of Lana's leather slippers, the beading caked with dirt as if she'd been ferreting around in a garden.

"Digging a new well?" Zal asked. "Laying foundations for a palace? Or a railway perhaps?"

"Never." Lana pressed her lips together as she squeezed her arm.

As amusing as the exchange was, Leksi's thoughts had snagged on Lana's words.

"When you say restore the old gods, you don't mean literally, do you?" she asked.

The stories about the slumbering snake were just that: fictions concocted to explain the mystery of magic. Yes, the gods existed, and magic was the force they bled into the world, but Leksi was no wiser than the humans when it came to understanding the true origins of her extended family. Human lore said the Great Serpent, Inyoti, encircled the void and during Inyoti's first ecdysis, each of the six gods were created, fashioned from scale-stuff to rule over their designated element: Water, Earth, Fire, Air, Time, and Death.

Leksi had tried asking her mother, but if Death knew any better, she'd kept it to herself. Far more likely that Death, like the others, had no idea how they'd come to be.

"Of course I do," Lana said. "The gods will be revived and Inyoti exalted."

"You think you can wake Inyoti?" Emri asked with awe and disbelief in his voice.

"Yes," Lana said. "The Serpent will wake and I will lead the city into a new age of spiritual enlightenment." Her eyes were calculating, shiny not with the fervor of zealotry so much as the burning coals of ambition. "Just imagine all that untapped potential, the power—*my* power. It's going to be glorious. I'm going to deliver this city a future worth embracing."

Leksi and Zal simultaneously muttered a Nethertaal oath so strong the windows cracked, the dogs howled, and the humans shed bloody tears.

Chapter Nineteen
Zal

Zal had never liked the myth claiming gods were made from reptilian dandruff. Surely he and his family had more noble origins than that.

"Do you think it's possible to find—never mind revive—Inyoti?" Emri asked. A bath and vittles had certainly revived the sciomancer, who no longer needed Zal's shadows to steady him despite the lopsided earth.

Clouds shrouded the evening sky, the temperature cooling with the sun mercifully subdued by approaching night. They stood shoulder to shoulder staring into the excavated depths of Lana's earthworks. Not for the first time Zal wondered if one could dig deep enough to eventually tunnel out of the mortal realm and into the Nether. All his previous attempts had resulted only in disappointment, and dead miners buried by collapsing tunnels.

The land behind Lana's house had been churned by machines and worked by dozens of people. Most of the workers had scarred cheeks and wore leopard-pelt karosses over their shoulders. Lana must've recruited half of Qhemba, and every earth-aligned arkani the Sodality hadn't skewered. Their presence chafed. Every magic-wielder here was one Zal had failed to gather to his own cause.

"Va'ili?" Emri prompted.

"Anything is possible," Zal said, staring into the depths.

"You don't know?" Emri asked. "Forgive me, Va'ili, but being what you are, I thought you'd know if the legends were true."

Zal shrugged, enjoying the feel of silk as it whispered across his freshly scrubbed skin. Lana had provided fine clothes indeed, as well as scented soap and oils. Emri glowed, his damp hair hanging loose and long, daylight making it a citrus-scented shimmer. He still wore black, the borrowed trousers and tunic a looser fit with fewer layers, no less dramatic in contrast to his silver hair.

"As a Netherling, I didn't contemplate our origins much. My mother was Death, my father the storm wind. Well, that's what I believed before—" Before Leksi had revealed the truth of his hideous conception. Either way, he was the demigod of Chaos destined to wreak havoc in the mortal realm. "I knew about various relatives." He waved a dismissive hand. "But we have little to do with each other. We all keep to ourselves, content in our aspect. It was only when I came to the mortal realm that I learned the human myths," Zal continued. "And heard stories about the Ancestors, how humans believed they could wield magic because they'd been impaled with a sloughed scale." He scoffed.

Having never met Inyoti nor seen any evidence of the big snake's existence, he'd always considered it a fabrication. Death and her ilk simply were, always had been—essential and inevitable. The idea he might be the result of some cosmic ecdysis slicked his insides with an inexplicable discomfort. If the gods had been created, they could be destroyed, and not simply drained of magic or drowned in deadly waters.

"You don't think it could be true?" Emri asked, a whisper of disappointment in his voice.

"Humans need stories to explain the things they don't understand about their world," Zal said. "One story has as much chance of proving true as another. Even the worst lie often carries a kernel of truth."

"You don't find it odd that despite differences in names and rites, that everyone believes life originated with a great serpent?" Emri continued, and Zal raised a brow.

"Perhaps not everyone," Emri conceded. "But all those I've ever met in joRania and Savat seem to agree on similar fundamentals."

It was a dragon in some cultures, who belched fire into the void, igniting the stars. A legevaan in others, that clawed open the ether, the gods rising from the spill of steaming entrails. Zal preferred that story: an echo of his own rebirth in the mortal realm as he stitched himself together from gore.

In the tales from Tsiraya, the serpent was more like an eel, life begun in the primordial ooze of the ocean, shocked into being by the sea-serpent's lightning-zap of magic. All variations of a similar theme; all prone to the vagaries of human imagination and the inevitability of change over time.

Time. Zal gritted his teeth hard enough to send an ache into his skull.

"What do the Yekkä believe?" he asked, trying to ease the

tension in his jaw.

Emri chewed on his bottom lip for a moment before answering. "In the oldest stories, there was a crocodile who swam through the ocean of stars. The Yekkä word for star is very similar to sand though." He said the two words, the tonal inflection so slight Zal's Nether-stung ears could barely distinguish the difference. "The crocodile shared magic through song."

"A singing crocodile?" Zal asked.

"With a voice so beautiful, life itself sprung from the melody." Emri's smile wavered. "I wish I knew more about my people's mythology, but I was raised on joRanian religion."

"Who also believe in a snake."

"Cobra, actually: its hood the universe. Its tail coils around gold and diamonds; thus, those who hoard wealth honor the god."

"Indeed." Zal had witnessed human progress, their beliefs shifting as their understanding of themselves and the world improved, values shed like old skin to suit the swinging pendulum of morality and politics. One day the humans of Savat might relinquish all notion of a gargantuan void-snake as the origins of life, but until then, the progeny of deposed monarchies would dig holes in their backyard.

He crouched to gather a handful of dirt, letting the dry particles sift through his fingers. His mines ran deep, the shafts plummeting into cold and darkness in search of gold and gems. There was a time when people didn't like the idea of mining, convinced the earth's riches belonged to Inyoti. Society had been dissuaded of that notion once their quality of life improved with the influx of wealth ripped from the ground.

"Riksa's trail ran north," Zal said, thinking out loud. "Could she be here?"

"Possibly," Emri said with the tell-tale tilt of his head as he listened to voices only he could hear. "If Lana has dug up something old and magical, then that could interfere with my divination. If there is something primordial lurking below, it could even mask Riksa from me entirely."

"What do your spirits think?" Zal asked, studying the sciomancer as the breeze combed the man's hair into shiny ribbons.

"They're restless." Emri's eyes glowed brighter as he deepened his connection to his ghosts. "They feel something, but whether that's the fossil of a god or simply some ancient magic-imbued artifact..." Emri shrugged, his eyes darkening again. "Whatever it is, the force seems disruptive."

"That's how we know we're close," Lana said as she walked across the broken earth to join them. "The spells of even the brightest arkani are starting to behave a little strangely," she added with unnerving excitement. "Surely you can feel it?"

Zal sensed a thrum as if bees were building a hive within his organs. He'd thought it a result of Leksi's borrowed power—the taste and texture of it distinct from his own. But his shadows whispered and Leksi's monsters thrashed; neither ever hummed nor maintained this incessant vibration.

"Have you ever considered Inyoti might prefer to remain asleep?" Zal asked as he pressed his hand to the earth.

"Then They can sleep and I will become Inyoti's sworn protector. We'll build shrines across the city and a new temple right here where penitents can bring their offerings."

"And you'll be high priestess, keeper of the Great Snake?" Zal asked.

"Inyoti's Anointed," she said, her expression distinctly beatific. "And divine sovereign of Savat." This woman really believed she was some sort of chosen one.

"And Ailia?" Zal stood, dusting off his palms.

"My most trusted advisor, and second in command."

Which was undoubtedly why Ailia had sought to usurp Zal's magic. She'd never settle for second best.

"Are those fanes?" Emri asked and Zal looked up, following the sciomancer's line of sight.

Boulders had been stacked together in crude altars, with candles, shells and other tokens set between the uneven surfaces of the stones. One set of boulders had been splashed red. A broken bird's wing and the skull of a rodent sat on top. A thrill shivered through Zal's chest at the evidence of respect, if not adoration. Perhaps that explained why the blood sang in his veins.

"Of course," Lana said. "When I am queen, the city will remember to honor the gods as we used to."

"All the gods?" Zal asked, the buzzing in his chest growing.

"We honor each equally, though here we offer more to Earth." She traced the accompanying sigil with her fingers in the air, honoring the goddess of ground and greenery, the very antithesis of his own aspect.

"And Death?" Zal asked.

Lana traced the sacred sigil. It felt like warm honey dripped from a lover's fingers into Zal's starving mouth. He swallowed, hungry for more.

"What about Time?" Emri asked, earning a glower from Zal. He had no desire to acknowledge his father nor benefit from worship to the entity. He'd only met the god once and remembered a slender figure with tousled hair as black as the void and eyes swirling with color. He squeezed his own eyes shut and rubbed at them vigorously as if he could erase the touch of his progenitor from the orbs. Both sat firmly couched in their sockets now, neither dripping greasy tears.

"Time, too," Lana said, although she wisely didn't inscribe Time's sigil. "We acknowledge all the gods."

"Thank you for honoring us," Zal said.

"You?" Lana looked perplexed. "Ailia never did say what your affinity was, only that you were a powerful arkani who had suffered a horrendous ordeal and been irrevocably… altered." She'd no doubt meant to say broken and wouldn't have been wrong.

"Arkani?" Zal snorted. "Is that what she told you?" They'd never agreed on what Ailia told others about the cloaked recluse who ruled from the shadows of his citadel, only that it was best not to reveal the truth to outsiders. Having adopted Ailia from her poverty-stricken family as a child, he'd raised her on stories of his true nature, stories made more digestible by a slow and piecemeal delivery. As she grew, she'd come to accept Zal's tales for fact. Later, they'd only revealed his identity to those who swore fealty.

He hadn't always been so careful. After Gafina, when he'd resembled something closer to human and less a walking wound, he'd proclaimed himself a demigod at every shrine and fane. He'd expected instant worship, for the penitents to fall prostrate at his feet. Instead he'd been chased from the temples, beaten and scourged by those calling him a heretic or charlatan. Some took pity on him, believing his mind as broken as his body. Pity wasn't the same as worship, but it came close enough to soothe fresh bruises.

Zal had learned quickly that it was better to feast on human belief in secret, insinuating himself with the Death cults in the joRanian capital. Surreptitiously, he fed on their zeal and devotion, calling himself an arkani as he took advantage of the city's seedy underbelly, accumulating power and wealth, changing allegiances between cults as required. He'd been tempted so many times to reveal his identity, to become the focus of their adoration, but he'd resisted and thus endured—if not enjoyed—several decades of that life.

Perhaps it was time now for honesty with this would-be queen who seemed determined to both honor and exploit the gods.

Lana's gaze narrowed. "You are ghost-touched, obviously." She gestured to Emri before turning to Zal. "But if you aren't arkani, then what?"

Emri gave Zal a questioning glance, waiting for Zal to nod before speaking.

"Va'ili is no mortal magic-wielder," Emri said, his words

tipped with steel. "You stand before the son of Death, and demigod of Chaos."

Lana giggled, the sound so incongruously childish emanating from the regal woman.

"A demigod?" Her gaze raked Zal from head to foot and back again. "But you were ill; you were damaged. You still are."

"Even gods can bleed," Zal said with a wry smile. "But those who wound us tend to end up worse off." Not always, though. Far too many times, he'd suffered at the hands of mortals and been too weak to fight back.

"Gods are immortal, impervious," Lana said.

"Not when corporeal," Zal said. "The mortal realm has a most unwelcome effect on us."

"If you're the son of Death, then prove it." She raised her brows expectantly.

Zal breathed deeply, luxuriating in the lack of agony as his lungs expanded, his shadows thickening with the power he drew from Leksi. He hadn't extended himself like this in centuries, all his effort confined to holding himself together and maintaining his flock of shadow-stained arkani. Now though, his magic unfurled like vulture wings.

A cry rang out from nearby workers as the shadows continued to swell, darkness emanating from him as thick as sea fog. Some cowered; others dropped to their knees in supplication which only bolstered Zal's burgeoning power. Beside him, Emri had dropped to his knees too, the naked adoration on the man's upraised face setting alight every nerve ending in

Zal's body.

"You are... you are magnificent," Lana said as she slowly dropped to her knees. "Forgive me for ever doubting."

Yes, this was how it felt to be a god. This was how it should always be: humans bowing before his greatness, raising their voices in prayer, their hands in supplication. There was hunger in Lana's gaze though, her eyes narrowed as if she was calculating how much Zal's godhood might be worth.

"Showing off?" Leksi said in Nethertaal, destroying the moment.

Zal deflated, his magic dissipating like a soap bubble burst by grubby hands.

"Glad to see my power being put to good use," she added.

"Always so self-righteous." Zal was in no mood for her sanctimony. "Don't pretend you don't enjoy their adoration too."

"I find it repugnant," she said, her words at odds with the desire rippling along their tether.

"You only hate how much you love it," he said.

"We gods are such pathetic creatures," Leksi said with unbridled derision. "I cannot wait until I'm no longer one."

"Va'ili's sister, you're also a demigod?" Lana asked, still kneeling.

"Oh, please get up. Neither of us deserve such piety."

Speak for yourself, Zal wanted to say, but held his tongue. He turned to Emri instead and cupped the man's face, feeling the soft hairs on Emri's cheek against his palm as the sciomancer leaned into his touch. Zal swooned, momentarily overwhelmed.

"Thank you," Zal said and Emri rose, his dark eyes misted with spirits and magic and… Zal turned away. He'd seen that look on Ailia's face once and thought it love. But love was nothing but a dagger tucked up a sleeve, waiting to cut when one expected a caress.

The other workers slowly rose as well, unsure what to do. Humans weren't used to having a god among them and some of them looked terrified. Zal couldn't help but smile. There was only one thing better than human adoration. The spice of their fear laced the air with a unique piquancy, and Zal licked his lips.

"As you were," Zal commanded. "Do continue." His shadows flitted among the diggers, prodding them to action.

"If only I'd known," Lana started.

"Enough," Zal said and the woman shut her mouth. Perhaps they could use her faith to their advantage. "Now that you know what we are, you will help us."

"Of course, Va'ili and—" She hesitated as she regarded his sister.

"Call me Leksi."

"Daughter of Death and embodiment of Nightmare," Emri added. Leksi looked decidedly ungodly in the blandly beige servant's tunic she'd chosen to wear over similarly dull and sensible trousers. She was going to excel at being human.

Lana stroked the serpent tattoo adorning her arm, her fingers tracing a sigil of protection onto her skin as if her petty spell-craft could dissuade a demigod.

"I will serve you," Lana said. "You have my word; as a loyal servant to Inyoti and all the gods, I will do as you wish."

"Perhaps you could start by not blowing up the Synod then," Leksi said.

"But they are apostates and blasphemers. Why do you let them live?" Lana asked.

"It's not about the Synod; it's about Savat," Leksi continued. "And about Ailia."

"What about Ailia?" Lana asked.

"She betrayed me." The words twisted through Zal's chest like a corkscrew. "She attempted to steal my magic and use it for her own agenda."

"But her agenda is mine: to rid Savat of the Synod and restore Savat to its former glory. No more restrictions on magic, no more discrimination, no more attacks on arkani. That's what Ailia wants. It's what we've been working toward for years," Lana said.

"Years?" Zal stilled, overcome by the realization this betrayal had been brewing far longer than imagined. "And you *never* suspected?" His question was aimed at Emri. For the first time, Zal regarded the sciomancer with suspicion. Either Ailia must've been far more cunning than Zal gave her credit for to hide her intentions this long, or Emri was equally duplicitous.

"Forgive me, Va'ili." Emri grimaced and shook his head, his voice whisper-soft as always. "On Ailia's orders, I managed the daily needs of the citadel and searched for a means of opening a path to the Nether."

"Sounds like she deliberately kept you busy," Leksi said.

"At very least, at a distance from her own investigations it seems," Emri said. "But I never had any cause to doubt or question her."

"And did you discover anything useful?" Zal asked. He only had himself to blame for being too complacent in his delegation, content to brood and sulk and spend his days engrossed in books when not exhausted by simply trying to hold himself together, his power spread thin across his followers.

"I was making some progress," Emri said, cautiously. "I was hoping to use the spirits to forge a path back to the Nether."

"You can do that?" Leksi asked.

"It seemed feasible," Emri said. "I thought there may have been a way to link the recently deceased to the ancient spirits already in my possession, but—I'm sorry." He bowed his head and Zal laid a reassuring hand on the man's shoulder before he could stop himself.

The tingle of surprise and amusement emanating from Leksi caused his fingers to twitch and hand to drop away, but not before Emri looked up, relief and gratitude etched into every line on his face.

"What do you mean, in your possession?" Leksi asked, ruining the moment. "I thought the ghost-touched communed with transient spirits."

Emri opened and closed his mouth, but before he could answer, shadows tore across the sky, plummeting toward Zal like a hawk falling on prey.

"Va'ili, what is it?" Emri caught Zal when he staggered

from the impact of his minions.

He fought to parse the deluge of shared images and chatter, his harried shadows desperate to share all they'd witnessed.

"The city is burning," Zal said as he saw through shadow eyes. "Qhemba." He corrected. "Hyenas everywhere." So much chaos, people screaming, homes engulfed in flame, fleeing feet tangling in frostweed, bodies shredded in puddles of anomalous magic—his magic, spreading like a canker through the township, through the entire city.

"Qhemba?" Leksi's panic seized him by the throat, throttling him as he tried to make sense of the secondhand fracas. "Zal, tell me." She grabbed his shoulders, shaking him.

"They're using arkani to set the fires," he said. "But the magic is reacting badly, unpredictably." Altered in ways no human arkani could foresee thanks to his blood. "People are fighting back, but they can't; the chaos—they're tearing each other to pieces."

"I have to go. Bring me a fresh horse. Now!" Leksi's voice was a roar, the monsters inside her thrashing in eagerness, feeding on her own fear.

Zal struggled against the sudden giddiness, his own desire for chaos rising like a squall. His pleasure at the carnage his shadows had witnessed threatened to engulf him as surely as the fires of the township riot.

"You can't go," Zal said when a farmhand came running with a horse for Leksi.

"This is your fault," she spat. "I'm going to save Tamisk and the people I genuinely care about. The people I swore to protect, and not just use for my own selfish ends. You want my magic, you better do something about this too." She flung a hand at the earthworks and Lana before mounting.

"You're just going back to feast on their fear," he said, lips curling in a snarl equal parts derision and hunger.

Leksi screamed, her face contorted in a rage, which swept through Zal in a cauterizing wave. She wheeled the horse around and was galloping away before Zal had the chance to stop her, to beg her not to take her power and leave him bereft once more.

His knee buckled as Leksi's magic ebbed away, his spine bending against the sudden influx of old pain. Scars strained against their seams, his sinews shearing as he struggled to hold onto her receding power. He was going to need it. The burning city wasn't all the shadows had shown him.

"Va'ili?" Emri joined him in the dirt. "Are you—"

"I saw her," Zal said, breathless, as he cobbled together magic both borrowed and broken. He pressed a hand to his chest, the sigil stinging, blood soaking through the silk shirt where his skin had split. "They have her at the palace. I saw them dragging her—" Through the streets, bloodied and bruised, the amulet hanging heavy from her neck. "The Sodality has Ailia."

No mortal is with or without magic/music. No mortal is god-touched or denied. Magic/music resides in all of us. Some know it and can access it. Others live in ignorance. To release the magic/music within requires sound devotion. We must bathe in the cosmic frequencies, our bones the resonators, our minds in tune with each other and the Creator from whose scales we weave life's tapestry. Each of us a note in the divine chord, that profound harmony in which we dwell.*

Excerpt from *The Manual for Music/Magic* by Kerisil of Enlouaya, translated

*The characters for 'magic' and 'music' in Olde joRanian are the same.

CHAPTER TWENTY

NIKI

Stifling a yawn, I tried to focus on the messy scrawl of my notes. I'd been at it all day, or night. I'd lost track of time again, the kakaki blasts blending into the din between my ears, my thoughts a cacophony.

My vision blurred with fatigue neither coffee nor khat could combat. Both, in excess, made my hands shake, which didn't help either, but there was no time for rest. And I was done waiting. The Esteemed had promised me unlimited access, and if she failed to deliver that, then I would just have to take it. No one had told me I couldn't go to the library. As one of the most learned minds in the palace, surely I wouldn't be turned away.

Gently, I shook Moli awake. She'd fallen asleep on a book of ancient sigils, the ink smudged on her cheek.

"Do you know where the library is?" I asked.

Rubbing her eyes, she nodded, then signed, *We're not allowed there.*

"Take me anyway," I said and she hesitated, worry creasing her brow. "If I don't produce results, I'll be dead anyway."

With a sigh, she gathered herself into wakefulness. Together, we padded down the deserted hallways, as no doubt many of the others were still sleeping off their Solstice indulgences. If only I could afford to take a day off. At least the itch had been more manageable today. It had taken up residence in my chest, an irritation like indigestion. I didn't want to think about what the errant wisp might be doing to my insides. If it was a scrap of primordial magic, it could be causing some bizarre evolution within my tissues—one I was powerless to stop.

Moli led the way in silence and I followed. Oddly, we encountered no guards on our traverse of the palace, only the sound of our footsteps disturbing the quiet. Eventually, she paused outside a suitably impressive set of doors, carved in high-relief depictions of Savati history.

You go, Moli gestured. *They won't kill you, but I…* She swallowed hard and I nodded, then thanked her with my hands before cracking open the heavy doors.

The library was smaller than I'd expected but no less impressive, with its circular construction and decorative pilasters. The entry level had an arrangement of desks, reading chairs, and cushions scattered on plush carpets while the upper levels contained a multitude of books on neat shelving. Pale light streamed in through the stained-glass window, suggesting dawn was on its way. The interior was otherwise unlit, the details of the painted ceiling lost in darkness. I had no time for ogling anyway, but I took a moment to inhale the peculiar aroma of leather and paper, ink and knowledge that always suffused a library. Perhaps after First Council—if I was still breathing—I could return to appreciate the collection in all its glory.

I prowled through the gloom, my heart thudding with anxious anticipation. Not sure where to start, I approached the first desk, disappointed to find it laden with legal documents. Another was strewn with maps showing various mining sites. None of the desks contained anything relevant to my pursuits.

I continued my search, passing several display cases housing various artifacts: exquisite masks, snatches of desert fabrics, an array of ceremonial items from across the continent, and even a few musical instruments. I paused to examine an orutu, its single string gossamer-thin with age. The case also contained a ceremonial kora in pristine condition, an assortment of flutes, and a large sesheshet, its metal jangles flaked with rust.

Before I succumbed to the compulsion to touch the instruments, a muffled cough and the yellow glow of a reading lamp drew me to an alcove where a gray-clad Sodalite sat at a desk, scowling. They muttered curses as they struggled to subdue the unwieldy scroll they were transcribing.

"Need some assistance?"

The Sodalite screamed and dropped their pen, splattering ink across the polished floor.

"Sorry, I didn't mean to startle you."

"You're not supposed to be here," the Sodalite whispered. "You're not even wearing the gray. How did you get in here?"

"I walked," I said, stepping closer to see what they'd been working on while they mopped up spilled ink.

"You can't look at that." The Sodalite snatched at the scroll as I picked up the cloth-bound codex they'd been writing in.

"You have excellent penmanship," I said, scanning the content. Not what I needed though. "I'm looking for translations pertaining to music, specifically Scryali. Do you know where I can find them?"

"No. Absolutely not," the Sodalite said, but their gaze darted to the alcove adjacent to their own. "You have to leave. Immediately. If you don't, I'll call the guards."

"Call the guards then," I said with a wave of my hand, already heading for the neighboring desk. If the Esteemed wanted answers, she'd forgive my trespass.

The lamp ignited when I sat down, clearly spelled. The codices and scrolls on this desk were neatly sorted with a basket of even more scrolls beside the chair, presumably still in need of translation. I cracked my knuckles and dragged the codex at the top of the pile into the corona of light. Ignoring the Sodalite's continued threats, I began to read.

Several pages later, the translations had only proven more baffling than helpful and yet, the writings of Kerisil of Enlouaya suggested I wasn't entirely alone in my presumption of a God-chord or its connection to magic. Unless it was all a horrible misinterpretation. In the flowing vertical script of Olde joRanian, the collection of brush strokes denoting music or magic looked an awful lot like the collection of flourishes meaning sorrow. Perhaps this was less a treatise on music or magic, and more a proposed system for managing mental malaise.

Apt either way, considering my current state of mind.

I scratched vigorously at my chest, not caring if I bled while I tried to assemble my scattered thoughts into more logical architecture, like notes gathered into chords, dissonant or euphonious. My thoughts clashed, adding to the discordant tumult within my skull.

Trying to focus, I dug my nails in deeper to quell the burn behind my sternum as the text swam before my eyes. I reread the passages translated from Kerisil's treatise. Some of the rules outlined in the text—if intended for music—were familiar at least, and had clearly influenced composers throughout the ages. The instructions for chords were simple enough, using intervals dictated by the given key as expressed in a scale, which delineated the relationship between the pitches.

Scales, scales, scales—the word caught in my brain like a ragged claw. Scales like those shed by the great Inyoti, a serpent's detritus sinking into human hearts to give them magic.

I reread the first page again. *Weaving life's tapestry from scales.* It seemed an odd turn of phrase considering the nature of reptile skin. I massaged my temples, mulling over the words. What if it had been a *musical* scale, and not a serpent's? The words were the same in both Savati and Tsirayan. Perhaps the original meaning had been confused in the creation of the old myths in joRania too.

No, my exhausted mind was reaching for the ridiculous, addled by the incessant shadow-noise. I scrubbed my hands over my face then rubbed the tender spot on my jaw as I returned to my original premise: magic had nothing to do with gods or elemental affinities. It all came down to mathematical frequencies and the harmonies produced from layered vibrations.

My *Fantasy No. 12* had excited the arkana particles and

resulted in an incendiary reaction. But it had released too much magic all at once in a way I had failed to account for with the reverberation plates, which is why the candles had ignited—if not quite as planned.

So, what was the shadow marking those arkani—and me—then? I couldn't help but think Scryali had somehow figured it out.

In need of soothing, I started humming her hexatonic children's song, and, gradually, the itch in my chest subsided. Chords… harmony…

Rushing to the display case, I retrieved the kora and sank onto the nearest cushion before settling the bowl of the gourd into my lap. This one had 22 strings, its voice rich and bright as I reverently plucked the weathered strings.

A pleasant coolness pooled in my knee, then shifted, a languid seepage defying gravity. I sang Scryali's ditty again, testing various harmonic accompaniments, taking note of the changing sensation beneath my skin.

There was one interval I had yet to try, one I had so far ignored since it was supposed to weaken spells. While it was only technically banned in incantations, most Savati music avoided the tritone, the interval an affront to Inyoti. Although the original Qhembalese tuning system for the kora had initially included the tritone, that scale had fallen out of modern use, too, but Scryali had been known for her transgressive use of dissonance.

Gently, I adjusted the kora, straining against the leather rings to tweak the tension on the strings. I plucked the so-called Serpent Tone and winced. No bolt of lightning struck me down, nor did the shadow beneath my skin immediately respond.

Perhaps one tritone wasn't enough. I added to it, expanding the interval into a chord, each new pitch adding fresh dissonance. Closing my eyes, I began to sing the ditty, gradually expanding the series of notes as I improvised my own rendition. The music absorbed me, the vibrations palpable in my back teeth, a thrumming that traveled through my jaw and up into my skull. It took me a moment to register the cessation of the cricket screech, the abrasive noise finally soothed into something closer to music. Cold simultaneously permeated my torso as if I'd chugged a gallon of icy water. I peered down the loose neck of my shirt to see the shadow unfurled across my chest like feathers.

I stopped singing and stilled my fingers. Immediately, the gray smudge congealed and began to itch, the music in my head splintering into chirp and growl.

Before I had time to process the result of my experiment, footsteps pounded in the corridor. A bolt of terror shot down my spine, but what could the palace guards do to me when the Esteemed herself had ordered me to find answers? I set the kora back in its display case, not wanting the ham-fisted hyenas damaging the antique when they came to drag me back to my laboratory, then turned to face the repercussions of my actions.

Yatto led the charge, flanked by two palace guards, all three of them sweaty and out of breath.

"You know you're not supposed to be here," Yatto said, his mouth twisting into a snarl. When Jaq wasn't around, he shed all pretenses of pleasantness. "Seize them." He pointed at me and the guards sprang forward, grabbing my arms before I could process the command, or the satisfaction in Yatto's expression. The burning itch in my skin intensified.

"Bring the prisoner," he said, and the guards wrenched me forward.

"Prisoner?" I managed through gritted teeth. "Surely—"

"The library is off-limits to the likes of you. We've beheaded others for less," Yatto said, his breath hot and sour as he spit the words in my face, reminding me of my father and how he enjoyed looming over me, seeing me shrink at the certainty of violence.

I'd similarly loomed at his deathbed, watching him gasp his last. What I wouldn't give to see Yatto wracked with pain and the knowledge of imminent demise.

"The translations were taking too long," I said, straightening my spine, refusing to shrink before this man. "I only did as the Esteemed commanded. I only wanted to do the work—"

"Enough." Yatto cut me off. "Let's go." He gestured to the guards.

"Where are you taking me?" I asked, my voice strained.

"The dungeons, of course." Yatto smirked before striding away.

Once more at the mercy of burly hyenas, I was forced to follow, my limbs taking a moment to remember how to function now that I was no longer shrimp-hunched over the instrument. I felt an ant-march prickle beneath my skin as the shadow moved. Thankfully, it remained hidden by my clothing, saving me from further condemnation.

As fear tightened its grip, I contemplated running—but even if I could get away, where would I go?

Back in the darkness, I picked my way across the floor stained black with mildew and old blood, the air thick with the stench of sweat and excrement, copper and the tang of fear welling now from my own pores as Yatto had me taken to an interrogation chamber. My gaze fell on the table where an assortment of blades, pliers, and hammers had already been laid out. If the guards hadn't been holding me in a bruising grip, I would be a puddle on the floor. What could they possibly hope to gain from torturing me?

The lamps flickered in the wake of our arrival, throwing ghastly shadows across Jaq's face where she stood in the middle of the room, arms folded and expression grim. A pair of red-clad constables hovered behind her.

The relief at seeing my friend evaporated when her searing gaze grazed me head to toe.

"What took so long?" she asked. She wasn't wearing the hand-me-down gray tunic and trousers like mine. Her clothes were fitted, her blouse embroidered with the sigil of the Sodality on the pressed collar.

"Long way from the library," Yatto answered when I couldn't, too busy trying to understand what was happening.

"The library?" Jaq looked furious, her features made more severe with her hair slicked back from her face and knotted in a single twist down the center of her head. "Can't say I'm surprised, only disappointed." Her words sliced into me. "Let's not waste more time." She stepped aside, revealing a bloody body dangling in chains bolted to the wall behind her.

"What's happening?" I asked, finally giving voice to my confusion as the guards who'd dragged me from the library finally relaxed their grip on my aching arms.

"Seems we can't trust anyone these days." Jaq grabbed the prisoner's hair and wrenched the head back to show me the face.

"Who is that?" I asked.

"You don't recognize a member of the Synod?" Jaq tsked, her tone oddly imperious. "This is Ailia Ogegesoa."

The name was an old one, belonging to the original Qhembalese people who'd barely survived the colonization of the peninsula that was now Savat.

"She doesn't have any facial scars." Of course my mind would snag on this minor detail.

"We'll give her some," Jaq said with derision.

"Why is she in chains?" I asked, bewildered, not least of all by Jaq's behavior.

"She's an arkani." Jaq flung the woman's head back and I winced when her skull cracked against the stone.

"Arkani? On the Synod?" How was that possible?

"Almost impressive, neh?" Yatto said, earning a dark look from Jaq.

"Even more impressive how members of the council and the constabulary failed to recognize this woman for the traitor she is," Jaq said.

"We screen all council members," Yatto said.

"Evidently, not well enough."

"Blame the Department for Arkanic Affairs for faulty devices," Yatto said.

If the screenings involved using the same sort of arkanospy the constables had used on me during my arrest, then the devices weren't worth the metal they were made from.

"Why am I here?" I asked, interrupting Jaq and Yatto's increasingly acrimonious exchange.

"Thought you'd like another living specimen," Jaq said. "To take her apart piece by piece, and let her insides answer what her mouth refuses to."

"I don't understand." My mind reeled. I wasn't the one in chains about to be dissected. Somehow, I'd been spared—exactly as I knew I would, were it not for Yatto's intimidation tactics.

I scowled at him, wishing he was the one I was about to eviscerate.

"Hopefully, you will soon. Bring a table and more light." Jaq snapped her fingers and the constables jumped to obey, dragging a table better suited to autopsies from a dark corner while another guard left to presumably fetch more lamps.

Jaq was clearly in charge, but how? I knew her family had

money, but it hadn't been enough to save her from this predicament and surely wouldn't have granted her this level of command even if she'd willingly joined the order.

"With First Council only a few days away, I thought you'd be a little less tedious, but you seem determined to try my patience," Jaq said.

"I—" I had no words, my mind frozen.

"Oh, come on, Niki. It's not that complicated. You cut, I'll question." She shoved a scalpel into my hand while Yatto and the constables secured the unconscious woman to the table. "Or must I truly do everything for you?"

"What?" I stammered, my head full of shadow-racket and my heart walloping against my ribs. This must be a fever dream or some fatigue-induced hallucination. Nothing made sense, but the blade in my hand felt real enough. A guard returned with more lamps, the smell of the oil nauseating, the sudden brightness lancing my eyes.

"We're days away from First Council," Jaq continued. "And you need to provide answers if you don't want to end up like dear Ailia here."

I closed my eyes and counted my breaths as I tried to calm myself, but it was impossible to feel anything but rising panic.

"Honestly, I don't know what my mother saw in you," Jaq said.

Her words punctured me like porcupine quills, the barbs lodged deep.

"Your mother?" I managed to whisper, my mind swirling.

"For more than a year, I've watched you bumble your way

through research, endured your trifling theories, and your vrotting, ear-bleeding *music*, and still—nothing. You're clearly not the genius we thought you were. Just a disappointment."

The air left my lungs in a dizzying rush as my veins shriveled and my heart instantly atrophied.

"A disappointment?" I asked, capable only of repeating Jaq's hateful words.

"My mother believed you were onto something, given the modicum of success at the old temple. She was convinced that with the right motivation and resources, you'd be able to unlock the secrets Scryali took to her grave." Jaq sighed. "You seemed closer than anyone else." She shot Yatto an accusatory look I couldn't begin to parse. "You were our best hope at deciphering all this." She gestured vaguely at the shackled arkani. "And yet here we are, so unless you fancy a life in chains, I strongly suggest you start dissecting this traitor and pray you find the answers in her flesh."

I stared at the blade in my hand. Confusion made my head throb and my guts roil. Jaq, my only friend and confidant, my colleague and the closest thing I had to family. She'd been my first and only friend in Savat. All that time we'd worked side by side, I'd never stopped to question why someone like her would take a bumpkin like me under her wing. It had been a ruse, of course. How foolish I'd been.

"How long can a person survive vivisection?" Jaq directed her question at Yatto. "I don't want the arkani to expire before she's told us everything she knows about my mother."

"Your mother?" I asked again.

"Kazwe Olonza," Jaq said, which only made my head spin faster, the cacophony between my ears becoming a roar. "She's missing." I had to strain to hear her through the din. "Went off on some clandestine mission and now she's gone, no doubt taken by ungrateful dissidents like this dog's mother—" she pointed at Ailia, "who thought she could corrupt our city council."

"Kazwe Olonza is your mother?" Kazwe Olonza, vice-chair of the Synod and leader of the Sodality. The jagged pieces slotted into place, completing an ugly picture I couldn't believe I'd failed to see.

"Yes," Jaq said. "She needs to prove to the Synod the Sodality should take charge of the city, embrace the future and all, but you're taking too vrotting long." She glowered at me. "At least now we have a real chance at uncovering whatever treachery Ailia and her ilk have been plotting. So best you dig out something we can use, Niki," she said, shedding all pretense of friendship. "Or we might have no further use for you."

They'd broken Ailia's hands, every finger smashed and swollen. Even if they let her live and allowed her a physicker's care, she'd never carve another sigil.

They hadn't taken her tongue yet. That would come later, once Jaq had her answers, if she didn't just kill the arkani and be done with it.

No, Ailia's death wouldn't be quick. The Sodality had been betrayed, the Synod duped by one of their own, the structural integrity of the city undermined by a woman who'd somehow hidden her magic-wielding from everyone. They'd make an example of her, a public spectacle even more grotesque than the impaled arkani already adorning the gates.

With trembling hands, I started with the clothes, slicing through rich fabric crusted with blood and filth from the dungeon floor, relieved and grateful it wasn't me strapped to this table.

"So slow," Yatto said, and my resentment of the man solidified into hatred even as I willed my hands to work faster.

Beneath the layers of imported silk, I found a strip of spotted pelt. It was old and worn, knotted around her waist where it wouldn't be seen, as if her Qhembalese blood was something shameful. Perhaps she'd feared others on the Synod wouldn't take her seriously if they knew her heritage. There were those in Savat who still believed the original people of this country were somehow less than the foreigners who'd come ashore in search of riches.

Like most people in my village, I had a mixed heritage. There, we were all blends of local and imported blood, but no one cared unless you had the gift—or curse—of magic.

I sliced away the bodice, blushing as I revealed the living flesh beneath.

"Oh, what's that?" Jaq reached for the amulet lying exposed on the woman's chest. She cried out and leapt back, shaking her fingers as if she'd been stung.

The constables drew their pangas while Yatto only raised a questioning brow from where he sat backwards on a rickety chair, looking decidedly bored.

"It scorched me." Jaq held up her hand, fingertips bubbling with blisters.

With the tip of the blade, I cautiously touched the thong threaded through the wooden medallion. When the contact produced no adverse effects, I used the blade to raise the amulet from the woman's chest. There were blisters on her skin beneath it—some dried, some still oozing.

"Is it magical?" Yatto asked.

"Obviously," Jaq bit out as she stalked back toward the table. "Did you see this when you found her?" She directed her question at the constables.

"No, imzi," the constable addressed Jaq with the honorific usually reserved for high-ranking officials. "We found her near the palace. We thought she was injured, but when we tried to help, she fought us with spells, although something wasn't right."

"With the magic," the other constable added. "Never seen an arkani looking so vexed. It's how we got hands on her though, so good thing she bungled it."

"Fought with nails and teeth too." The constable touched his face. Four long gouges ran from temple to jaw. The scabs caught the light in strange refractions. I must be imagining the gemstones growing from the wound. My fatigued brain must be succumbing to hallucination.

Jaq studied the constable too, then grabbed his chin and

jerked his head to the side. "Just like the rest of this city," she said, derisively. "Ailia must be the cause of it, or perhaps a victim of her own spell gone awry. Would serve her right."

"What do you mean?" I asked.

"This nonsense." She pointed at the constable's face. "It's all over the city. They're trying to sabotage us, to destroy everything we've built."

So there were gems growing from the hyena's face. I blinked and shook my head.

"Who?" I turned my attention back to the amulet.

"Qhemba," Jaq said. "While searching for my mother, the constabulary discovered fanes to the old gods and several arkani hiding in the shacks. Seems the whole township has been plotting rebellion. Something must've gone wrong though." She gestured to Ailia. "There are pockets of strange magic polluting the city." Her lip curled in disgust.

"Not to mention all the weird flowers," Yatto added.

I twisted the blade, accidentally flipping over the amulet. Yatto was blathering on about botany but I wasn't listening, his voice drowned out by my screaming thoughts. There was a sigil on the amulet.

A choked whimper escaped my throat; the screeching in my head settled into the serrated syllables of a language both familiar and obscure.

"What is it?" Jaq was at my side. "Isn't that the same sigil from the music score?"

I nodded again as I bit my tongue, harder and harder until I tasted copper and the pain cleared a path through my brain, allowing me to think again.

Scryali's sigil, the one she'd used repeatedly in a composition to end the world, now on an amulet connected to misbehaving magic. Out of habit, I began to hum the same hexatonic children's song.

"What the vrot?" Jaq said, elongating every syllable.

I looked down into the open eyes of the arkani. They were mesmerizing and chilling. I stared as a shadow moved within them, darkness consuming the irises holding the lamp glow like twin flames. Still I hummed. I couldn't stop, the compulsion too strong even though my throat itched. If only I'd brought the kora with me. I needed *more*.

"I need an instrument," I said.

"This isn't a soiree," Jaq snapped and I gave her a withering gaze, momentarily forgetting she was the daughter of Kazwe Olonza and heir apparent to the Sodality.

"If I can test my theory, I might provide some answers." I tried not to let my growing agitation show. "I need my kora."

"Fine," Jaq said. "Yatto, go get the instrument."

Yatto grumbled something about Jaq not being head of the Sodality yet but still did her bidding.

"What's your theory then?" Jaq folded her arms.

I scrambled to corral my scattered thoughts as I rubbed my jaw, Scryali's refrain playing on repeat in my mind, now with added lyrics I couldn't understand.

"I think Scryali's sigil denotes a chord," I said. "The Godchord."

"Scryali was delusional." Jaq looked utterly unimpressed.

"Perhaps, but I think she discovered a way to control magic through the use of a very specific chord."

"What's so special about it?" Jaq asked.

"I think it's built on fourths like the quartal chords used to harmonize more powerful spells, except it uses the forbidden tritone. The Serpent Tone."

"I thought that weakened spells," Jaq said.

"In the writings of Grand Arkani Anjaria Moy..." Writings I had dismissed as not very helpful. "The tritone caused unpredictable reactions during spellwork. Perhaps that's why it was truly banned."

"And you think this mystical, forbidden chord is somehow connected to whatever that is?" Jaq pointed at the amulet.

"I suppose we're about to find out," I said as Yatto stomped back into the room and handed me my kora. Gladly, I discarded the scalpel in exchange for the instrument. My very first kora had been a rare and precious gift from my parents, my father teaching me how to tune and play while my mother sang. I'd never felt closer to them, my heart swelling with the hope they'd finally love me. Despite how easily I took to the instrument, their disappointment in me only grew. Music alone would never be good enough, not when they wanted magic.

If only they could see me now.

"You may want to stand back." If this worked, I had no idea what would happen. It might not be enough to simply play the right notes. They might need to be played in a specific order, each interval slotted into place like the teeth of a key in a lock. With six notes, there were—I tried to mentally calculate the number of possible combinations. There were far too many. Perhaps the order didn't matter as much as the resulting overtones. Perhaps the quality of the resonance would be enough to de-arkanisticate the particles, if there even were any.

In the amulet, perhaps? In the shadow beneath my skin?

Perhaps this would be my swansong, the chord liberating the shadow from my flesh in a gory explosion that claimed my life in the process.

Perhaps, perhaps, perhaps—my brain throbbed and skin burned, both full of shadow. And Ailia glared up at me with murder in her eyes as Jaq glowered with growing impatience.

Taking a steadying breath, I hummed Scyrali's tune and let my fingers caress the strings. I quickly abandoned consonance in favor of the tritone, delighted when Yatto winced. Ailia squirmed, the blemish on her skin darkening and the itch in my own throat intensifying along with the clamor in my skull, but still the music failed to conjure any magic.

With a sigh, I surrendered to the music the way I had in the library. I closed my eyes, letting the music wrap me in its strange currents. A familiar buzz of vibration began in my back teeth and this time I didn't fight it, letting the music overwhelm my senses and wash through my thoughts, listening to the sharp syllables crack like frost without trying to understand them. Vibration—sound—was the source of all creation. We all thrummed, entrained to the firmament and part of the resonant universe, each of us a tone in the sonic tapestry uniting us all—perhaps even magic.

Improvising with nothing but instinct and my ear to guide me, I alternated between augmented and diminished fourths with a few perfect intervals thrown into the mix for good measure. The vibration intensified and sent tremors down my spine. I opened my eyes to find myself staring into Ailia's. Shadows welled like inky tears and spilled across her face. Only these trails were beneath her skin, flooding down her throat to puddle on her chest beneath the amulet.

The fine hairs on the back of my neck rose in a prickle. Yatto moaned and held his head, as did the constables. Jaq visibly paled but stepped closer to observe as I continued to play, letting the gyre of harmonics sweep me up in its embrace.

The amulet began to smoke, the wood—and the arkani's skin—charring as the chord reverberated off the stone walls, the echoes layering dissonance upon dissonance. My body felt strange, not entirely my own, as the itch spread up the back of my throat and into my nose like an oncoming sneeze. My tongue itched too, the way it did whenever I ate cherries, the muscle flexing and contracting, shaping the sounds vibrating in my teeth into the eerie, elongated vowels and whip-snap consonants of the syllables inside my skull.

The shadow peeled off the arkani's chest, tendrils wrapping around the amulet like fingers as that too lifted into the air. A dark mist poured out of my mouth, the shadow that had infected me tangling with the one rising from the arkani. I tasted aniseed and burdock, the bitterness of frost and the crisp iciness of winter. The shadows writhed, but their touch felt oddly comforting.

Time slowed, thickening like the porridge my mother used to make. She'd stirred it constantly, keeping a steady pace to stop clumps from forming until it was ready. My music was the wooden spoon now, my heart keeping time as magic curdled the air.

"You have no idea..." Ailia's words slurred in phonetic syncopation. "The magic. It's mine. You can't have it!" Her cries morphed into a counter-melody, a quarter beat behind my own as if she were trying to nullify the music, but her descant only added to the dissonance.

"What are you doing?" Yatto asked, his fists clenched.

"Niki, stop." Jaq attempted to grab my arm, but her hand stopped a hair's breadth from making contact as if she'd encountered an invisible pane of glass. Her eyes widened as she reached for me again, her gestures almost comical. When I stopped singing to suck in a breath, the shield gave way and she wrenched the kora from my grasp. The instrument landed on the floor with a sickening crunch, the wood and harmony shattered, the strange spell broken.

The shadows knotted about the amulet disentangled and I inhaled my own smoky fragment as the other dropped like a wet cloth back onto the arkani. As did the amulet, thumping into bruised skin to lie smoldering. Ailia screamed and thrashed, knocking the scalpel from the table.

Even without my instrument, the God-chord echoed in my head, the harmonies writhing in my bones as if something inside me had been liberated. I reached for the amulet.

The slick puddle of shadow glommed to my fingers as if I'd plunged my hand into ice water, and it sent a shudder of pleasure up my spine.

"No. It's mine. You can't have it!" Ailia continued to scream, spittle flying, and teeth gnashing like a mongoose caught in a snare.

"Niki, put it down," Jaq said. "It's not yours."

Fury sizzled through my veins. The amulet was absolutely mine and I wouldn't let her steal it from me. It fit into my hand so perfectly, the weight a comfort, the sigil pressed against my palm pleasantly cool as the shadows conjoined and twined up my fingers.

"She said drop it," Yatto said, taking a menacing step toward me.

This time, I wouldn't be so easily cowed. He was nothing, when I held infinite possibility—and power—in the palm of my hand. I retrieved the scalpel from the floor, as Yatto and the constables stepped closer.

My research. My music. The amulet was mine now, too, and they would have to pry it from my corpse if they wanted it.

"Niki, please, it could be dangerous. You should put it down," Jaq said slowly as if I were an irate toddler refusing to share a toy. "Look at what it's already doing to you."

I dropped my gaze to my hand. The darkness had spread up my wrist. The music continued to resound in my head, the sibilant syllables distinct, if still incomprehensible. But I didn't need to understand the words to glean the sentiment.

The amulet was mine, and no one else could have it.

Yatto lunged, his hands like claws. The shadows hardened, bruising me from the inside out. He grabbed at my arm and I flailed in self-defense. I was still clutching the scalpel though, and he only brandished his fists. Finally, I'd see him humbled, the smirk wiped from his mouth.

But it wasn't Yatto I stabbed.

Taking advantage of our tussle perhaps, Jaq slid between us, her gaze locked on the amulet. I swung at Yatto who blocked my arm, knocking me off balance as I refused to release the amulet. I stumbled into Jaq, the sharp blade sliding into soft flesh.

For a moment, silence. In the cell—and in my head—as Jaq staggered back. She blinked wide eyes at me, her hands already sticky red where she grappled at the hilt protruding from her stomach.

"No!" Yatto caught her as she toppled, blood spilling from the wound.

I hadn't meant to hurt her. Despite all her lies and empty friendship, I'd wanted it to be Yatto writhing in agony. Not Jaq.

The constables reached me, only to slam against the shield of screaming shadow now engulfing me. They toppled, slipping on slicked stone. The constable with the ruby-flecked face shattered on impact, a gruesome scatter of gemstones amid chunks of granite and bone-shaped sandstone.

While the other constable vomited diamonds and opals, I wrenched on the amulet, snapping the thong around Ailia's neck and ignoring the woman's enraged screams, before turning to leave.

Yatto cradled Jaq, his face ashen. His expression morphed from anger to fear as I approached, and he started to mutter familiar words even as he tended to Jaq.

He was *praying,* the same supplications beaten into me as a child to gods he was supposed to shun. His gaze flicked briefly to the bloody scalpel lying between us, but I kicked it out of reach before striding out of the dungeon in possession of both the amulet and a cloak of protective shadow.

The Principles of Inyoti as recorded by the first arkani blessed by the Ancestors to carry that most sacred fragment of the Serpent God within their hearts. Thus are the tenets upon which we build our society.

Fourth Principle—Trust, Cooperation, and Solidarity: *Members of society build mutual trust by working collaboratively toward improving the quality of life for all. Working together for the greater good, to maintain harmony and overcome challenges, to minimize moments of discord and strife ensures the survival of the community.*

Chapter Twenty-One

Zal

Ailia could never leave the world without Zal sensing her departure.

She'd been by his side for the better part of a century. The child who'd frayed his patience even while his chest swelled with inconceivable pride, the girl who'd exhausted him with her petulance and determination, and the woman who'd filled his heart cavity with a warmth he'd thought was love—warmth that had since drained away, leaving only ache and emptiness in the wake of her treachery.

If she were dead, he would know it, feel it like a brick to the back of the head, like being flayed open again and again, turning white snow scarlet.

"I have to know," he said to Emri.

The sciomancer stilled, head cocked in consideration. "I'm not fully recovered, Va'ili. After the bonding spell—"

"This is your specialty, is it not?" Zal asked with impatience. "Your true power and purpose?"

"It is," Emri admitted. "Were I at full strength I wouldn't hesitate, but as I am, I can't guarantee results."

"I wouldn't ask if I—" Zal would not admit his desperation. It was fury at the thought of being robbed of revenge making him despair. Fury—not grief, he tried to convince himself.

"The Sodality wouldn't kill a Synod member," Lana interjected. "Not immediately. Especially not if they know she's an arkani."

No, they'd kill her slowly, sure to make a spectacle of it, a warning to the public and demonstration of their power. There was hope she lived, then.

"Emri," Zal said, and the sciomancer nodded without further argument.

"In the shade. I'll need water and food for after, and someone to steady me if I lose consciousness," he said, already walking toward a thatched lapa where there were refreshments set out for the workers.

"I'll be right here," Zal assured.

"Lose consciousness? What's he going to do?" Lana asked, keeping pace beside Zal as he hobbled after the ghost-talker.

"What he must," Zal said.

Emri didn't bother with a chair, sitting cross-legged on the ground with his back resting against one of the wooden pillars. Gingerly, Zal eased himself onto a low stool beside the sciomancer, ignoring his protesting body mostly bereft of Leksi's magic.

Lana folded her arms, observing, as Emri closed his eyes and began a chant similar to the one he'd used for the tracing spell. It seemed a more powerful incantation, though, one Zal felt thrumming in his teeth, a sympathetic quivering that struck each bone as if his skeleton were a balafon being played once more by that invisible hand.

His shadows jostled, their tremulous forms adding a peculiar accompaniment to the sciomancer's song. For moments that dragged into what seemed like hours, Emri sang, his voice faltering as he struggled for breath. Blood dribbled from his nose and tears trailed red down his cheeks gone gray with strain. More than once Zal wanted to tell him to stop, but thoughts of Ailia fermented in his mind. Was she alive or dead, he had to know.

Emri continued, the song wobbling as he struggled, head drooping as if too heavy for his neck. Zal laid a supportive hand on the man's shoulder despite how much even this simple movement caused his joints to ache.

"Stop this," Lana said when blood trickled from Emri's ear. "It's too much."

"Come on," Zal whispered, not sure who he was beseeching. "You can do this, Emri."

The sciomancer's head jerked up and the song stopped. He stared unblinking, his eyes turned white with moon-glow, the effect so eerie even Zal shivered as Emri's opaque gaze latched onto his.

"*Va'ili*," he said, but the voice wasn't his alone. A second voice had been superimposed on the sciomancer's tongue. "*Va'ili, did you even notice I was gone*?"

"What's happening?" Lana asked. Several workers had paused to observe as well, and anger rippled through Zal. He'd never seen Emri possessed, although he knew it was possible. Not all ghost-touched could control the spirits. Some succumbed, minds frayed by the whispers, their edges of self blurred by the relentless presence of the dead. Emri had always been so strong and so in control of his Ancestor-bestowed magic. Emri had warned him, though, that fatigue made him vulnerable to the restless wraiths.

"Sometimes the spirits talk back," Zal said. "Sciomancers are conduits after all. The connection can go both ways." He peered through the glare in Emri's eyes, trying to glimpse the spirit who'd usurped his body. "Tell me who you are and what you want," Zal said, his shadows creeping closer, ever protective.

"I wanted justice." The voice was sibilant in its sorrow. *"I wanted to make things right for us. I wanted you to love me, to love us. We were loyal to your cause. Did you miss me?"*

"The constabulary took you," Zal said, making an educated guess. He should've kept better inventory of his followers. In the beginning, he'd known every acolyte by name. He'd learned their histories and their languages if they weren't from Savat. He'd cared about them, made them promises, cultivated their adoration. He didn't know when he'd started taking their devotion for granted.

"Yes," the voice fractured with pain.

"Where did you die?" Zal asked.

"In darkness. They broke my fingers, took my tongue. They cut away at me, piece by piece. My legs, my legs," the voice moaned. *"They ripped your promise from my skin."*

Where was that scrap of chaos now, Zal wondered. "Did you see Ailia? Do you know where they're keeping her?"

"Ailia, Ailia, always Ailia, and precious Emri." Emri's hand

jerked, index finger slowly curling into a hook. The man's whole body was shaking with strain.

"We died. For you, for you, for you," the voice repeated. Emri's hand jerked again, a sigil started as the words became a hum, the tune uncanny in its familiarity.

It transported Zal back in time, the centuries erased as easily as a scuff mark on a shoe. He was with Scryali again, entranced by her music, amused by her theories that a simple scale might be the key to unlocking primordial magic—*his* magic. That tune though. His shadows writhed as the hexatonic sequence he'd all but forgotten filtered into his ears. He drew in a breath that didn't hurt quite as much as the refrain washed over him, through him, a tremor of arousal coursing through his depleted veins.

Abruptly, the tune transposed and it felt as if ice water had been poured down Zal's spine. This wasn't Scryali's music, but rather the microtonal layali typical of traditional joRanian songs. Again, he was shunted into the past, to that very first temple where he'd been nothing but a puddle of gore, the chants and prayers a slow-working panacea. He'd heard music like this every day on the streets of joRania, and every night in the slums where Gafina lived.

The tune solidified into a new and different voice. *"Release me,"* the spirit intoned in the beZebi dialect rarely heard in Savat. *"You stole what was never yours. Return it."*

"You'll have to be more specific," Zal said, struggling with the curlicue syllables of the joRanian language. Zal had committed many thefts over the decades. Several of the books and artifacts adorning his citadel shelves hadn't been acquired by honest means, never mind the lives he'd stolen to replenish his magic.

"Release me, you moon-eyed, ghost-addled, soul-snatcher," the voice demanded, tone imperious. It seemed Zal wasn't the only one who'd pilfered and purloined. Emri shuddered, head knocking against the pillar as blood oozed in viscous rivulets from his eyes and ears.

"Who are you?" Zal asked, curiosity getting the better of him despite Emri's increasing distress.

"You will undo what you have done. You will release me." Emri's arm twitched like a marionette's, his shaking hand once more struggling to scribe a sigil.

Zal caught the sciomancer's fingers. He focused his own magic, intending to release the menacing spirit, but Emri's grip tightened as he whispered, "Don't."

"Come back to me then," Zal said, dredging another near-forgotten language from the quagmire of his mind. "It's enough," he said in the lilting syllables of the Yekkä nomads. "Banish this wraith and come back to me, Emri. Please."

Emri tensed, his body going rigid as he fought for control. Zal pressed his hand against the man's chest, feeding what little power he had to spare into the scrap of shadow beneath Emri's skin. Slowly, the sciomancer's shivering subsided. He stilled and Zal caught him, not caring about Emri's blood staining the fine silk of his shirt or the way his shoulder twisted out of its socket with an audible pop. He allowed himself a moment to luxuriate in the cool press of Emri's body and the gossamer swish of the man's hair. Zal inhaled, ignoring the scent of floral soap to savor the glacial aroma of death—so reminiscent of the Nether—which perpetually clung to the sciomancer's skin.

"Is he..." Lana watched, arms crossed, face stricken.

"He lives," Zal said. Emri's heart beat quick but steady beneath his palm, his breath warm against Zal's neck.

As Zal cradled the recovering sciomancer, he took some comfort in the fact it hadn't been Ailia trying to possess, but that didn't mean she wasn't dead. Zal glanced at Emri's red-splotched face, wondering why he insisted on keeping an angry joRanian ghost like a venomous pet.

"Va'ili?" Emri finally spoke and Zal exhaled in relief.

"Here." Lana offered him a cup of water and Zal reluctantly released Emri so he could drink.

"I'm sorry—I never intended..." He closed his eyes and smoothed back his blood greased hair. "I'm usually strong enough to keep my ghosts in check."

Zal's mind swarmed with questions but only one truly mattered. "What about Ailia?"

"I couldn't find her," Emri said, scraping a scab from his eye. "Either she lives or she's already beyond my reach."

Zal doubted she'd have willingly walked into the Nether if she'd been tortured and murdered at the hands of the Sodality. If anyone would resist Death, determined to become a vengeful spirit, it was Ailia.

"She lives," Zal said. "I'm certain of it." But for how much longer?

"I saw what they did." Emri squeezed his eyes shut and inhaled. "I felt Gilla's pain." He rubbed his shins as if to ensure his legs were undamaged.

Gilla. A fire arkani Zal had recruited a few years ago whose face he couldn't remember.

"We can't let that happen to Ailia," Emri said. "I know she wronged you, but she doesn't deserve to suffer at the hands of the Sodality."

If anyone was going to break her fingers and cut her into pieces, it would be Zal. He'd kill every godless Sodalite who dared to touch her.

"We have to go to the palace," Zal said. "They'll hold her there, until they can make a spectacle of her murder."

"First Council is in four days," Lana said. "They'll probably execute her there, make it a real show with everyone present." The would-be queen frowned and absentmindedly stroked the serpent inked on her arm.

"We need to go now then," Zal said. She was most assuredly already being tortured, a thought that hurt more than any of Zal's open wounds.

"Why? Our plan can still succeed. This changes nothing," Lana said.

"Once I have Ailia, you can do as you please," Zal said. "Assuming First Council still goes ahead with the city on fire."

"All the more reason for the Synod to meet," Lana said.

"Think they'll wait four days?" Emri asked.

"Not if the Synod declares an emergency," she said.

"Then we have to hurry." Emri struggled to his feet, swaying, and using Zal to steady himself. "Thank you, Va'ili," he whispered.

"No, thank you," Zal said. He wanted to apologize, too, for forcing Emri to use his magic when he was clearly exhausted, for forcing Emri to experience the suffering of an arkani Zal should've done more to protect from the Sodality, but Lana interjected.

"It'll take time to transport the gunpowder," she said. "We were planning to leave tomorrow night."

"And march up to the doors of the palace with a wagon full of explosives?" Zal asked, his patience worn thin with worry and anger.

"Of course not." She gave him a withering look that any other time might've cost the human her eyes, but Zal was sore and too preoccupied holding up Emri to punish her for insolence. "My family built that palace. The Sodality are ignorant squatters. They don't know the true layout of the palace, the hidden passages, of which there are many only accessible with a sigil or spell." Lana smiled. "As a true royal, I would know."

Clever. Wise even. When—if—Zal ever returned to rebuild his citadel, he would need to undertake some clandestine construction of his own.

"We'll go now," Zal said, wondering if either he or Emri would have the strength to make it to the palace. He'd go alone if Emri was too weak. He'd survived worse, and he would endure this if it meant wrenching Ailia away from their enemies. "Do you have maps? Can you tell us how to get in?"

"No maps," she said. "And to tell you, I'd have to trust

you." Her gaze narrowed.

Zal straightened, sudden rage dulling the pain in his protesting joints. His fury became palpable, a vinegar smear across his tongue as he glowered at this petty human with her ridiculous notions of waking ancient gods and usurping power.

"I am Chaos," Zal said, drawing what magic he could from the connection with his sister. The sigil on his palm throbbed and he pulled harder, as if reeling in a whale on a flimsy rod. His shadows billowed around him, and he delighted as Lana gaped, her fear spicing the air like sweet tamarind.

"I am the son of Death and Time." The bitter truth of his birthright stung his lips, but there was no point denying it. "You will obey me or perish."

Lana dropped to her knees, muttering prayers. Her obeisance was a balm, alleviating the incessant ache clenching his body like a fist.

"Tell us how to access these secret passages and you will—" He hesitated, not sure if the spawn of Death could offer anything but curses. "You will be honored by Death and her children."

"Come now, Lana." Emri placed a hand on her trembling shoulder. "Best not to keep Chaos waiting." The faintest twitch of a smile played on Emri's lips, and Zal glimpsed a darkness in the sciomancer he'd previously dismissed as a side effect of the man's proximity to Death. Perhaps there was more to it though, and perhaps Zal would be wise to be wary of someone who'd always seemed the epitome of loyalty. He'd never doubted Ailia either.

An hour later, Zal and Emri had changed clothes again, eaten to replenish their strength, and learned all they could about the secret passages. Lana had suspended digging for the day, already mobilizing her forces to begin transporting the gunpowder.

Zal felt oddly spry and unencumbered. After his little display at the lapa, the workers had begun bowing to him, muttering prayers, and placing more offerings at the fane to Death. Zal had feasted, their prayers as filling as the copious quantities of food Lana had supplied. While it wasn't nearly enough to eradicate all his pain, Zal could walk without limping and his joints no longer threatened to escape from their sockets. Emri still looked haggard as they headed to the stables.

"I'm fine," he argued, despite the bruises darkening his sunken eyes. "Two horses will be faster."

"Not if you topple from the saddle and get trampled. We ride together." That way the sciomancer could rest safely nestled in Zal's arms, which had nothing to do with Zal's desire to breathe in the subtle fragrance of the Nether wafting from the man. "The horses are descendants of royal stock. They're strong and swift." Zal chose a fiery-eyed stallion with heavily feathered feet and a swirl of white between its eyes like an interrupted sigil. The horse was huge, muscles bulging beneath a satin-black coat as it pranced, light-footed despite its bulk.

Zal mounted first, then hauled Emri up in front of him.

"Sleep if you can. You'll need all your strength once we get to the palace," Zal said and took up the reins, making sure

Emri was secure between his arms before turning his eager mount toward the city.

He sent a cadre of shadows streaking across the veld to search for Leksi, to share their plan with her, and report back on happenings in the city. If Ailia died before they could secure the amulet, or if the Sodality in their infinite ignorance attempted to use the amulet, the consequences could be devastating.

Urging the horse into a canter, Zal tightened his hold on the already snoring sciomancer and bit his tongue, silencing the prayer for Time to be on their side.

Chapter Twenty-Two
Leksi

Greasy black smoke billowed above Savat. The city stank of burning wood, scorched metal, and singed flesh. Not to mention the reek of Zal's magic, so much more pungent when ignited by arkani flames. And it wasn't only Zal's. There was another foetor mixed into the miasma Leksi almost recognized.

The air crackled with magic, making every hair on her body stand up.

"You could stop this," she appealed to Air in Nethertaal, as if her father would deign to concern himself with the fate of humans who'd turned their backs on the gods. It would take a monsoon to douse these flames.

She dared not call on her uncle and keeper of the Waters. A mighty wave would extinguish the fires but kill just as many, and leave a wake of even greater destruction. Earth couldn't do much except open her gullet and swallow the place whole, and Fire—she was no doubt convulsing in spasms of ecstasy as the city burned.

Death couldn't help the living; it was beyond her purview. She would be waiting, though, perhaps already lounging beside the river watching the currents fill with the iridescent souls of the recently deceased. Her storks would be busy.

There'd be no rest for Grief today.

As for Time, Leksi would rather see the city and every single inhabitant charred to a crisp than call on *him*.

That wasn't entirely true, but she'd have to be nothing more than fish food in the Waters of Consequence before she begged Time for help.

Trusting her instincts, Leksi prowled through the streets, her heart racing with an unwelcome mix of disgust and glee. As much as she wanted Zal's claims to be nothing but lies, she knew there was no escaping her nature, not while magic gnashed its teeth within her.

The city had become a living nightmare, but this wasn't her doing. She inhaled the human terror, hoping it would quell her hungry beasts. Again, that putrescent odor, different from Zal's, assailed her senses. Each of their magic carried such a distinct and unpleasant aroma, but she couldn't quite place this, equal parts foreign and familiar.

She pushed forward, wading through a tide of fleeing citizens. Some headed to the coast, to pile into boats and wait out the fires from the safety of the sea. Others fled north, to the mountains perhaps and sands beyond, or to wine country where a zealous princess was digging holes in search of a sleeping god.

The city was succumbing to chaos, but Zal wasn't only to blame. He'd been here for centuries, his presence taking an inexorable toll on the people until Ailia had come along and expedited the inevitable.

For all the good it would do, Leksi wanted to wring the

arkani's neck herself. Part of her wanted to punish her brother, too. This far from him, she could ravel up her magic and deny him the barest dregs. Instead, she left the channel open. He wouldn't be able to do his part to save the city if he could barely stand.

She passed streets choked with frostweed and dismembered bodies, dodged rats sporting all manner of magical mutations, and kept her distance from the city's cats. The creatures roamed in gore-streaked clowders, stalking unperturbed through the carnage. Her thoughts drifted to Ansa and The Anchorage, which probably lay in smoking ruins now.

If Tamisk had made it to her friends in Qhemba, she'd be in the eastern quarter closest to the sea where Tsirayan immigrants usually settled. Leksi hurried, fighting her way through mobs of Qhembalese locals clashing with the constabulary. Cudgels rose, pangas fell, rifles bellowed, and bullets zinged through the air, sometimes hitting flesh, sometimes turning into flowers or bats as they passed through clouds of magic.

She could only hope Salja and the others had enough sense to stay hidden. If Tamisk was with them, she'd have gotten them to safety: to a boat, out to sea, taken them all the way to the Tsirayan atoll even if she'd vowed never to return to her homeland.

Leksi coughed behind the makeshift scarf she'd made after tearing off the sleeve of her blouse to tie around her face. She fought the urge to rub her eyes, letting involuntary tears wash away the ash. A gust of wind cut through the smoke like cat claws on fine curtains, revealing a familiar figure wielding a cudgel.

For several heartbeats, Leksi could only watch in awe as Tamisk beat back a cackle of hyenas, absorbing half as many blows as she delivered. Her clothes were soot-stained and tattered, her biceps bore raw welts where her skin had been seared by fire, and blood matted her hair into sharp spikes.

Leksi had never been more in love.

Her parasites roiled, ebullient at the sight of violence, at the fresh bouquet of blood spilling from a broken mouth. Teeth skittered across the cobbles, snatched up by snarls of frostweed and transformed into pearlescent petals.

But Tamisk was flagging despite support from other humans. The smoke was too thick, the hyenas too many. Leksi cried out a warning, startling Tamisk mid-kick. The Tsirayan faltered and caught the blade Leksi had been too slow to intercept. She grabbed the hyena by the throat, her nails extending into talons, her canines elongating to puncture her lip, allowing tendrils of magic to escape her furious veins. Those nearby screamed as Leksi's magic infected their mind with fresh terror.

Under her fingers, bones and cartilage shattered, and soft tissue turned to pulp. The constable's eyes widened, piss soaking their trousers, as they stared into the face of Nightmare. Leksi inhaled their terror before unceremoniously discarding the corpse. She licked her lips, swallowing her blood and magic before turning to Tamisk. The Tsirayan knelt with one hand pressed to her belly, the other pressed to her forehead as if she were trying to gouge out whatever nightmares Leksi's magic had conjured.

There should've been blood—and a lot of it—from a gut wound, but sea foam gathered around the slit in Tamisk's abdomen, pink-tinged and shrimp-scented.

"Where's Salja?" Leksi asked. If the healer-arkani still lived, there was a chance Tamisk would too. She studied Tamisk's face, trying to gauge the odds. At least her eyes were her own despite the crust of tiny barnacles adhered to her face.

"At Jinka's," Tamisk said. Leksi knew where the woman lived and it wasn't far. She scooped Tamisk up despite her protests; she wouldn't let Tamisk die here, not like this.

Hair singed, skin soot-streaked, and lungs burning from smoke inhalation, Leksi plowed her way through the riots to the abandoned eastern quarter. Many homes here had collapsed, whole rows reduced to cinders. Although Tamisk was limp and heavy in her arms, feet dragging more than stumbling, Leksi guided them through the debris, searching for Jinka's thatched hut—for Salja, for any survivors at all. It was hard to believe she'd been here just a few days ago for the Solstice.

The rubble was confusing, one jumbled street indistinguishable from another. With Tamisk barely conscious, Leksi resorted to calling Salja's name. She'd never been so resentful of silence. Not even the screech of a gull or croak of a crow. The birds all kept their distance from the flames and belching smoke. Only the ocean rumbled, the tides indifferent to human suffering.

A moan. At first she thought it was the wind through the

ruins. She paused, listened, waiting for the crash of the breakers to fade, and heard it again. Animal or human, it didn't matter. Something was alive.

"Come on, Tam. Just a little further." She kissed Tam's temple and dragged her lover forward toward homes huddled together, the mounds of brick and thatch like the rumpled hem of a flared skirt where the ruffles of rock slowly gathered into cliffs hugging the bay.

Some had survived the fires, and Leksi hoped one of them was Jinka's. Judging by the shape of the cliffs, she was in the right place. They'd been here for dinners and parties, sharing stories and laughter what seemed a lifetime ago.

The first people they came across were dead, some with hair turning to kelp, others with shells for eyes and frostweed erupting from half-open mouths. Closer to the cliff, a few still lived.

Leksi took a moment to crush the throat of a flailing constable, their fingers turned to sea cucumbers. Mercy, she told herself. Putting someone out of their misery wasn't the same as murder.

"Leks, I can't," Tamisk gurgled.

"Just a little further."

Within the dwelling, Leksi finally found what she was looking for. At the back of the hut where the bare cliffside had been used as a wall, Salja was digging through smoldering timbers.

"Help me," she said, glancing back at Leksi. "It's Zadi. She's buried." Salja picked up a chunk of rock that might've once been a foot. Small and narrow, like Zadi's.

Leksi eased Tamisk down beside a larger chunk, propping her up as gently as she could. She then forced herself to peer past the splintered wood and tumbled stone, to see the echoes of a human in the scraps of thatch and puddles of sludge solidifying into sparkling gems. The shapes were all wrong, the body folded into itself like the paper flowers kids made for Solstice.

"She's dead," Leksi said. "But Tamisk isn't and she needs your help."

Salja sagged with a sob and Leksi studied her face, hoping she had enough strength left for one last spell. The girl's one eye was framed by lashes turned to anemone fronds, while the other eyelid had sprouted a fan of fine feathers.

"Please, Salja. You have to try." Leksi squeezed the girl's hand. It was freezing, the veins like lines on a map beneath her pale gray skin.

"They fought," she said, every word a struggle. "I stayed. Waited to heal. I tried to heal..." Her head lolled toward the jumble of debris, her thin chest rising and falling with the whoosh of bellows. "I'm sorry," Salja said with a final exhalation.

Leksi felt the girl's death as the door between worlds briefly opened to claim her.

"Go well," Leksi said. "May the waters find you worthy." She tried to close Salja's staring eyes, but the feathers fluttered as if dreaming of flight and the anemone lid refused to stay shut, the tubular lashes gently sucking at Leksi's fingers.

"Leks?" Tamisk said with a tidepool burble.

"I'm here." Leksi cradled her lover, her bones spongy within bloated flesh. Her body was nearly all reef now, her salt-scent rich and cloying. Leksi took her lover's hand and kissed each crab-claw phalange.

"I thought they'd be safe here," Tamisk said. "I went to help. Bofile and Salja insisted on joining."

Despite everything, Leksi smiled. Of course they'd joined the protest. They were survivors. They hadn't escaped the conversion camps and worse only to cower when the constabulary came to call. Even if it had gotten them killed, Leksi couldn't help but be proud of Tamisk and her charges so willing to fight for themselves and the ones they loved.

"We left Zadi with the younger ones—we left them."

"It's not your fault," Leksi said.

"We should've seen it coming," Tamisk said, her words punctuated by pained gasps. "You could've done something sooner."

Leksi absorbed the admonishing blow, the truth in Tamisk's accusation a hammer to her sternum. The cracks in her bones radiated from the impact as blame settled across her shoulders.

"Is Salja…?" Tamisk left the question unfinished.

"Dead. Zadi too." If the others were amid the rubble, Leksi couldn't recognize them. She should've seen this coming and hadn't; she could've done something, and now she'd have to live with the consequences of her inaction for all eternity.

She wouldn't make the same mistake again.

"I should've—" Tamisk started.

"Shh," Leksi soothed, stroking the tangle of Tamisk's hair. "Do you remember when we first met?" she asked. "Do you remember the poem you said that night?"

"Home is a shark's mouth, but the shore is where I cut my feet on scattered teeth," Tamisk whispered, her words bubbling. "Thought I was so eloquent."

"You were. I was enthralled from the moment you stepped onto that tiny stage. I was in love by the end of the second verse."

"The stars, the salt of a distant ocean." Tamisk tried to move her fingers, but the joints had stiffened with chitin. *"For even the gods have wept, their tears the sea."*

"Yes," Leksi said, tears pricking at her own eyes. "I've never forgotten."

Tamisk sputtered a few more words before her head dipped and she closed her eyes.

"The audacity to ride our waves then claim them as your own." Leksi hugged Tamisk tight. *"To rewrite our stories in another tongue, but the water remembers and sings us true."* Leksi continued the recitation, feeling her lover's chest rise and fall, rise and fall, then stutter and still.

"May the waters find you worthy." Leksi squeezed Tamisk's hand and brushed a kiss on her lover's barnacle speckled forehead. "Ra'ava akimvopi anim'ny matorimaso kizadra ny ayazonak izhay, di'amdidipo sotsare ho'eo anim'ny faokiri ranazak izhay; izma meliti hi'aitsika aninpidana ha no tekera ifray," she added, reciting the Tsirayan farewell for the dead in the Salt tongue then laying Tamisk's hands gently in the woman's lap.

She rose on shaky legs, her knees soaked with the brine oozing from Tamisk's tissues already claimed by the sea. She didn't want to leave her loved ones to the cats and urban scavengers, abandoned in the wreckage beside the bodies of their enemies, but there was no time to fuss over proper funeral rites. She'd always believed she'd exit Tamisk's life long before death could claim her mortal lover.

Eyes burning and limbs leaden with grief, Leksi forced her feet from the ruins, kicking aside the transmogrifying remains of the hateful hyena. She stepped onto the broken street and stared out to sea. Above her, the sky seethed, leaking ash like snow.

For even gods have wept. Leksi clenched her jaw, tasting the death of Qhemba in the grit between her teeth as she drew a deep and damning breath. For the first time in several lifetimes, her monsters settled, calm and sated, content to sleep in her hollows, but Leksi was far from satisfied.

Zal might be chaos, but it was Riksa who reveled in violence, and Leksi recognized the stink now. It was the putrid stench of her sister's magic that tainted the air. If Leksi wanted to stop Savat from destroying itself, she'd have to find Riksa before the civil unrest could blossom into war.

...scholars have long believed in two separate magicks, the blood of the universal womb and primordial essence... mortals wield is some sort of diluted variation... I whole-souly disagree.

...power within every mortal's grasp... pure vibration... so profound it would shatter the universe...

A surviving fragment, allegedly from the notebook of Fetrina Scryali, date unknown; text incomplete due to fire damage

Chapter Twenty-Three
Niki

All the commotion had drawn more guards to the dungeons.

I walked with purpose, humming to keep the panic at bay, hoping I would pass unmolested despite my blood-splattered attire.

"You. Stop." A guard grabbed me, but their hand only skimmed across the carapace of shadow still encasing me. I brandished the amulet, which pulsed like a heart against my palm. Wood should not have been able to beat, and yet there was something *alive* throbbing between my fingers.

"What the vrot?" The guard raised their cudgel but hesitated, gaze riveted on the wisps of darkness slicking my skin.

"Careful, or it might infect you too," I said through gritted teeth and the guards all stepped back. Without hesitation, I scrambled up the stairs, the climb made all the more awkward for the amulet in my hand, but I couldn't bring myself to shove it into a pocket. I couldn't let it go at all. My fingers were curled in a vice-like grip on the hexagonal block of wood, flesh fused to grain. More screams echoed behind me, drawing the guards' attention as I clambered up the remaining steps.

Free of the subterranean darkness, I urged my burning legs

down the hallway, glancing out of the narrow windows to get my bearings.

Despite my thoughts whirling like seagulls about my head, shrieking at me to flee, I headed to my laboratory. I wanted my notebook and the research I'd already completed on Scryali's sigil—the same one carved into the amulet, obscured now by my clawed hand, still pulsing.

Magic. Magic. Magic. My footsteps kept time as the word looped in my mind, the syllables matched to Scryali's tune.

In the lab, I awkwardly gathered up my notes and stuffed them into a satchel, not caring if pages crumpled. As long as I could still read the ink.

I whirled at the sound of footsteps, brandishing the amulet, but found only Moli, her hands raised and eyes wide.

What's happening? She signed.

"I need to get out of here. Do you know the way?" I swung the satchel over my shoulder.

Her gaze dropped to the amulet.

What is that?

"I don't know, but I can't let the Sodality have it. I need it," I said. If they wanted it, they'd have to snap my dead fingers to pry it free. "Can you show me the way out? Please, Moli. We don't have much time." I bounced on the balls of my feet. Every moment I delayed gave the guards a chance to catch up.

Moli shook her head, fear creasing her forehead. *They'll catch you. They'll hurt you.*

"I'll have to take my chances." I strode toward the door, but she blocked my path.

Main doors, she signed. *It's faster.*

"Can you show me?"

Again she hesitated, wasting precious moments.

"Either show me where to go or get out of my way." My voice crackled with sudden anger. Moli's gaze narrowed before she took off like a rabbit, leaving me panting and sweating as I tried to keep up, weighed down by both the satchel and the amulet and a body unused to exertion.

Given the early hour, we managed to avoid the few patrols making their rounds. Either those in the dungeon had not yet raised the alarm, or the arkani had escaped and incapacitated them. I thought briefly of Jaq, a pang in my chest knowing she might be dead, but then I remembered who she was and her deception swept through me like a scythe.

My only friend, the only person I had let get close, the only person I had ever chosen to trust—

Moli reached for me, her hands skating across the shadow cloak, unable to yank me back around the corner where she'd crouched, hidden. Lost in my thoughts, I hadn't been paying attention and jogged into the path of several Sodalites.

"Where are you going in such a hurry?" the tallest one asked.

I glanced down the corridor. We were almost there, the main doors looming, freedom tantalizingly close.

I'd never been a very good liar and words failed me now. The Sodalite narrowed their gaze, noticing my satchel and the amulet in my hand.

"What's that?"

"Research," I said.

"Then best you get back to the lab," another Sodalite said.

If I shoved past them, I might have enough energy left in my legs to make it to the doors.

"That's the one! Stop them!" Guards appeared behind us. These ones were carrying muskets, barrels raised.

"I'm sorry," I said to Moli who stared up at me with wide, imploring eyes.

I'd have to take my chances with the Sodalites and trust the guards wouldn't want to risk hitting any of the gray-clad by taking a shot at me. I darted toward the doors as nimble as a gnu with a broken leg. One of the Sodalites managed to tackle me to the floor, the shadows not entirely impervious to tangled limbs. My elbow smacked the floor first, then my knee, the pain explosive and tearing a scream from my lips. The amulet in my hand smoldered, wisps of smoke peeling from the wood like unfurling ferns. Despite the agony coursing through my body, I began to sing and the corridor filled with echoing overtones of the God-chord.

Magic darted from the amulet and lashed at my attacker who writhed on the floor.

The roar of a musket made me cower, the percussive retort disturbing the harmony. Even as I braced for impact, I kept singing, my voice an endless loop of fourths even as panic soused my senses, all thoughts reduced to survival and escape.

A second musket fired and time seemed to slow. I watched the bullet streak toward me like a hawk plummeting toward prey. I shouldn't have been able to track its movement, but the air had turned to syrup while I droned those same eerie and elongated sounds borrowed from the voices in my head.

I held up the wisping amulet, a smudge like a mirage forming an oily corona around my fist. In another heartbeat, the bullet pierced the mirage and fractured, a dandelion dispersal of metal shards.

Time resumed its regular pulse and I sucked in a much-needed breath, gasping and coughing as I struggled to my feet. Not wanting to trust the strange magic I'd somehow wielded, I bolted for the doors. There were guards there too, alert and waiting as I approached.

I belted the notes, my throat raw from cycling through the tones of the God-chord, trying to suck in air through my nose while simultaneously singing. Dizziness made splotches of my vision, but I kept singing and barreled past the guards—through them—the shadows shredding flesh in my wake. Not pausing to consider the carnage, I shoved open the doors and hurtled toward freedom.

Chapter Twenty-Four
Zal

Secondhand grief swept through him, the force of his sister's pain like being disemboweled.

Her home, her lover, her city—she believed she'd lost all three.

But Savat remained, even if smoke lay like rumpled blankets across the obdurate spires, the charred stink spoiling the sea breeze buffeting Zal's face as they drew closer. Dawn pierced the darkness, turning the ash-choked air as red as flayed flesh, the threat of heat already humidifying the morning and only intensifying Zal's discomfort. At least he was closer to his sister now, their connection stronger and her magic more accessible.

"Are you all right, Va'ili?" Emri asked over his shoulder as Zal hunched against the onslaught of shared agony.

"It's Leksi," he said, breathless, trying to siphon some of her magic while not being overwhelmed by her emotions. The effort left him feeling like a samovar boiled dry. He wondered if her loss would make her more amenable to his cause. With or without her, they had to breach the palace and find Ailia.

Following Lana's directions, Zal guided the horse around the outskirts of the city until summer-thick foliage proved too much for the beast. Standing on shaky legs, they shared a meager breakfast and drained the water-skin. Zal drew on more of Leksi's magic, surprised by the lack of resistance. It swept away his fatigue faster than the strongest cup of coffee and soothed his lingering aches more efficiently than scale leaf.

"Are you all right?" Zal asked as he tentatively stretched his stiff muscles, joints popping.

"Well enough, Va'ili," Emri said. "Sleep helped, as will this." He produced a wad of khat from a pouch secreted in a pocket. "There's plenty for two."

"All yours," Zal said. With access to Leksi's power now, he didn't even feel the need for scale leaf.

"Thank you, Va'ili." The sciomancer's gratitude sent a tingle across Zal's scalp. This was the type of stimulation Zal wanted, and no herb or tincture had ever come close. He was becoming more sensitive to moments of worship, Lana's fanes and pious workers no doubt having something to do with it. How he'd craved faith and fear; how he craved even more.

Leaving the horse, they surreptitiously navigated the trails lacing the cliffs below the palace, using the dense shrubbery for cover. With the riots providing ample distraction, the walls would be sparsely guarded with few eyes turned toward the sea.

At least the path was shaded, sparing Zal from the vicious sun, which had left his nape blistered despite Leksi's talisman. It took longer than he'd hoped to pick their way to the secret cove, occasionally having to wade through shallows or hop along slippery rocks before reaching the cave that would lead them into the depths of the palace.

Once in the cool embrace of shadow, Zal crumpled at the water's edge and splashed his face, not caring if the brine made him stickier than the sweat already coating his skin. He regarded the sciomancer, who was similarly kneeling beside the water. Zal watched Emri drag graceful fingers through the tangles of his long hair, re-braiding the strands with practiced dexterity.

"When this is done, I'll have questions for you," Zal said. Before he could ever fully trust the man, he needed to know what the sciomancer was hiding, and why he insisted on keeping a truculent ghost leashed like a rabid dog.

"I imagine so." Emri looked away.

"Will you manage the spellwork?" Zal asked.

"I'll manage," he said.

Although the khat had seemingly made Emri more alert, Zal knew all too well how it felt to survive on scraps, every minor use of magic costing a broken bone or shriveled organ. But Emri only needed time and sleep to recover; Zal needed a spell to strip his siblings of their power so he could make it permanently his own.

If they didn't reach Ailia, if they didn't discover the final piece of her working, then he'd be trapped in pain and weakness forever. There was no time to wallow or wait for strength to return though, and Zal's never would, unless he took it from someone else.

Siphoning a little more from Leksi, he hauled himself to his feet and offered his hand to the sciomancer. Emri took it, his fingers cool and grip firm.

"We can do this," he said when they were face to face, their gazes locked.

"I can give you more." Zal touched Emri's chest and felt the magnetic pull of his shadow where it nestled beneath Emri's skin.

"I don't need more," Emri said. "What I have is already enough."

Zal studied the man's face, trying to quell the fist of disappointment squeezing his insides. He'd already gifted Emri more of his magic to break the ghost's hold. He wouldn't do it again, unless Emri wanted him to or his life depended on it. Zal stepped away and withdrew Lana's hastily-drawn map from the saddlebag slung across his shoulder.

Six doors, six spells, then a winding passage Lana couldn't guarantee hadn't been discovered by the Sodality. It would lead them to a hidden entrance in the southern reaches of the dungeons. From there, they'd have to find their way to Ailia. Zal's shadows would either feast or fail, depending on how many enemies stood between him and his quarry.

"Should we have brought a lamp?" Zal asked. He could see in the darkness, but he wasn't sure about the sciomancer.

"I have Death's eyes," Emri said. "I can see well enough."

They padded quietly along the rough-hewn passage, the darkness thickening around them. Emri emitted a lunar effulgence, his ghosts cloaking him in a spirit shimmer, his eyes all the more lambent for the lack of natural light.

Zal followed as Emri navigated, sometimes having to turn sideways to squeeze around narrow corners, often ducking to avoid splitting his skull on the dagger-sharp ends of stalactites. Zal trailed his fingers along the rock, ridged and lichen-furred.

"It feels like we're being swallowed," Emri said. "Like we're walking down the gullet of some fanged beast."

"The gullet of a petrified serpent taking a nap?" Zal teased, nails catching at tufts of moss and peeling them away in soggy ribbons. Emri returned his gaze and they exchanged wry smiles, which sent a pesky, if not wholly unwelcome, warmth tripping up the back of Zal's neck.

The first door was a wall of warped wood, swollen with damp and impregnated with magic. The boards were scored with six sigils: one for each of the gods.

"This is it." Emri nicked his hand with his blade, pressed his blood to the wood, and sang the refrain Lana had made Emri memorize. The words were on the map—the syllables nonsense—but apparently relevant.

A shimmer of ghosts riffled around the sciomancer as Emri cast the spell. The door groaned, boards protesting as magic turned them to splinters.

"Lana said nothing about destroying the doors." Zal took a tentative step over the remains.

"She likely didn't know," Emri said, breathless. "No spell lasts forever; nothing does."

"Not even gods?" Zal asked.

"Faith erodes. Magic fades." Sweat pearled his upper lip and a bloody tear slipped down his cheek. "To live is to change."

"Only Death is permanent then."

"Is it?" Emri raised a delicate brow as a plume of spirits rose from his fingers.

"Five more doors." Zal didn't want to contemplate the loss of the sciomancer. His followers had come to seem interchangeable, if not disposable, but not Emri. He was one of the treasured few Zal would grieve.

"You may have to carry me," Emri said.

"Gladly," Zal said. Even if the added weight broke every bone in his body.

By the time they reached the sixth door, Emri was sweating blood. His eyes were red-limned, his nostrils scabbed, and ears oozing. As promised, Zal carried him.

"This is killing you," Zal said, startled by how much sorrow cinched around the heart-shaped rot in his chest.

"You'll find I'm hard to kill, Va'ili," Emri said, then retched, coughing up pink-flecked foam. He pressed his sliced palm against what should be the sixth and final door. All the others had been wood; this was stone.

Zal held Emri upright, feeling the shudder pass through his slender frame as the sciomancer took a bracing breath and began to hum. He faltered and the spell fizzled, incomplete. The door remained shut.

"I'm sorry, Va'ili," Emri murmured, then folded like a flower. Zal eased him to the floor, propping him gently between the stones. His clothes were soaked, his face a scarlet mess, but he was still breathing.

Zal tore a length of fabric from the hem of his borrowed tunic and bound Emri's palm then slipped the saddle bag beneath his head as a crude pillow. He tucked a strand of silver hair behind the sciomancer's ear, resisting the urge to trace the lines of ink sweeping up Emri's neck.

"Death cannot have you," Zal said. "I won't allow it. Sleep, Emri. I'll come back for you." Either Zal would return with Ailia in a state to restore Zal's magic and he'd be able to revive the sciomancer, or all would be lost anyway.

Zal regarded the stone door. He was a demigod, not an arkani. While he wasn't capable of working human spells, surely he could wield enough power to get past a lump of rock.

Dispensing with both blood and incantation, Zal called on his shadows and pulled deeply on his sister's magic. He might not be able to break the spell, but he could break the door. He was chaos, entropy, and what was that, if not ineluctable demise? Even rock eroded and crumbled to dust; Zal merely had to accelerate the process.

He pressed his palm to the stone door, his shadows bleeding out of him in a dark patina, searching for the tiniest crack or divot in the smooth sandstone, staining the colorful striations with Zal's intent.

Obliteration, he thought, closing his eyes to better focus as he imagined peeling back quartzitic layers, shearing them into shale, reducing them to pebbles, to dust.

The rock quivered, as if the walls were the hide of an animal twitching to remove a fly. He pushed harder, the force of his magic pounding inside his skull, the rush in his ears like a screaming harmattan. The ground convulsed and the door crumbled, but that wasn't all that moved. A surge and ebb, surge and ebb—the rise and fall of a chest, the slow pulse of a waking heart deep inside the earth.

Zal pitched forward, his hands on his knees as Leksi's magic ebbed away. It left him gulping for air, his whole body thrumming with the sharp pain of a recently stubbed toe. He forced his tired eyes open to peer down a passage reinforced with wooden beams. The old-fashioned torches on the wall were unlit, the air stale and tainted with rot. It seemed the tunnels hadn't been recently used and were likely unguarded.

Another tremor undulated the ground beneath his feet, as if the rocks had momentarily turned sinuous, the motion nauseating. Was it the result of his unchecked chaos ripping open the seams of the city, or something older? Just once, Zal would appreciate not having to shoulder the blame.

Leaving Emri unconscious but definitely breathing, Zal trudged along the corridor. There was only one path and it led him to the dungeons, the earth gradually giving way to a carpet of frostweed.

The air was soaked with the rich pungency of death, a heady mix of sweet putrefaction and freshly spilled copper made all the more delightful by the bitter scent of the Nether blooms. Zal licked his lips.

His shadows glommed around him protectively as he stepped into the dungeons, stalking passed barred cells. The prisoners were dead. Some sprouted mushrooms, while others had turned to rockeries. More were made statues of petrified flesh, some nothing but sticky globules hanging suspended like gory apples from invisible trees. Those were only the recently deceased. He didn't need to place a hand on the stone to hear the screaming dead. It was a good thing Emri had stayed away. He'd be overcome by the raucous ghosts, trapped where they'd died in agony and indignity.

Here was a history written in blood and carved from shattered bone: arkani at the hand of the Sodality, indigenous Qhembalese at the hands of foreign sovereigns, and the unlucky who'd been made the playthings of royal magic-wielders eager to test their skills on flesh.

A few of the fresher corpses must've been his arkani, the escaped shadow scraps flitting eagerly back to Zal. With every regained fragment, Zal grew stronger. Not enough to heal the sigil sliced into his chest nor to stop the insidious pilfering of his power, but enough to strengthen his withered muscles without having to borrow magic from his sister.

At the end of the row, the cells gave way to larger rooms and the site of a more recent skirmish. The quiet was ominous, the silence of bated breath and stealthy paws creeping up on unsuspecting prey.

Zal studied the remains, flesh warped but not yet stiffened by rigor. His heels crunched over scattered gems, releasing the tell-tale waft of magic—his own and another's, her signature scent unmistakable.

A rhythmic thudding disturbed the quiet. Somewhere in the dungeon, a heart still beat.

He paused, peering into the gloom. A creature hurtled out of the darkness, teeth gnashing at his throat. Zal staggered back with the impact, the weight of his assailant sending them both thudding to the floor. His shadows cushioned his landing, the frostweed billowing razor-edged spores into the air as he and the attacker tumbled.

He grappled with the smaller form, catching a knee aimed at his crotch with his thigh, deflecting jabbing elbows with his own arms, until he managed to catch the hands flailing at his face. The fingers were broken, the digits pulpy in his grip.

The attacker cried out when Zal squeezed, pausing their assault long enough for him to recognize the face under the tangled mop of hair.

For decades that stretched into centuries, Zal had tried to recover who he'd been and rebuild the boy Death had razed, but he'd been doomed to failure. Even if he'd managed to recover every last scrap of bone and flesh, he would never be whole. The puzzle pieces would never fit when the picture had irrevocably changed.

He'd been beautiful once. Like all his siblings, he'd been fashioned from frost and darkness, sculpted from Death's black womb blood. With Time his true father, he'd received a dollop of additional cosmic radiance. A beauty shattered and violently destroyed, a beauty he would forever grieve no matter how much of his former self he retrieved from the cracks and hollows of the mortal realm.

Mother had broken him, left him irreparable, ugly, and

unlovable. Or so he'd thought. But Zal had learned to be resourceful, to use his wit and charm to manipulate and cajole, to convince humans to trust and adore him for reasons beyond the superficial. And they had.

Some had even loved him over the years. He'd felt their adoration sealing the fractures in his bones, thickening wizened tissue, or re-threading snapped sinews. Still, it had been more than a century before any human had wanted to touch him or demonstrate their fealty through carnal means. He'd taken what little pleasure he could from their flesh, tongues and lips offering a different kind of prayer.

But it wasn't until Ailia—an arkani resplendent in her full power—had come to him dressed only in moonlight and longing that Zal finally understood a primal form of worship. She'd never lied to him, never called him beautiful when he was wound and wreckage, but she'd kissed every scar, caressed every break and bruise, as gentle as she was determined to show her devotion. And he'd let her, becoming intoxicated by her love and drunk on her passion, her faith in him to seat her on a throne.

For decades, he'd spent nights enthralled by her body and entranced by her belief. He knew the shape of her, every dip and hollow, every mole and scar, how to make her laugh or sigh or scream. She knew him too, of course, had cataloged all his weak spots and how to use them to her advantage: how to make him moan, to whimper, and to beg.

He'd been the one worshiping her, her name a prayer coaxed from his panting lips, his devotion to his most precious arkani spilling out of him in shadow-spume to soak sheets and skin.

"Ailia," Zal said, her name an accusation now, and not a benediction as she pulled free from his grasp.

She was filthy and blood-drenched, her face bruised and clothes in tatters. The remains of sigil-marked manacles clinked about her ankles, the iron chains transforming into wriggling tentacles, the metamorphosis accelerated in Zal's presence.

"Zal," Ailia said with a recalcitrant jut of her chin. "I'm surprised to see you standing. Perhaps I underestimated your resilience."

"As I underestimated your ambition."

"At least I learn from my mistakes." With her broken hands useless for spell-craft now, she dragged a toe through the soupy darkness instead, attempting to draw a sigil despite the manacles stifling her power.

Zal could learn from his errors too. With a thought, he sent his shadows slithering toward her. She cried out when they swept her off her feet and ensnared her limbs in oily coils. She thrashed as they dragged her closer, body contorting in eel-like serpentines. Zal gripped her ankles, releasing just enough power to relieve her of the loathsome manacles. He would best her with her arkani power intact, or not at all.

She began to hum and fire surged from her damaged hands, searing the shadows which hissed and howled as they retreated. The flames leapt from Ailia's flesh to ignite the torches within the torus of her spell, incinerating swaths of frostweed and any human flesh not yet petrified. Blinded, Zal recoiled, his shadows shrieking.

Ailia launched herself at him, incandescent with heat and rage. With a screech of syllables, she scrabbled at his clothes with broken fingers, managing to singe away the fabric of his shirt and scorch the exposed swath of his torso where the sigil gleamed raw and weeping in the torch glow.

Stunned by her ferocity, Zal struggled to defend himself as a new song burbled up her throat. It was the one she and Iqno had sung in his chambers, the one she'd used to pry away his power.

Only she was alone now, and the sigil was incomplete. The spell wouldn't work, but Ailia was powerful. It was why he'd chosen her, loved her, and been undone by her. The magic pounced at his side, and he felt his molars snap as he grit his teeth, stifling the scream tearing up his throat as her spell sunk talons into his side.

Even now, battered and degraded, she hungered for his power. He held her at arm's length, enduring the sizzle of her flames against his palms. He welcomed the pain, the clarifying agony incinerating the foolish hope he'd harbored that this was simply a misunderstanding, and not a betrayal.

"Give it to me!" she screamed.

His power had changed her. He'd tried to warn her. The primordial magic of the demigods could not be wielded by humans. Scryali had tried and he'd watched her mind shatter, witnessing her slow unraveling as his chaos consumed her. Now it was happening again. The anger he felt over Ailia's betrayal flowed out of him, a sudden backwash leaving nothing but grief and exhaustion in its wake.

"I want it," she continued to babble between aborted attempts at the incantation as her strength flagged. She wasn't wearing the amulet. Either it lay discarded in the dungeon somewhere, or more likely, it had been taken by her captors. "I need it. Give it to me." She lunged again, but Zal held her back with trembling arms, siphoning a little more of his sister's power.

"Why?" Zal asked, never more aware of the void where his heart should've been. "So you could be queen?"

"Queen?" she laughed, a raucous crow-croak. "I want to be a god."

Just like Scryali, she had succumbed to delusion.

"Where's the amulet?" he asked, his gaze resting on the empty hollow between her collarbones.

"An arkani took it," she spit. "Filthy, thieving brat."

"One of mine?" he asked.

The question triggered her fury and she redoubled her efforts. She lashed out with her feet, catching him in the thigh, groin, stomach, shin. The fires burned brighter as the sigil twisted open the spigot on his power. The frostweed burgeoned, catching escaping droplets of blood and chaos on their pristine petals. Zal unleashed his shadows, letting them slither through the misplaced meadow, slicking themselves in cold and entropy before shackling Ailia once more. This time they formed a noose, and Ailia's eyes bulged when Zal clenched his fist, tightening the knot around her neck.

Her face slackened, lips turning blue as the torches dimmed, her magic failing. He pulled her close when she sagged, easing them both into the bed of waiting frostweed. He held her, his hand pressed to the softness of her belly. He flattened his palm there, feeling his shadow flutter in her otherwise barren womb. It unfurled against his touch, straining for release.

"This arkani—were they one of ours?" He eased his hold, allowing her to draw breath.

"No." She gasped when he dug his nails into her flesh. Shadow dribbled free from the puncture wounds, and Zal welcomed it home, using the returning power to plug one of the many wounds Ailia had reopened. She stilled in his arms, body heavy as the shadow she'd carried for longer than any human slipped free of her folds. "No, Zal, please," she whimpered. "You can't."

Zal inhaled the returning mote of his power.

"Save me," she rasped. "I know you can. I want to live forever. Please." Her voice wavered.

"Only if you tell me how to reverse the spell," he said, his lips brushing her ear, his eyes smarting.

"You can't," she said. "It's a—" Her breath was shallow, her heart stuttering. She was fading now, denied the primordial scrap sustaining her geriatric body.

"All spells can be countered," Zal said.

"It was meant to end the world… Scryali's work…"

Scryali. Of course this had been her invention. What was a spell to strip a god of power when she believed she could compose apocalyptic melodies? He should've known, should've done more to stop her, to understand her. Instead he'd let the monarchy execute her and cut his losses.

"Where is Riksa?" he asked, not wanting to dwell on past failings.

"Don't know," Ailia said. "She was only a distraction."

Zal shifted as frostweed spread into his hair and sent probing tendrils curling around his ears.

"I'm sorry," she said and he held his breath. "Sorry I didn't do it sooner," Ailia continued. "I was so close—I almost had it, and you, so pitiful and pathetic—" Her words turned malediction as she listed all the ways he'd left her wanting.

Zal removed his hand from her empty belly, letting it rest on her throat where the shadows parted to make space for his fingers.

"You're not worthy of immortality," she said. "Of godhood. You're not—"

He shut his eyes, tears cutting acid trails down his cheeks as his fingers flexed. Ailia fell silent.

Even the ghosts in the walls were quiet as his shadows pressed close, offering comfort. Zal waited for pain to seize him by the jugular, for that sweeping agony Leksi had felt to similarly engulf him. He waited to be drowned in sorrow, to be smashed against rocks by the breakers of mourning, but his grief was a feathery rime, an inexorable crystallization of his insides that left him feeling sharp-edged but brittle.

Numbly, he released Ailia into the embrace of the frostweed.

If he lay down beside her and let the flowers of the Nether

claim him, perhaps he'd finally be transported home. Perhaps he'd be held under by a long, cruel beak and torn into algae fronds by the river, joining Mezra in an eternal unmaking, never to be forgiven or tossed ashore to be reborn.

Maybe he could sublimate here, gnaw open his veins and bleed out pure chaos, let the mortal realm succumb to entropy as he slept, and damn them all to an ignoble end.

But Emri lay in the tunnels, alive and waiting, and somewhere beyond the warped walls of the dungeon his sisters roamed—Violence and Nightmare stalking Savat. There, too, an unknown arkani was in possession of his stolen power, leaving a city—a world—teetering on the brink.

And there was still Time.

Reluctantly, belligerently, Zal rose, and dusted off the Nether creeper clinging to him like cobwebs. Too bad he couldn't rid himself of Ailia's final words quite as easily. They scuttled inside him like spiders, injecting him with necrotizing venom. He was pitiful and pathetic, weak and unworthy.

He gathered his shadows, stepped over Ailia's transmogrifying corpse, and turned back along the tunnels. Despite familiar fears still curdling his thoughts and old scars made fresh wounds, Zal would prove himself worthy of his godhood and the devotion he craved.

Chapter Twenty-Five
Leksi

Leksi peered at the sky, squinting at the sun past the brim of her hat. There'd been no kakaki blasts today, the passage of time marked only by the guttering of flame. Further north, the fray continued. When the wind blew south, it carried the roar of muskets and cries of the anguished.

The Qhembalese were still fighting. The city had endured war before, and it had survived insurrection, but all those battles had been the result of human strife. This was different. Zal had spilled chaos across Savat, and Riksa trailed violence in her wake. The results were incendiary in the worst possible way, and now Leksi, nightmare made manifest, was the one left trying to quell it.

Her brother's shadow found Leksi while she was digging through the collapsed remains of a shack. The ink-spill varmint chittered the same way her monsters did, its Nethertaal even more clipped and acerbic.

She listened as she worked, searching for survivors. There were others helping too, and she handed over a semi-conscious child to a woman with a scarred face and singed hair. A soot-streaked arkani, gaze glazed with exhaustion, staggered past. He doused lingering flames with a ragged refrain and trembling hands. She expected to see despair in his eyes, but when he turned toward her, she saw only a grim determination staring.

The air thrummed with magic, a mephitic mix of mortal spell-craft and primordial excrement. The charged vibrations were like a cloud of mosquitoes buzzing around her ears, landing intermittently on her skin to bite and irritate. She swatted at her arms, but there was nothing there except her brother's shadow waiting for her response.

The people of Qhemba didn't need her hands searching through the wreckage; they needed her hands throttling the embodiment of war who'd brought this upon the city. Leksi didn't want to face either of her siblings though. It was easier to shift cinders and retrieve bodies, to stop thinking, stop feeling, and focus on saving others instead of ruminating on how she'd failed Tamisk.

"Take me to him then," she said, and the shadow peeled from her shoulder, its edges folding into bat-like wings. She followed its zig-zag flight, leading her down to the water where Tsirayan fisherfolk welcomed Savati residents, loading people and their meager belongings into their dhows with gentle smiles. Some survivors piled into rowboats or unfurled sails on dinghies, the waves dotted with the desperate who'd chosen to flee instead of fight.

Leksi claimed a small rowboat for herself, hoping it wouldn't be missed. While the Tsirayans headed toward the safety of the atoll, Leksi followed her brother's pet as it skimmed the water, heading west.

She was barely out of the bay when the tether connecting her to Zal twanged once with exquisite agony, then stilled. She waited for more, braced and holding her breath, but there was only a permeating numbness. Dread coiled like a sleeping viper in the pit of her stomach, wrapping her monsters in a quivering embrace.

She rowed. Her shoulders burned while forearms strained against the unfamiliar motion of the oars. The skin blistered under the relentless glare of the sun, but she ignored her pains. Instead, she breathed in time with the dip of the oars as she crossed from the calm turquoise of the eastern sea onto the chilly chop of the western ocean. The waves spit sea foam in her face, gnashing at her boat with briny teeth.

Cresting the swell, she spied more vessels in the distance. A flotilla, or armada—impossible to tell. It was equally impossible to tell which direction the boats were traveling but Leksi suspected Lana and her gunpowder were on their way.

By the time the shadow guided her into the cove, her palms were raw, her back was screaming, and her clothes were soaked with salt. She tumbled gummy-legged onto the sand and hurried into the cool maw of the cave. Her eyes adjusted to the gloom, her vision flaring with Nether-sight as she stepped into darkness as thick as the oil joRanians extracted from the punctured desert. Zal's shadow glommed to her neck, whispering her forward despite the dread growing heavier in her gut.

Carefully, she squeezed along the narrow tunnels and probed along the tether. Zal was close, but she couldn't tell what he was thinking or feeling. Perhaps the numbness was because he'd finally succumbed to his injuries and fallen into a death-like stupor.

Leksi stumbled over splintered timbers, jarred by the sudden, unbidden recollection of the fallen beams which had become Tamisk's grave. Leksi probably should've scraped up her lover's remains and given them back to the sea. Not that burial rites made any real difference when the dead always ended up in the Nether.

There was nothing charred here, though—only the lingering musk of mortal magic. It grew stronger with every passing archway. There'd been doors once, she realized, now torn from their moorings or left in piles of rubble. The dark smears were blood. Frostweed sprouted, tumbling from a messy handprint to spread tendrils across the path and up the walls.

The shadow detached from her neck, flitting along a widening corridor leading her into the dungeons. The scene was as gruesome as she had anticipated, made worse by the spreading frostweed and pockets of chaos warping the human remains limned in the glow of torches.

Voices drew her forward.

Emri sat at the single desk, hands pressed flat to the scarred wood, his eyes white and glowing, his entire body outlined in ghost-glow.

Zal paced, cutting an uneven path through the Nether meadow and casting furtive glances at the sciomancer every other step.

"Hello, brother," Leksi said.

Zal paused and regarded her through the waves of dark hair obscuring his face. He looked exhausted, but at least he was standing. "You came," he said, surprised.

"You called," she said.

"Still, you didn't have to come."

"Prefer I go?" Leksi made to retrace her steps.

"Stay. We need you," Zal said, and she knew that admission must've hurt. "If you still want to save the city, that is?" He raised a questioning brow.

"Tamisk is dead," she said, the words an axe cleaving her in two.

"I know," he said. "I felt it." He pressed a hand to his chest as if he could fathom the depth of her grief. He'd never apologize, even though the string of recent catastrophes were beads on twine all leading back to his meddling fingers. "Hence my question."

Perhaps his numbness had been in response to her own pain, his inability to cope with loss, even vicariously, necessitating a withdrawal from their connection. The physical bond remained, though he seemed to be drawing less of her magic now. Some other source must've strengthened him.

"Unlike you, I don't want to tear the whole world apart because of a personal grievance," Leksi said.

"You just run away from the things you don't like," Zal said, and Leksi bristled at how easily he irked her.

"Perhaps we could set aside differences for the time being?" Emri said, gently, as if minding querulous children. Which they were, although Leksi loathed to admit it. The sciomancer winced and shut his eyes, swatting away a bloody tear before it rolled down his cheek.

"You all right?" she asked.

"Magic takes its toll," he said, before resting his head in his hands. Zal placed a hand on the man's trembling shoulder, the gesture painfully tender.

"Did you at least find Ailia?" Leksi asked.

"Yes," Zal said. "She's—"

A sudden stinging, as if a wasp had emptied its venom into her desiccated heart.

"Also dead," Emri said, his voice the softest burr. "And already gone. She didn't linger." He stirred the air with a bloody, bandaged hand. So Ailia was dead and escorted to the Nether on mantis-wing, or so the Qhembalese believed, the indigenous psychopomp surviving foreign invasion to become the Savati fetch as well. joRanians believed the dead departed on the backs of white owls, while the Yekkä thought sand-cats responsible for ferrying souls to the Nether. It didn't matter when Death's door was open to all.

Leksi braced for her brother's reaction, for something, *anything*, to spill out of him. Slowly, he met her gaze. She wanted to see her own grief reflected in his gaze, to know she wasn't alone weathering this catastrophic loss of love, but his eyes swirled with shadow, making his expression blank and unreadable. She probed their tether and hit a wall as solid as the rock beneath her feet.

"Did you find the amulet? Did Ailia reverse the spell,

before she—" Leksi couldn't bring herself to say it, not with the void of his stare pinning her in place.

"Neither," he said. "Seems a renegade arkani absconded with the trinket."

"One of yours?" she asked, rankled by his seeming lack of concern.

"Apparently not," he said.

"So you're still leaking magic?" The sigil was visible between the scorched threads of his shirt.

"Less now, but yes."

"Without Ailia you have no way to reverse the spell," she said, and her dread unfurled.

"We can still reclaim the amulet, but first, the Synod. Lana is on her way," Zal said.

"Have you forgotten about Riksa?" Leksi asked. "Qhemba lies in ruin. Half this city is burning. Untrained arkani and people armed with sticks and stones are waging war against the constabulary bearing muskets. It's a bloodbath out there, and no doubt Riksa is strolling through the carnage with a big old smile on her face."

"All the more reason for Lana to level the palace and the Sodality along with it," he said flatly.

Leksi sifted saliva through her teeth. Something didn't add up. Riksa had been Zal's prisoner, but he hadn't dragged her kicking and screaming from the Nether. She'd already been in the mortal realm of her own volition.

"Do you know why Riksa is even here?" Leksi asked. "How did you manage to capture her?"

"I didn't." Zal's gaze slid past her to the sciomancer, whose spangled hair was so bright it hurt her eyes.

"We didn't know who she was at first, of course," the sciomancer said. "She befriended some of our younger recruits and started asking questions, wanting to know about the shadows we carried, the marks of the one we called Va'ili." Emri scratched at a scab on his jaw. "We reported to Ailia first, then to Za—Va'ili." His desert accent softened the syllable of her brother's name, partial as it was. No human could utter his full name and expect to live. "It was Ailia who figured out what she was."

"Ailia has a knack for intuiting a person's affinity for magic," Zal said. "Had," he amended, and a muscle twitched in his jaw.

"Ailia knew we'd found someone special," Emri continued, "and came up with the plan."

"Of course she did." Leksi sighed. How naïve her little brother had been.

"My power grants me some influence over beings of the Nether," Emri continued. "Ailia prepared the spells necessary for Riksa's capture, and I subdued her long enough to fit the chains on her wrists, but—" The skin around his eyes tightened, the harsh shadows making canyons of the creases. "I always thought it was too easy."

Mezra was the cunning one, conniving and sly, but Riksa could be manipulative when it suited her.

"She came here looking for something," Leksi said. "For us?"

"I never could pry the reasons from her," Zal said. "And

not for lack of trying."

"I'm not sure physical torture was the best strategy with the embodiment of violence," Leksi said.

Zal frowned, perhaps only now realizing the missed opportunity. If he'd only been able to see past his own pain, he might've realized pulling teeth and removing fingers was never going to work on a sibling who relished bloodshed.

"So you never figured out what she wanted?" Leksi asked.

"Power," Zal said. "She thought she had Ailia's loyalty, believed Ailia planned to use the spell to strip me of my magic and give it to her." He shrugged. "We all crave power, in one form or another."

"I don't," Leksi said.

"Maybe not as magic," he said. "But you built a sanctuary, you rescued the lost and vulnerable, you became their god and held the heart of a human in your hand. Different, sure, but power nonetheless."

Oh, how she hated him. "No, that's—"

"Don't pretend you don't enjoy it, that you don't long for it," Zal said, drawing out the syllables. "To be adored, worshiped, venerated."

"To matter," Emri added. "Even humans crave that."

Leksi bit her tongue hard enough to taste copper. She wanted to believe she'd only ever longed to be free of her magic, but that dream lay crushed by the death of Zal's precious arkani.

"Without Ailia and a way to complete the spell, you won't be able to keep your promise to me," she said.

"Not unless we find the amulet," Zal said.

"With what's happening out there, that arkani could be dead in a gutter, your amulet devoured by Mother's flowers." She extricated her foot from a hungry swath of blooms. Her bootlaces wriggled, already transformed into tiny snakes.

"I think that's why Riksa came here," Zal said. "Humans turn to the gods in times of hardship. What better way for Riksa to restore the city's faith than by starting a war?"

"Precisely," Leksi said. "If power is what she wants, we should be doing everything we can to avoid violence."

"If we destroy the Sodality, we stop the war," Emri said, making it sound far too simple.

"Or maybe we make everything a thousand times worse," Leksi said. "There's no guarantee the people will welcome Lana back, not when she plans to reinstate the monarchy. A foot on your neck is a crushing force whether it's a boot or a golden slipper."

"All humanity ever does is inflict suffering on each other, one way or another. There's no preventing it," Zal said with surprising resignation.

"So instead we cause it?" Leksi resisted the urge to slam her fist into the wall, or into Zal's jaw. "And what happens to your followers in the aftermath, or don't you care?" She couldn't let him do this. Savat was still worth saving. There were good people out there defending their homes, fighting for their lives, for a future free of dogma and dictatorship.

"All arkani will be safe with Lana on the throne," Zal said.

"The people got rid of the monarchy for a reason. They

won't want this regression. You'll leave Savat without governance. You'll make the city vulnerable." Leksi took a step toward Zal. She'd shake sense into him if she had to. "This city has long been coveted by its neighbors. You don't think one of them will swoop in while it's mired in chaos?" she asked, but she knew she was losing.

"Cities rise and fall," he said. "Nations collapse and new ones emerge from the ashes."

"The way belligerent Netherlings claw their way back to life from a puddle of viscera?" she asked. She didn't know how to make him see they had the opportunity to do something good here and, yet again, he was about to make a mess of it.

"Exactly." He smiled as footsteps echoed up from the tunnels.

A moment later, Lana's horde spilled into the dungeon, led by an arkani. They were flanked by farmhands and miners brandishing swords and pistols instead of shovels. Behind them, several others wheeled in barrows and carts full of explosives.

"Welcome," Zal said with an expansive sweep of his arm. "I trust you know where to set the powder."

"We have our instructions." The arkani barked orders, directing the barrows into position.

"Where's Lana?" Leksi asked.

"Safe, of course," the arkani said. "Ready to lead us into a better, brighter age."

Paralyzed by indecision, Leksi watched as the rest of Lana's lackeys set out the barrels, each strategically placed according to blueprints brandished by the arkani.

Leksi had seen half the city flee—she'd seen the despair and devastation on the survivors' faces—and yet she couldn't relinquish the kernel of fragile hope daring to smolder in her chest. She'd seen the people's determination too, their care for each other and for Savat.

"We can't do this," she said, voice barely a murmur.

"It's already done," Zal said. "You might not want to be here when it goes boom. Or maybe you do." He arched a brow at her. "Stay and be obliterated then. Perhaps once you spend the next five centuries gathering up all your shattered pieces, you'll finally understand." He twirled his hand in the air and his shadows coalesced into a staff, which he offered to Emri. The sciomancer clutched the shadow-rod, clearly needing it, weak and depleted as he was.

Now was her chance.

She studied the barrels of black powder. Each bore sigils. Fire, she guessed, wishing yet again she'd learned more about mortal spellcraft.

"No fuse?" she asked.

"I'm the fuse," the arkani said, holding up a finger like a match. "Once I complete the incantation, I'll have more than enough time to make it to the cove." They stroked one of the sigils. "You might want to leave now though."

"First Council isn't for another few days," Leksi said.

"The Synod has convened early," Zal said, already at the mouth of the tunnel. "Given the current insurrection, the government is holding an emergency summit."

"As confirmed by your shadow spies?" Leksi asked.

"And the dead," Emri said, eyes shining silver again. "There are so many ghosts, it's hard to parse the clamor." He winced as he touched his temple.

"Several of the guards proved less loyal to the cause once they were ghosts," Zal explained. "They were quick to spill Sodality secrets."

"The Sodality is meeting tonight," Emri said.

Tonight. Now. She tried to remember the shape of the annulment sigil she'd drawn on Zal's chest. She traced it in her mind, finger twitching in readiness. The incantation was harder. She'd never had much of a talent for music, but she had to try. There had to be another way than causing more death and destruction, but if she was going to prevent that, she'd need to distract those who'd try to stop her.

Her monsters unsheathed their claws and Leksi released the hold on her magic.

"What are you doing?" Zal asked.

"Whatever it takes to save the city," Leksi said.

"We had a deal." Zal's face contorted.

"Void without Ailia or the amulet." She shrugged, mimicking his insouciance, then strode toward the barrels. The humans cried out in panic as Leksi released her hold on her magic. She tasted the fear lacing the air, every sweet and spicy flavor as it slicked the back of throat and greased her tongue.

Crouching before the barrel, she slipped back her human façade like a cowl to reveal a sliver of her true form. With a sharp nail, she gouged the annulment sigil across the one marking the barrel. She sang—or rather she tried—but she inhaled a mouthful of shadow. Zal's vermin glommed to her teeth, choking, silencing.

She roared against the darkness suffocating her and pulled on his magic, tearing it from his grasp. She should've known how unstable his power would make hers, should've anticipated the sudden surge of magic fattening her veins. She should've known better than to try and channel so much magic not her own, exhaling her brother's chaos across multiple barrels of gunpowder primed to ignite.

The barrels detonated with a sjambok snap as the world ripped away in a blaze of blinding white.

Music is fundamentally mathematics. Notes are numbers and thus their relationships may be described in proportions and seen as ratios. The simpler the proportion, the more pleasing the notes will sound. The more complex the proportion, the more dissonant the music becomes. Consider then the syntonic comma if you will, the most complex proportion illustrating the disparity between just and tempered tunings. This is why precise tuning is essential for spellwork and why Qhembalese instruments should not be used for incantations. Arkani must consider their surroundings as unintended overtones may produce unwanted magical side effects.

Excerpt from *Tempered Tuning for Advanced Spellwork* by Ymela Adjawaja

Chapter Twenty-Six

Niki

With my heart threatening to burst from my chest, sweat drenching my shirt, and leg muscles screaming, I finally made it to the safety of my secret refuge.

The cramped little study was located in the disused attic in the tower of the university library. During my second year, I'd come looking for forgotten textbooks and abandoned treatises the Sodality might've missed when they purged the stacks. I found nothing but dust, fish-moths, and solitude.

Over the years, I'd made the attic my own, rearranging furniture and installing lamps. More importantly, I'd kept this place a secret. Although I'd trusted Jaq, I'd needed a place to sit quietly with only my thoughts and no possibility of distraction.

I sat now, knees pulled up to my chest and hand clutching the amulet cradled against my shins. My fingers were numb where they fused with the wood, entangled like the parasitic filaments of mistletoe digging into their unwitting host.

It was worse than being locked in the cellar with only the threat of my father's belt keeping me quiet through the fear. It was worse than being in the dungeons, the shadows shifting and creeping closer. Here, in what should be a sanctuary, I was overcome.

Breath snarled in my lungs, my veins icy traceries beneath my skin as I shivered, the shock of all that happened finally taking its toll. I rested my head on my knees, exhaustion a vulture settling on my back and tearing at my mind. I closed my eyes, just for a moment, just until I could catch my breath, until my heart stopped pounding, until…

I slept.

And dreamed.

Of darkness and flitting shadows, of an iridescent river snaking through a desert. Of snow and blood and smoke.

I finally woke to the smell of burning. The narrow window looked toward the Qhemba township and the ocean beyond. Black clouds obscured the view, smoke rising in columns from the quarter crowded with thatched huts and wooden shacks. While the acrid tang of burning buildings reached me in the tower, the flames were far away and posed no threat. I was safe. For now. I exhaled and studied my hand, my fingers still knotted into wood.

The city was burning, and yet it all seemed so meaningless when I held the answer to the mystery of magic in my hand.

Slaking my thirst with the cold dregs of tea gone muddy in a sigil-marked thermos I'd brought with me on my last visit here, I shook off the remnants of sleep and got to work, trying to arrange my notes and thoughts into a sensible order.

Bololo's theories on arkana particles.

Ngakula's assertions about hexameter.

Adjawaja's revelations concerning the mathematics of

music.

Makhezi's understanding of sigils.

Not to mention Scryali's own postulations.

My mind churned while shouts and gunshots rang out in the distance. Had they found Kazwe Olonza, and uncovered some Qhembalese plot to destroy the city?

Was Ailia Ogegesoa still alive? And Jaq?

There was far too much I didn't know.

I studied the amulet and my fingers melding into wood.

I'd worked with magically imbued objects before, like the phonograph in my studio, various instruments, even tomes spelled against the ravages of moisture and beetles, but none of those items had ever behaved like this amulet.

Again, I began to hum, but without an instrument or the benefit of echoes to add harmony, my singing produced nothing more than a slight tingle in my fingers. Still, here was irrefutable proof that someone without any training and no innate ability could wield potent magic with nothing more than music.

Arkani weren't blessed by the gods or better than anyone else. It was simply the vagaries of nature and the accident of birth that made them natural resonators, aliquot strings capable of stirring magic from the ether. But it wasn't only innate. If that *scale* was the key to unlocking magic from arkana particles, then anyone could learn the right notes, use their bones as resonators in involuntary sympathy, and tune themselves to that primordial power.

Had the ancient Qhembalese known this all along with

their traditional tuning systems known to produce greater dissonance?

A creak on the rickety tower stairs shattered my concentration. I turned toward the door as it swung open on groaning hinges. The person on the threshold was pale and gaunt, with white blond hair as fine as spider silk clinging to their skull. They smiled, lips paring away from gums missing teeth.

Despite their wizened visage, there was a haunting beauty to them, their sharp angles accentuated by the tunic hanging from their thin shoulders. Their legs and feet were bare, their toes just stubs of bone. Were they an escaped prisoner perhaps, who had followed me from the palace?

They were missing their left hand, the wrist a gnarled stump. Their right hand ended in graceful fingers, the nails long and pointed.

"Please, don't stop." The voice was a frost-crackle making me shiver as if winter had slipped into the tower and rimed my flesh. I glanced toward the slit of a window. The sky had turned to slate, painted with ash and twilight. There'd been no kakaki blasts today, only the report of muskets, the sounds of fighting closer now, but the living cadaver in my doorway was far more disconcerting and posed the more immediate threat.

"Ah, lovely isn't it?" They sucked in a breath and their cheeks seemed to fill out a little, their hair thickening, and the whorls of tissue at their severed wrist smoothing into new growth.

"Who are you?" I asked.

Again, the person smiled, or grimaced, their lips splitting

to limn the stumps of their teeth in red, their beauty turning grotesque.

"More importantly, who are you? Do you even know?" Despite their corpse pallor, their eyes were bright, their gaze pale and piercing. "Do you know what you're holding? What you're wielding?"

"Magic," I said, and the ghoul laughed, blistering my ears with a mirthless cackle. "But I'm not an arkani," I spit, surprised by my own defensive need to make sure this stranger understood.

"All the more reason to give me the amulet." They held out their hand.

I couldn't part with it even if I wanted to, my fingers shadow-stained and lignified.

The ghoul pounced, trying to wrest the wood from my grasp. We tussled, a frenzy of teeth and nails like a pair of alley cats fighting over scraps.

If I hadn't been rolling across half-rotten floorboards fighting for my life, I might've felt the tremors sooner. If I hadn't been spitting my assailant's blood and torn flesh from my tongue, I might've smelled the blistered-metal odor in the air.

It was only when the first explosion shook the tower as if it were nothing more than a wooden block in a child's fist that we paused our violent squabble.

More explosions rocked the building. Walls that had stood for centuries cracked as the earth bucked and roiled. The fissures widened; the air was sucked from the room and ripped from my lungs. The stranger screamed, mouth moving, teeth gnashing. I couldn't hear anything over the thunder of blood in my ears.

It became a roar, then a whoosh. I turned toward the window, the glass melting as the side of the tower sheared away in a single sheet of failed architecture.

The stranger lunged, gouging sharp nails across my fore-arm, releasing shadows and smoke. A new and terrible agony tore up my arm as magic-imbued wood splintered.

Then we were falling.

The Principles of Inyoti as recorded by the first arkani blessed by the Ancestors to carry that most sacred fragment of the Serpent God within their hearts. Thus are the tenets upon which we build our society.

Fifth Principle—Forgiveness and Reconciliation:

Those who threaten the harmony of society must be held accountable. They must also be allowed to redeem themselves. True reconciliation does not harbor grudges. Once harmony has been reestablished, reconciliation is considered complete and all individuals must move forward, continuing to strive toward the greater good.

If harmony cannot be achieved, those responsible must face the ultimate disharmony of death. When the soul is deemed worthy by the Ancestors, they may be reborn to society and try again.

Chapter Twenty-Seven

ZAL

Zal woke to a mouthful of sand.

He lay still for a moment, trying to remember how to breathe, or if he even needed to. His body tingled, stretched thin as a blood smear on stone. He'd woken like this before, broken in a temple, his parts scattered.

Not again, not again, not again—each thought was a scorpion sting.

Tentatively, he felt for his edges, following capillary trails through a gauntlet of bone and muscle, organ and sinew, until he reached the margins of skin hemming his flesh. He was not quite whole, nor was he shattered.

His shadows spilled from his center like slop from a dropped bucket. Languidly, they flowed back toward him and Zal gathered his strength, recompiling his body into a more manageable configuration. Body aching and joints protesting, he settled into human form.

Blinking grit from his eyes, he surveyed his surroundings. Sand rippled away from the crater of his impact as if he'd been dropped into the desert by a bumbling eagle. Unlike the sapphire expanse above the desert separating Savat from joRania, the sky here was dishwater-gray, familiar stars struggling against the cinereal haze.

Zal dug his fingers into the grit. The snow was gone, the frozen veld of his childhood melted into aridity, but the constellations above and the frigid kiss of dead air told him he was home. He was finally back in the Nether, and everything about it was wrong.

Gingerly, Zal rolled to his knees, testing each limb. He didn't need to be human-shaped here; he could spread and unfurl, billow and congeal as he wished, but he'd grown partial to his bipedal form. Zal rocked back on his haunches and grabbed fistfuls of his hair. It was thick and coarse, tumbling to his shoulders as it had before he'd been unmade. He wasn't a Netherling, though—no longer that wastrel boy who'd destroyed his sibling. He touched his left eye, which sat firm in its socket, his vision clearer than ever.

He rose, surprised when the Nether itself didn't strike him down for his unsanctioned return. No whipping wind or wraith army had been sent to thwart him. He received no sudden scourge of levin. Although he doubted Death had forgiven him, perhaps she no longer cared about her spawn begat in violence.

With the stars as his guide, he headed for the river, which would lead him to Death's necropolis. The air was heavy with the weight of spirits, and ghosts smudged the emptiness in shimmering mirages, which parted like spider web as Zal trekked across the dunes. He crested a rise and paused.

What had once been a majestic grove of towering baobabs stood forlorn and decrepit. The massive trees looked as if they'd been whittled by a cruel hand, their trunks shrunken and hollow, the trees buckled beneath their crowns of spreading branches. In the center lay a glistening coagulation of spirits—a shroud caught on broken twigs obscuring the figure within.

Emri lay between the desiccated baobabs, his hair pulled free from its braid to tangle with the silver ghosts wrapped around him in a sepulchral chrysalis. Ghost-touched though he was, Emri was mortal and shouldn't be in the Nether, not like this. When souls died, they tumbled from life, down the falls marking the Nether's threshold, to land in the Waters of Consequence. If Emri had died, he'd be facing the storks.

"Leave him be," Zal said in Nethertaal and the spirits obeyed, splitting open at his approach. Zal reached inside the coccoon and touched the sciomancer's cheek. The fine hairs on his face were silky soft against Zal's palm, the skin surprisingly warm despite the icy air.

"Emri?" He pressed his fingers to the side of the man's throat, feeling for the thrum of life. Impossibly, his heart was beating, his chest rising and falling beneath tattered clothes. "Can you hear me?"

Somehow, they'd both been sideswept across the realms. A living human, here in the Nether. Death must've allowed it. Unless she didn't know. Or perhaps she had ceased to care about her crumbling realm entirely.

Emri groaned and shifted, face scrunching as consciousness returned in increments. Perhaps the Ancestors had protected him; or perhaps his proximity to Zal—and his hand on the shadow staff—had shielded him from the force of Leksi's magic.

Zal suppressed a shudder at the memory of the fear she'd wielded, monstrous teeth skimming his skin as she'd tried to steal his power. He'd fought back, locked in a tug of war, before a flash of white erased reality.

Emri stirred again, fingers finding Zal's. Zal returned his grasp, pulling the sciomancer from the sand and cradling him against his chest.

"Where are we?" Emri said, the words burbling out of him in his native Yekkä.

"You're in the World of Shades," he said, using the Yekkä name for Death's realm.

"I'm dead?" Emri said.

"You are very much alive." Zal rested his hand on the hollow of the man's throat, then lower, where the laces of his shirt had come undone. The shadow remained ensconced in Emri's flesh. Perhaps it had been that piece of Nether magic carried within that had spared him a psychopomp's attention.

"So many voices." Emri clapped his hands over his ears. "They're all talking. It hurts."

"Stop," Zal commanded in Nethertaal and the spirits clamoring about the sciomancer stilled. "He's mine. Leave him be." In the Nether, Zal could claim his godhood, and—while his power wasn't fully restored—he was stronger here. The ghosts dispersed, rippling skeins fading into stagnant air.

"Thank you, Va'ili." Emri blinked, his gaze devoid of the ghost sheen. It was odd looking into his eyes, so dark they were almost black, the pinprick pupils barely discernible, yet still so unmistakably human.

Zal released the sciomancer, instantly resenting the loss of the man's touch. "Can you walk?"

"I think so." Emri popped the cricks from his neck, and raked his fingers through his moon-spun hair, trying to tame the disheveled tendrils. "How did we get here?"

"Leksi," Zal said. "She tried to annul the spell but caused the barrels to blow instead. She never was good at magic." And yet had given him what he'd craved for decades.

Now that he was back in the Nether, knowing what he did, Zal's anger fizzled. The hurt he carried lingered, a festering wound that would never heal, but the hatred he'd felt in the wake of his mother's cruelty had shifted. He still longed for vengeance, but Death no longer seemed the most deserving target of his rage.

Leksi then, for attempting to thwart him.

Riksa, for plotting against him and corrupting Ailia.

Or the unknown arkani who'd tortured Ailia and dared to steal his magic.

They all deserved to suffer.

"How do we get back?" Emri asked.

There was only one way in or out of the Nether. "We need to find the river," Zal said.

"They're still talking to me." Emri cocked his head, as if listening to a spectral brightness hovering against the gray. The Nether had always been wrapped in permanent night, a realm of cold and darkness. Death's land should not be sand and stillness, and certainly not stained by this crepuscular light threatening to become dawn.

Something was wrong, a thought confirmed when the helpful ghosts led them across the plains of beige to a furrow between the dunes. The once blue waters, pellucid and simmering, had cooled to sludge with souls gunged against the shore like overgrown algae. It reeked of rot and putrescence, strong enough to make Zal's eyes water as Emri wretched.

There, a figure at the muck's edge, not quite human, with an elongated muzzle and too-long fingers ending in scythe-like claws. Leksi turned where she knelt, her talons trailing through the slime of the dead. "Tamisk," she said, her face contorting back to human. "She'll be stuck. They all will."

And Ailia, too, Zal thought. Their dead lovers were both trapped in the rancid currents.

CHAPTER TWENTY-EIGHT
NIKI

None of the stars made sense. Regularly abandoned in the woods as a child, I'd learned to measure the passing hours in the inexorable spin of Elephant and Two-tailed Monkey, Yawning Baboon, and Dung Beetle.

None of the constellations above me now, though, resembled any of those. Impossibly, I found myself beneath an alien sky with cold sand beneath my empty hands. The amulet must've been ripped away when the world turned white.

Slowly, I raised my fingers. They were still streaked black, but red as well, my flesh torn—several nails were missing, too. My palm was shredded, and I could only hope the injury would heal well enough for me to play the kora again.

I'd fallen from the tower. I shouldn't be alive, let alone able to move, or think, or feel the agony throbbing in my mangled hand. I should be a dough-batter blob on the street and yet here I lay, conscious and contemplative, beneath a map of strange stars.

Was I breathing?

I sucked in a mouthful of dusty air to be sure, coughed, and spit up grit. It tasted of copper and salt, and something sweet too, like watermelon left too long in the summer sun. It was cold, the air a frigid kiss on patches of bare skin where my clothing had been torn in the fall.

Braced for the inevitability of liquefied ribs and obliterated organs, I rolled onto my side. When my body didn't turn to mush, I managed to prop myself onto my elbow.

"Well, you are just full of surprises." The ghoul who'd accosted me in the attic crouched beside me. They looked decidedly less cadaverous now, their cheeks plump where before they'd been hollow. Their eyes flashed pale as frost, and their left arm ended in a hand again. Between their fingers, they held the remnants of the amulet. "Thank you for this. Not exactly what I wanted, but it'll do."

I cradled my own savaged hand, already healing at an accelerated rate I couldn't explain. Was I dreaming?

"Where are we?" I asked, the pain receding enough for me to take in more of my surroundings. Dunes stretched in every direction in swaths of beige under a gray sky—neither twilight nor dawn, as if time hung suspended here. "This isn't Savat." Obvious, perhaps, but I wanted to be wrong.

"This is the Nether," the ghoul said.

"So I'm dead." Of course I was. There'd been an explosion powerful enough to knock me from the highest tower. I couldn't possibly have survived.

But this wasn't how the stories went. Dying meant being swept across the veil and into the currents of Consequence. Or death was simply cold, hard oblivion. It was not waking up in a desert wounded and in pain, feeling the blood pound in your throbbing temples.

"You should be blood splatter and crushed bone," the

stranger said, scrutinizing me as if I were a specimen on the autopsy table. "I should've sensed it, but I was a little preoccupied with that amulet you stole," the ghoul continued. "That should've killed you too. The arkani you took it from was highly skilled, and it almost undid her. Primordial magic isn't meant for humans."

"Primordial?" I aped, my thoughts racing.

"The amulet contains magic from a demigod."

"That's not possible." But the cogs turned in my mind, teeth finding purchase as understanding clicked into place. Scryali believed in a primordial power and her ability to tap into it, to wield it using a hexatonic scale and the subsequent harmonies.

"You were holding evidence to the contrary," the ghoul said. "Humans are endlessly creative and confounding."

"Who are you?" I asked.

The stranger regarded me with a searing gaze, and I imagined I could feel their indecision, that mix of wonder and consternation bubbling inside their mind.

"I believe we might be cousins," they said. "My name is—" The word was a fist, each phoneme a knuckle cut bloody against sharp teeth. I spoke it back to them, my tongue blistering and gums stinging.

"I'm impressed," they said with a crooked smile.

"Is there a less painful abbreviation?" I swallowed a mouthful of iron-flecked spit.

"Riksa. And since you seem determined to speak Savati, use *she, her* pronouns for me if you must."

"Riksa." I tried it out, grateful when my teeth didn't snap. "What are you?"

"A demigod. A Netherling," she said.

"Is the magic in the amulet yours?" I asked, trying not to think too hard about the fact I was conversing with a deity in a realm beyond the mortal one. Any moment now, I'd wake up in the attic and this would all prove nothing but a vivid dream—or nightmare.

"No." She twirled the damaged talisman. "My brother's."

"Brother?" My head hurt, thoughts spinning in a tightening gyre.

"The one leaving dirty fingerprints everywhere." She reached for my stained hand and the shadow shifted.

"I was infected by a god's magic? Is that what makes us—cousins?" I asked even though it was all too much for my overwrought mind to handle. I rubbed my hand where it had been adhered to the amulet and felt oddly bereft in its absence. The wound had healed, although my palm was gnarled scars, the skin tight when I tried to stretch my fingers. I eyed the amulet, wondering if I could snatch it back.

Riksa laughed, the sound like rocks smashing together and breaking into pebbles.

"You called me cousin. I just want to know why." I bit back the 'please' despite everything my parents had taught me about the gods and their need to be adored, admired, supplicated.

My parents. Were they here? Frolicking in the dunes, shimmering in the air as mirages? Or had they already been born again into new bodies? If the stories were true, then they'd be in the river, drowning and pecked apart over and over again. It had barely been six years since their deaths. Six years of suffering wasn't nearly enough for all they'd forced me to endure.

"Beg me and I might tell you," Riksa said, looming over me where I still sat slouched in the sand. Her legs were slabbed with muscle, as was the rest of her—her body exuding power and control—but I was done being bullied. I lurched to my feet and met her gaze, peering down at her from my superior height.

"I've never begged for anything in my life." Not for mercy or favor or recognition. "And, god or not, I will not beg you. I will *never* beg."

Riksa's lips peeled back from her long teeth. "That's what Zal thought, but you should've heard him screaming and pleading in the snow as Mother split him like a pomegranate, plucking out his organs like sweet little seeds."

"Zal?"

"My brother. *Our* half-brother," she said and again twirled the amulet.

Our brother. The words were flies buzzing around a corpse, my sense of self the dead meat.

"No."

"You are most certainly god-spawn. Not quite a changeling," Riksa said, sounding amused. "Your mother was human. But your father—" she paused, gaze narrowed. "I wonder if all Time's bastards look so alike."

Time?

God-spawn?

I was losing my mind, unraveling as Scryali had, lost in delusions. Perhaps it was a side effect of working with magic, the result of the hexatonic vibrations addling our brains. I clutched my head, panic rising up my throat and breath turning soupy in my lungs. I started to hum, the same ditty that had seen me through the darkness of the cellar and palace dungeons. Was Scryali's melody the cause of my mental rot?

And yet my feet kept time against the tune's hemiolas as I paced patterns in the sand. The shimmering air responded, lugubrious voices joining in a chorus.

"Stop that," Riksa said, but I couldn't. The voices grew louder, a dirge weaving through the ether, a circle song, twisting and looping, forward and back, all encompassing.

If only I could go back to that moment in the dungeon with Ailia. If I'd known then what the amulet was, I would've been more careful. Go further back, and I could've avoided the shadow slipping into my skin. But even then, that wasn't the beginning. I could've avoided arrest and entrapment if only I'd known all this before that night in the temple.

The ground quivered beneath my feet, the sand dancing. Green shoots protruded between my bare toes. I kept singing and the vines kept growing, roots spreading, reaching, grasping. Stems strengthened and leaves unfurled.

"What are you doing?" Riksa yelled, but I kept singing, shifting the tonal center through various modulations.

If I'd known all this, I might never have come to the city, might never have pursued the heresy Scryali started, could've accepted being a disappointment and learned to live with that, bowed my head and said my prayers.

God-spawn. God-spawn. God-spawn.

What of my legacy now? I'd wanted to be remembered, to matter, to have my name preserved in the annals of academic greatness. I'd wanted my name to echo through the ages, to leave my mark on history. Was there still time to go back and undo all the damage but retain this knowledge, to write a treatise on the perils of attempting to tame magic, before my legacy became nothing but a cautionary tale?

My thoughts spiraled and the sands receded like a wave from the shore as I hurtled backwards toward light and life. My shoulders met resistance, a membrane in need of tearing. I sharpened my song, accidentals like a blade, ready to slice.

"I said stop." Riksa's human features sloughed away, a reptilian molt revealing a hideous creature all scale and claw, and glistening viscera. My song faltered as she fell on me, her fangs sinking into my throat.

Chapter Twenty-Nine
Leksi

Leksi's head felt full of feathers, her skull split open like a threadbare pillow case. Her fingers were greasy with soul-scum, the waters clogged and festering.

"Tam won't be able to get out," she said. "She'll be stuck forever. Where are the storks?" Without them, every soul remained trapped. "Where is Mother? What happened here? We have to do something." She flung viscid dead from her fingers in sudden disgust. "We have to fix it."

"Fix it?" Zal's nostrils flared as he stood, hands on hips, glaring at her. "Like you wanted to *fix* Savat?"

"No. I—" Feathers spun. Leksi tried to snatch them up, to stuff them back where they belonged. She remembered the barrels, remembered the sigils and her own trembling finger carving imperfect lines into wood. She'd meant to stop the explosion and spare the humans the strife her sister wanted.

But Leksi was Nightmare—and she'd released her power, the barest smidgen of it—and yet, it had been more than enough to be their undoing. Only, she'd forgotten she wasn't immune to her own magic. Now here she sat watching the curdling waters, some of her worst fears made manifest.

Not all of them, though. Not yet.

Zal moved, a flash of shadow against the too-bright sky.

He shoved her hard and she tripped, falling face-first into the viscous shallows. He held her down even as she screamed, thrashing against him, but he was so much stronger here. They remained tethered, however, and Leksi jerked on his power. It was enough to make him stagger and she wiggled from his grasp. She kicked at his legs and he fell to his knees, reaching with long arms to grab at her hair. She scratched and bit, bucking away from him, but he held on, dragging her down once more. They'd fought like this as children, their tussling having a nasty habit of mimicking death throes.

Zal elbowed her in the ribs; Leksi kneed him in the groin. They both pulled away from each other gasping. Then he snatched up a handful of her hair again, his face reflecting the mirror image of her own rage and pain.

"Is this what you did to Mezra?" Leksi asked.

"They had the decency to drown," Zal fired back, but his venomous words were undone by the rush of guilt sizzling along their psychic bond.

"You forget I can taste your shame, little brother."

Zal released her and wiped his hand on his chest as if he could rub away the memories. Leksi crawled from the waters, coughing up scraps of spirit that skidded back into the water, unable to find purchase in the mud.

Zal remained in the shallows, bent forward with his hands on his knees, as Leksi scooted further up the bank.

"So much sorrow," Emri said, his hands sticky with soul stuff, stretched into shiny strings between his fingers like melted cheese. "I'm guessing the river shouldn't be like this?"

"No," Zal said.

"And we need to fix it," Leksi added while wringing the thick water from her tattered skirts. She tried not to think about how much she might've swallowed.

"Assuming we even can fix it." Zal combed scum from his hair before trudging to the shore. "It's worse than I thought," he said. "With Mezra, the storks were waiting. They should've come for us now as well. We should've been pulled under."

"Next time you feel the urge to wallow in the consequences of your poor choices, you can leave me out of it," Leksi snapped. She really should've rolled Zal over the cliff when she'd had the chance.

"As if your choices haven't contributed to all this." Zal gestured to the dilapidated realm.

"We need to find Mother," Leksi said. "Or Riksa, if she isn't reveling in whatever has become of Savat." Whatever happened to the city, it was Leksi's fault—not that she'd admit that to Zal and gift him the satisfaction of her guilt.

"This way." Zal started upstream with Emri trailing after him. The mortal should've been one of the congealed in the river, not strolling through the Nether as if it were the palace gardens on a summer afternoon.

It was all so very wrong: the staunched waters, the sky, the light.

Time had no dominion over the Nether. Hours and days meant nothing here in the land that should've been locked in perpetual midwinter. Fire's realm had summer, Earth held autumn, and Water held spring. Air moved freely between all the realms, and Time… Leksi only knew her uncle had no home, existing in whatever void cradled the worlds like a cupped hand. Perhaps he shared a bed with Inyoti, the serpent of Life who chose to sleep instead of taking responsibility for its alleged creations.

While Leksi and Zal could've moved more quickly in less human form, they maintained a slower pace for Emri's sake and passed through what should've been meadows of frostweed and woodland pearled with snowberries. The frostweed lay in desiccated clumps, the woodland a slouch of kindling, the berries all shriveled in the inclement warmth.

Eventually, the river broadened into the primordial swamp where the marabou storks usually resided with Grief, their keeper and tutelary of the Nether.

The falls were as sludgy as the shallows. The dead oozed over the cliffs where once torrents had gushed. The waters of Death, the waters of life—a constant cycle of loss and renewal, now all but dried up. The storks too. At first Leksi thought they might be sitting on nests or taking a nap with their miserable faces tucked into their wings. As she drew closer, she realized with fresh horror that the storks had turned to stone.

"I thought they were boulders." Emri rested his hand atop a curled neck. "Are they birds?"

"They were." Zal ran his hand over petrified feathers, each stork an eerie statue.

Leksi kept expecting them to wake and ruffle their wings, but they remained frozen. The Nether was too quiet. The only sound, the congested drip of the falls and the rustle of ghosts in stale air.

"To the necropolis then." Zal had already turned away from the river, limping determinedly toward their home.

When Leksi had left this realm, she'd turned her back on a palace carved of ice and obsidian. Death's court was a marvel of spires, the necropolis rising from snowy mounds like a giant's cadaverous fingers reaching toward the sky. Now though…

"No." The word was a strangled whimper in her throat. "This can't be."

The necropolis had collapsed, the spires toppled into rubble strewn across the sand. Where previously the facets had glinted with reflections of ghost light, they now lay dull in the gloaming, the sculpted ice melting into oleaginous puddles, the stone friable to the touch.

Leksi rubbed black dust from her fingers. Both her worlds had been reduced to grit and ash.

"Was it always like this?" Emri asked. "So… desolate?"

"It used to be magnificent," Zal said, a pang of sorrow twanging between them.

"How did this happen?" Leksi turned to her brother who looked as despondent as she felt.

"I'm surprised you even care," he said. "You turned your back on all this."

"To escape myself," Leksi said. "I never wanted this. Never imagined—" But she'd never truly contemplated the consequences of her actions; she'd only wanted to avoid the truth of what she was and escape the dark purpose foisted upon her. Perhaps this is what happened when a god stood guilty of dereliction of duty. With human worship waning, perhaps Death and a single remaining daughter hadn't been enough to sustain the realm.

"Death is here," Emri said. "But she is..." He paused, spirits trailing through his fingers like mist. "She is unwell."

Zal led the way again, cutting a track through the rubble and splashing through ice-filmed puddles. His footprints filled with feathery rime, and Leksi followed until they reached the center of the wreckage.

Death huddled between the largest chunks of chipped obsidian. Her garments hung thick and heavy, her once black raiment turned to mourning white. Her horns—usually decorated with bird skulls to form a crown—sagged flaccid through the fabric, moldering with velveteen rot. Her crown of skulls had scattered in the dust.

In her arms, the limp form of Grief. The stork's black feathers had grayed as if the creature had been soaked in an alkaline bath, its long neck so pathetically frail, and the beak pitiful instead of terrible.

Zal seemed paralyzed, staring at the diminished god so small in her sorrow. She'd been weeping, her tears tangling with the puddles of her melted palace in threads of brittle frostweed. Leksi stepped forward, crushing wilted flowers beneath her feet.

"Mother?" she said, her voice booming in the silence. She received no response. Not even a twitch of surprise. "Mother, please, it's me." Leksi said her full name, resenting every syllable, but hoping it would jolt Death from her stupor.

Still nothing. Leksi turned to Zal, who stood wide-eyed and unblinking. Gently she probed their tether, trying to understand what he was feeling. A chaotic jumble greeted her, too much and all at once, each emotion splashing into another like rapids tumbling over rocks.

Emri nudged Zal forward, his hand on Zal's back offering the support Leksi wasn't sure he deserved. He'd destroyed Mezra. It was easier to focus her resentment on Zal—to blame her brother for all this—than to remember the day she'd abandoned them.

She'd rather forget how Mezra had been waiting at the bottom of the falls, how they'd blocked her path and begged her not to go. They'd pleaded with her to stay until she'd threatened them with claws and fears. And even then, Mezra had stayed to watch her climb the rocks with Grief and the other storks gathered in the stream, bearing silent witness as she deserted her realm.

Zal cleared his throat and rubbed his hand where his Nether gem should've been. "Hello, Mother," he said, his voice the soft crush of fallen snow. "The exile returns."

A rustle then, like the dried pages of an old book being rifled by clumsy fingers. Or feathers turned to slate and flaking.

It was Grief who stirred, not Death. The bird twisted its neck at an ugly angle to stare at Zal with an expression at once vacant and woeful. It opened its beak in a wretched keen before its amber eye rolled back in its socket.

"Mother?" Zal nudged Death with his toe, nudged then

kicked.

"Zal, don't," Leksi said weakly.

"Aren't you filled with rage that I dared to defy you, Mother, coming back against your wishes?" He kicked even harder, enough to break off a chunk of their mother's robes. "Don't you want to punish me, to carve out the rest of me?" His voice broke on that last part, and Leksi felt it like a fault-line through the center of her chest, the remains of her heart flinching in involuntary sympathy. "Mother, please." He crouched beside her now and reached a trembling hand toward her fingers knotted in the stiff wings of Grief. "Mother, please, I'm so—"

"Ah, little brother, still begging like a sniveling child, I see." Riksa strolled through the ruins in a billow of garments the color of blood. Another figure trailed behind her, their neck stained scarlet and brown.

"Welcome home, siblings," Riksa said, her smile a sinister display of teeth as she raised her hand. Zal cried out, falling as if his legs had been broken by the sweep of a giant hammer. Leksi felt the pull on his magic, the cord between them tightening.

"You never did appreciate your power," Riksa said, her fingers curled around a wooden token.

The amulet.

"Do you even know who you truly are?" she asked. "Death and Time, now there's a potent mix. You could've been the best of us, but you squandered what you had." She scoffed. "No matter. It's mine now." Colors danced across her fingers in ribbons of nebulous light. "And I know how to use it.

Chapter Thirty
Zal

The shadows flocked to him, drawn by his distress. Riksa had the amulet. Either she'd taken it from Ailia or she'd taken it from the arkani who'd tortured her.

Zal's whole body ached with the effort of fighting the spell still siphoning his magic. It tore through him, like fish hooks lodged in flesh, tearing furrows as cruel hands reeled in the line.

Riksa might hold his power in her hand, but he had his shadows and a tether to Leksi. He had Emri too, who'd stepped closer, standing beside Zal protectively, ghosts swirling around him.

"And what do you plan to do with all that chaos?" Leksi asked.

"Restore our realm, of course," Riksa said. "Look around. *You* did this." She pointed an accusatory finger at Leksi. "The deterioration began after you left. You broke Mother's heart; you abandoned us, and your birthright. And you." She turned her burning gaze on Zal. "Thanks to you I was left alone here, to bear the burden of Mother's duty while she wallowed in misery."

"Love what you've done with the place," Leksi said, and the lines tearing at Zal slackened as Riksa's focus shifted.

"You abandoned us," she said. "You don't get to judge me."

"As if you didn't go for a jaunt in the mortal realm yourself," Leksi said.

"To find you!" Riksa spat. "To find some way to fix this." She gestured to the unmoving forms of Death and Grief. "She's been like that for an age or more. Weak and pathetic, mourning the loss of her children and withering away as humans fail to keep faith."

While his sisters continued exchanging verbal ordinance, Zal's attention shifted to the stranger.

"The resemblance is—uncanny," Emri said, his gaze flicking between Zal and the interloper.

"Who are you?" Zal asked, suspicion forming a throbbing embolus in the center of his chest.

"Oh, my apologies," Riksa said. "Let me introduce another one of Time's misbegottens." She switched to Savati. "I believe their name is Niki. Like dear old Zal here, they were equally ignorant of their origins, until recently. Go on, Niki, say hello to your brother."

Niki gurgled a response and clutched at their throat.

"Right. Sorry about that." Riksa shrugged. "But you gave me no choice. Accident of shared blood I suppose, but Niki here could wield your magic, Zal. Had to sing to do it, and I couldn't have that, so—" She mimed slitting their throat.

Zal rose on shaky legs, taking the measure of Time's alleged bastard. Niki's gaze met his own and it was like looking in a mirror, one with ripples in the glass causing subtle distortions in the reflection. They shared the same dark hair, strong jaw, and sharp cheekbones. They both had eyes rounder than Leksi's and Riksa's, their lips fuller where the sisters' were razor-thin. They were both tall, too—of equal height, if only Zal could fully straighten his spine.

If it weren't for the missing chunks of throat already knitting into scar tissue, Niki could've passed for a younger version of Zal—the person he might've been had his mother not flayed him to ribbons. He couldn't help but wonder if Niki's conception had been like his own. It brought a cold sort of comfort to think he might not be the only one born of such depravity.

"Are you the arkani who hurt Ailia?" Zal asked, forcing every word through his gritted teeth. He wanted vengeance. He needed to hurt someone, to make them suffer as he did, day after day—century after century—without reprieve. "Tell me!" Zal demanded.

Niki hesitated, nostrils flaring as they shot a murderous glance at Riksa.

"Zal, dear, did you miss the part where I tore their throat out?" Riksa used a long nail to dig a morsel from between her teeth. "But I did find them fleeing the palace in possession of this lovely trinket." She brandished the amulet. "So make of that what you will."

"About that amulet," Leksi interjected. "Assuming you do have noble notions of restoration, once you've used Zal's power to redecorate, what then?" she asked with astonishing placidity while Zal churned in an alloy of mixed emotion.

"That'll be a good start," Riksa said. "But it won't be nearly enough. Not in the long run. It's important to consider sustainability. We're all powered by this realm, which is why war is the only long-term solution," she continued. "In times of despair, people turn to the gods. They take comfort in ritual and prayer, they build altars in our names and make offerings."

"They kill each other too," Leksi said.

"Yes, and hopefully that'll get the river flowing again. It's really starting to stink."

"So many will die," Emri said, wistfully. "So many already have."

"What are a few hundred human lives if it restores Death?" Riksa asked. "Do you think humans will survive if the imbalance continues, if the river gets clogged with souls? No one likes a blocked sewer."

"Storks and spirits," Leksi rubbed a hand over her face. "It's already clogged, and you want to send more souls down the cliffs?"

"People have started praying again. Fanes are going up as buildings tumble down. It's all rather poetic. Human faith—that's the renewable resource our realm needs in order to sustain itself. Mother knew that. She just didn't care anymore." Riksa stroked Death's head and Zal saw Death's fingers twitch.

"What happens if faith isn't restored fast enough?" Zal asked. "If prayers and offerings aren't the aperient you expect?"

Riksa frowned as if the thought of failure had never occurred to her. "War will see their faith restored. Slowly, perhaps, but unequivocally. You'll see. I'm doing this to help humanity. Sacrifice a few to save the many."

"Sacrifice Savat, you mean?" Leksi said.

"It could be any city," Riksa said. "But you two have made Savat an easy target. Violence has been simmering in those streets for years. It took so little to bring it to a boil."

"Why don't I believe this is truly all you want?" Leksi asked.

"And here I was hoping you'd help," Riksa said with a pout. "Maybe lend me your power and expedite things. Fear can be such a powerful motivator. Oh well, Zal's magic will have to do. It should be enough to get this started at least, and finally revive Death." She chortled at her own terrible joke. "Or release her from the grip of her own incompetence."

"It's not incompetence," Zal said. "It's grief." The bird's talons were lodged deep in his mother's chest, each clinging to the other, inseparable in their petrification.

Zal understood the paralyzing grip of despair, the despondency of not knowing how to survive devastation. It was only his desire for vengeance that had driven him through the agony, sustaining him when he had nothing else. If only Death would wake, perhaps then he could convince her he'd never been the one she truly resented. Perhaps then Death might finally take her own revenge.

"Honestly, I was hoping you'd fight me. I've been dying to dismember you for what you did to Mezra, to Mother, to me." Riksa smiled, all fang. "Or do you still maintain that what happened was an *accident*?"

Zal hesitated, denial already on his lips. Death stirred, a ripple in the white shroud obscuring her skeletal face, and

Zal swallowed. There was no point lying anymore—not to his siblings and not to himself.

"Mezra was being an ass so I pushed them," Zal said. "I wanted them to suffer." Admitting the truth brought bittersweet relief. "I didn't like losing, and Mezra laughed at me." And Zal had retaliated like the spiteful child he was, shoving his sibling into the river, watching Mezra flounder as sharp beaks caved in their skull. Zal could've helped, at least tried to intervene. Instead, he enjoyed the spectacle, smug in victory as his sibling unraveled.

"Mezra laughed at you so you condemned them to eternal unmaking?" Riksa gawped.

"I know," Zal said, screwing his eyes closed against the unwanted regret slithering from the smelt of his mixed emotions. "It was petty and ill-considered. Mezra was just being what Mother made them, but so was I. We were young and foolish."

"As if that exonerates you." Leksi scoffed.

"I know what I did was wrong." Zal turned to his sister, the one who wanted nothing to do with her family and yet still bound herself to him out of necessity, if not love. "I'm trying to tell you, I *know*," he said. "I know I deserved Mother's retribution. I deserved exile." His admission was a blade opening the abscess where his heart should've been, the wound suppurating guilt and remorse in a gruesome torrent. Death shifted, fingers peeling away from feathers one swollen knuckle at a time.

"And I'm sorry," Zal said, pressing a hand to his chest

where the sigil still burned. "I'm sorry."

"Oh, spare us," Riksa said. "If you truly want to make amends, then you'll give up your magic and let yourself perish so the Nether can flourish."

Perhaps she was right—and yet, when Zal felt his magic slipping through his grasp, he instinctively tightened his grip, not wanting to relinquish what was rightfully his.

"Not so sorry after all, it seems." Riksa sneered.

Would it be so bad to let go, to let himself unravel and fade to nothing? He glanced at Emri, then Leksi, before his gaze finally settled on his mother. His existence had caused so much harm. It would've been better to have never been born at all, but since he couldn't undo that, giving up his magic was the best alternative.

"To restore the Nether, then, and replenish Death." Zal released his hold on Chaos.

"No!" Leksi grabbed his arm. "She's lying. This isn't some selfless act of love for the Nether or some twisted act of altruism to save humanity. She's using you, Zal. All of this is for her own agenda. Can't you feel it?"

Through the psychic commotion, Zal tried to focus on the strand connecting him to Riksa, but she recoiled before he could catch her intentions. He sensed Niki too—like kelp drifting on the tide, instead of the usual unwanted noose of Death's filaments netting her children together. Niki was a strand he could snatch up if he wanted to, but for now, he left it hanging.

"Believe what you want, darling sister," Riksa said. "But

you're either with me or against me." She wrenched his magic away and, depleted, Zal fell—onto sand instead of snow.

"You are an affliction on humanity. War and Violence never brought anything but suffering and torment," Leksi said. "I know; I carry the shape of their nightmares within me. I've seen what they dread—I've tasted their fear. Force the people into war and maybe they'll turn to the gods for solace, but do you really want adoration borne of terror?"

"I'll take worship any way it comes," Riksa said. She sucked in an unnecessary breath. "Ah, I can already taste it. Their prayers on the wind, the influx of the dying, the river swelling. If we don't act soon, there might not be enough souls recovered from the waters to repopulate the city, and then I might need to extend my reach. To the atoll perhaps, or maybe beyond the desert. And with each city, town, or village that takes up arms, I will be venerated."

"You'll be loathed," Leksi said.

"Love or hate, I'll be in their thoughts." Riksa shrugged. "As long as it's Violence in their hearts and Death's name in their prayers."

"I knew it," Leksi yelled. "This is about your ego and your own thirst for power."

"Someone needs to step up."

"Children," Death's voice fell like a scythe as stone shifted and the god raised her head.

"No!" Riksa roared. "No, it's my turn now. You failed us." She flailed her fists, bashing at Death. "You broke. You let Time violate you, and then you let that filthy result destroy you." She glowered at Zal before using her nails like pickaxes, chipping away at the statue Death had become. "You could've fought; you could've avenged yourself. We would've helped you. We could've drowned the runt in the river as an infant. You could've cut it from your belly the moment you knew, but you didn't. You let this happen because you are weak." Riksa brandished the amulet, her eyes changing color as she drew on Zal's power and released a stream of chaos into the ether. It fell on Death and Zal scrabbled after his stolen magic, bones breaking and sinews snapping.

Leksi pulled too, adding the strength of her will to Zal's. Briefly, warmth puddled in his core, but Riksa was strong and wouldn't let go.

"Va'ili, your shadows," Emri said. He held Zal's hand, the bones grinding together as Zal's body became the battleground for his sisters' war. "Let me help you."

With a whimper and a thought, Zal instructed his shadows to obey the sciomancer. He looked up into Emri's face, into his eyes obscured by ghost-glow cataracts. Darkness condensed in his sockets as tears of light and shadow streaked his face.

"Which one do we fight?" Emri asked, his voice full of echoes.

Zal hesitated, caught in a moment of indecision. Leksi had abandoned them, but Riksa had tried to take what was rightfully his. He hated them both.

Riksa grabbed a handful of his shadow and ripped it apart. Zal thought he'd already endured the worst agony imaginable, but this was acid and fire, a sundering from deep inside as if the marrow were boiling in his bones.

Emri began to sing, his rich voice splitting into the familiar multitone tune. That finally got Niki's attention at least, the sibling Zal might otherwise have forgotten was even there. They staggered toward Emri, hand still gripping their ruined throat, mouth opening and closing like a suffocating fish as Emri sent a spear of shadow and blinding spirit streaking toward Riksa. It plunged into her shoulder and she screamed in rage, releasing a string of blistering invective.

Emri altered his song, drawing more souls into the fray, but the spirits of the Nether would never be able to defeat a demi-god in her own territory. Riksa evaded the shades, batting at them like a swarm of tsetse flies, using Zal's magic without restraint. His power tore through the necropolis, obliterating the rubble and turning swaths of sand to sheets of fulgurite.

"Stop!" Leksi screamed. "This won't restore the Nether. You'll destroy it, and us along with it."

Leksi... Zal didn't have the strength to speak, but he flooded their connection with a plea for the help only she could give. She turned to him, already shaking her head when Riksa lunged at Zal, her human veneer replaced by her true brutish form.

While Riksa may have been able to wield Zal's magic against others, she had gravely miscalculated what it meant to turn that power on Chaos incarnate when he stood within the realm that had birthed him. She had also seemingly failed to account for the other aspect of his creation—the one Zal could resent, but not deny.

So when Riksa barreled into him, her fangs sinking deep, Zal enveloped her, the force of their collision punching a hole through time and space as he finally embraced his true self.

Chapter Thirty-One
Leksi

Leksi was witnessing her family's annihilation at the hands of the big sister she'd once adored.

Death couldn't die—not in the human sense of the word—but she could succumb to the disorder of Chaos, her physical form turned to dust and her power subsumed by the Nether. Zal couldn't die either, but he could be ripped into shreds as easily as old paper.

Riksa leapt, transforming mid-rush into a slobbering hound of war, her jaws snapping shut on Zal's throat. His arms closed around her as if he welcomed the bite, and Leksi felt the impact as if Riksa had latched onto her own neck. The shift in Zal was a landslide—his Chaos becoming something different, something *more.* It sent the three of them reeling, hurtling through the membranous cerement separating the Nether from its neighbors.

Their feet sent up plumes of acrid ash as they skidded into the realm of Fire. Lava bubbled in soupy streams down the flanks of convulsing volcanoes, the roar of disgruntled tectonics a constant thunder in Leksi's ears as she struggled to get her bearings. The air reeked of sulfur and she was grateful she didn't have to breathe.

They weren't supposed to be here—not uninvited like

this. Fire was ornery at the best of times and would see them aggressively evicted for trespassing in her realm. But her bellicose aunt wasn't Leksi's immediate concern.

Zal and Riksa wrestled in a tangle of too-long limbs, their bestial screams indistinguishable as they grappled, biting, scratching, rending. At least it seemed Niki and Emri had been spared the dimensional dislocation, or had perished somewhere in the liminal space between realms.

Zal rose, momentarily victorious despite his many wounds inflicted by Riksa's teeth. Skeletal black wings extended from his hunched shoulders. The black bones of the unexpected appendages were sheathed in orange flame and his head bore a similar corona of fiery wisps, his skull visible through the glow. He was immense and terrible in this guise, and Leksi was grateful she wasn't the target of his ire as he fell upon Riksa, who'd become an entity of many mouths, each fanged and gnashing.

Zal couldn't win—not in a fight against the embodiment of violence. They tore at each other and Leksi stared, relegated to spectator. Even if Riksa succeeded in stripping Zal of power, refurbishing the Nether, and rekindling human piety, she would never be satisfied. Wars waned, beliefs fluctuated, and people would once more forget to love or fear the gods. Riksa would have to keep stoking the embers of that strife. And when Savat was reduced to a wasteland, she'd turn her sights elsewhere, chewing up city after city to feed her ego, glutting on pain and devastation.

One of Riksa's many maws ripped into Zal's wing, and the

flame-feathers guttered. Zal dropped to one knee, his exhaustion palpable, and Riksa hauled herself from the ashes of his crushed pinion, singed and bloody but fueled by the conflict instead of depleted.

This had to end before it began. If Riksa fully consumed Zal's magic and made it her own, she'd be invincible.

Leksi's limbs elongated, bones sprouting from flesh into needle-spines, her teeth rearranging themselves into serrated rows. She charged at Riksa who now had Zal in a chokehold.

How did it come to this? How was she here, embroiled in the very thing she'd so desperately tried to escape? She couldn't escape herself though—her own nightmare made manifest as she bit at her big sister, trying to break her hold on their little brother. It was all so unnecessary, and yet Leksi didn't know why she'd expected Riksa, of all entities, to consider a diplomatic solution.

"How dare you!" Fire lumbered toward them clad in magma, her basalt eyes smoking.

Leksi curled protectively around Zal in an attempt to escape their aunt's wrath.

Riksa sucked on Zal's power and Leksi pulled back in a futile tug of war. Zal screamed and, before Fire could spit-roast them, he once again catapulted them across the divide. Shearing through the realms would no doubt leave a wake of destruction. The worlds weren't meant to be so violently traversed. If they survived, then there were going to be consequences.

Still entwined, they erupted from the ocean, ejected in

a spout from an underwater geyser. The force of their flight punctured the sky before they plummeted back into the salty fathoms.

Leksi tried to speak but choked on a mouthful of brine. Riksa was beyond being reasoned with anyway. When frenzied like this as a child, it had only ever been Mother who could soothe her ferocity. And even Death had sometimes thought better of trying to tame the malevolent thing she'd created, resigned to let Riksa's tantrum run its course—usually in the mortal realm.

Now, Riksa and Zal circled each other, their lithe bodies undulating with the currents. A trail of bioluminescence flowed from the sigil in Zal's side, visible even as he became a saw-toothed leviathan with fins like scythes. Riksa was a mess of stinging tendrils, dragging Zal closer to the vicious beak her face had become. No matter how many of her appendages Zal severed with tooth or fin, she sprouted new ones and continued to smother him.

Leksi wafted in the current like a cloud of plankton. She'd already used her magic more than she'd ever wanted to. Her monsters strained against her hold, desperate for release, excited by the fray. If she unleashed them now though—away from the Nether and addled with Zal's magic—she wasn't sure she'd ever be able to tame them again.

Zal's desperation sliced through her thoughts and Riksa's glee followed like a sour chaser, pouring through the unwanted connection Leksi shared with her siblings.

As Zal weakened, so Riksa strengthened, her form shifting

with every siphoned morsel of magic. She grew even larger, a hideous assembly of teeth and tentacles locking Zal in a death roll. Leksi stretched herself to the limit, transforming, and opened her gargantuan mouth. If the only way to stop them was to devour them both, then so be it.

Her jaws closed on emptiness as Zal tossed them like a stone skipping across a pond. They somersaulted through the damp undergrowth of a jungle, loam coating her tongue, leaves and twigs knotting in her hair. They only came to a halt when they slammed into the base of the mountain Earth called home.

Leksi gaped at the devastation left in their wake: the splintered trees, flattened flowers, and bloody smears of creatures caught in their passing. Worse still, tiny waves lapped at the shimmering edges of the trail where the border between realms had been ruptured. The air shimmered too, the tatters of the veil like jellyfish fronds catching at the tree branches. The foliage instantly withered.

"You really thought you could beat me?" Riksa held Zal by the throat. He dangled, limp and defeated in her claws, reduced once more to the bloody, broken thing that had clambered out of the grave to ruin Leksi's life.

"I'm going to see Savat razed," Riksa continued. "A temple on every corner erected to the God of War, of Blood and Violence, of Pain and Death. They will forget about you—your name and essence excoriated from human history as surely as you were rejected by the Nether. Any survivors will become my army, to conquer in my name across sea and sand until every knee buckles before me, humans and gods alike. They will finally see that Death reigns supreme. Inevitable. Inescapable. Eternal."

This wasn't how it was supposed to work, Leksi thought. All things in Time. All things in cycles. Birth, death, and rebirth. Times of strife, but also times of peace—a constant balancing act.

Zal whimpered as Riksa sunk her talons into his chest where the sigil lay obscured by ichor and muck. Leksi was out of options, but she wouldn't be strong enough here. She needed to be in the Nether, connected to the essence of her magic. She hoped Zal had enough power to breach the veil one last time.

She poured all her longing into her connection to her brother, channeling it so only he would sense her desire and understand what she needed.

Riksa was so focused on enjoying her seeming victory, she paid no attention as Leksi snuck up behind her.

"Now," Leksi said. She glommed onto her sister like the sticky residue of a bad dream not even the brightest dawn and strongest cup of coffee could slough away. Zal met Leksi's gaze, all the nameless colors leaching away to gray then white as he flung them once more across the divide.

"I'm sorry," Leksi whispered, though she doubted her siblings heard her for all the roaring in their ears.

Leksi tucked and rolled to her feet, instantly relieved to be home. She shook herself as if she could dislodge the travesty infecting her mind, but the truth was written in her marrow.

This was where she belonged.

Reduced to peeling scales and broken feathers, Zal lay crumpled, his eyes sunken into the hollows of his skull. Behind him, Grief stirred, shedding dust from stony wings regaining feathers. Slowly, she withdrew her hooked feet from Death's chest and turned her baleful gaze on Leksi.

"What did you do?" Emri asked with a sob as he knelt beside the gore-stained husk that had once been Chaos.

There was no time for explanations though. Riksa had survived re-entry and now set her sights on Leksi.

"I'm sorry," Leksi said again, this time for Emri's and Niki's benefit. Perhaps for her mother's too, although if anyone might endure, surely it would be Death—but no one was entirely immune to fear.

Shedding her human form, Leksi let the Nether strip away all pretense. There was no other way to stop her sister. It had to be done. Using her fingernails, she dug into the soft squelch of her belly and tore herself open. Her nightmares tumbled from her rotten womb—beaked and clawed, fanged and nebulous—some nothing more than wisps of mist or tongues of flame. They attacked indiscriminately, no one spared from their savagery.

Zal was set upon by jackal-faced abominations, which yipped in glee as they plucked at his brittle seams. Had she been stronger, better, Leksi might've tried harder to resist the pleasure of seeing her brother succumbing to terror.

Instead, she sashayed toward Emri who batted weakly at what looked like a giant owl—one of the golden-winged raptors that haunted the dunes of the great desert. It fell upon him and Leksi closed her eyes, relishing the sciomancer's strangled screams.

Niki gasped and writhed, hands on their throat as a flock of flaming weavers attacked their body, stitching shimmering threads like blades of grass into her unlucky cousin's flesh. How absurd that Time's child would fear gods and magic so profoundly. Leksi inhaled their distress, sighing in long-denied satisfaction.

"I am War," Riksa roared. "I am Violence. I fear nothing." She threw her head back, laughing as nightmares stalked toward her on velvet paws, ropes of saliva escaping grotesque jaws.

But Leksi knew that wasn't true. If she was stronger, better, she might've spared a moment's sympathy for her sister about to be undone by her denial, but Leksi was Nightmare and would not deny her nature. Not this time.

With a snarl, Riksa unsheathed claws like daggers. "Let me show you, sister, how easily I destroy your pets." She attacked, a vortex of razors, as she whirled through the conjured monsters. Leksi sidestepped an errant blow, watching with bleak satisfaction as Riksa exhausted herself against beasts that refused to fight back.

"Fight me!" she shrieked in frustration when the diaphanous nightmares knit back together. Her sister's annoyance thrummed along their connection, a furious conflagration, and still the nightmares did nothing but press closer.

Leksi's palm smarted where the sigil binding her to Zal

flared in a final, feeble paroxysm as Riksa drew on borrowed magic. Wielding the last vestiges of Chaos, cold fire erupted from her fingers, incinerating Leksi's monsters.

"See? I'm not afraid of you. I'm not afraid of anything! You cannot defeat me." Riksa smiled, but there was a flicker of uncertainty in her eyes.

"Dear sister, it's not me you have to defeat," Leksi said. Again, the cinders reconstituted and the renewed nightmares advanced once more, cat-like and purring.

"No! Fight me! Why won't you fight me?" Riksa trembled with fury, batting at the purring monsters. They butted her with too-large heads, smothering her with affection.

"I don't understand," Riksa whimpered as the beasts licked at her bloody hands, brushing against her legs and butting her ever closer to the river and her demise.

Riksa slipped on the soul-slick shore, the sluggish currents sucking at her feet. "How do I win if they won't fight me?" She pounded her fists in the iridescent scum before being bowled over by an exuberant nightmare intent on cuddles. Riksa screamed, her exasperation shifting into terror as the waters gripped her ankle, then her knees. She tried to flee but it was too late; the river had her in its grasp. Grief waded through the quagmire, her black wings spread wide, her head bobbing as she clattered her spear-like beak.

"No! Not like this. I am War!" Riksa railed.

"Be at peace, sister," Leksi said.

With a guttural bellow, Grief skewered Riksa through the back and Leksi found herself smiling as her sister thrashed, unable to yield. There were only two things Riksa had ever been afraid of: a lack of conflict and ending up like Mezra. She might've spared herself the latter indignity if only she'd had the courage to admit her weakness, but courage could only bloom in a fear-seeded soul.

With Riksa gone, the nightmares turned on Leksi, as she knew they would. She offered no resistance to her monsters when they insinuated themselves in her every crease and crevice, filling up her ears and welling in her eyes. She strode back to the necropolis where she found the desiccated remains of her brother. Niki lay where they'd fallen, whimpering, and Emri slowly unfurled from the fetal position, his cheeks awash with snot and tears from whatever he'd endured at the hands of her power. And then there was Death, face-to-face with her own worst nightmare.

Time looked as he had that day on the banks of the river. For centuries, Leksi had rebuked herself for not coming to her mother's aid. Now, she couldn't intervene. Fear had dominion over all and could only be defeated by the one afflicted.

Death rose, shaking off her torpor. The white garments turned to gray, the hems blackening as if soaking up spilled ink. The nightmare dressed as Time advanced and Leksi braced herself for the jolt of pleasure she'd receive if her mother succumbed—for the simultaneous pang of guilt and sorrow knowing she'd been the one to destroy Death herself.

But Death stood her ground, glaring at the shade wearing Time's face. The nightmare shrank in Death's gaze, diminishing as she swatted away his groping hands and shoved past him. Instead, she knelt beside what had once been Zal and gathered him into her arms.

The nightmare followed, shifting into a younger version of itself: the son instead of the father. It drifted toward Zal and Leksi froze, trying to understand what she was seeing—never mind feeling—as the nightmare she'd conjured folded itself into her brother.

Cradling Zal like a child, Mother began to sing a haunting melody Leksi hadn't heard for centuries.

Niki gurgled, trying to say something, but only bloody froth bubbled between their lips. They sat beside Emri who seemed equally awestruck, ghosts shimmering around him, his eyes glister-white.

Death sang and the sky darkened—gray returning to black, the stars renewing their sparkle. The temperature plummeted as Death plunged her fist into her chest with a sickening crunch. Between her fingers, she held up a gobbet of throbbing black meat. With her other hand, she opened a seam down Zal's withered body and pressed the steaming sliver of her heart between his ribs.

"Daughter." Death gazed up at Leksi with black eyes. "For too long I feared the wrong thing." She pressed a kiss to Zal's naked knuckle, and, slowly, the bone began to twist and grow, his Nether gem reforming. "I have faced my fear," Death said. "And now you must face yours. You must make your choice."

"Mother, I—" But what choice was it, really, when to face her fear meant becoming the one thing she detested above all else? She dropped to her knees, cinched in the python embrace of her nightmare.

"Make your choice." Death took Leksi's hand. "Or it will be made for you."

Leksi contemplated her brother's remains, watching the web of capillaries beneath his sallow skin turn black then blue as Death's heart beat inside his chest.

"I never wanted this," Leksi said.

"Sometimes the thing we never wanted is the very thing we need," Death said. "Sometimes, we can learn not to hate it." Her gaze dropped to Zal. "Perhaps, even, to love it."

Leksi wasn't sure she'd ever be able to do that when making this impossible choice would rob her of everything she loved. She'd never see the mortal realm again—never feel the warmth of sunlight or hear the laughter of children, never smell the streets of sultry Savat soaked in spice and human sweat. Her eternity would be ice and darkness, her existence confined to the Nether; but if her sacrifice would restore order across the realms, could she be selfish? If she truly wanted to mitigate the harm her very existence caused, then Leksi knew what she had to do.

A single tear carved a hot rill down Leksi's cheek as she turned to face her mother. "I will face my fear," she said, and made her choice.

Death smiled, and brushed the tear from Leksi's cheek before she dissipated, fading into the shimmer of the gathered ghosts.

Leksi didn't fight the transformation, letting the primordial power that had always terrified her rearrange her bones and recalibrate her magic. She let herself become the one thing she'd never wanted to be—not sure if she was conquering her fear or succumbing to it.

Antlers grew from her temples, shedding gory velvet as they spread into a heavy crown. Darkness wrapped her in a shroud—garb snipped from the very fibers of the Nether to armor the new queen of the underworld. The Nether was hers now, and she would be its keeper.

It started to snow then, flakes swirling to land as softly as a mother's love. The air moved, quickened to a breeze, and whisked snow across the barren sand. With an audible sigh, the Nether slipped back into winter, into balance, as Leksi accepted her fate.

The Principles of Inyoti as recorded by the first arkani blessed by the Ancestors to carry that most sacred fragment of the Serpent God within their hearts. Thus are the tenets upon which we build our society and foster community.

Sixth Principle—
Servant Leadership:
Leaders within society exist to maintain harmony and serve the people by upholding the principles of the community. Decisions must be democratic and must reflect the will of the people while always striving toward the greater good.

Chapter Thirty-Two

Niki

I was going to live forever. Possibly. My recently acquired relatives weren't entirely sure if my semi-humanness rendered me susceptible to mortality, or if my human death would simply grant me eternal life beyond the veil—in my father's realm, perhaps. Either way, it seemed I'd become the manifestation of what I'd always craved: the demigod of Legacy.

Demigod.

The word was absurd, the notion even more ridiculous. I wonder if my mother had known her devotion to the old ways might result in a conjugal visit from a god. Had she invited Time into her bed? Had she even known I was the result of a divine coupling—that it was god-spawn she relentlessly punished and derided?

Ever since we'd stepped out of the Nether, the nascent magic sat uneasy inside me. It had been quieter there, a hummingbird thrum as Emri led us to the rift where he and Zal had torn through the fabric of the worlds. There were so many tears—the Nether wounded and bleeding—wounds Leksi would need to stitch closed while we did our best to rebuild the city.

On that front, we were already making progress.

I navigated my way through the cleared streets, my satchel heavy against my back and my head full of hope. The city would never be the same again, its features irrevocably changed. The palace was gone, the entire cliffside collapsed in on itself, becoming a canyon of jagged chunks tumbling into the sea.

The surrounding areas fared a little better. Some homes were still standing; others proved salvageable. Many more still needed to be rebuilt. The medley of spells hadn't only ignited the gunpowder meant for the First Council. The detonation had set off a series of chain reactions, catching at pockets of chaos magic like a spark on dry grass. The damage was significant, but at least the puddles of Zal's power had mostly been used up in the process.

My circuitous route took me past the university. It had lost its eastern wing, including my tower attic and all my research. Not that I needed it as much anymore. I'd never have to take apart another arkani to understand the true nature of magic. I could study myself and the other surviving members of Zal's order. They'd been at the citadel when the barrels exploded, escaping the worst of the damage. Most of Zal's arkani were only too happy to let me observe their magic at work, answering my numerous questions and experimenting with music to satisfy my scientific inquiries.

Even Emri eventually acquiesced, however grudgingly. He sang for me, allowing me to record snippets of his voice for further analysis. His abilities challenged and confounded so many of the established theories. Studying him was proving less boon, more headache—but he was part of the larger conundrum, and if I wanted to solve the grand mystery of magic, I needed to understand all its forms.

My own magic was a constant vibration now, as if a hundred tiny birds had taken up residence within me. Their wings flapped in syncopation between breath and heartbeat, their wings beating harder now as I arrived in Qhemba.

In the weeks since the blast, the people here had rallied, joined by arkani less afraid to use their magic to assist in clean-up efforts. Several streets were already being rebuilt, supplies generously donated by Tsirayans. Slowly, their dhows were returning Savati residents happy to come home to a city no longer ruled by the Synod or Sodality, with the constabulary all but disbanded. The people had reclaimed power and were no longer afraid of cudgels or muskets when the hyenas were like everyone else—now struggling to pick up the pieces of their shattered lives.

The Qhembalese sang as they worked: incantations to ease aching muscles, to lighten loads, and to soothe blisters. Some even offered up old orisons: prayers to the elemental gods and to Death, prayers of thanks and supplication. Riksa had been right about one thing: hardship did rekindle the people's faith. I only hoped this disaster could truly unify the people of Savat now, despite their fractured beliefs.

I traced the scars on my throat and tested my voice, wanting to join in the chorus. I tried, producing only a croak and a wheeze. My voice was still healing. Even demigod flesh had its limits and needed time to rejuvenate.

Time. My true father—and an even bigger mystery. Being excruciatingly aware of all the things I didn't know, with no way to find the answers, was a chafing aggravation.

Somewhere to the north, a kakaki sounded, the hour echoing across the city. With the drowsy sun sinking into a bed of clouds, I continued east to the one structure that had sustained no damage at all.

The ancient Temple to Inyoti sat at the end of an avenue now peppered with fanes to each of the gods. In the beginning, the fanes were dismantled as quickly as they were erected. Many in the city remained vehemently anti-magic and anti-god, cleaving to the rhetoric dished up by the Sodality; but as days became weeks and now months, a new tolerance had developed in all but the most skeptical of hearts.

I paused, considering what offering might entice my father-god to make himself known. Not shells or sea glass, not fresh fruit or candles, no yellowed teeth or votive offering soaked in blood. I pressed my palm to the stone, offering only myself. I needed to understand the circumstances of my birth, to know what I was, and the true nature of my fledgling magic. My inheritance; his legacy. Not that my demigod status was something I advertised. For now, I remained Nikima Tjadamo: the expert scholar and newly appointed council member.

The Temple of Inyoti teemed with people. I slipped inside, hoping not to draw attention to my almost-tardiness. The most important folk were already milling up front where six seats were arranged in a semicircle facing the audience. Six chairs on the new council, six Principles of Inyoti, six notes of the serpent song. It was hardly subtle, but few people seemed to care.

I made my way around the periphery, searching for the stillness that hung on Emri like a cloak. Not one for socializing either, he stood off to the side dressed throat-to-toe in black as usual with his silver hair hanging in twin braids over his shoulders. The black lines of his tattoos ran up the side of his neck, tapering off across his ears. He turned at my approach, his ghost-glow eyes always catching me off guard.

Acknowledging me with a nod, he stepped aside so I could slot into the recess beside him. It was as close to a corner as one could get in a circular structure.

"Ready?" he asked, immediately reminding me of that fateful night when Jaq had asked me the very same question.

I nodded. Now that the initial phase of my research had been completed, Lana demanded a public demonstration—one that wouldn't get me arrested or threatened with execution. I'd inadvertently become an advocate for the emancipation of magic. More like the emancipation of the people, really—freeing them from the notion that the ability to wield was exclusively a birthright. All it took was an ear for music and the God-chord, which I intended to prove tonight.

Just because magic was accessible to everyone didn't mean wielding it was easy, though. Becoming adept would still require training. I was leading the cohort tasked with establishing free magic schools, as well as providing updated sigilaries and songbooks for home study. A lofty goal that would take months, if not longer, to come to pass, but a goal I believed in with every fiber of my godliness.

"Are you sure this is a good idea?" Emri asked in his customary low voice I had to lean closer to hear. He smelled of lemongrass and the crisp coolness of autumn despite his layered garb. How did he manage not to work up a sweaty stink in the heat all wrapped in black like that—was it his ghosts and constant tether to the frigid Nether?

"Anti-magic sentiment is a hard poison to neutralize," he continued. "The people might not be ready."

I rolled my eyes, not wanting to let my own doubts show.

"Then you should've worn indigo," he added.

I want to look ordinary, I signed—my gestures the clumsy configurations of a novice. I'd deliberately chosen to forego academic wear to better blend in with the citizens of the city. *I'm no one special.*

"Just a liar, then," Emri said, his tone making me bristle.

Not a liar... I curled my hands into fists, my knowledge of sign woefully inadequate for expressing my indignation. He watched my hands, his gaze only grazing my face when necessary for interpreting my gestures.

"You're a demigod trying to convince people birthright has nothing to do with magic," he said, raising a slender and extremely judgmental brow.

Magic belongs to everyone, I signed.

"Is that what you learned chopping up arkani for the Sodality?"

I wiped a hand over my face before rubbing mercilessly at

the tender spot on my jaw. I'd admitted to what I'd done, apologized, and vowed to make amends—to help the people of Savat with all I'd learned—and still, it wasn't enough. Magic would never again be a power reserved for the privileged or despotic, something I was going to demonstrate today; yet Emri seemed determined to resent me.

He had a right to be angry considering what I'd done to those he'd considered friends and family. If only I could make him understand, though. I'd seen the scars on his body, exposed by the tattered rags of his clothing in the Nether. The pain of his history was written in his skin. I only wished I could tell him about my own experiences. My father's belt hadn't cut nearly as deep, but I wanted Emri to know I understood at least a little of what he'd been through and why he was still so afraid.

It would've taken me hours to try and string all that together with my fingers, though, and my wrists ached at the mere thought.

I'm sorry, I signed instead. It was the first sign I'd perfected.

"Prove it," he said in his rasping monotone.

I planned to do that and more—to not merely atone for all my past mistakes but to never never again let my ambition make me lose sight of what truly mattered.

A kakaki announced the hour. It was time, and I filed into position behind the other council members, my magic thrumming.

Lana was the first to step into place, dressed in turmeric yellow. It was the color once favored by the monarchy, her statement bold and unmistakable.

"Welcome, welcome everyone," she said, smiling as she gestured to the rest of the new council members to take their seats.

Instead of swooping into the devastated city with declarations of sovereignty, she'd arrived with wagons of food and blankets, medicine, and tools, ingratiating herself with the people so no one minded when she eventually took charge. Although she remained crownless, she had claimed Savat all the same; and no one was going to argue with the one person capable of feeding all those made recently destitute. Of course, she'd omitted to take responsibility for the gunpowder plot that destroyed the city in the first place.

"Sibling," Zal said with a wry smile as he hobbled past me, his mahogany cane tap-tapping the uneven rhythm of his steps. He wore a leather patch over his missing left eye, which made him look roguish—especially when paired with the rest of his fading facial scars and waves of graying black hair.

As always, Emri walked beside him, hands ready to catch Zal if he stumbled. The sciomancer had become my brother's living shadow, replacing the magical flock Riksa had obliterated in the Nether.

With all of us in place, Lana continued. "In Inyoti's name we are gathered here today to discuss the progress we're making in restoring our beloved city to its former glory. We've also come together to continue discussing how best to govern our new Savat—a city rebuilt by and for the people. Let's begin by giving thanks to Inyoti, our serpent creator with whom all life began, who has blessed us with the gift of magic and the understanding to wield it."

I glanced around as Lana led the prayer, noting those who scowled and folded their arms in defiance. My magic stirred, roused by the music. It was Emri's voice that sent shivers up my spine, though, his split-tone throat-singing unlocking something primal in me—and the crowd—as the vibrations excited every arkana particle in the air.

There was an answering rumble in the earth. Aftershocks and tremors were a daily occurrence. No one paid them much attention anymore, but this felt different. I pressed my hand to the rock curving overhead and felt the echoes in the stone—a zinging that traveled from my palm into my heart.

Over Zal's bowed head, I locked gazes with Emri. His eyes burned white, a corona of ghosts shimmering in the air around him. He felt it too.

When the prayer concluded, the tremors subsided and Lana smiled out at the crowd, a crocodile showing off sharp teeth.

"Today we welcome our own Nikima Tjadamo—scholar, musician, and maven of magic—for a demonstration I think everyone will find most interesting." She waved one of her lackeys forward to set a sad-looking potted orchid at the edge of the platform. The audience craned their necks to get a good look.

This was it: a chance to prove everyone who'd ever doubted me wrong. A chance to show off the years of work I'd invested in developing my theory of fully accessible, equitable magic. But the moment was tainted by deception. I wasn't human. I never had been. I might never have achieved much at all if I had simply been Niki from the village.

As much as I longed to be honest, revealing my true nature now would undoubtedly cause more harm than good. First, we needed to establish trust, faith, and stability. Eventually, Savat would be ready to know demigods walked among them, but not today.

Besides, I wanted to be known as Nikima Tjadamo, the brilliant academic. Not as Time's bastard. I wanted my own legacy, separate from my father's, and that began today as I demonstrated a method for activating magic using music built on the God-chord without spell or sigil.

Several hands shot up when Lana requested volunteers, while I set out the instruments and sheet music. I'd tried to make it as simple as possible—the explanation for what to do described in terms even the most uneducated might understand—with Emri on hand to verbally explain should the need arise.

I chose one of the more enthusiastic volunteers, then pointed at a person who sat slouched in their seat looking decidedly unimpressed. With a surly roll of their eyes, they sauntered forward and plonked down beside one of the balafons.

My hands shook as I gestured for the volunteers to begin. Movement at the doors caught my attention and I braced for the shrill of a constable's whistle, for hyenas to burst in and drag me back to the dungeon. Impossible, since the palace had been consumed by the waves, reduced to nothing but wreckage on the seafloor.

No hyenas entered the temple, only a slim figure with their hood flipped up, their face obscured by shadow. For no discernible reason, a prickle of unease made my guts clench.

Taking a deep breath, I focused on the music, letting the thrum of my magic soothe me as the volunteers began to play. The surly one fumbled the notes—perhaps deliberately—but I ignored the errors and gestured for the impromptu ensemble to continue.

The composition was simple with two hexatonic melodies producing harmony based on the intervals of the God-chord. *Revive*, the music said. *Grow*.

The players settled—even the reluctant one—when the music started working. As the melodies wove intricate harmony, so the orchid's stem thickened, the leaves turning from brown to green. Given the temple's impeccable acoustics, the music swelled and reverberated, the notes all but glistening in the air as I closed my eyes, momentarily lost in the overtones.

Titters from the audience drew my attention back to the plant. The orchid bloomed, six perfect flowers opening pale pink petals. The audience erupted, smatterings of applause punctuating the clamor of awe and irritation. One woman at the back yelled, "Charlatan!" and another, "Heresy!" while many more took to their feet, stomping and clapping.

"Well done," Zal said, startling me when he patted me on the back, and I nodded, smiling, giddy with pride. Here was everything I had worked so hard for: my theories proven true, my legacy a gift to the people to improve their lives. This was only the first step, though. For now, a person still needed to create the sound, but I was convinced recordings would have the same effect if only phonographs were able to reproduce the music with greater accuracy.

The volunteers stopped playing and the magic dissipated, the conjuring extemporaneous, the effects evanescent. I was still working on a way to make musical magic more permanent without the use of sigils. I glanced toward the doors again, noting the hooded figure hadn't joined in the applause or cries of derision. As the orchid wilted, so the audience calmed and the person at the door pulled back their cowl, revealing a familiar face.

Jaq.

I thought I killed her. I saw her bleeding in Yatto's arms. Perhaps I'd underestimated the man's ability as a physicker, or Jaq had found healing some other way. I thought she'd been buried in the ruins of the palace, nothing but a memory and regret. But here she stood, watching my music work magic. Her eyes narrowed, her gaze as sharp as the scalpel I'd slipped into her belly.

Chapter Thirty-Three
Leksi

Leksi strolled through the Nether, taking her time to inspect every corner of her realm. She should've known the damage a magical explosion like that could do—should've destroyed the barrels at Lana's estate long before they ever made it to the city riddled with chaos.

"What is done is done," Tamisk said. She wafted beside Leksi, a glow vaguely shaped like a person, her voice the clatter of seashells in a child's bucket. "Your guilt helps no one," she added, and Leksi smiled, glad to be chided by the ghost of her former lover. Glad to feel less alone as she traversed a meadow of snow and frostweed.

It had taken an age to find Tamisk, even with Grief dutifully searching through the quagmire of unsorted souls clogging the river. For a while, Leksi feared Tamisk was stuck in the mortal realm, but eventually Grief had disentangled her from the effluvium. Tamisk was immediately returned to shore, to be reborn when she wished. She'd chosen to stay, for now, a companion as Leksi fulfilled her duty to the living and the dead.

Grief had yet to find Ailia, which troubled Leksi with a nagging sense of disquiet. Not that she had thought to spare for the arkani when it was her responsibility to seal the rifts between the realms. The largest breaches were easy to find. She only had to follow the trail of escaping souls to the tattered margins of the Nether. Using her own nails as needles, she darned the fraying threads with starlight and rime, hemming in the dead once more.

So many had escaped, though. Too many to count. And not all of them had earned redemption. Some of the damned had managed to crawl out of the mire while the storks were incapacitated. Those that had prematurely fled the Nether couldn't be reborn into new bodies—only Death could sanction that—but they could haunt the living. Emri might have his work cut out for him, corralling any malevolent spirits tormenting Savat and banishing them back to the Nether.

That didn't address the matter of souls slinking off to the other realms where Leksi had no right—not even with her new crown and title—to go wandering. She hoped her relatives were fastidious in their realm-keeping and would sweep Death's detritus back to the Nether.

Leksi trailed her fingers along the border. The smaller rips—soggy with salt water or wreathed in flame—were trickier to find but no less important to suture. There was a reason the realms were separate, ruled by gods within their own aspect. To have primordial magic bleeding from one to another was to court disaster. Her finger snagged on a fray. No briny dribbles or creeping foliage marked this rift. She pressed her eye to the shredded fabric of the universe and peered into the void beyond.

"What is it?" Tamisk asked.

"I don't know." Leksi picked at a thread, the tear widening to give her a better view of what lay beyond.

"Be careful." Tamisk's warning came too late as the thread in Leksi's hand pulled free, the veil laddering like a stocking. She snatched for the strands, but they slipped away, the veil unraveling.

"Oh dear, niece."

Leksi spun to face Time—not a nightmare dressed in god-guise, but the loathsome oaf himself. His cheeks were dusted with freckle constellations, and Leksi recognized some as the ones that shone above the Nether. There were more, though—the stellar clusters disappearing beneath the billowing shirt that hung loose on his lanky frame. Every patch of his exposed, amber skin held more stars, which seemed to shift and flow in strange orbits.

"You were not invited," she said, her fury instant and incandescent. This was her realm. She had dominion here and he was not welcome. She prepared to shove him both physically and magically from the Nether when he raised an admonishing finger.

"Uh-ah-ah, I wouldn't do that if I were you." He hooked his thumb in the widening tear and looked at her with mismatched eyes. One was the solid black of an empty void; the other was bright with colors Leksi couldn't name—the way Zal's had been before he'd succumbed to Nightmare.

"Do you know what's out there?" Time asked. "Since you seem so determined to rip open this seam."

Leksi's hands balled into involuntary fists.

"Don't let him get to you," Tamisk said. "You can fix this."

"Oh, little ghost, not every wound can be stitched closed," he said in a voice both ethereal and irritating. "I have traversed the eons; I can skip across centuries in all directions, and I have seen it all—the beginning and the end. I was there at the birth of humanity, and I have seen their planet shattered like glass, but this—" His eyes widened as more strands of the veil snapped beneath his fingers. Leksi flinched, feeling the decortication of her realm as if her own flesh was being stripped away.

"Do you know what it is then?" she asked. "Do you know *where* it is?"

"No," Time admitted. His smile was Zal's, only keener, deadlier. "And isn't that exciting?"

Chapter Thirty-Four
Zal

Even though the sun no longer hurt him more than any other human, Zal still found comfort in darkness. At night, with natural shadow pressed around him, he didn't feel as bereft without his Nether creatures, nor did he feel so whittled thin by his demotion.

"Admit it," Zal said as he and Emri made their way through the cleared streets. "It was an impressive little display."

"The plant withered the moment the music stopped," Emri said, reluctant as ever to acknowledge Niki's achievements.

"Why do you insist on hating my sibling?" Zal asked.

"Hate is a strong word, Va—" Emri caught himself. There was nothing godly about Zal any more. His sojourn in the Nether and tangle with his siblings had rendered him utterly, abjectly human. Mortal, aging, and decaying. He no longer deserved to be called Va'ili—or any other honorific, for that matter.

"It's not that I hate them," Emri said with a beleaguered sigh. "I resent them for what they did to our arkani, and I find them insufferably arrogant. I knew people like Niki in beZebi." He named the seaside capital of the joRanian empire, a city of glittering spires tucked between ocean and desert. "People who justified barbarity in the name of progress. They didn't care what they did, who they hurt, what they took, so long as it benefited them." The bitterness in Emri's voice stung Zal's ears.

"The ghost you carry," Zal said. "Were they some egotistical, imperial scholar then?"

When Emri didn't answer, Zal continued. "If you murdered a muti-making academic who hurt you in the name of science, then trapped their ghost in the mortal realm to stop them from ever finding rest or redemption, I wouldn't judge you. I understand the desire for vengeance." *And how easily it can seem like justice;* but Zal kept that thought to himself.

"Thank you for understanding." Emri folded his arms. "Not many would."

Zal waited, but when the sciomancer didn't offer any more on the matter, he returned to their previous topic.

"For what it's worth, I think Niki genuinely wants to help others, despite their arrogance," he said. He wasn't used to defending his kin. Niki wasn't like the others, though. Ambitious, yes, and calculating, but having not been born of Death, they weren't the embodiment of suffering the way Zal and the others had been. Niki was Time's child and Time was monstrous, but Niki had a human heart, which hopefully held a greater capacity for compassion than cruelty.

Zal flattened his palm to his chest, not yet used to the dull thudding of the renewed organ behind his ribs. He smiled at the irony of this slice of Death having gifted him a second life.

"I'm just afraid of what Niki might do to achieve their goals," Emri said. "Ailia was ambitious too."

"Don't worry. I'll keep a closer eye on them," Zal said, winking his remaining orb.

Emri chuckled, a low rumble that spilled a permeating warmth into Zal's chest. His cane lodged in a cracked cobble, and he stumbled, but as always, Emri caught him before he could fall. Zal inhaled the man's frosted-meadow scent, delighting in the cool touch of Emri's fingers.

Without the benefit of magic, Zal was permanently broken; his body healed old injuries slower than he acquired new ones. He was mortal now and middle-aged. No tincture, tonic, or spell could change that. Eventually, he'd succumb to Time, as all humans did, and tumble over the falls to face the consequences of his life choices. To face Grief and his sister, who had assumed Death's abdicated throne.

"All right, Zal?" Emri asked, and Zal leaned into the sciomancer's arms, lingering longer than strictly necessary as the throbbing in his knee and hip subsided. Pain remained a constant—no longer an ebb and flow, but a permanent susurrus in his inflamed joints.

"I'll be fine." He steadied himself before they continued their traverse across Qhemba toward The Anchorage. The streetlamps hadn't been replaced yet, and Zal could no longer see in the dark, but Emri carried a spelled lantern emitting a lilac effulgence to light their way.

The Anchorage had fared better than many other buildings during the explosion. A former military installation, it was sturdy with thick timbers and heavy stone. The roof had caved in, but that had already been cleared. For now, the building remained open to a sky rashed with stars.

A chorus of meowing greeted them as they entered the former courtyard, stacked with pallets of building supplies—local and imported, and all paid for by Zal. He'd made a promise to Leksi, and while neither of them had gotten what they truly wanted, he owed his sister. He rubbed the scar on his palm where Emri had carved the binding sigil. Their magical connection had been severed—as had their psychic one—when Zal had been ejected from the Nether for the second time. But a promise was a promise, and rebuilding her sanctuary while funding the reconstruction of Savat was simple enough. It also kept Lana in check.

She wasn't the only benevolent benefactor of the city; she wasn't the only one appreciated and lavished with gratitude—a thanks Zal didn't feel he deserved. If only the people knew it was their savior's gunpowder and Zal's leaked chaos magic that had resulted in the demolition in the first place, they might not be so adoring. As it stood though, Zal kept Lana's secret and she kept his—a pact made of mutually assured destruction.

Zal had craved worship. Now the people made daily offerings at the fanes dedicated to Death, and their faith was all but meaningless to him. At least it would empower his sister.

"I swear there are more of them every time," Zal said, pausing in his limping approach as cats tangled about his legs.

"She's gathering an army," Emri said and approached the pallet where Ansa sat, regal and round-eyed. For a moment she regarded Emri as if weighing his worth before emitting a purr so loud it was more of a roar. She head-butted his chest and he returned her affection with generous ear rubs and back scritches.

"How many souls did you catch today?" he asked.

The cat didn't answer, but Zal knew they shared some unspoken understanding—a way to keep count of all the errant souls Emri had been tasked to return to the Nether. When they'd found Ansa at The Anchorage, much altered by chaos, the sciomancer had quickly formed a bond with her. She and the other city felines seemed only too happy to hunt down pesky spirits like rats on a ship and shepherd them back to Emri.

Now Ansa turned her too-bright, too-human gaze toward the corner of the courtyard. The ghosts there hung like flimsy sheets on a clothesline, snagged on the branches of Leksi's medlar trees. Setting down the lantern, Emri removed his blade, silver glinting before it turned red where it opened his wrist.

Zal rested against a pallet, content among the cats still rubbing at his legs and battering his shoulders with their soft heads. They were Death's creatures after all, so perhaps they recognized some lingering aspect of his former self. He closed his eyes, listening to Emri sing, appreciating the magic as much as the music—even if he could no longer feel it the way he once had.

He'd been learning all he could from Niki, getting to know his long-lost sibling while discussing the intricacies of magic and Niki's various theories on the subject. Zal hadn't been able to contribute much, and wished he'd paid more attention to both Scryali and Ailia when he'd had the chance. Regret piled upon regret, but he'd told the scholar all he could remember and given them all of Ailia's research.

Despite all that, Niki seemed determined to wear away what little vitality Zal still possessed with their questions about primordial magic. As exhausting as it could be, talking about his life as a Netherling and the power he'd once wielded was helping him cope with the loss of all he'd been. Zal rubbed the knuckle that had been devoid of its gem for so long it still surprised him to find the stone restored. It was no longer a living piece of the Nether—not magical except for the way it grew from his body—but a multi-faceted reminder that, in the end, Death had forgiven him and gifted her misbegotten son a piece of her frigid heart.

With blood and song Emri banished the ghosts, returning them to the Nether where they belonged.

"How many?" Zal asked.

"Fewer than yesterday." Emri rolled his sleeve down over the shallow cut. Picking up the lantern, he continued to lead their survey of the building, pausing to discuss various aspects of the redesign.

Zal had plans to expand The Anchorage, to provide housing for the homeless and transient, as well as restore its former tavern status. The neighborhood could use a watering hole and minstrel stage.

He paused, squatting down awkwardly to inspect a patch of frostweed. While the blast beneath the palace had ignited most of the larger puddles of his unstable magic, nullifying its strange and deleterious effects on the city, a few pockets remained.

He grazed his hand across the flowers, releasing their corpse-scent. He gagged, where once he'd have appreciated the putrid aroma. Coughing, he tumbled backward onto his arse with all the grace of a marula-drunk baboon, his hips creaking in painful rebuke.

"Need a hand?" Emri offered Zal his own, the lantern light splaying geometric shadows across the sciomancer's smiling face.

"Give me a minute," Zal said, trying to catch his breath. His sister's nightmare had given him a thorough mauling. If he hadn't already been so weakened by his battle against Riksa, he might've had the strength to fight his fear, but he'd been unable to summon either energy or courage, and so his magic had been devoured. "I miss being what I was," he said.

"A bitter demigod trying to hold the broken pieces of himself together with capricious magic?" Emri teased gently.

"Now I'm just broken with nothing to hold me together but wrinkling skin. Permanently damaged and dying." And rather quickly, too, judging by his graying hair and sagging muscles.

"We're all dying," Emri said, who had retained his youthful appearance despite having lost the scrap of Zal's magic. "And we're all permanently damaged, one way or another."

"Yes, but your damage is more aesthetically pleasing," Zal said, and instantly regretted it.

"You know I'd trade my looks in a heartbeat if it meant never having to endure all the things that left me scarred," Emri said in that whispery voice Zal longed to hear across a pillow. He longed to feel the brush of Emri's lips across his skin, just as he longed to trace every scar and line of ink from the tips of the man's ears to his toes—but it wasn't to be. Emri had made that clear.

"I'm sorry," Zal said, surprised by how easily he could say the words these days. "That was callous of me."

"Apology accepted." Emri offered Zal his hand again, and this time Zal took it. "Home to the citadel, or are we sleeping here tonight?" he asked.

At home the beds were soft and the caves quiet. Staying in the city meant sleeping on a straw-stuffed mattress on a rough pallet and being woken by the dawn-crack cacophony of a city under construction. But it was late and Zal was tired. They wouldn't find a tumbrel to take them to the mountains at this hour, and the mere thought of mounting a horse in his current state made him wince.

Sitting on their beds with the lamp set between them and a cluster of cats curled around them, Zal and Emri shared a flask of hibiscus tea while Zal smoked a spliff of scale leaf. The Tsirayan weed curbed human pain as much as it did spells gone wrong.

"Think it was really Jaq *Olonza* at the temple?" Emri asked, stretching out his long legs alongside Zal's.

"Even if it was, I don't see her posing much threat except to Niki." Although, knowing what little he did about the girl's mother, he imagined Jaq quite capable of bearing a grudge.

"You murdered her mother," Emri said.

"A thing few know. I think I'm safe from the girl's ire."

"She did manage to deceive Niki for years. Perhaps we'd be wiser not to underestimate her."

"Me? Wise?" Zal smirked.

"Old dogs can learn new tricks." Emri's fingers brushed Zal's as he took the flask.

"So I'm old, too?" Zal asked.

"Positively ancient, but there's life in you yet." Emri's smile warmed Zal better than the steaming tea. "We could ask a few of our arkani to watch Niki. Make sure they're protected moving about the city, that sort of thing," Emri added.

"Thought you didn't like my little sibling."

"I don't, but that doesn't mean I want them at the mercy of the Sodality."

"The Sodality barely exists anymore." Zal blew smoke rings for the tabby beside him to paw at.

"Not everyone loves Savat's newfound piety. Jaq may be able to gather up the remaining members," Emri said.

Although spared from the worst of the blast, Zal's order of arkani was diminished as well—the shadows having faded from their skin the moment Zal turned human. Previously, he would've dismissed the sciomancer's concerns, but it was his hubris that had gotten him into this entire mess in the first place.

"If she does resurrect the Sodality, then we'll deal with it. Her survival changes none of our current goals," Zal said.

"Goals to rebuild Savat, banish pesky ghosts, and—" Emri raised his brows expectantly.

"I'm too old and decrepit for vengeance," Zal said.

"And a terrible liar," Emri said. "I know what you want. I've seen the books you've been reading and the tomes you send arkani to steal from the university archives."

"Borrow," Zal said.

"I've heard the questions you ask Niki—ones they're too naïve to find suspicious," Emri continued.

"Eavesdropping is rude," Zal said, expecting to see Emri grinning, but the sciomancer sat pensively, his brow furrowed.

"You don't think pushing Time into the river would work?" he asked, his voice gentle but his words like blades.

"Mezra and Riksa were Netherlings. Time is something else." Zal stubbed out the glowing cherry and contemplated rolling another spliff. The first had dulled the ache; another would leave him feeling pleasantly floaty, as if buoyed by the shadows he no longer had.

"Do you really think there's a way to kill a god, then?" Emri asked.

"I sure hope so."

"Vengeance—"

"Justice," Zal snapped. This was definitely justice. But he would be wiser in this matter and pursue it himself. He knew better than to trust others with such a delicate task. "For what he did to my mother," Zal said. "Perhaps to Niki's too. Even gods should be held accountable, and if not by the progeny they've wronged, then who? You've seen the fanes. People *worship* that monster."

"The fanes that get torn down faster than they go up?" Emri asked with a raised eyebrow. "Petty, but understandable."

"Thank you, by the way," Zal said. "I'm far too slow to get to all of them."

"You're welcome." Emri smiled and Zal's chest expanded with ridiculous sentiment. "So, we're going to kill a god."

"We?"

"Obviously, Zal."

His name in the man's mouth sent a jolt through his inchoate heart. He watched as the sciomancer undid his braids and combed his hair free, fighting the longing making his hands twitch.

"You're not afraid? Of what Time might do if he knew what you planned?" Emri asked.

"I already endured my greatest fear," Zal said. To be rendered magicless and permanently severed from the Nether. At least until he died a mortal death, which seemed a paltry consolation. "Facing my father can't possibly be worse."

Emri's fingers stalled in their combing, his body tensing as he pulled his knees toward his chest and wrapped his arms around his legs. He looked so young in that pose, and Zal caught a glimpse of the child he must've been.

Zal longed to hold him—to cradle the sciomancer the way Death had cradled Zal in the Nether. Too soon her arms had crumbled, her embrace failing, but he'd had those precious moments with her, and she'd whispered the words he'd needed to hear.

"If you'd like to kill everyone who harmed you, we can add their names to the list," Zal said. "If we can slaughter a god, we can certainly kill a few joRanians."

"No," Emri said, emphatic. "I've worked to stay hidden and forgotten."

"And the ghost you carry?"

"A reminder of *why* I stay hidden." Emri bit out, his hair catching the lamp light to shimmer in a purple pall, obscuring his face.

"That's your nightmare, isn't it?" Zal asked gently, nudging Emri's foot with his own. "To be found and killed or—captured? Returned to joRania?"

"Yes." Emri exhaled. "They wouldn't kill me. Not quickly. Perhaps in increments." He rubbed his legs, his trousers hiding scars. Like Zal, Emri had had pieces of himself carved away, flesh reduced to carrion scraps. At least Zal had managed to recover most of his scattered bits; Emri had only been able to fill the loss with ink.

"But you were in the Nether. You faced your nightmare," Zal said. "It's done. It can't hurt you. *They* can't hurt you. They have no claim to you now, not ever."

"I didn't face it, though," Emri said. "My nightmare didn't manifest the way everyone else's did. Not yet, at least."

"What do you mean?" Zal asked, both curious and concerned. His sister's pets rarely failed.

"I met my fear, but I didn't defeat it. I just delayed its coming. And they do have a claim on me." He lifted the edge of his shirt where it tucked snugly into the waistband of his pants to reveal a knot of scar tissue. It had been tattooed over, the brand obscured. "I'll always be their property," Emri said, his voice hoarse with restrained emotion.

"We don't treat people like that in Savat," Zal said.

"Not any more. That's why I came here," Emri said. "And after all these years—I can't imagine ever going back."

"If they come for you, we'll be ready," Zal said. "You're not alone. You have arkani on your side; Lana and her army; Ansa and her ferocious felines." He scratched the ears of the nearest dozing cat. "You have one brilliant, if annoying, demigod scholar on your side, and even Death herself at your disposal. And you have me, such as I am."

"Thank you, Va'ili," Emri said, this time not correcting the false title. Zal let the adoration in Emri's voice and the gratitude on his face wash over him, quelling his pain far more effectively than any spell or spliff ever had.

I won't let them take you. I won't let them hurt you, Zal vowed. If he'd still had his magic, he would've made the promises out loud, but diminished as he was, he worried he might perish before he could keep them.

They settled into a comfortable quiet then—Zal resting his head against an ancient timber, his gaze on the stars; Emri stretching out long legs opposite him so that their knees brushed each other's. He watched the constellations as they wheeled through the sky, and listened to the hushed world around him, grateful to be alive but so very afraid it would all too quickly be wrenched away.

Time passed, measured in glowing trails across the void,

the rumbling snores of cats, the deepening breaths of the sciomancer, and the rime-thick beats of Zal's heart as he slipped into dreams of patricide—and the golden owl watching them from the splintered rafters took flight on silent wings.

EPILOGUE

Dawn ruptured the eastern horizon like a bullet tearing through flesh, spilling bloody viscera across the ocean. Dark sails billowed, staining the white-capped water with lengthening shadows.

On the sails, the image of a golden owl—its wings spread and talons reaching, its hooked beak stained red.

On the deck, a woman with hair like spun sunshine and eyes sapphire blue waited with her arm outstretched as her bird returned, swooping low over the waves on sun-spangled wings. It landed and snatched the shred of meat from her fingers, swallowing greedily before sharing all it had seen and who it had found.

THE END

ACKNOWLEDGMENTS

This book began several years ago when I became infatuated with the lesser-known underworld characters of Finnish mythology. In Finnish folklore, Louhi is the goddess of Death and Disease. Impregnated by the wind, she bears several children named for diseases; however, the one considered the 'worst' remains remains mysteriously unnamed. Death banishes this child from the underworld to become a scourge upon humanity. It was this unnamed exile who immediately captured my imagination and became the disaster on legs I called Zal.

Although I initially pitched this book as a cozy fantasy where factious siblings worked through their trauma over copious quantities of coffee in a halfway house for the magically disenfranchised, I am immensely grateful to my agent at the time, Lindsay Leggett, for helping me dig deeper and discover the darker, better story longing to be told.

This was only the second novel I've sold based on a synopsis and sample chapters, so I am immensely grateful to my publisher and editor, R. B. Wood, for believing in this story and seeing its potential. With both R. B.'s and Anna Koon's editorial guidance, this book became what just might be the best thing I've ever written. The entire team at Ruadán Books has been a dream to work with and I can't thank them enough for all they've done for *Born of Malice*. I am so very grateful to have a publisher determined to uplift marginalized voices, celebrating books featuring disabled, BIPOC, queer, and neurodivergent characters by authors who share those identities.

I also want to thank Clara, my new agent, for picking up where Lindsay left off, championing this story with as much fervor.

As for the cover, I am absolutely blown away by the magnificent artwork J. Edward Neill painted, perfectly capturing Zal and Leksi as well as the exquisite darkness of the story. I couldn't have asked for a more striking cover and am so incredibly grateful I get to now hang the original painting on my wall.

Now onto beta and early readers…

Jamison Shea! You absolutely rock! This book would not exist were it not for our summer sessions spent yammering about publishing and beating our keyboards at the Heritage Café. Jamison writes gory, depraved horror so exquisitely, I couldn't help but be inspired. Some of the more gruesome body horror moments in *Born of Malice* are all their fault. #sorrynotsorry

Similarly, I owe a resounding KIITOS PALJON to Dr. Sara Norja, who holds a PhD in Alchemy (how cool is that!) and provided incredibly detailed feedback on the more academic chapters. Niki became a much richer and more realistic character thanks to Sara's insights, and I learned a lot about scrolls and codices.

To Stephen, thank you for taking the time to read my book and for always providing such constructive feedback as well as a very kind blurb. Massive thanks also go to my friend and author buddy, Cheryl Ntumy, for always being a willing and thoughtful beta reader and for providing a blurb that makes my heart swell with pride.

Others who have been tremendously supportive of my writing and who helped make this book happen in ways they might not even be aware of include Nicole, Ella, Nerine, Azaliz, Tero Porthan, the Nine Lives authors, the Dragon Writers, and all the members of the Saućti Collective, from whom I have learned a tremendous amount about writing Afrocentric stories, and celebrating the diversity of the African continent in my fiction.

I'd like to thank my family, especially my mom, who fostered my early love of reading and writing, and who has always encouraged me to write the stories of my heart even when they're a little gruesome.

And lastly, I wouldn't be able to write at all were it not for the unconditional love and support of my husband, Mark, who has encouraged me every step of the way on this publishing journey, who gives me the time and space to write, who listens when I need to vent about plot issues or characters misbehaving, and who kindly keeps me caffeinated during long hours at the keyboard.

Finally, thank you, dear reader, for choosing my book. I always love hearing from readers, so please feel free to reach out on socials if you wish. You'll find me in all the usual places.

I cannot write without music, so here are a few of the songs I was listening to while writing this book. Immense gratitude to these artists and the many others who provided the de facto soundtrack to *Born of Malice*:

"Legacy" by Kaleo

"Dethrone" by Bad Omens

"Carrion Flowers" by Chelsea Wolfe

"Claws in Your Back" by Julien Baker

"Not my God Anymore" by Harpy

"Alone" by The Cure

"Prayer" by Amanati & Roniit

"Dimensional Bleed" by Holy Fawn

"Usurper" by NXCRE & The Villains

"The Right to Destroy Myself" by Okada

About Xan van Rooyen

Xan van Rooyen is an award-winning, autistic, and non-binary storyteller from South Africa, currently living in Finland. Xan has a Master's degree in music, and—when not teaching—enjoys conjuring strange worlds and creating quirky characters. You can find Xan's stories in the likes of *Three-Lobed Burning Eye*, *Daily Science Fiction*, and *Galaxy's Edge*, among others. They have also written several books including *Waypoint Seven* (Mirari Press), *My Name is Magic* (Tiny Ghost Press), and the forthcoming Dorian Gray retelling, *Exquisite Decay* (Tiny Ghost Press). Xan is also part of the Saúútiverse—an African writer's collective—with stories in the multi-award-nominated anthology *Mothersound* as well as the *Saúúti Terrors* anthology (Flame Tree Press). Xan has also had a number of non-fiction articles published, which you can find in the Locus Award-winning *Afro-Centered Futurisms in Our Speculative Fiction* (Bloomsbury, Australia) among others. You can find Xan online here: https://linktr.ee/xanvanrooyen.

Also By Xan van Rooyen

Waypoint Seven
Scardust

YA

Exquisite Decay
My Name is Magic
I Heart Robot

Delicious. Dark. Fiction.
the brink
Sophia Adamowicz
Winter in the City
A Collection of Dark Speculative Fiction
Edited by
R.B. Wood & Anna Koon
The Black Fire Concerto
Mike Allen
120 Murders
Meg Gardiner
Josh Malerman
Silvia Moreno-Garcia
Paul Tremblay
and more...
Edited by Nick Mamatas
Portraits of Decay
A Novel By
J.R. Blanes
A Collection of Dark Speculative Fiction
Spring in the City
Sinister Societies
Six Novellas of Secrets and Horrors
Michael Burke • Tom Deady
Errick Nunnally • Cindy O'Quinn
Sarah Read • Mercedes M. Yardley
Edited by Linda Hartley • Foreword by John Skipp
"It's an eerie gem."
Five Funerals
by Jeff Somers
Foreword by Nick Mamatas
"Darling is an unflinching horror novel—an unsettling story about what constitutes true evil."
Darling
Mercedes M. Yardley
Ruadán Books